Steven R. Boyett

STEVEN R. BOYETT

MORTALITY
BRIDGE

Mortality Bridge

Steven R. Boyett

Subterranean Press 2011

First Edition

ISBN
978-1-59606-375-4

Subterranean Press
PO Box 190106
Burton, MI 48519

www.subterraneanpress.com

CANTOS

Not every man knows what song he shall sing at the end,
Watching the pier as the ship sails away, or what it will seem like
When he's held by the sea's roar, motionless, there at the end,
Or what he shall hope for once it is clear that he'll never go back.
                                                    —Mark Strand

THE PRELUDE IN HELL

WET AND FACEDOWN ON THE sand the blank man shivers. Close behind him is a constant gentle hiss of water rushing past. He lies there blinking. Looking down and trying to remember—anything. His name. Who he is. Where. How he came to be here. Why he is wet, why cold. Why he doesn't know or remember.

He stands and wipes grit from cheek and brow then grimaces and gasps. His cheek is swollen and bruised, his forehead scabbed. The back of his head throbs. He touches there and finds a painful swelling. His entire body cut and bruised and stiff and aching. Sand abrades the lacerated soles of his feet.

What has happened to him?

The sky is starless black. No cloud or moon or differentiation. As if all surrounding is contained within some cavern.

The blank man turns toward the inky river. On the far bank begins a vast reach of blotchy ice that seems to glow with its own faint light here in this vast yet enclosed dimness. Something's moving in the water.

He must have just been in the water because he's soaking wet. But he doesn't remember being in the water. He doesn't remember anything before coming to here on the sand.

He surveys the shore. This side's very different from the other shore. Here the ground is like a beach. The hardpacked sand is blond. The breeze is light and warm and when it shifts from off the plain of ice across the river it contains a hint of chill. He could almost be on a beach just after sunset. If there were a sun. If there were an ocean. If this were a beach.

The clothes he wears are filthy despite being wet. He bends to sniff and nearly gags from the reek. Well there's plenty of water a dozen feet away. Might as well make use of it and wash himself and his clothes.

He faces the water and begins removing his clothes. He holds his jacket up before him to discern what tale it tells like some maltreated tapestry. Ripped and hugely stained with blood dried brown. He wonders if the blood is his. Something heavy in the right jacket pocket. He removes it and stares blankly at a fifth of Jack Daniel's whiskey in his hand, bottle full and seal unbroken. He reads every legible word of the white on black label. The smaller print impossible in this noxious light. He frowns and sets the bottle on the sand. Pulls off his flayed black T-shirt and winces at pain in his shoulder. Touches it as if examining someone else. Swollen and discolored and tender. His hiking shoes look fine but when he pulls them off his threadbare socks are stiff with dried blood. His buttonfly jeans are filthy but sound. He isn't wearing any underwear. He yanks down his pants and tears out a plug of scab where a gouge on his thigh has bled and dried stuck to his jeans. He screams and does a little rain dance on the gloomy shore.

Further mysteries are produced. A waterlogged pack of Swisher Sweets containing seven cigarillos, three of them salvageable. A saturated box of matches. A folded piece of soggy writing paper with a deckled edge, blue ink smeared beyond deciphering. A wet leather wallet holding cash, platinum charge cards, and a California driver's license with a thick silver coin taped to the back. Two round indentations in the tape where two other coins have been removed.

He frowns at the license. A blackhaired man with deeptoned skin and a constant five o'clock shadow. Nikkoleides Popoudopolos. Faintly familiar. Is that supposed to be him?

MORTALITY BRIDGE

He rubs his bristly jaw and feels his wet and curling hair and brings a strand of it before his eyes. Best he can tell in this faint light it's black. He rubs his face with both hands to form an image from his touch but lacks the tactile vision of the blind.

A silver locket hangs around his neck. He unclasps it and dangles its flattened oval before himself and watches dull red light glint from its turning surface. Like a man trying to hypnotize himself. He thumbs the catch but does not open the locket. His attention caught by thick hard calluses on his fingertips. He holds them up before him and touches them against his lips to feel their rough. Bites down on one but cannot feel it. Bites down harder and does, barely.

His knuckles are scabbed. Has he been mugged? Survived a planecrash? Shipwreck?

He shrugs. It'll come back or it won't.

He opens the locket and something glinting falls to the sand. He squats and sweeps his hands across the fine grit. His knees hurt and the gouge in his thigh bleeds freely. The skin around it waxy.

There. He lifts it carefully from the sand and holds it in his palm and blows it clean. A narrow gold ring, unadorned but with a half twist in the band. He knows this means something but not what. He presses the ring against his cheek and shuts his eyes. Jemma had been out of town visiting her father, Hank. Missing her and thinking of the immutable past and the oncoming wall of the future he had visited a jeweler off Rodeo Drive. He'd demonstrated what he wanted with a strip of paper. You give it a half twist and then join the ends, see? His finger sliding on the surface, traveling round the twist like some funhouse ride. It's a twosided object that only has one side. Because of how it's joined. Offering up the paper strip. Marriage, see? The jeweler smiled and nodded, not understanding any of it but knowing money when it walked in his door, and told him he could pick up the rings in five weeks.

The blank man's hand closes over the ring. He'd wanted to marry her but for some reason couldn't. Why not? Some fear not of marriage but of what it would portend for her to marry him. And she had never known he wore it near his heart for that day when perhaps he could remove it from the locket and slip it on her finger and clasp her hand and never let her go.

But here is the ring. So clearly that day never came.

He tries to conjure her face but cannot fix an image. What he does remember pangs his heart. But at least a name has caught in his memory's sieve. Jemma. His precious Jem. Something to hold on to.

The wind shifts and he gets downwind of himself. Let's take that bath, buddy pal. You can play detective when you smell better.

He clutches his filthy clothes to himself and leaves his small pile of artifacts on the warm sand and heads toward the river. He tests the water with a toe and the toe goes numb. This is gonna be bracing. He takes a deep breath and wades on in until he's

sitting naked on the inner shore the blank man shivers, wet and staring at the sand. He blinks. Freezing water hisses past before him. He clutches a wrungout bundle of wet clothes. Beside him on the sand a full bottle of whiskey. A wallet. Cigarillos. A box of matches. A silver locket. Are they his? The clothes he's holding are dry and ragged and stained. Are they his? Why doesn't he know?

He opens the wallet. Cash and credit cards, an odd coin, driver's license bearing a stranger's picture with a long Greek name and an unfamiliar address. He looks at the picture and touches his own face. The pictured face is shaven. His own is prickly with an early beard. The remaining items hold no meaning for him either, though he pauses over the gold ring in the locket. Maybe he can trade or sell it for something useful.

He has a small and tender bump on the back of his head. A cheek and shoulder feel a little bruised. His feet are sore. A fresh pink scar puckers his thigh.

He realizes he's thirsty. He considers the whiskey. But alcohol has never quenched any kind of thirst he's ever had. He knows at least that much. No, a big long drink of water first.

He stands and walks down to the river, where he bends and takes a good long look at

whiskey wallet cigarillos matches locket. The naked blank man blinks at unfamiliar things. The ragged clothes on which they're piled are dry though he is not.

He stares at the driver's license and touches his thickbearded face. He frowns and shrugs and flips the license away. Cracks the whiskey bottle and sniffs. Now this he recognizes. He puts his mouth to the bottle and lifts the bottle high and swallows. Poison, jesus christ it burns like lye. He staggers gagging toward the river where he splashes in the shallows and bends with hands on knees and vomits whiskey and little else. He dryheaves for a while. When the sickness passes he cups his hands and splashes water on his

face up on the sand the blank man stares at murky redblack air. He sits up gasping as if remembering that he has an appointment and has overslept.

A dozen feet away downshore a man stands watching him. Short and muscular and hairy. His beard mere thickening of his curly black hair. Eyes a piercing blue. He is armored in bronze. Cuirass, plated girdle, greaves, leather sandals, a helmet with flared nosepiece and a horsehair crest on top. In his hand a long wooden spear tipped with a flat bronze blade shaped like a narrow leaf. On the sand at his feet a long black case, feminine in shape, with silver latches and a handle on one side.

The armored man watches the blank man struggle to his feet. The blank man glances at the unfamiliar objects on the sand before him. Empty whiskey bottle on the sand. Jewelry. Some litter. Oddly the most familiar thing the blank man sees is the armored man he faces now. He feels perhaps he knows him. Knew him anyway some lost where.

The air is hot and the blank man begins to sweat. The armored man stares past him and his bright eyes do not waver and his tone is flat and without color as he says Hola, Orfeo.

The sound of the name opens a door in the blank man's mind. An ancient door long locked and safeguarding a room held deep within a house containing many rooms. He raises his hand palmout in the old way and in the language of the Achaian before him says, "Hola, friend. Are you come to tell me who I am?"

The helmet swivels slowly but still the eyes do not meet his. "A man may only tell himself that thing."

"What, then?"

"I am charged with several duties." The stern face gives the impression of a grudging smile. "First I bear two gifts."

"There's an old saying about Greeks bearing gifts."

"I have heard it many times." The Achaian fumbles in his cuirass until he draws forth a roll of human parchment that has flattened in the metal breastplate. He offers the scroll and the blank man hesitates and then takes the parchment and unrolls it and reads the illdrawn letters inked in red dried russet.

Buddy pal:

Here's the short version. Your name is Niko. You're a real true Rock Star. The reason you are is because you signed a deal with us a long time ago. We'll skip the fact that you've got the chops to have made it to the top without us. Your problem, not ours.

You were also quite the alcoholic junkie asshole back in the day, but your name in red on the dotted line took care of that double plus good. Well, the alcoholic junkie part, anyway.

So you straightened up and flew right and got rich and famous and everything else you bargained for, but then you went and fell in love with some babe. Maybe you forgot the "implicit chattels" part of your contract, or maybe you just didn't care. I don't know. Anyway, she got sick and died. You're not a very roll-with-the-punches kind of guy, and you got pissed off and came down here to bring her back. Which should explain a lot about your current condition, physically and otherwise.

A while back you fell into the river Lethe and forgot who you are, because the water washes away a lot more than dirt. At least I think you fell. You might have jumped. Either way, you keep on going back to the river, and every time you do it's like hitting reset. Blank slate time.

You've been doing this a lot longer than you'd want to know.

Armor Boy's been sent there to throw you in the river with a chain around your ass to keep you from ever remembering any of this and resuming your little quest. I didn't send him but I was able to use him to give you this message and your Dobro. I'm hoping it'll help bring you back to yourself, but for all I know you've forgotten which end of the thing to hold.

MORTALITY BRIDGE

Don't let Armor Boy's sparkling conversation fool you. He brought the gifts because I made him, but he's mainly there to kick your ass. Try not to make it easy for him.

Sports book now puts it at 9,000 to 1 against you—IF you hand this guy his hat.

Got a lot riding on you, cowboy. Don't let me down.

No signature. Niko sounds his heart for some response but he finds none. This note concerns some stranger.

He looks up from the sweatstained parchment. The armored man stands patient and unblinking, a living statue on the sand. "Do you know what this says?"

"I do not care what it says."

"I see. Well, thanks for delivering it." Niko smiles. "Have a nice day."

A glint of amusement in the bright blue eyes. "My duty is not discharged."

"Ah. Well. Worth a try."

The Achaian merely stands there. His gaze includes Niko only in the sense that Niko stands within his field of vision. As if the Achaian can see a horizon on the endless plain on which they stand.

Niko gathers his belongings and nods at the Achaian. "See you," he says, and makes to step past him but the bronzetipped spear comes to the fore.

"Can't we talk about this?"

"I am not sent for conversation."

"But we are countrymen."

"There are no countries here."

"Well we are ancients of a sort."

"There are no ancients here."

Was there a falter in that gaze? "I have no quarrel with you. According to this I'm after those who sent you."

"I am those who sent me." The Achaian takes his gaze from that haunted private distance and looks directly at Niko for the first time. His expression yields nothing. "This time with you is a respite from afflictions I endure without surcease. Nothing you can say or do will sway me from that reprieve."

Niko's slow nod belies the sudden prick of anticipation and fear within his chest. "All right. One thing more?"

The armored Achaian merely stares. Niko indicates the carrying case on the sand. "This note says that belongs to me."

"It is your second gift."

"Okay then."

The Achaian sets the black case on the sand without taking his gaze from Niko and steps back three paces and transfers the spear to his left hand.

Niko eyes the spear as he steps toward the case and kneels before it on the warm sand. He flips a latch and the Achaian tenses. "I don't think it's a weapon," Niko says. And undoes the latches and opens the case and regards the gleaming metal thing encushioned there.

"Not a weapon?"

Niko shrugs. "No more than any musical instrument. I think it is a kind of lyre. See the strings?"

"If the strategy is to bore an opponent to death perhaps. Music is a wasteful vice."

"I'm going to take it out."

The Achaian shrugs but does not relax his grip upon his spear. Still Niko feels that the Achaian will not murder him but means to engage him according to some code. He pulls the heavy unfamiliar instrument from the case and holds it awkwardly as he squats there on the sand. Polished metal glinting dull red light. He frowns at the long neck with its inset metal bars. Raps the metal body with his knuckles and it gives a dull and hollow gong. Well, if it is a kind of lyre then it stands to reason the strings are meant to be plucked.

He cradles the foreign metal thing and just before his callused fingers touch the strings he has a sense of the instrument fitting itself against him with the nonchalance of a longtime lover settling with her partner into bed. Cold metal body. But the startlement of that sensation dissolves in the wash of memories that inundate him when his hands touch the strings and deliver him to himself and the dread knowledge of who he is and what has led him into Hell.

I

BABY PLEASE DON'T GO

SHE LET GO HIS HAND as the pallet slid into the narrow
tunnel. "Niko?"

"Right here, Jem." He squeezed her foot beneath the cover
pulled so tight she looked like a streamlined mummy.

"It's really small in here." Her voice muffled in that cramped space.

The technician's voice came tinny from the intercom. "You
okay?"

"Umm. Yeah. I think so." Percocet thickening her tone. "It's like
wearing a knight helmet. Like a joust."

Behind thick glass the technician nodded. "The regular CT
unit is down for scheduled maintenance. Bessie here's our backup.
She hasn't let us down yet. But we can try again another time if it's
bothering you too much right now."

"No. We've come this far."

"Okay. I'm going to activate the scan now, all right? I need you
to hold perfectly still, okay? Try to keep your arms straight and
don't move. Can you do that?"

"Do you have to close the door?"

"No, we'll keep it open for you."

The Muzak played some watered down song by Gerry and the Pacemakers. Niko squeezed Jem's foot to maintain contact as they listened in the nervous interlude.

A muffled laugh. "Just wait'll they do this to one of your songs." She began to hum a cheesy lounge act version of "Notes on Her Sleeping" and Niko smiled even as his face went tight and his eyes began to sting. "I think they already have," he said.

"Okay," said the intercom. "Here we go." There was a slight vibration.

"It smells like vanilla."

"There's some evidence it reduces stress," the intercom said.

The leaden laugh again. "Better use the whole can."

Niko patted her foot and felt the corn on her big toe. Countless gigs in high heeled shoes. He pressed and her foot kicked.

The intercom said Hold still please.

"Sorry."

"You're doing fine, Jem." Niko squeezed her foot again and bit his lower lip. He should get another Grammy for this. Or an Oscar. Best Vocal Performance by a Son of a Bitch in a Lead Role.

Hidden engines surged invisible energies through her head.

"I can't feel my arm." The fear in her voice tore a plug from his heart. They'd told her there was a slight chance of allergic reaction to the iodine. One in ten thousand, nothing to worry about. But she'd had to sign waivers.

The intercom said It's normal for limbs to get pins and needles when forced to hold still, nothing to be alarmed about, we'll massage them as soon as you're out.

But there had been that single moment of mortal dread, Jemma lying without moving in a tube with metal inches from her skin, iodine coursing alien in her veins and her limbs numbing. And Niko thinking o god is this it, can this be it.

When they got home the Percocet kicked in bigtime and Niko helped her sag upstairs and tucked her into their huge bed and kissed her brow and dialed down the light and crept out of the room and eased shut the door, stopping to look back at her through the narrow slit and feeling like a father peering in on a sleeping child. He left the door cracked open and the intercom on in case she woke disoriented.

THE WEST HALL was lined with framed concert posters, many of them decades old. Drippy letters and high contrast dayglow colors. Niko's name on all of them. Or the names of bands he'd played in long ago. Before the four letters of his shortened name alone became enough to fill arenas. Jemma'd put the posters up here. He had thought it much too vain. Decades of his pawned off life arrayed along these walls. Legendary days. Those early Perish Blues gigs, the fevered howling yearning. Fights broke out during his solos. He made the room crazy just by playing his guitar. Made the crowd want to fight or fuck or both. He just stood there playing. And somehow just standing there made the music stronger. Surrounded him with energy. Incredible such anger and such anguish could be wrung howling from the neck of a guitar throttled by a young man who just stood there like the center of a cyclone oblivious to its debris.

On the strength of their live gigs Perish Blues recorded Say Hey on the Decca label. A single got decent local airplay but the band just never caught. The feeling was they had something live that recordings could not capture. Niko's playing was ferocious but he was bagged half the time, he forgot playlists, missed rehearsals and even gigs, tiraded incoherently. He felt restless and the band was discontent.

Perish Blues disbanded and their lead guitarist felt bad about it and felt good about it too. He sat around his apartment and drank and thought about getting another band together and didn't. He played sessions with a few wellknown bands but didn't get around to much else.

He'd met Jemma around the beginning of his fiery arc. She'd sung backup in some now forgotten band that opened for his, at one point trading call and response with their lead guitar. He simply couldn't believe her voice. The beautiful pain of it. Niko so broke he had to borrow money to get his Fender out of hock to play the gig and still he asked her out. Then the long series of attempts to be together. Our staccato love, he'd joked.

Jemma left him after one of his more mundane binges. Though by then it was more correct to say that Niko was on one long bender that ebbed and flowed. This time out was not as spectacular as the time he'd thrown their furniture and clothes out on the curb, the time he'd hurled a paperweight into a blacksmoked mirror, the time he'd doused his Fender with butane and torched it on the balcony of their matchbox apartment off of Gower. This was just another drunk, a sad and stinking unshaved weekday drunk where Jemma had come home to find him crying incoherently about what a nogood shit he was, emptying himself until he slept and then awoke alone all wound in sour sheets like a corpse within a shroud. A C-clamp hangover tightened on his temples as he waited and waited for Jemma to bring him morning coffee the way she always did rain or shine, pleased with him or mad, a little ritual enacted in their daily life together. And when the coffee didn't come he knew that she was gone. He called her name regardless but of course there was no answer. A hollow silence lay about the place that was precisely her subtracted measure. She had finally had enough. Last night just the final night in the parade of nights spent waiting for him to come home, sweeping broken glass from tile floors, bringing him a basin to throw up in, trying to convince him he was not the demon he imagined himself, holding him through his senseless crying jags and patiently thinking she could fix him. For Jemma was a fixer. She could not bear to see potential squandered. Which had sparked her interest in him in the first place and kept her with him past the point of any reason. At least until she'd understood she couldn't fix what wanted to be broken.

However bad he got he always seemed to come through whole while those around him lost some unseen thing. You always land on your feet, she told him. And the ones who catch you fall.

With Jemma gone there'd been little to stop him slowly drowning in a whiskey river. He told himself he was only dulling the pain and the pain was pretty bad. Better put me under, doc, a local anesthetic just won't do.

But when he slept his callused fingers clutched a pillow and caressed her absent contours like a phantom limb. She fired his brain like a lovely fever and throughout his long descent he felt her burning out there in the world apart from him. He'd lie drunk and crying in the bed just big enough to hold them both or howl the Strat he'd borrowed after torching his own, two a.m. and another whiskey bottle consigned to the graveyard of failed consolations. He'd lie on the thin worn carpet and stare up at the waterstained ceiling and make pictures out of earthquake cracks, fissures on some vast and endless plain, or he would cruise the empty glitter of latenight Sunset in a blurred and weaving stupor with the puttering station wagon's radio cranked until the music left no room for thought. Niko driving down the unabating night and knowing she was awake in the shabby North Hollywood house she'd rented with her friend Bonnie. Knowing her bedside light was on beside her. Knowing she could feel him out here burning too.

For months he dieted on trashy novels and tv and stayed indoors. Reading the same paragraph over and over he would wonder Where are you tonight Jem, are you thinking of me, are you alone?

Friends told him he was crazy to punish himself like this. They told him to put it behind him. But he kept Jem alive in his mind precisely because he wanted to feel the pain. The pain cut through the haze as proof that he could feel at all.

One day there was a knock on his apartment door and he opened it and blinked in the bright afternoon sunshine bleary and hungover and already getting drunk again. A tall thin man dressed like some kind of psychedelic drum major with a bushy afro stood holding a guitar case and grinning as if he'd just told a really good joke and was waiting for the laugh. "Hey," he said. "Can Niko come out and play?"

Niko stepped back into the house. "Naw. But you can come play with him."

And so they jammed long into the night. They had never met before but they had common influences and mutual admiration. Niko played his new Dobro while Jimi played his beatup Gibson and they howled at the moon and raised the devil and drank like fish and laughed like thieves and cried the blues. It never occurred to either of them to record the session. Its frail unwitnessed evanescence made it all the better in a way. Lost in pure creation without a thought about the world without. Before the night was over Jimi dug out his rig and asked if Niko indulged and Niko said yeah sure why not, old Mr. Daniel's isn't getting the job done anymore.

He would only snort. Injecting was hardcore. Injecting was for junkies. It made him itch and it made him sleepy and it made him float a half an inch above the floor but best of all it made him just plain go away. He dove into a river of oblivion and lay contented in the bottom mud. Jimi staggered off sometime near dawn, leaving Niko with a little powder present in a cellophane twist. The gift that kept on giving.

Soon the rush just wouldn't happen when he snorted so he started shooting. He became a kind of alchemist. Into his veins went china white and out his hands came sorrow and pain and terrible beauty. He fronted shortlived bands and couldn't get a deal and played some of the best guitar of his or anyone's career. And all the while out there somewhere shining faintly in his battlemented heart was Jemma. She was doing well he knew. Background vocals for successful acts. On the road half the year, studio time in L.A.

Niko would imagine showing up backstage at some gig of hers. He catches her eye as she sings off to the side, she falters at the mic. The tearful backstage reunion. But he knew it wouldn't happen because he hadn't really changed.

He shot up alone, he shot up with friends. Celebrities, strangers, people he didn't much like. If he wasn't playing a gig he was lying down at home or crashed on someone's couch. He lived on junk food and whatever else was in arm's reach. Sometimes after gigs he brought women home and failed miserably in the sack. If he cared enough to try at all. But they helped to fill the howling silence waiting for him every time his footsteps echoed in his new apartment in the hills beneath the Hollywood sign. He lived on tv dinners and spent bleary afternoons unshaven and unbathed with his new soap opera friends, blathered for hours on the phone to people he didn't even like just to hear a voice, hired managers, fired managers, contracted hepatitis, trashed a contract meeting by showing up drunk and telling a major producer to go fuck himself, drove someone else's manager's Cadillac into someone else's swimming pool, frisbeed someone else's gold record out the window of a VP's office at a friend's record label, watched someone OD at a party that got raided not five minutes after he stumbled away.

He had felt her out there all that awful lost and forlorn time, quietly burning, and knew that she would not come back until he came back to himself. And that didn't happen till he signed away the most fundamental part of himself and killed his brother Van.

ALL THESE HALLWAY posters. All this past. Niko looked away. Jemma couldn't have known what kind of awful scrapbook she had put together in this hall. Let it go.

He left Jemma to her medicated sleep and hurried down the hall and down the sweeping curve of staircase. Through the cavernous living room and into the study. The house was open and airy and Mediterranean but the study was Victorian and dark, brass and polished woods. Tracklights highlighted gold and platinum records in plain wooden frames between pilasters on one wall. On the mantel three gold phonographs on wooden trapezoids, a Lucite pyramid on a black block base, a silver astronaut planting an MTV flag. Him and Jemma hugging Goofy at Disneyland. Jemma with her eyes closed singing background at the mic, blobs of Vari-lite rig behind her. Her portraits of sleeping people, murky acrylics distorting shapes like funhouse mirrors. Newly inaugurated president shaking his hand there on one end of a maple bookcase. Etta James hugging Jemma on the other. On the battlements of maple bookshelves stone gargoyles vigilant before mystery and horror and occult. Her doll collection spaced out among cookbooks, selfhelp books, art monographs. Floppy ragdolls dangling stuffed legs over the wooden precipice like overseeing patchwork angels.

And Jemma's pencil sketch of him. Seated on a rude stool in his studio with the Strat high on his thigh, eyes closed and fingers poised and a length of ash on the burning cigarette pinched on the guitar head. Shock of hair obscuring one eye as his head inclines. Historical artifacts, ladies and gentlemen. Note the longlost days of this immortal youth when cigarettes were the least of many vices, when the hair was jet and hanging in the unkempt fashion of the day, not thin and flecked with gray. He'd looked as old back then as he is now. Older.

The day Jem gave him that portrait. So tentative. They'd been together only a few months. He'd looked from his drawn face to hers so worried and in his heart he'd felt a driven nail of terror because she already loved him more than ever he would her. No one owned a key to that deep place. He would not allow it.

Niko looked away. This panoply of static things. Totems in some pharaoh's tomb. Jemma upstairs fading.

On a marble pedestal in the form of an ionic column stood the weathered remnant of a lyre under glass. Its tortoise shell beneath the dust-shouldered belljar. The mystery of it. He'd bid ruthlessly through intermediaries when it came up at Sotheby's. He had to have it, he didn't know why. It brought him close to something old and deep. What hands now dust had plucked forth what notes long carried away?

Niko pulled a volume from the bookcase by the lyre and pressed a button and the bookcase opened inward.

Many mansions harbor hidden rooms and tunnels. Panic rooms and getaways, dungeons and shrines. Used with great solemnity and rarely secret at all. But Niko's little room was truly secret. The woman he had shared his life with never knew about it. Perhaps she had her own such rooms. Perhaps she kept them hidden in her heart.

Niko stepped through the bookcase like a storybook child.

The tiny room contained a single chair behind a little walnut desk carved with sleeping faces on the corners and the legs. A laptop incongruous amid fountain pens in display holders, a blotter and a crystal inkwell and a green bankers light. A framed photograph of Niko with his brother Van. Here is Niko eighteen or nineteen, thickly bearded, hair long ringlets. His little brother tall and gangly, closecut hair a cap of curls, sixteen or seventeen if he's a day. Both of them smiling as they pretend to punch each other, playing at a rivalry that really did exist. Van how many times have I awakened screaming because I saw you there unseeing? And to think I laughed at first. Watched the red bloom unfold in your eyes and slow blood trickle out your nose. My brother I was mean to and played army with and rode a bike beside, whose underwear I threw out in the rain once at the municipal pool, and this is the picture I am left of you. Van what would you say if you could see where all that spun forth from that awful day has led? You were there at the start of it all. You were the start of it all. The horrible bloodflower in your eye. I didn't kill you but I was why you died and all my life I've been ashamed. Driven, driven down. Are you waiting for me there across some bridge of penance? I will find out soon enough.

Niko sat at the desk and slid out a drawer and removed a document. Sixteen yellowed stapled pages. Courier tenpitch type, floating caps archaic evidence of a manual typewriter, every lowercase e gummed in at the top. Every word of it tattooed upon his mortgaged heart.

He glanced at the date and shook his head. A life ago yet only yesterday as well. He turned to the last page. His signature still there of course, scrawled in red gone russet over time. He still owned the pen he'd signed it with. A 1920 J.G. Rider pearl and abalone pump action fountain pen with a 22-karat gold medium nib. The contract's lower right side smudged brown where his hand wet with blood not his had rested when he signed.

His nervous fingers riffed the contract pages. Should I bring it? To what end? I know every word of it by heart and still am not sure what my options are.

But he took the contract with him when he left his secret room.

Back in the study he called Jemma's father. The CAT scan went fine, Hank. She's sleeping now, they gave her Percoset. We won't have the results for a couple of days but I'll call you soon as we do. No reason to panic yet. You bet. I'll tell her. Take care. Talk soon. Then he stared at his phone and thought about who he had to call up next.

II

CROSSROAD BLUES

H E WENT DOWN TO THE Crossroads with his contract by his side. His burgundy Bentley Continental GT Speed sat idling in the empty lot while he stared through the sloped dark windshield at the restaurant.

Crossroads of the World had been built to look like a paddle-wheeler and it almost did. Driving along Sunset Boulevard near Paramount Studios Niko had passed it many times over the years and paid it little attention apart from noticing its ugliness and vainglorious name displayed in bright blue neon on a retrofuturistic steeple. He never would have set foot in it were it not for his meeting here today.

He took a deep breath and let it out and switched off the ignition and grabbed his vintage Hermes valise and got out into what passed for winter in Los Angeles. The car door shut with a reassuring and expensive sound and Niko headed for the restaurant. Behind him the Bentley chirped like a fat contented budgie.

THE CROSSROADS WAS crowded and bustling and loud. Glasswalled and sunny. Waitresses older than the architecture hurried about bearing unreasonable burdens on serving trays to men in designer jackets and two hundred dollar T-shirts sitting proprietarily in their booths and at the counter and gesturing violently at no one as they argued into cellphones or ignored their boothmates while they texted.

Niko glanced outside. But for his car the lot was empty. He frowned at the crowded restaurant and clutched the valise tighter.

A waitress hurrying by with an armload of steaming food nodded at the sign near the register that said PLEASE SEAT YOUR-SELF. Niko walked to a booth as if moving in some whitewashed dream. A waitress with shellacked hair and librarian glasses and a name badge that read MADGE gave him a menu and took his order for coffee.

The two men in the booth in front of his scribbled in red ink on a yellow legal pad they passed back and forth. "No no no no," said the one facing him. Sallow and cadaverous with perfect hair and trim black coat, white arrowcollar shirt, dark wraparounds. He jabbed his lit cigarette at the legal pad. "You can't put it like that. What's in it for us if you put it like that?"

Niko tuned them out. L.A. coffeeshops see more deals than a Vegas blackjack table.

The man with his back to Niko looked like some Sunset Boulevard glamrocker throwback. Longhaired and strongjawed and skinny. Black boots with silver caps and heels and chains and everything but chrome exhaust pipes. Once upon a time Niko had looked like this guy's second cousin.

While Hair Boy spoke, Trim Coat nodded and smoked and looked as if he had better things to do. Niko considered moving to another booth. Like a lot of former smokers, drinkers, catholics, and whores, being near the source of previous pleasure could be a royal pain in the ass.

But damn near everyone else in here was smoking too. Gouts of it rose above the booths. Behind the counter two ancient waitresses faced each other with unfiltered cigarettes pinched in their fisted fingers like Gestapo interrogators, their makeup straying outside the lines like kindergarten coloringbook drawings. L.A. restaurants had long been smokefree zones.

Niko fidgeted in the booth and Madge brought his coffee and said Ready to order hon?

"Just coffee for now. I'm waiting for someone."

"Aren't we all." Madge pocketed her order pad.

The scalding coffee tasted even worse than he'd expected and he almost dumped in a load of cream but then stopped himself and lifted the lid on the little metal pitcher and sniffed and put it back. He drummed his fingers on the seatback and stared at the empty seat across from him. Conscious of the valise beside him. As if it held a coiled viper.

The lunch rush picked up and the Crossroads got crowded. Madge headed toward him with a determined look. Niko wondered if he were vain and foolish enough to leave without the meeting taking place.

The waitress reached his booth with pad in hand and opened her bright red mouth to tell him Sorry hon but I can't hold the booth any longer but a figure stepped in front of her and eased into the seat across from him and adjusted the cuffs of his cream-colored raw silk jacket and beamed at Niko from behind dark sunglasses. "Mexican omelette, beautiful. Rye toast burnt, hash browns extra crispy. Coffee of course. If it's the bottom inch of the pot and it's been on the burner at least an hour you'll make me one happy camper—" he glanced up at her name badge "—Madge."

The waitress smiled. "And you sir?"

"I'm fine."

"Fine." The trendy retro shades looked him over. "Nick-o, look at you. You're wasting away." And smiled up at the waitress. "You make an outstanding chicken fried steak as I recall."

"Best in town."

"He'll have that."

She scribbled and nodded smartly and left.

The man watched her go. "I do love waitresses. Always pamper you, always have that cash on hand. It's that mom thing I suppose." The smile turned on full wattage. "So." Flatware rattled as he para-diddled the table. "What brings us here before our appointed time, Niko-teen?"

Niko sized him up. The precise scruff of hair. The uniform tan with not a zit or freckle to be seen. Retro shades perched on a model nose. White linen shirt not too pressed and not too rumpled. A Rolex Oyster Perpetual Daytona Cosmograph occupied his left wrist. The outfit had changed with the times but Phil had not aged a day in the quarter century since they'd first met.

Niko was trying to be mister cool but he wanted to throw up. Van's head was still against the steering wheel, the eyes so like his own still stared at nothing, and he still laughed when he first saw it. The bloodrose still bloomed in one dulled eye. No time had passed in that tableau.

He wiped his palms on his thighs. "Jemma got a CAT scan last week."

Phil shook his head. "All this time and this is how you say hello." From somewhere he brought forth an iPhone in a beige leather case monogrammed with a single letter M. He tapped the screen and frowned. "Jemma, that's the wife, right?"

"We're not married."

A wide smile. "For purposes of conversation."

Madge arrived with Phil's coffee.

"She started getting headaches. Having dizzy spells, short term memory lapses, problems concentrating."

Phil spooned sugar and dumped clotted creamer into his coffee and stirred it with a finger.

"Sometimes blurred vision."

Phil blew across his coffeecup and sipped and toasted Madge who had already left them. "A month ago it started getting worse. She'd stare at nothing for twenty minutes and then pop out of it without being aware the time had gone by. Like a little epileptic fit." Phil drained his coffee in one gulp and looked around for their waitress. "Two weeks ago she fell down when we were out shopping. She didn't even reach out to stop her fall. Just fell. She nearly broke her nose on the concrete."

The empty coffeecup pushed away and the iPhone went back into a pocket. "Well we all have our little problems, Niko-lodeon."

"Her doctor thinks it could be some kind of cerebral virus. But you know what it is. Don't you."

A hand spread across the linen shirt. "Me? I'm just a gobetween, Niko-rama. A glorified mailman. I pick up and I deliver."

"Then deliver this."

The smile vanished and the man grew absolutely still. "Careful, Niko-san."

"Just one word."

"I'm all ears."

"Don't."

"Don't? Not even please don't?"

Madge returned and refilled their cups.

"Thanks, beautiful. I'll bet you'll make some guy very happy someday."

"I've made too many guys happy already."

He brayed like a mule. "Bam! Let me shake your hand. You can call me Phil for short."

She avoided his hand like an Aikido master. "I wouldn't call you Phil for long."

Phil watched her go and shook his head. "That's so great. These girls. They've seen everything. You gotta love em." He saw Niko reaching into his valise and grew annoyed. "Oh have a heart, will you? Have some selfrespect."

Their food arrived and Phil looked up wide eyed at Madge. "Madge my darling dear, I am going to devour this fine meal as if you prepared it with your own loving hands."

"Don't blame me for it."

Phil dug in and talked to Niko with his mouth full while he gestured with his dirty fork. "Trust me when I tell you that we have the best lawyers ever born. A lot of them. And they've been over our boilerplate about a million times each. But you and every other armchair Daniel Webster think you're going to be the one to find the loophole and beat the rap. Well you're not." Egg sprayed from Phil's mouth. Niko watched him devour his omelette like a man who had not seen food for a long time.

The son of a bitch was right about the contract. In the bad old days after Niko had cleaned up but before he'd owned a nice big house in the Hollywood Hills he'd once taken the contract to a lawyer named Carlton Howard, whom Niko's manager Avery

Kramer had recommended. Howard was thin and graysuited and gold cufflinked, round spectacled and baldspotted. For all that he had the same leonine largesse and sleepyeyed look Niko would later learn to recognize in sparring partners who could kick his ass at will. Niko gave him the contract with much trepidation. It had never been out of his possession. He told the lawyer that the document was part of an elaborate prank and that he wanted to be sure it read like the real thing.

Howard called him back a few days later. "I've read your little prank, Mr. Popoudopolos, and I must tell you that what Shakespeare is to the stage this contract is to law."

"That's bad?"

"Hardly. It contains some of the most effective contractual language it has been my fearful pleasure to read. I'd rather fight the law of gravity than go up against this thing. Did you know it won't photocopy?"

"No kidding."

"I tried to make a Xerox of it to show some associates. I've never seen anything like it."

"Me neither." Niko closed his eyes. "So if it were real would you sign it?"

"I personally would not wipe my ass with this thing. But it's a masterpiece." Howard chuckled. "Sign it hell. I'd frame it."

PHIL POINTED HIS fork at Niko's valise. "Really, Niko-polis. I expected more from you." He dabbed his mouth with a paper napkin. His plate now spotless. "So what exactly is the purpose of this meeting? To tell us Don't, like Jimmy Cagney? Keep ya mitts offa my goyl?"

"Jem has nothing to do with this. She's not part of—"

"Read the fine print, Niko-saurus. Section three sub a little i. Valued chattels attached." Phil leaned back on the seat and drummed his fingers.

"Your business is with me. Leave her alone."

Phil slid his shades down his nose and leaned forward and looked at Niko over the frames. Bald eyes wanting iris or pupil, eggwhite sclera redwormed and dull. "Or else what, you pusfilled maggotfeast?

You're meat, asshole. And you've been our meat ever since you signed on the dotted line. What part of Sell did you not understand?"

Niko quailed beneath that cueball gaze. A look around the restaurant showed the diners tending to their own affairs. One of the oddest things here in fact was that he'd not been recognized. Nobody seemed to know him, everybody passed him by.

Phil slid his shades back up and resumed his former velvet tone. "What you've got there in your dorky lawyer bag is a receipt, shitbag. With your signature guaranteeing delivery. We can run a DNA test on the ink if you want." He smiled. "So get off your high horse and listen up, Niko-sabe." He pointed a pinky at Niko and his tone allowed no contravention. Niko smelled burnt matches on his breath. "Our business, as you put it, is with what the philosophers like to call your irreducible self. Such as it is. And guess who's part of that now." The hand lowered to the table. "What, you thought you had a get out of jail free card if you didn't marry her?" The braying laugh again. "You're the one who fell in love, Don Juan. Maybe you should have kept your pecker in your pocket." He moved his plate aside and slid Niko's untouched chicken fried steak in its place. He picked up knife and fork and dug in like a dire wolf while Niko tried to think of what to say or do. Phil glanced up at Niko and held his knife and fork before him in a cross. "Here comes the whiny beggy part. I hate that as much as I hate coming up this way, so spare me before I choke on my lunch here." The utensils turned outward with his shrug. "You signed and we delivered and now it's your turn and you want to welsh. I've heard this song so many times it gives me a headache." He chugged his coffee in one gulp again and slammed the empty cup on the table. "Every damned one of you tries to renege. You've even tried before."

"How could I have? I haven't even seen you since—"

"Not now, pinhead. Different times, different guises, different means. You don't remember because that birth thing fucks you guys up something awful. And I end up meeting you in the woods or in some cheapo movie graveyard at midnight or in some artery clogging choke and puke—" he indicated at the restaurant with the knife and fork "—and I sit there listening while every one of you maggot banquets tries to cheat his way out of a binding contract freely entered into. But somehow we're the bad guys. Well piss on that." Phil abandoned the utensils and picked up the gravyclotted slab of batterfried meat with his bare hands and his mouth opened impossibly wide and he dangled the steak obscenely over it like a rat held by the tail and he dropped it into his gullet and swallowed loudly without chewing and then picked up the plate and licked it clean. He wiped his fingers with his napkin and pulled another from the dispenser to pat his lips. Then he dropped the napkin to his plate and leaned forward again to tick off points on his slender fingers. "Now here's the straight dope, Niko-lette. You don't make demands. You don't ask favors. You don't even call me up again. Are the clouds parting here?"

"You have no right. She didn't—"

"Tell a lawyer. Tell your priest. But don't tell me. We signed you and you went and made it a package deal. Buy one get one free."

"Don't do it to her. Do it—"

"—to me." Phil slapped his own forehead. "Doubleplus no, Niko-loser. Get it? Is it the fuck or the you that isn't coming through here?"

Niko only stared and felt a soft collapse inside.

Phil toyed with the ice in his drinking glass and it began to quickly melt. "You poor things." He drummed the table. "Well, there's nothing more to—" Phil's iPhone rang and half the men in the restaurant patted their pockets and glanced around. Phil produced the phone from nowhere and glanced at it and frowned. "My three o'clock." He flagged their waitress and drew a big checkmark in the air.

Niko got up from the booth and tossed a twenty on the table. Phil's hand shot out and clamped Niko's wrist like a shackle and he grabbed the twenty with his other hand and curled Niko's wrist up and pried open his fingers and pushed the money back into his hand. "My treat," he said and let him go.

IN THE PARKING lot the Bentley shook with Niko's trembling.

So Jem had fallen sick with something doctors couldn't diagnose. Something they had said might be a virus in the hope that giving it a name would provide a target for their weaponry. But it had no name. Was not something you could look at through a microscope. Niko knew this in his bargained heart. The thing Jem hosted uninvited somewhere in her brain was going to eat at her till she was gone. And it was all his fault. Undeniably all his fault. The gold nib that had traced in red the unique glyph of his own name so long ago had infected her as sure as if they had been hepatitic junkies sharing needles.

How could you do this? To Jemma. To Jem.

His loathsome demon whispered But you couldn't have known. No one told you it applied to her. Love's not something you control, buddy pal. You didn't sell her. They're taking her. You got done in by the fine print. You got lawyered.

Niko punched the center console. Fuck that. Fuck that. You can't sit here and try to spread this blame around. You own this one, cowboy. You have a bill of sale to prove it.

And what about Jem, asshole? Just who the fuck are you really crying for here? Poor Niko, him's girlfwiendums go bye bye and he'll be aww awone.

More than once he had decided he would start a fight with her and drive her away, be such a prick that she gladly packed and left without a backward glance, the way she had those many years ago. And many times he had resolved instead to tell her everything. The accident. The Deal. The whole enchilada. Tell her what happened that day with his brother Van and show her the secret room and let her read the contract and then stand back and take his medicine. But then he would think about the day that she came back to him. An offseason weekend in separate cabins on Lake Arrowhead. His strength recovered and his life on track. The trip had started off like some negotiation and ended up the best day of his life. The memory of it sapped his strength to set in motion the machinery that would send her off again. He was a weak and selfish man. That's what addicts are, Niko, weak and selfish people. That view kept you safe inside a bottle or a needle for a good long time, didn't it?

What he'd done instead was try to keep the status quo. He'd told himself as long as you don't marry Jem she's safe. Keep her hidden in a camouflage of unimportance and the retribution that is rightly yours will pass her by. It's your name on the line, not hers.

And now outside the Crossroads of the World where he had begged for Jemma's life and failed he gripped the leatherwrapped wheel of his expensive car and understood at last that he had only fooled himself. Had hung her fate on technicalities and semantics. As if to get away with this through turn of phrase. But in truth he knew his contract to the comma and there was no escaping that, spoken vows or not, the union of their souls itself had set Jem's path indelibly with his.

Ah god. Ah god. He'd been so sure. So certain he would get away with this. Scam his way through and land on his feet the way he got through everything else. But it just didn't work out that way did it old boy? And there's nothing you can do about it now and nowhere else to shift the blame. Jemma's sickness is the very confirmation of your love. And it will kill her. And more than merely kill her will consign her to some unknown awful and eternal punishment against which mere oblivion is a mercy.

The enormity of what he'd done towered before him. The arrogance of it. The unequivocal truth was unbearable. How do you like hitting the wall of the immutable, asshole? How's it feel to know that you can't charm your way out of this one? What's the next lie you'll tell yourself? Your king's surrounded and your pieces are gone and still you sit here planning your next move. Nobody would give a good goddamn if it was just you dying here. Who'll miss one more alcoholic junky guitar player? There's no lack of washed-out rockstars in this town. You could form a union. But you've got Jem's blood on you now. And you still don't even have the stones to tell her why she's really dying.

And now at last he was afraid, mortally afraid.

He started the car. Some old song was on the radio and he poked it off. He massaged his face.

But even so. Even so. I won't just give her up without a fight. I won't give up until I've nothing left to give. Until I've truly lost instead of merely stopped. Now will I draw careful plans and strategies and place myself upon the stage to act against the power that is taking what it has no right to take.

There's nothing I can do while Jem's alive. Okay. Fine. But after that?

After that.

Niko clenched the steering wheel and felt a desperate notion born. If I can call them up then I can hunt them down. If I can't stop them taking her then I'll pursue her. I will find her and I'll bring her back. However far it takes me. Whatever price it costs.

Seen from outside he was a man woolgathering in his car a few minutes after lunch before returning to his busy world. The unsuspected battles within each of us.

Niko banged a fist upon the steering wheel. A plan then. An objective. Some faint hope. He put the car in gear and then he stopped. Gawking through the windshield like some mislanded astronaut. In front of him lay broken glass and boarded windows. Sagging beams and peeling handbills over dirty stucco tagged with spraypaint. Crossroads of the World was long abandoned and well fallen into ruin.

III

SHE'S GONE

SEVERAL TIMES THE PRIVATE NURSE buzzed at the gate and startled him awake on the chaise lounge he had dragged beside Jem's bed. Their bed. These last few weeks Jem had become so sensitive to light and sound and touch she couldn't bear to sleep beside him. She had always liked to hold his hand at movies and public events, would lightly rest a hand upon his ankle on a sunchair in the garden drinking morning coffee. As if needing reassurance of his presence. Now she flinched at every touch. The sheets are rough, she said. He replaced them with high threadcount brushed egyptian cotton. He replaced them himself because he'd dismissed all the help except the private nurse a week ago. He replaced them every day because she broke a fever every night.

He kept the room heat high because she said that she was always cold. She drank liter after liter of water and sweated constantly. Nauseated and no appetite. The bones emerging in her face and her color bad. She'd lost twentyeight pounds since the CAT scan and hadn't had them to spare to begin with. Often she made noises that made Niko think that she was having nightmares and he'd lean across the bed to reassure her and she'd be awake. Had been awake for hours. Sensitive to everything. Water was freezing and tepid teas scalded. The room too bright and her bedclothes bunched and his footsteps loud on the deep pile carpet. Her world burning brighter even as it waned.

Niko kept his vigil by her bed and talked to her. She'd grown short of breath and did not talk much. Short tired sentences often trailing off as medications claimed them. He talked about their lives together and adventures they had had. Would have. The great good fortune of their lives, of being alive. News of the world, their friends, their industry. He tried to keep it light but every word felt like goodbye. He called her father and held the phone against her ear and she said a few words but mostly listened. Hank a broken-hearted bear who had been nothing but kind to Niko despite all that Niko'd put his daughter through. Tolerant and forgiving and firm and stern when need demanded. His wife dead of pancreatic cancer these eight years. The man made smaller in the years since then. Tentative. Aware that everything valuable can be broken. Will be broken.

She called friends and spoke to them through him. She'd been texting them but that had dwindled. Some came to visit though he discouraged this. The great unspoken in their eyes. She didn't need to see that. When the reporters started calling he stopped answering his phone.

He helped her to the bathroom while she still felt good enough to walk and changed her bedpan after she did not. He changed IV bags and swabbed insertion sites and gave meds as the nurse had shown him. The litany of medications now well known to him and only palliative. A month ago it had been Tylenol for headaches and chronic fever and joint pain. The headaches became migraines which had led to Imitrex. The joint pain became general which led to Lyrica. Shortness of breath and chest pain led to asthma inhalers which did nothing. Reglan for nausea. Her skin began to hurt and sometimes even burn. She spiked fevers several times a day and soaked the sheets with night sweats. She became dehydrated and had no appetite. IV glucose and fluids, Vicodin and then Percoset for pain. Marinol briefly to horrible effect, hallucinations and panic. Now it was morphine and nowhere left to go.

He did everything he could to be with her and make her comfortable, and conducted his researches and arrangements while she slept. Phone calls and emails and websites and rare books. Fed Ex packages delivered through discreet third parties. Notes and diagrams and incantations. He became disturbed by how familiar all these preparations felt. Keys and summonings, abjurations and imprecations. Icons and dead languages. Things he'd never been exposed to in this life and could not have known. Yet know them he did. He did not learn so much as remember. As if the more he dug the more some tiered self surfaced like recovered strata of despoiled Troy.

He worked in the study and left the intercom on in case she called out and kept his cellphone near to hand in case she texted him. Sometimes that was easier for her than talking. Her voice the first thing he had loved about her. Wise beyond its years and freighted with the world no matter what it sang about. Now threadbare and so much diminished. As Jem herself was much diminished. She slept more than she was awake. It all got worse.

SOME NIGHTS IT weighed on him too much. The unforgivable nature of his complicity. The exquisite folly of what he was going to attempt. On those nights he'd simply play his Goya on the button-down leather couch in the study. He had a fine small studio across the courtyard but the thought of even going in there filled him with dread. Like desecrating a tomb. He'd play the guitar on the couch and let his sorrow rage despair and grief emerge as notes upon the quiet air to linger well beyond his fingers' muting on the strings. The counterpoint of hope among them. All of it delivered from six tuned strings and a hollow lacquered wooden body far more easily than speech could ever convey. And throughout it all the sense of final things, of winding down. Of waiting for some tardy guest. Every gesture emblematic. Every note farewell.

For the first time in decades he heard the bottle's siren song. The memory of whiskey trickling down his throat, the warm purr spreading in his veins. It would be so easy. In the next room was a cherrywood bar, Waterford decanters and matching highball glasses. Jem had thought he should get rid of the bar, toss out the booze or give it away, remodel the room into something very else. She needn't have worried. Since the Deal he hadn't touched a drop.

But one night he found himself sitting at the bar and turning a decanter in his hands, the caramel liquid disk seesawing as cut facets caught the light. The thick round stopper sideways on the glossy wood. He frowned. Had he? He took stock of himself. No. No. But still. He raised the decanter to his nose and breathed in and coughed. He thumped the decanter onto the bar and restoppered it and went back into his study and sat down again to play.

THE PHONE CHIME woke him. Jemma's ring. He'd fallen asleep on the couch again. He sat up and picked up the phone and pressed it and it lighted. `Whats it like outside`. He looked around the study. Ancient leatherbounds and scattered notes. Trophies, portraits, ragdolls guarding books. The Goya leaning on a bookcase. He drew aside an opaque curtain and squinted out the window at the courtyard. Bright Los Angeles morning. `Looks nice`, he typed. He pressed send and got up and used the bathroom and splashed his face and stood looking at it dripping in the mirror until the phone chimed again. `Can I see?`

SHE WAS SITTING up and typing on her phone when he came in. Her color better but much else wrong. She turned the phone screen toward him. "Clear, sunny, seventyeight degrees, air quality index mild." This the longest she had spoken in a week.

"Another shitty day in paradise."

"Can we go outside?"

He looked at her. Gaunt and pale, dark circles around her eyes, breathing strained. She did not look as if she could make it as far as the bedroom door. "We can try," he said.

The nurse was not due again until tomorrow. Niko pulled the sheets aside and Jem swung her legs over the side of the bed. He put her slippers on and started to make some Cinderella joke but stopped. He disconnected the IVAC monitor and gathered the clear IV tubes and picked up the metal pole and put his free arm around her and was startled at the hardness of her shoulderblades against him. He helped her off the bed. She could stand. She took a test step toward the door and stopped and nodded. He said Okay and stayed beside her and carried her IV pole, the plastic bag swinging from its loop as they moved slowly from the room. Her hipbone a hard knob against his thigh. He moved in unison with her and held the gathered tubes like someone operating a lifesized marionette. His ankle kept hitting the IV pole casters but it was easier to carry it than to pull it along. His framed past slowly sliding by them in the hallway.

The flared sweep of staircase was work but he held her and waited while she caught her breath and then continued down. He imagined having an elevator installed or one of those gliding bannister chairs. Then he caught himself. What the hell was he thinking?

Through the cavernous living room and the long main dining room, so little used in recent years. Through the french doors and onto the patio. The landscaped courtyard beyond. The whole place suddenly obscenely large.

He sat Jem in a white adirondack patio chair and set her IV beside her and made sure she was comfortable and then went to the kitchen to get her a bottle of room temperature water. The huge spotless space, all the stainless steel. Like some underutilized restaurant.

Going out again he stopped. Jemma ghostly in the sunlight on the wooden chair, the IV pole beside her. The simple heartbreak wrongness of it. Look at her, you son of a bitch.

He gave her the water and dragged another chair beside her and sat on the edge of it and watched her drink most of the water in one go. He took the bottle back and asked her if she wanted more.

"I'm good right now."

"You look a little better today."

"I feel a little better today. You don't know where the mountaintop is till you're past it."

"All downhill from there."

"That would be nice."

"You comfortable?"

"Considering, yeah."

"Other than that, Mrs. Lincoln."

She smiled a little. The new sharp contours of her face, the hard prominence of veins on her arms and on the backs of her hands. The daylight merciless.

"It's nice out here, isn't it?"

"It is. I'm not sure the sun's good for you."

"It won't kill me."

"Aren't you the comedian."

"I'm here all week. I'd like that water now I think."

He picked up the bottle. "Sure."

"Bring your guitar back too."

"You got it." A ghost bullet in the heart, but he didn't hesitate. He went inside again and got the Goya from the study and got a pair of sunglasses from a drawer and grabbed another bottled water from the kitchen. Back outside he waited while she gulped down most of her water again and then set her chairback more upright and put the sunglasses on her face. "Ooh look, I'm a movie star. Alfonse, strike up a fandango."

He set the Goya on his lap and started up a fandanguillo. She had an awful coughing fit and he stopped and then realized she was laughing.

"Aren't you the comedian," she said.

"I'm here all week."

"Play something."

Niko looked at the guitar. For the first time in living memory it felt like a block of wood on his lap. What notes and chords for such a time as this? What meter counts the winding down? He looked up from the guitar and felt a sudden shock of recognition. They had been in almost exactly these positions long ago. This moment nearly reenactment. He shut his eyes and remembered and his hands moved on the wooden body, remembering as well:

IN THE SILENCE after he cut the outboard they listened to the water gurgle against the hull. In the fading early morning gray the surface of Lake Arrowhead was haunted by a mist. They drifted, they bobbed, they breathed the rarefied air.

Niko closed his eyes and felt himself cradled, endlessly rocking. Floating on a lake high in the mountains. A wonder to a flatland Florida boy.

Between them Niko's Martin lay within its case. On the deck a thermos rolled and rolled.

He opened his eyes.

She faced him with her Navajo blanket across her knees, its thunderbird wings spread toward him. She reached for the thermos and poured fresh Kona. "You look good."

He took the offered cup. Vapor rose to join the mist. "I feel good." He lifted and drank and felt the coffee lighting up his veins.

"So. New band. New album. New single. National tour. No drugs. And you look ten years younger. What's your secret?"

Niko handed back the thermos cup. "I signed a deal with the devil."

"You signed a deal with Atlantic, anyway." She blew to cool the coffee.

"Same thing."

Water gurgled on the hull.

They opened a brown paper sack and ate thick bearclaws and washed them down with strong fresh coffee. They floated without speech or navigation as they ate and drank and watched the sun burn off the mist.

"So," he finally said, "here we are."

Jem looked away from the rumpled shoreline drawing slowly past. She seemed a little disbelieving she was here, like someone recovering her memory in the midst of a vacation. "Here we are. I swore I wouldn't."

"I know."

She watched him and he looked steadily back. "But you really do seem changed. Since—" She gestured vaguely.

"You can say it. Since the accident."

She nodded but said nothing. Niko took her napkin and put it with his in the paper sack that had held the bearclaws and folded the sack then crumpled it.

They floated.

"I wish I could've met your brother."

Now Niko made his own vague gesture and looked out at the fractured mirror of the lake. "Yeah."

"It saved you, didn't it?"

"I guess it did. That's a hell of a price for going clean."

Her eyes teared as she nodded. "I'm so sorry."

He gave a little helpless shrug.

A fish chopped water near the boat and they both jumped. Jemma smiled a little and glanced at the case between them and they both knew it was time. He unlatched it and pulled out the Martin and tuned it and thought how he could play before a screaming thousand without a second thought yet here with Jemma astonishingly returned to his life and all between them fragile and uncertain he felt his palms grow damp.

Niko played.

Jemma watched him close his eyes and rock with their boat's rocking. She listened to his music, the morning birds, the water lapping on the hull. She thought of how he loved to watch her sleep.

The final notes had disappeared across the morning before he opened his eyes to find her watching him. He lowered the guitar. "Long time since I had to audition."

Jemma took a deep breath. "I think you got the gig."

They should have met each other in the middle of their little boat but they did not. They swayed and turned upon the water. They were laughing by the time he brought the boat back to the rental dock. It looked unfamiliar and Niko asked the old guy watching them if they were at the wrong dock. "Hell, you're at the wrong shore," the old man said, and pointed them back across the lake. They laughed harder and gunned the engine and fractured the lake's glassy surface heading back as the sun burned off the last of the mist.

It was the happiest day of Niko's life.

H E OPENED HIS eyes as if awaking from a dream but the playing continued and the dream went on. Slowly rocking back and forth. Jemma in the sunlight in her sunglasses with the IV pole beside her. Vamping along with him, slow blue notes robbed of the authority that had been their trademark. But the feeling was there. Their faint duet a fragile elegy on this beautiful California day. A motionless dance.

He struck a final open chord and set the guitar aside. She nodded and said, "I think I'm ready."

Back upstairs he helped her to the bathroom and then removed her slippers and tucked her in and reattached the IVAC monitor and turned it on. The nurse had taught him how. Complicit in their understanding. He got her yet another bottled water and gave her her meds and asked if she wanted anything else. She shook her head and he hugged her and got up and turned down the lights. Just as he was leaving he heard her say, "Did I get the gig?"

"You've always had the gig," he said, and closed the door on their last good day together.

Two days later Dr. Abkagian called. I'm afraid her latest labs show elevated BUN and creatinine. There's no doubt at this point. There'll be a kind of domino effect as her systems start to fail. Days at best. I've written scrips for morphine and your nurse will. She'll be comfortable and not in any. I wish I had better news but.

The nurse arrived with morphine and a kind of starched condolence. She recommended certain paperwork be completed before she started pushing opiates. Jemma started sobbing when he approached her with the DNR. Long dry rasping sobs. The paper's naked meaning undisguisable. She'd been strong till this. Holding out some hope. He held her and talked to her and cried with her and in numb wonder handed her a pen and watched her sign her name to complete the circle he had started with the signing of his own so many years ago. What a perfect son of a bitch you are.

And then the clear morphine push into the IV line. Her pain abated and she slept.

He told the nurse he wanted to be alone with Jem from here on out and asked her to show him how to administer the morphine. She walked him through it next time a dose was due, drawing the solution from the ampoules with a syringe and injecting it into her IV line. He asked her why she didn't administer it directly and the nurse said, "IV drip lets her have a constant dose. With injection she'd have peaks and valleys. And this solution is too strong for direct injection anyway; it's concentrated for IV drips." She pushed the plunger. "One of these every four hours. Too little or too late and she'll still be in pain. Too much or too soon and she could go into respiratory distress."

"That would kill her?"

"It would probably just be unnecessarily painful. It'd take about sixty milligrams for a lethal dose."

"I see."

She drew up doses for the next two days and left them in the bathroom by the sink. "I noted the nonadministered morphine as wasted," she said.

Niko nodded. She knew who Niko was of course and thought she knew what he was really asking but she was wrong.

Before she left she told him she was sorry and she wished him well. "You're very strong," she said. "But this is never easy."

After she left Niko went into the bathroom. On the sink a small white sack containing twenty capped syringes drawn with measured doses. He held one to the light. The clear liquid promising passage. He set it back among the others in the sack and left them on the bathroom sink. Then he sat beside Jem's bed to hold her hand and talk to her and be a presence for her as all else became an absence.

HE DID HIS best to stay beside her every moment but it wasn't possible. He had to get her meds, go to the bathroom, go downstairs to make quick meals. He hurried through all of these, tripped on the stairs once, burned himself eating. Ignored his phone and turned hers off. Talked to her and told her everything. His brother's death, the Deal, the shameful farce of his career. Confessed his soul and pled with her and with whatever powers lay outside them both. Apologized and begged forgiveness and offered bargains. Sometimes Jem seemed conscious but he didn't think that she could hear him. Anyway it was all too little too late, wasn't it? Easy for you to come clean now, isn't it, Niko?

He gave her meds and swabbed her IV site and changed the bag and bathed her with a soft washcloth. Fingers tracing hard bone close beneath her thin and bruising skin as if needing to verify what he saw. Once she seemed to be trying to speak but he wasn't sure.

On the evening of the second day after he'd dismissed the nurse he came back upstairs with some barely noticed microwaved dinner on a plate. The moment he walked in he felt the difference in the room. He set the plate down on the floor and hurried to the bed. Her quick strained gasps. He held her hand and said her name. As if calling her back home. Jem, Jem. Jem? Her hand jerked in his and then relaxed. She breathed out calmly like a sigh and released something unseen to the reclaiming world. Niko waited but there was nothing more. The moment come and gone so mildly.

Still holding her relinquished hand he let out a horrible long bay like some wounded cornered animal. His heart torn from its mooring. The bay become a sob he leans across the bed to hug her one last time. The heartbreak yield of her.

Now let her go. The clock is ticking, Niko. Let her go. Let her go or never get her back.

He knows it's true. He knows what must be done. He'd thought that he was ready but how could he be. Who could be ready for this? The grief that sunders him.

No. No. Contain it. You have to contain it. You have to turn your back on it. If you grieve now Jem is truly lost and all your plans mean nothing.

He straightens from the bed. Makes his hand let her hand go. Jemma's utter stillness so pitiful there. Deep breath. Keep breathing. He steps back from the bed. Breathe. Breathe. Now turn around. Turn away. "I can't," he tells the bed. The room. The waiting deep. "I can't do this."

Oh yes you can. You know very fucking well you can. You're the one who put her there. You goddamn well can get her back. Now turn your back on her and start this whole machine or just surrender now and save yourself the trip and live with what you've done.

He knows his demon voice is right. He takes a deep and shaky breath and says goodbye to her and shuts the bedroom door and pulls it tight until he hears the gentle click of latch. Soft as if to avoid her waking. Breathe.

Go.

IV
_____

BRIGHT LIGHTS,
BIG CITY

APED TO THE BACK OF Niko's driver's license are three old coins and a yellow Post-It with a neatly lettered phone number. Niko has to dial three times before he gets it right. The knot in his throat feels like a fist.

It's picked up on the first ring. "Delivery," a woman answers. "How may we help you?"

"I need a ride."

"Name, please?"

Niko gives his name.

"Password?"

Niko speaks a word not uttered in four thousand years. "We show a carrier is on the way already, sir."

He thinks about what this might mean. "Not that one. This ride's for me."

"One moment." Incantatory static. Niko feels something in his hand and looks down to see an empty syringe. When did he administer this? How long has he been holding it? He tosses the syringe and it clatters likes some insect across the beveled glass coffee table.

The woman's voice returns. "The current carrier is all we're authorized for, sir. We're very sor—"

"This has been willed," he says, "where what is willed must be."

A sharp intake of surprise. "Please hold, sir. We have to speak with a supervisor."

"I'm kind of in a hurry."

"Yes sir, we understand. Just one moment." An interminable minute. "We apologize for the wait, sir. This is very unusual, we hope you understand. We're sending you a driver right away. Our very best."

"How long?"

"Ten minutes at the most. The first carrier will probably arrive first."

"I see. All right. Thank you."

"You're most welcome. And sir? Sir?"

Niko brings the phone back to his ear. "I'm here."

"We just wanted to wish you good luck, sir. Good luck and good traveling."

HARD ABOUT HIM now the empty house lies still. Tick of the old Herschede grandfather clock in the foyer, its snoring Man in the Moon face and deep broad chime that always make him think of early childhood at his grandparents' house in Florida, which was why he'd bought it in the first place.

The bedroom door beyond the stairs. Jem I pray your pain is gone. I pray you will forgive me. All I've done, all I am about to try to do.

Two carriers on the way. Ten minutes at the most. Hurry. Breathe.

CLIMBING FROM THE San Fernando Valley on the San Diego Freeway the Black Taxi crests Mulholland Drive and starts the long descent across the pass and into orange city light. The big car passes through the Friday traffic and drifts right and exits on the Sunset ramp. Eastbound through Bel Aire and Westwood, through Beverly Hills and on the crowded Sunset Strip it eases forward unobserved.

All without is crowded light. Massive lighted billboards, club marquees, hotels, and restaurants du jour. None of it reflecting from the metal shape that rolls among them.

On the far side of the Grecian courtyard with its Japanese rockgarden Niko opens the door to his little studio. Muted overhead light shines down on a quarter million dollars in recording gear. Framed foam wedges and thick gray carpet on the walls. Tiny vocal booth there. The phone booth Jemma called it. In the small control room Niko pauses as he looks through the window into the recording room.

They stand arrayed along one wall like dusty weapons in an ancient armory. Fender, Gibson, Ibañez. Sunburst, lacquer, mother of pearl. Sixstring, twelvestring, doubleneck, bass. Last in line the Dobro rests gleaming like a new dime. Polished steel distorts the studio around it, warps the reflection of Niko's hand reaching past it to grab its hardshell case that leans against the wall behind it. The womanshape dull with dust.

Niko opens the case. Gray plush lining. He opens the little storage compartment. Metal slide, strap, picks and strings. He sets a hand against the plush as if in benediction. A moment only. Hurry.

He grabs the Dobro by the neck and fits it in the case and shuts the latches one two three.

In the living room he leans the case against the black Italian couch. He sets a hand upon the case and glances up the stairs. The sense of Jemma up there still.

His thumbs jerk with sudden pricking.

Motor rumble coming up the lengthy driveway.

On his neck the locket burns.

The engine cuts off and a parking brake zips and a car door opens and then closes with a solid heavy sound. Don't make em like that anymore.

Niko goes to stand behind the door.

Heavy footsteps up the cobbled walk.

He leans his cheek against the door and shuts his eyes. What waits on the other side. Deep breath. Don't resist. Useless fighting here and now. This is just an errand boy, a messenger. It has no authority. Your true arena waits somewhere not any where at all.

Leaden knock of knucklebone on wood against his cheek. Niko jumps back and is about to open the door when a man in a tailored chauffeur's uniform walks through it. Thin, pale, whitehaired, Nordic, nearly albino, smooth androgynous face bony as a Siamese cat. Niko backs up several steps. The driver touches the glossy bill of his cap with cold politeness. Its shadow falls across his eyes, always falls across his eyes.

Both men look upstairs.

From a jacket pocket the driver removes a small mason jar with a twopiece lid and a white jacquard silk kerchief. He glances at Niko and then glides past him. At the foot of the staircase he touches the vase on the newel in a lingering way that is somehow lewd. He grins a pale poisonbottle grin and glides up the carpeted stairs and down the hall.

Niko follows. At the top of the stairs the driver heads down the hallway and enters the bedroom without opening the door and Niko stops. What can he do? All this is writ and in its unfolding is a thing already done. Wait. Breathe. He clenches his fists and heads back down the stairs.

By the time he picks up the guitar case the driver is gliding back downstairs, obscuring with the kerchief a faintly glowing black-tipped feather now within the small glass jar. The driver wipes the jar mouth with his kerchief and returns it and the jar to his jacket pocket where it leaves no bulge.

Approaching Niko the driver looks from the guitar case to the depressed syringe on the glasstopped coffee table and grins insinuatingly and touches again the glossy bill of his cap and makes to go past Niko.

"Wait." Niko grabs the driver's arm and the driver stops and looks at Niko's clutching hand. Jaundiced eyes narrow and every plant in the house withers and dies.

Their gazes meet and Niko feels the churning horror ever waiting past the cliff edge of cognition. Some day you will sail beyond that precipice, that gaze tells Niko, and I will be there when you do.

Niko drops his hand from the tailored sleeve in sudden vertigo. "You're forgetting something." He sets down the guitar case and pulls out his wallet and takes out his driver's license and removes one of the three ancient coins taped to the back and holds it out.

The driver looks surprised. He holds his narrow hand palmup and Niko drops the coin into it, careful not to touch him this time. The driver holds the small bronze lepton to the light and grins a deathshead grin and flips the coin into the air, flicking it with a yellowed thumbnail to make it ring. The coin does not fall back down.

The driver touches his cap once more and leaves through the front door.

Heavy metal of car door closing, deep gargle of welltuned V-12 engine. Niko goes to the door to look at what sits idling in the circular drive. And shakes his head. Of course. In other times in other places it has been a reed boat, a palanquin, a chariot, a coach, a train.

Bugeyed headlamps glowing as it pulls out from the curb, polished glossy black but unmarred by reflections from the lighted drive, an immaculate 1933 Franklin Model 173 seven-passenger sedan with a gold-on-black California classic vanity plate reading 2L84U glides like a stalking jaguar around the marble fountain and passes among oblivious statues along the winding landscaped drive and slides like oil through the locked iron gate and out into the narcotic Hollywood night.

CLEAR YOUR THOUGHTS and make your preparations. The words you'll need. Ordered arcane syllables to unlock, undo, unmask. Guttural doggerel in lost languages like choking nursery rhymes. Their phrases surface now like chants from preschool primers.

He has her oh the son of a bitch he took her. You goateyed bastard I will eat your heart and spit out the pits.

Niko quickly changes into hiking shoes and bluejeans and a black T-shirt. A light jacket for the cool Los Angeles night. Should he bring a daypack? Food? How long will he be gone? A day, a week, a month?

Niko shakes his head. How could he know? How could anyone?

His fingers find the locket warm against his chest. Okay, travel light. No backpack, no supplies. It takes a month or more to starve to death, and if you're gone that long, well, starvation probably won't be at the top of your worries. The Dobro's gonna be a bitch in any case.

Weapons? Niko gives a disgusted laugh. Killing anything where he is bound would be redundant. Better to be hungry and wily, unarmed and afraid.

Something, he's forgetting something. And remembers.

In the pantry Niko finds the old box of jumbo milkbones and opens it and takes one out. Algae-green and big as a crescent wrench. He slips it into the inner breast pocket of his light coat. Weapons come in many forms.

Headlights sweep across the living room draperies and Niko glances out the window to see a car pull up to the distant gate. The intercom buzzes and Niko taps the button that opens the gate. He turns away from the window and surveys the room as a chuffing engine approaches outside.

Living room, staircase, bedroom door. Furnishings, mementos, objets d'art. Our life together. Who do you think you are? Where do you think you're going?

That baleful bedroom door shut soundly, rising like a tombstone down the upstairs hall. How can you just leave her here?

But no. Jemma's not in there. A feather in a mason jar.

A plaintive halfassed horn toots twice. Outside the door an engine hiccoughs and sneezes.

Niko picks up the guitar case and feels a little foolish as he taps the code on the house alarm. As if concerned with guarding objects. But what if it gets tripped and rentacops show up with Jemma there upstairs? No, no. Her body has to stay there undisturbed, has to be there when he gets back. So he punches in the code and turns his back on several lifetime's acquisitions, and when he leaves he does not look back.

Dented and dirty, some long ago fenderbender having set the dinged chrome bumper aslant in a smirk, a classic Checker Cab idles roughly in the driveway before the silent fountain. It looks like a '55 Chevy on steroids. All that can be seen of the cabbie is an arm resting alongside the lowered driver's window, faint orange of a lit cigarillo between two fingers.

When she hears the front door shut the cabbie hurries out and opens the cab's rear door for Niko. The interior light tints the dirty rear windshield to the yellow of an old newspaper.

The cabbie is short, acne scarred, ponytailed, tomboyish. A ghost of former glamor haunts her features. Her eyes are bright and alive in a face that has peered into a great many dark corners. Her expression seems ready to smile in a worldly wise and weary way, as if about to be told a joke she's already heard but still finds funny. Khaki shirt and loosely knotted thin black jazzman's tie, old leather sneakers probably white in some former incarnation. She nods goodevening as Niko approaches and she drops her remaining inch of cigarillo and grinds a battered sneaker on the smoking butt, then holds out nicotine stained fingers for Niko's hardcase with exactly the proper tentativeness. "Set that in the trunk, sir?"

Niko shakes his head and tries to place the cabbie's accent.

"All right." The cabbie sets her hand upon the opened door. The latent smile blooms. "Step into my office." A crescent moon of grime beneath each nail.

The hardcase leads the way as he climbs in. Springs creak beneath the old bench seat and hinges squeal past audibility as the cabbie slams the door. Dog notes, Jemma called it when session producers made her sing at the top of her range.

As the cabbie gets behind the wheel Niko takes in leather upholstery, creaking springs, engine knocking stallward, huge bench seat patched with duct tape peeling up on one edge to reveal the original color which Niko thinks of as banker's green. Lots of legroom. Smells of tobacco, leather, stale coffee from stained styrofoam cups on the floorboard, rims pressed flat with endless tiny crescent thumbnail marks. Litter of empty Swisher Sweets cigarillo packs and half-used matchbooks, gumwrappers, foodstained restaurant stubs, a pullout ashtray against the driver's seatback overflowing with gumwads and cigarette butts, broken pencil nubs, tarnished pennies, a torn Butterfinger wrapper.

The cabbie glances at Niko in the rearview but Niko doesn't notice. She grinds the cab in gear and eases round the waterless fountain and down the long enstatued driveway and then stops before the gate. Clanking metal as it opens automatically and the Checker Cab moves across the threshold and out into the careless world. Behind them the housegate rattles shut.

The cabbie's bright eyes in the rearview slat. "Where to, sir?"

Niko sets a hand against the locket underneath his shirt, the other on the hardcase firm against his leg. "Follow that cab," he says.

V

CROSSTOWN TRAFFIC

THE BIG YELLOW CAB SNAKES down from the Hollywood Hills and onto Sunset Boulevard and has a deceptively unhampered run down the Strip. Traffic's heavy but moving as they ride east toward Hollywood and into Friday night cruising and tourism. Turning north from La Cienega to Highland runs them into automotive quicksand and they inch through the intersection.

The cabbie seems aware of Niko's urgency. Near Franklin she works the cab into the beercan lane and ignores the angry honks as their car glides by crawling traffic. Every redlight turns to green at their approach as they head toward the Hollywood Freeway.

Soon the Hollywood Bowl marquee slides past in the center divider. Niko remembers the old terraced clamshell looming behind him with its enormous floating globe clusters like grapes in a giant's cornucopia, the frozen wave of audience before him, his trademark stillness in the midst of all the beehive hum, the surf roar of the crowd above his sustained demoniac feedback howl. Homeowners two miles away had complained about the volume. Nowadays he'd likely be one of them.

The Checker Cab turns a slow hairpin right and enters the access road leading to the ramp for the Hollywood Freeway southbound. The freeway's packed and barely moving. No one lets the cab merge as the entry lane tapers away but the cabbie eases into a space between a BMW and a Honda that Niko would have sworn could not have fit a motorcycle.

Niko tries to relax as they inch toward downtown but mostly he feels numb. Where grief ought to be is only silence, vacated space.

"Are you giving a show sir?"

Niko glances up. "Sorry?"

"Got a gig?"

Niko looks at the guitar case and laughs without a trace of humor. "You could say that."

The cabbie nods.

Niko makes his hand let go the case but a minute later it is tracing its contours again. Somewhere up ahead that mason jar contains its featherweight of soul. Do I feel her out there really? I think I do. Then don't let go of that.

He fidgets on the patched green seat and watches sluggish freeway traffic and old familiar landmarks. Capitol Records tower on the right at Vine. In the hills ahead the Griffith Observatory, the Greek Theatre. His laminated past.

Brakelights flash ahead and the Checker Cab groans to a stop near Western. "Sorry," says the cabbie.

Niko glares at stalled traffic.

The hot night is unusually humid. The freeway smells of oil, rubber, gasoline. Niko's fingers drum the guitar case. The cabbie glances at her rearview and seems to be considering. Without signaling she muscles the cab across three creeping lanes into the narrow breakdown lane and ignores the angry honks that follow in their wake. She snaps on the radio and Charlie Parker blows like Gabriel on smack. Engine valves rattle like bones in a box.

Near the Virgil offramp the breakdown lane is blocked by firetrucks and a paramedic van. A silver Arco tanker has overturned and sloughed across the right two lanes until the bulldog radiator ornament chewed the concrete retainer wall. The eighteen wheeler's cab is crumpled like a roadside beercan. The wet roadway gleams orange streetlight and a leaden smell of gasoline saturates the night. Firemen unreel hoses as jackbooted CHiPs pace before the halted traffic. Drivers talk on cellphones. Overhead a harpy helicopter rides a spotlight cone. Off the freeway a giant cartoon figure in a tophat looms atop the Western Exterminator Company building, hiding a mallet behind his back and admonishing a giant rat who holds a knife and fork.

Firemen cut away the big-rig's driver side door with the jaws of life. From out the smashed inverted truck cab comes a thin and sharpdressed man who holds a jar containing something palely glowing. Eyes in shadow and pale orange streetlight malarial on his face's lower half. A large and twisted doll hangs glistening in the cab behind him. Arms upraised as if in belated surrender. Niko wants to look away but cannot look away. The inert form so recently breathing, thinking, driving toward its life's conclusion without the slightest clue. Niko thinks of Van bent forward against the steering wheel of the station wagon and looking at Niko but seeing nothing anymore. Van who not ten seconds before the absurdly mild accident had been shutting Niko down about Las Vegas. The house of cards that is a human life.

On the radio now the sibilance of bottleneck slide.

The Black Taxi Driver wipes the mason jar clean with a white silk kerchief as heedless paramedics hurry past him into the truck cab. The CHiPs ignore him passing in their busy midst. A fireman cradling a length of hose now braces himself as it swells like a regurgitating python. He directs the spray across the freeway surface to dilute the gasoline as the Black Taxi driver strolls past him and toward the black 1933 Franklin sedan idling smoothly in the breakdown lane on the clear stretch of freeway on the other side of the wreck.

The cabbie drums her grime-crescented nails on the steering wheel in time with the radio's heartbreak blues and glances in the rearview at her passenger. "These old songs are still the best, I think."

Niko stares blankly at the cabbie and then realizes it is himself playing on the radio. Niko twenty years ago and hurt and pissed off and freighting every note with feeling.

The cabbie stubs out her cigarillo and feathers the accelerator. Valves protest like rowdy clams. "This isn't generally allowed," she says. She pushes a sequence of radio buttons and then eases the cab forward and cuts right and heads between stalled lanes. Cars are not a yard apart here yet somehow the Checker Cab passes between them. Niko fights an urge to yell. On one side the orangelit concrete retainer wall flows past a foot away from the cab. On the other the firetrucks are not a foot beyond the door. Ahead the trucks and wall are only a few feet apart.

Niko's vision blurs. His brain can't make it fit. "I see your radio gets some extra stations," he says.

The cabbie smiles tightly. "One or two."

Seconds later they are past the firetrucks, the wreck, the stalled traffic. Just past the wreck the Black Taxi sits purring on the other side of the road. Niko's heartbeat ratchets up a gear. The son of a bitch is right there, a hundred feet away. The marine layer is encroaching and a misting stillness lies hardedged about the miles between the two cars and the clustered downtown skyscrapers rising futuristic in the distance, lighting up the very air about them like some alien encampment.

Niko sees a match flare and then a cigarette glow behind the driver's window of the Black Taxi. The window rolls down smoothly and a long thin arm emerges, gold cufflink gleaming in a crisp white cuff, glowing cigarette clamped between thumb and forefinger. The cufflink winks, the finger flicks, the cigarette arcs away, and the Black Taxi smokes rubber and leaps forward like a dragster while behind it the discarded cigarette is a tiny meteor streaking an impossible distance back toward the wrecked and bleeding tanker.

Niko bolts forward and grips the cabbie's seatback and yells Go.

The Checker Cab lumbers forward and gains speed, engine valves complaining castanets. Niko looks back toward the wreck just as an aurora of paleblue flame springs from the pavement where the cigarette butt landed and races toward the leaking tanker like some kind of magic trick. Niko winces in expectation of some worldconsuming blast, but a fireman taps a hose-wielding colleague on the shoulder and points, and the man merely nods and turns with the hose and drowns the spreading curtain of pale flame.

Niko lets out his breath and turns forward again to see the taillights of the speeding Franklin half a mile ahead. Two cars drawn like moths toward luminous downtown.

THE LONG BLACK Franklin whips out from in front of a Fed Ex truck just before the Golden State Freeway divider and at the last possible moment angles across a broad expanse of lanes and nearly sideswipes a concrete divider at the Temple exit before it takes the exit ramp at twice the posted speed.

"Gee," says the cabbie. "Think he's onto us?" She cuts the wheel and the Checker Cab slews across three lanes to the Temple offramp. Ahead of them the Franklin runs the light and slews left onto Temple beside Our Lady of the Angels cathedral.

Niko snatches at the strap as the Checker Cab squeals around the ramp. The traffic signal just ahead turns green for them as they turn left on Temple. Tires screech to either side as drivers panic-stop for a light that went from green to red without a yellow inbetween.

Ahead of them the Franklin turns a sudden right. The Checker Cab howls around the corner in a fourwheel drift and now they're heading down Hill fast, driving through the Civic Center past generic slabs of government buildings. A few hundred yards ahead the Black Taxi slows to a crawl and then speeds away. The cabbie guns the engine.

Niko grips the back of the front seat. "Where's he trying to get to?"

"Red Line tunnel." The cabbie points down. "Underground."

They pass the entrance to the Red Line station on their left and Niko sees long steep escalators and staircases. "He's trying to get in there from here?"

"Not with us on his tail. He'll head to the next station at Fourth. We're riding above the Red Line route right now."

A few streets over to their left is the quaint old gumshoe movie backdrop of City Hall with the Lindbergh light revolving like a lighthouse beacon warning traffic not to founder on some downtown shoal.

They cross Second Street and the light turns green for them. Bunker Hill a clump of skyscrapers above them and to the right.

The twin towers of the California Plaza with their neonbanded tops. The palegreen robot of Library Tower. The glossy tiled tube of Second Street tunnel whips by. Beyond this a black and orange gateway reading ANGEL'S FLIGHT RAILWAY stands alone along the sidewalk at the foot of the hill, railtrack slanting up to meet a matching gateway on the hilltop at the California Plaza. On the track two black and orange railway cars are shaped like parallelograms to fit along the slope.

"He's slowing down again."

The cabbie nods. "Red Line station on both sides at Fourth. And he might give that a try." She points to a building up ahead on Fourth Street. Niko stares out at trompe l'oeil window-washers cleaning painted-on windows. "The old Subway Terminal Building. In the Twenties there was a mile's worth of subway running under Bunker Hill. The tunnel's still there, they broke into it when they dug the foundation for the Bonaventure in the Seventies. Runs all the way to where Beverly and Second meet."

"Why isn't he going faster?"

"He's trying to time it so he loses us at the lights." As if to illustrate her point the traffic light turns yellow as the Franklin speeds across Fourth Street. The Checker Cab is close behind and the light turns from yellow back to green. Two cars run the light in opposite directions and without even looking at them the cabbie taps the brakes just so and avoids a broadside.

"I like your greenlight trick," says Niko. Because if he doesn't say something he will scream.

"Good one, huh?" They pass the defunct Subway Terminal Building and the cabbie waves her cigarillo at it. "There's a huge copy of The Thinker in the lobby of that."

"Do you sell maps to the stars' homes too?"

She arches her eyebrows in the rearview. "The Thinker was originally the figure on top of Rodin's Gates of Hell. Which he never finished." She smiles. "You should look up what he was working on when he died."

Niko studies the cabbie's profile as they chase the Black Taxi toward the Jewelry District. Crow's feet but her eyes seem young. Beautiful color really. Forehead that wrinkles when waiting for an answer. Beautifully sculpted lip, the upper wanting to favor one side. Barely glancing at traffic as she drives. She knows this cab and its surround like an old pair of jeans. Dark hair without gray. Hardworked hands. How old is she I wonder.

They pass Fifth Street and the Red Line station entrance across from the yellow and purple building blocks of Pershing Square. The Black Taxi puts on speed and cuts left onto Seventh.

The cabbie hangs a long and screaming left to follow. "I bet we're really pissing him off," she says. "There's no point in him getting in there if we just follow him on through."

"Where's he headed now?"

"I'm betting Union Station. All roads lead to Rome. It's what I'd do if I was still driving black cab."

The bottom falls out of Niko's stomach. "When was that?"

"Oh, a long time ago. In London." She hits the gas and the engine misses once then surges and they pull around a Prius with a Harley-Davidson sticker on its rear windshield.

Niko relaxes a bit. Driving black cab in England and driving the Black Taxi are two very different occupations. "You were on the knowledge?"

The cabbie glances back at him. "Boy, not too many Americans know that phrase."

Both cars thread through sparse traffic down Seventh past jewelry stores, past grand old movie palaces fallen to ruin or converted to swap meets. The State. The Palace. The Orpheum.

Ahead the Black Taxi fishhooks left onto Wall.

The cabbie shakes her head. "He should've gone down San Pedro. This puppy deadends at Third." The Checker Cab chortles around the corner and avoids a shopping cart in the middle of the road.

Police station on their left, listless crowd near the L.A. Mission on their right. A man in a torn shirt steps off the curb in the midst of some tirade and brandishes a crutch at them as they speed past Korean toy marts.

They're at Fourth and Wall when the Franklin's brakelights flash where Wall deadends at Third. Niko thinks the Black Taxi will turn left onto the oneway street but instead it screams a one eighty, headlights sweeping cansprayed doorways and aimless homeless people and scores of soiled sleeping bags arrayed along the sidewalks like the detritus of some apocalypse. The black sedan now faces them with wheelwells smoking like a monster breathing in the cold.

The radio's playing some forgotten song.

"Boy, on the knowledge." The cabbie shakes her head as the Black Taxi rushes toward them in their lane. Ahead and to their left is Boyd Street but they'll never make it in time. "For most of a year I slept with a map of London taped to my ceiling." Niko stiffens in expectation of sudden impact and metal roar. "Hundred percent on my exam too." The cabbie leans forward and presses a sequence of radio buttons. The froglike headlights grow before them. Niko stomps a nonexistent brake and draws a hissing breath as metal interpenetrates oncoming metal. Molecules that would collide instead find empty spaces in the hurtling metal, empty space of which most things consist. The utter wrongness of this instant realignment tastes of bitter iron.

The cars pass through each another.

The sharp planed face of the Black Taxi driver flashes through him and he feels a terrible wrenching at his core, voracious entropy and churning chaos, leaching cancerous famished death that thrills to strip him from the fabric of his being. For a single breathless thoughtless moment he knows what it is to be hulled from self and sealed inside that mason jar.

And past.

The cabbie pops a match against a nail and lights another cigarillo. She yanks the wheel and stomps the brake. Niko slides right on the broad bench seat as they power onto Boyd.

The cabbie grins at the rearview. "And you thought the greenlight trick was something."

Nighttime Boyd Street is a corridor of zombies. Shambling figures leached of color who threaten empty air before them with their fists, stand and stare at nothing, inventory shopping carts and grocery bags. Souls consigned to sad perdition before their death has found them.

The cabbie weaves the big car through their wary ranks like a ship through risky shoals. They ease past vestibular Boyd, then pick up speed as they turn left onto Los Angeles Street. Still accelerating as she cuts right onto Fifth and picks up the Black Taxi speeding west ahead near Spring. Engine valves clatter like raked poker chips. On the radio Jimi Hendrix scratches out the "Steel Town Blues."

Traffic lights turn green or stay green for them as they rush down Fifth through the old theater district, once more heading toward the cluster of skyscrapers and Bunker Hill.

Jimi Hendrix never recorded "Steel Town Blues."

They hang a right on Hill and there the Franklin is, waiting at the traffic light at Second.

"Well well," the cabbie says. "The fiendly stranger in the black sedan."

"Why's he stopped?"

The cabbie slows down, suddenly in no hurry to overtake the Franklin. "Listen," she says. "There's one place where he won't have to force an entrance. The old Belmont Tunnel where Beverly, Glendale, and Second all come together. It's a portal where the old Pacific Electric Railway used to go to ground. The old subway from the Twenties."

"It connects to the Red Line?"

"It connects to the same thing the Red Line connects to." The cabbie swerves around a wide-eyed mendicant standing in the middle of the road holding high a cloudy squirt bottle and a filthy rag with no more thought than if he were a roadcone. "Same thing all tunnels connect to if you know how to work em."

The light at Second Street turns green but the Franklin still sits motionless.

"Why's he letting us catch up to him?"

"He knows he can't shake me so he's about to push back." The cabbie catches his eye in the rearview. "This might be rough."

They're coming up on the Franklin now.

Niko throttles the strap. "I'm holding on."

"You'll need to hold on to more than that."

Ahead of them the twelve-cylinder engine revs and the tires shriek and the Black Taxi hangs a left at Second and howls down the night before them. The Checker Cab follows, baying tires blending with the mournful wail of Jimi's ghostnotes on the haunted radio as they pursue the Franklin down the throat of the Second Street tunnel. Glossy tiled walls pale orange and wetlooking in the sodium lights.

The tunnel dims, the throat constricts. Niko starts to ask the cabbie to turn on the headlights but stops when he realizes he can't even see her in front of him. Her everpresent cigarillo glow has vanished. Peripheral dashboard light is gone as well. The pressure of the seat beneath him and the hardcase against his hand his only reassurance of the solid real. The only light the twin red taillights up ahead.

They brighten into burning suns and the assault begins.

CHRISTMAS MORNING AND *Niko dumped his stupid Mr. Mechano to grab the just-unwrapped Sears & Roebuck guitar from Van's hand and his mother told him You should be ashamed of yourself while little Van looked too bewildered to even cry.*

Niko bathed in the light of his past thinks Oh you lousy motherfuckers.

Jemma's face when she came home to their ratty little Hollywood apartment to find him drunk on the kitchen floor pathetically piecing together blue shards of the Cookie Monster jar that fell when Niko pulled it from the top shelf to use her emergency cash to buy himself another fifth.

Even knowing these little videos star someone Niko murdered long ago he feels the turning worm of shame for who he was.

Stephen's sleepy smile in the motel room holding up the hypodermic and pushing out the air and Niko fixed already and sitting on the floor with his back against the wall halfnodding off saw how big the dose was and said Hey as Stephen slid the needle underneath his tongue and shot and sank back in the chair and stared at the ceiling and stopped breathing. And Niko took the dead man's rig and smack and cash and left and never told a soul.

The unremitting truth. Well hell with you. I can weather this. I already did.

Niko smiling meanly in the quiet early morning as he slid Van's cheap guitar behind the right rear tire of Dad's new Ford because last night his father told him Nikkoleides your brother doesn't mind you playing it sometimes but it still belongs to him now give it back.

He shuts his eyes but the images still come.

The strain behind Jem's smile as she clutched tight his hand and slid into the little CAT scan. Niko smiling back while his demon voice said Take a bow, buddy pal, 'cause this is your work.

Faces gone these many years now, withered in the transmutating earth. He can smell Dad's Old Spice, see the defiant tilt of Van's jaw, hear Mom's voice across a continent of wire, *You were there when he died and now you won't come home to throw in a handful of dirt, what kind of brother is that, what kind of son can you be,* Jemma skeletal on the bed and pain a distant lightning in her eyes, *But you always land on your feet, Niko,* Van's eyes unseeing and a flower of blood in one of them and why wouldn't his brother blink it away, the boneless flop when Niko shook him with the very hand that might have stopped the death of one of them and the damnation of the other, *Sign right here, Niko-meister, keep the pen,* you fucking bastards I can fight anything you throw at me except myself. The dead arrayed behind me pointing.

The Checker Cab breaks from the tunnel into city night. The assault of memories cuts off and all is visible again. The two cars that are more than cars and yet not cars at all race down Second toward the convergence of streets, of worlds, of myth, toward the portal where in 1925 the old Pacific Electric Railway used to go to ground.

VI

SUBTERRANEAN HOMESICK BLUES

The RAILS BENEATH THE TIRES sing a happy hornet's song below the syncopated beat of Robert Johnson calling out the "Coal Shaft Blues." Far ahead and dimly seen the Franklin's taillights glow like rateyes in the Stygian dark. The rusted rails are very old, the tunnel older still. The route they take is not on any map above the ground.

Robert Johnson never played the "Coal Shaft Blues."

The humming rails unspool from out the skein of night itself. At some point they have linked up with the Red Line tunnel, for the rails within the old graffiti covered subway tunnel entrance where they drove into the midnight earth became modern level smooth and prestressed concrete sections gleaming as the headlights pulled them from the dark. But now the rails are raised and rusted resting loose on rotting wooden crossties. The conjoined fate of hurtling trains. Now the cabbie drives the Checker Cab upon two iron lines conscripted to the ground by iron spikes driven by what indentured hands for reasons that no living mind of man could fathom. Without guides and by her kinesthetic sense alone the cabbie holds them true and Niko marvels at her casual expertise. Now the chase is pure and plain, no stunts no tricks no strategies. Now is but a set of rails that narrows to a distant point above which shines the twin red lights of their objective.

The tunnel has darkened in the absence of signal lights or the cold bluewhite of an approaching or receding station. Now there is only the weak wash of the Checker Cab's headlights, pale yellow as manila paper. What lies in their purblind view has changed from prestressed concrete to what looks like brown brick slick with darkgreen algae and large patches overgrown with moss and creeping vines.

Shapes that have been stirred to motion by the passing of the Franklin can be glimpsed in halflit regions of the jellied tunnel walls. Now they turn their Morlock eyes upon the Checker Cab's approach and stretch toward them unavailing mottled malformed limbs. The cab passes and the creatures flatten against the curved tunnel walls and shield their luminous lantern eyes with clublike hands.

If somehow Boyd Street were cut off from the world like Loch Ness from the ocean and its shambling zombie guardians left to carry on, over time might they become what Niko sees here. But some he passes cringe against the tunnel on four legs. And some on four legs rise to sniff the agitated air with long and tapering snouts. But these tunnels cannot be that old. But this tunnel may be old as man.

The cabbie has the air on full but it's only pushing the hot air around. Beneath that is a foundry breath of sulphur, tinge of rot.

"Sorry about the AC." The hornet hum increases as she rolls her window partway down. The sudden reek so thick it seems to invade the cab as visible curling tendrils.

The cab's not driving all that fast, twentyfive or thirty miles per hour. Any faster and the cabbie probably couldn't keep it on the rails. Niko wants more speed of course but as he sees and hears the milling and averting shapes go past he's grateful for what speed he has.

Sudden purple splats across the windshield. The cab jerks right and they thump off of the rails. The cabbie yanks the wheel and steel rims scream along the iron. She switches on the wipers and they smear fan shapes across the windshield and stutter back. In the wavering headlights Niko sees a creature pale and cratered as the moon and then the left front fender slams it with a solid sickening crunch of bone. A hairy clot lands on the left rear window and crawls sluglike and dripping in the slipstream.

The cab bounces over the righthand rail. The fender grazes brick and plows a furrow of moist matter that streaks the headlight and tints it like a gel spotlamp. From behind them comes a pop and then a slowing rumble fills the tunnel as the Checker Cab jounces to a stop.

"Tire." The cabbie zips the emergency brake and cuts the engine and kills the lights and gets out and trudges to the back of the cab, leaving Niko in the dark.

Slick patches covering the tunnel walls give off faint algae phosphorescence.

Niko hurries from the cab. It feels like days have passed since he first climbed in, though it can't be more than an hour. Far ahead the Franklin's taillights dwindle. Damn it.

The cabbie pulls the spare tire from the trunk and leans it on the bumper. Niko asks if he can help. The cabbie bends into the trunk again. "You might wanna see what you can do to keep the lookie-loos away." She straightens holding a two ton hydraulic service jack and an old red plastic twelve volt lantern with a rubber nipple over the switch.

Niko glances back up the tunnel. "What'll they do?"

She pulls the jack past him and it squeaks and jounces like a nervous little yipyap dog. "I don't know." She squats and rolls the jack beneath the cab. "Never stopped to find out."

"Okay." Niko leans into the cab and turns the headlights on. Exposed shapes scurry or hump or flow or limp a startled retreat. Slime on the headlamp tints the tunnel's right side seasick green. Niko goes to the front to examine the damage. The left bumper is pushed inward and sports a large fresh lumpy splotch. Wiry black hair sprouts from a clot sizzling on the radiator grille with an awful smell of burning pork.

While the cabbie jacks up the cab Niko gropes around the large and lightless trunk to find a rag to wipe the headlight clean. Boxes, jumper cables, gascan. Did he just hear something behind him? He finds a bag of rags. He straightens and turns and gapes up at the slick hide of a greateyed thing hunched in front of him.

"Candybar?" it says in a guttural hopeful voice. It shifts toward him and raises a ropy glistening arm from which small things fall to writhe upon the wet ground.

"Uhh," says Niko.

"Jeremy love candybar." It clenches its clubfingered fist and lumbers forward. "Jeremy Hershey bar." It looks like a great gray-green shag carpet grown slimy in the rain. It may once have been a man the way a hippopotamus may once have been a horse. Pale owlish eyes with pinpoint pupils. Floppy-tongued shoes dimly recognizable as Converse Hi-tops. "Butterfinger Pay Day Almond Joy." It steps again with a great heaving sucking sound. Niko smells something like weekold diapers and dumpster cabbage. He backs away from the cab and steps on something hard and round. A prybar. Hellyeh. He picks it up and holds it high and feels ridiculous and afraid.

A flashlight beam strikes Jeremy's undifferentiated face and Jeremy leans back and covers the cartoon ovals of his lidless eyes with splayed wet hands.

The cabbie scrambles to her feet and stands beside Niko with the lantern trained on Jeremy. With surprising speed and grace the creature leans forward and bats the lantern from her hand.

Niko lunges like a fencer and the prybar strikes resistant flesh. He pushes and feels a small pop as the prybar sinks into Jeremy's side all the way up to Niko's knuckles. Startled Niko lets go and steps back.

Red-edged in the cockeyed taillights Jeremy stands staring dumbly at the wrench head of the prybar protruding from his middle like a radio knob. Niko gets the clear impression of a frown. "No candybar?" Jeremy grips the knob and pulls the length of metal out. A great gout of indigo follows to spray in pulsing arcs as Jeremy examines the glistening prybar and says Awww. A pissing sound as gushing ichor strikes the tunnel wall. Awww. Jeremy lumbers away bleeding with the prybar dangling from his bigfingered hand.

The cabbie is still watching the retreating island of Jeremy's back as she holds up a shapeless foilwrapped Chunky bar. "I was gonna give him one. I always carry em."

Niko isn't quite sure what to say.

The cockeyed headlights show a dozen more approaching shapes two hundred yards away.

Niko and the cabbie fetch the flashlight and quickly change the tire. The cabbie tightens the lug nuts and lowers the jack and heaves it in the trunk and slams the lid. She and Niko hurry back into the cab.

The engine won't start.

"Don't do this to me," says Niko.

"We'll take care of it." The cabbie turns the key again. The engine catches and dies.

Niko looks at the approaching creatures. "I think you need more candybars."

"It's flooded." She stomps the gas and turns the key and lets the engine turn over and lets up on the gas and stomps it again, somehow feeling for the timing, and sure enough the engine catches and chutters weakly a couple dozen revolutions and then picks up. She eases the cab back out to the middle of the tunnel and lines up with the rails and jerks the wheel left-right to make the cab hop up on them. "Nothin to it," she calls back.

Ahead of them more Jeremys shirk from the light and slink against the tunnel walls as the cab rides past. One of them picks its scabrous nose with a soggy finger shoved in past the middle knuckle as if lobotomizing itself. Another swings a squirming rat by the tail like a bolo and lets go as the cab drives by. Niko hears it thump against the side of the cab.

"You all right?" the cabbie says.

"I don't know whether to laugh or cry."

"Yeah. It's like that down here."

Niko's rough slim hand caresses the curves of the hardcase beside him. No taillights shine before them now. Lot of catching up to do. He settles back on the seat and feels the old urge rise, the small burn in his stomach's pit. And suddenly he wants a drink so bad he can literally taste it. Whiskey.

The drone of rails moans through the cab as he outstares the pitiless dark.

"L.A. RIVER OVERHEAD."

Niko startles from his reverie as the cabbie taps the ceiling of the cab. He wonders if the Red Line runs beneath the river. How to know? Where he is could not be found on any map. Except perhaps the maps enscrolled in the collective dream of what may lie outside of life. A cartography of bone and laminate of blood.

In any case he understands the significance of crossing running water. In this deep place, in this conveyance, with this unyielding driver. Customs must be honored and passage must be paid in kind and sterling. So Niko pulls his driver's license from his wallet and removes one of the two remaining coins taped to its back. Its glint dull in the tunnel's phosphorescence. Drachma, lepton, obolos. He'd obtained them through an online broker to whom he gave thorough and particular descriptions. Metal, denomination, condition, age. Knowing from his research he would need to pay his way. But the coins when he received them proved upsettingly familiar though he couldn't have said how. These transactions merely reenactments. By intimations and degrees he is coming to feel himself directed by an older self that has watched and planned and only let Niko know as much as he needs to. A wiser deeper self that even now is moved and moving him to action.

This coin is silver, stamped with the head of a gorgon. Niko presses it against his lips, then taps the cabbie's sweatdamp shoulder with the coin and holds it out in front of her. She accepts the silver drachma without looking, bites it as tradition demands though also as a kind of cowboy joke, and flips it ringing into her change tray.

"Much obliged," she says.

Niko pictures the dirty sluggish water running overhead, glinting in sunlight he may never see again yet still may come to dread glimpsing prematurely. He knows the light has played a part in ruining this quest before. But he hasn't made this quest before. But he has.

He leans back in his seat and wonders why he isn't more afraid.

VII

Walking the Dog

E ND OF THE LINE."

Niko jerks awake and is startled to realize he has slept in the first place. Lulled by tire hum on narrow rail in shadowed tunnel. He feels faintly guilty. As if sleep betrays resolve.

He rubs his eyes and works a sluggish tongue around the sleep-taste in his mouth. He feels thick and slow, almost hungover.

The Checker Cab is idling with its engine knocking. Niko cranes forward to peer through the crudcaked windshield. Dull red intermittent light throbs like a painful wound, caressing bloodred highlights off the contours of the driverless Black Taxi parked beside a tall white marble wall that teems with figures carved in deep relief. Farther on along the sculpted wall an enormous wrought iron gate. On the lintel above the gate a red neon sign flashes.

ALL SALES FINAL

NO EXCHANGES

NO RETURNS

Above the sign an enormous marble figure of a pensive devil perches thinking, pointed chin on taloned fist and huddled in his jointed wings. Horned and brooding.

Chained to an iron plate bolted to the wall beside the gate is a very big dog.

A few yards past the dog a wooden ladder leans against the marble wall. On it stands a largeheaded balding man with a full beard shot with gray. Mallet in one hand and chisel in the other. The mallet strikes the chisel and a moment later Niko dimly hears the sound above the engine's idle cough.

Of the tunnel there's no longer any trace. At some point they have emerged from it or it has widened to become this unfathomable cavern around them.

The cabbie leaves the engine running and gets out to open Niko's door. Looking not at him but at the Franklin parked undamaged by the wall. Her expression one of mild hatred.

Niko emerges like a man who can't believe he's just survived some kind of epic accident. Preternaturally aware yet faintly disbelieving. He stands behind the yellow shield of opened door, barely aware of the cabbie beside him. Eyes only for that Franklin. That wall. That gate. That dog.

The dog is staring at the cab's headlights as if contemplating pouncing. There is no certainty the tanklike Checker Cab would survive if it did.

The cabbie leans in and turns off the headlights and steps around Niko to pull his hardcase from the back seat. Niko steps out from behind the door and the cabbie nudges it shut with her hip while holding forth the hardcase. Niko accepts it and for a moment their gazes meet, flinty blue and walnut dark, and when their hands touch briefly in the transfer of the case's handle from her grip to his he feels again a sense of ritual. The passing of a torch perhaps. Acceptance of a boon.

"Got it?" says the cabbie.

"Got it."

The cabbie turns to face the man at work upon the ladder. She glances at Niko with a mischievous look and cups her hands beside her mouth and calls, "Bonjour, Auguste."

The man on the ladder nods but does not look. "Bonjour, bon-jour." His mild voice faint with distance and drained of character in this cavernous space.

"Comment ça va?"

A shrug. "Ehh, bon. Trés bon."

The cabbie grins at Niko. "Quand finirez-vous?" she calls.

"Quand t'est finis."

She slaps the cab and laughs. "Sorry," she tells Niko. "He just cracks me up."

Niko frowns at the Frenchman on the ladder tapping away. Tap tap tap. The seething multitude in deep relief in the walls around the iron gate, red-edged chiaroscuro figures writhing in the stroboscopic light. Tap tap. Straining marble flesh toward the archway. Their hands the living stone incarnate yearning to escape the very structure of their being, tap. Beyond Auguste the wall is flat and blank and stretches off as far as can be seen. How long has this man been working on the dozen yards of figures that have been completed?

Niko feels awkward and inadequate as he regards the cabbie. "Thank you doesn't even begin to cover it."

She pops a match alight against a nail and lights another ciga-rillo. "Get outta here. I oughta thank you. All I ever get is milk runs. It's nice to stretch my legs."

Niko laughs mirthlessly. "Well, I guess it's my turn. To stretch my legs, I mean."

The cabbie glances at the paladin dog. "Well. Knock em dead, huh." She holds out a hand.

Which Niko clasps. "Too late."

She laughs. "That's good." And lets go.

The cabbie gets back in the cab and shuts the door and turns the headlights on. She pats the side of the cab as if it's a good horse and nods up at Niko. "Break a leg."

"I'll probably break a lot of them."

Crow's feet bracket her ageless eyes. "You do that." And she slowly drives away.

Niko is just turning toward the Black Taxi when the Checker Cab's brakelights flash and the backup lights come on. The cab whines toward him and the brakeshoes grind as it pulls up beside him and stops. The cabbie leans out the window. "Here." She tosses the half-empty cigarillo pack. "Who knows when you'll get hold of any more?" Then she's driving off again toward the tunnel and the daylit world.

Niko puts the pack in a jacket pocket and watches the receding taillights until the engine sound has faded out and the ensuing silence makes him feel despairing and marooned.

Alone now Niko feels the tension in and past the marble walls, a carnival charge in the whipcrack air. It's more than just the presence of the monstrous dog. It's a quality of the walls themselves. As if the living stone has absorbed the pain and fear and tyranny of all that they surround.

A small metallic ping gives Niko's heart a little kick. Not Auguste and his irregular hammering. A distinctive sound that he'd know anywhere. The crackle of a cooling engine.

BEFORE THE WALL's pale marble the Black Taxi looks like a shadow of itself. As if abandoned by the thing that cast it.

Niko sets the hardcase on the ground, which seems to be a flat expanse of ochre stone, and walks around the huge sedan.

It truly is magnificent. Lacquered and curved and pristine like something poured or grown. Niko looks but does not touch. Not yet, not yet. The dog behind him watching. Niko cannot help but wonder if the car itself knows he is here.

There's barely room to sidle between the Franklin and the wall. Niko doesn't want to touch either one. The stone wall crowded with huddled figures beautifully rendered in marble agony, damned souls locked in stone who huddle and teem and yearn toward the unfelt space denied them, groping from their anhedonic orgy for some dimly conceived paradise of emptiness. Though motionless they suggest motion, a surging wave of sculpted humanity impeccably rendered. The alabaster snarl carved on one wide-eyed face with crooked teeth. The flaring nostrils on one reaching figure always at the onset of a scream. Tension in the tendons of a reaching wrist. Niko remembers viewing Rodin sculptures at the Louvre and at the Norton Simon and remembers thinking that the figures did not look like sculpture at all but like human beings made of stone, moments frozen by a loving hand. He starts to turn away from the beautiful horrible wall, then stops.

Rodin. Auguste Rodin.

He shrugs and turns away from the basilisk stares, certain they are aware of him. As the Black Taxi seems aware of him. He cannot help but feel the car holds some kind of awful coiled potential waiting to be sprung like a warhead silent in its housing.

Something grabs his jacket when he tries to move on. He jumps back and whirls, raising an elbow against whatever holds him. A faint rip as his jacket tears.

It's an arm. A lifesized alabaster-muscled arm, marble fingers clutching frozen, leading toward a rounded shoulder eclipsed by a contorted blindeyed face halfdrowned in unformed stone.

Niko nearly laughs. You just snagged it, buddy pal, that's all.

Still. He didn't remember that arm being there when he'd started walking round the car.

Niko crabwalks out from between the wall and the monolithic car. Thinking as he looks upon the Franklin's dreaded form, What are you?

Impulsively he grips the gleaming doorhandle and then jerks away as if shocked, though he hasn't been. The handle is unblemished. He grabs again more firmly but the door is locked.

From behind him comes a growl so deep he feels it through his shoes. Niko glances back at the gate. The dog is up on all fours now and bristling. No question it could stop a truck.

Niko tries to ignore the dog as he bends and hoods his eyes and peers into the driver's window. The mason jar's not there of course, but how utterly damned he truly deserved to be if it had been and he hadn't looked.

Now the growl is multiple and Niko feels it in his chest. He straightens. Okay, we're in for the long haul, buddy pal.

He glances again at the gate. Takes a deep breath. Turns from the dark car to face the foaming dog strangling itself as it strains forward, restrained by that divided anchor chain attached to three humanleather collars big as weightlifter's belts. Chainlinks thick as Niko's thumb but Niko doesn't trust them. They've been there a long time. And it's a really big dog.

Past the dog the bearded sculptor on the ladder does not heed the monster's histrionics but continues working, mallet tapping chisel, the tinking sound subsumed now by the worldconsuming frenzy of the guardian and multiform dog.

Niko pats his jacket pocket.

The dog barks in threepart discord and trembles before Niko like a bowstring drawn and held too long. No limb of him is still. The creature angles forward at the rusted leash's limit, struggling, bulge-eyed, straining.

Niko says Nice doggy.

At the sound of Niko's voice the dog goes absolutely mental. Three wet snarls reveal huge fangs of yellowed ivory rotting at the gumline. Three spiked humanleather collars each a handspan wide stretch creaking.

"Got a present for you, Sparky." From his jacket pocket Niko pulls the jumbo milkbone taken from the kitchen of his worldgone home. He waggles it chest-high, eye-level with the furious bristling dog. "You want this, boy? Huh? You like that?"

The dog's mad eyes glaze over and foam runs down its muzzles thick as the head on a beer. It rears up on muscled hindlegs now, thrashing and gnashing like something sleeping a thousand years on the ocean floor snagged on some hapless fisherman's marlinhook.

"Come get it, sport." Niko fakes an underhand. "Cmon, come get it, Rex." The dog is fighting amongst itself as if contending for the chance to rage into Niko first. The wasp-nest tension, the rising note on the vibrating air.

Six wormveined eyes bulge as the insane dog's straining grates the massive iron plate. Above the basso profundo chorus of snarls Niko can hear metal creaking.

He underhands the jumbo milkbone to the berserk dog and white foam flies as feral jaws snap it from the heated air. Two more sets of beartrap teeth clamp on the central massive neck from either side. The hot air boils with snarls and thickens with a tang of copper.

Niko grips his hardcase and broadly rounds the brawling mass of dog to hurry to the massive gate. The moment he touches it the ancient iron grows hot in his grip. Insomniac rust smears his callused palm. There is no lock upon the gate, no handle. Niko simply pushes and it moves. No creak of hinge or metal groan. Hell's gate opens inward.

Niko looks up at the flickering neon glow above the archway. Red-edged against it that carven figure perches smirking, pointed chin on taloned fist and exulting in its outspread wings. Horned and smiling.

Niko shifts the case to his left hand and puts his shoulder to the gate and plants his heels and puts his weight into it and the iron gate shudders wide enough to admit a man. In patches of red light the ground across the threshold looks just like the ground out here, flat and baked and cracked. What difference had he expected?

Behind him now the snarling grows to yowls. Niko slides into the opening and his hiking shoe descends upon the undisputed floor of Hell.

Niko dodges as the massive gate slams shut. He tries not to think of the dull boom of its certain closure as omenous, or apocalyptic, or containing any note of doom.

VIII

WALKING AFTER
MIDNIGHT

I**T'S DARK OUT THERE.** T**HE** crashing echo of the gate's
decisive closure is all that fills the silent void surrounding Niko.
Somehow the closing of the grated gate has cut off the intermittent
neon light and all is starless and bible black. Before him might be a
wall or a crevasse or an endless plain for all Niko can see. For all he
knows horned cartoon demons leer and taunt with pitchforks just
beyond his reach.

The air is sweatshop hot.

Niko takes a tentative step forward. He can sense the wall
behind him, feel its mass and presence. Horrible as the wall is, he
feels a strange security knowing it is there, the only certain solid
thing between himself and utter isolation in a world that's never
known a sunrise, never felt a drop of rain. Endless uncarved marble
the boundary between damnation and mere mortality.

Niko turns his hand before his face as if motion might make visible what is not seen when still. He shuts his eyes then opens them
and cannot tell if they are open or shut. He stands there feeling

foolish and observed and tells himself he's merely acclimating, waiting for his eyes to adjust and his kinesthetic sense to absorb the notion that his universe might as well end at his skin.

The sudden churning fear. Jesus on a snipehunt Niko what the fuck are you doing down here?

He breathes in deep and summons up an image of a weightless feather in a mason jar.

All right. Okay.

He rubs gooseflesh beneath his coatsleeved arms despite the fact that there's no wind, no sound, no light, no sense of here or there.

Niko spent a night once in a sensory deprivation tank. A large plastic coffin sealed away from light and sound, holding amniotic saltwater on which he lay suspended and unfeeling. It was easy to believe he was the only thing in the universe, that he was himself a universe and beyond his reach lay untenanted infinity. He had lain still and waited. For what he did not know but that was the sense of it. Waiting. A sense of imminence, of always arriving. Floating soulless in the briny dark.

Then the hatch yanked open and light slammed in and there was Gus's drunken silhouette to deliver him slapped into the world and saying Hey was that a trip or what?

Like a disembarking argonaut Niko climbed out from the tank, wet and blinking at the alien world where he had beached, beckoning oblivion abandoned.

And there was Jemma naked on the sauna bench and keeping watch outside his little world, a faint worry crease between her eyebrows as she looked at him emerging, a curling paperback bookmarked by her thigh, and Niko had smiled remembering why he'd come back to the world and why he always would.

Now in sultry darkness with his back against the wall to end all walls he blinks and catlike shakes his head. It had been so real. Jemma had been sitting right there in front of him on the redwood bench, turbaned in a bluestriped towel, paperback dampened by her sweating hands.

"Stop." Startled by his own voice in this pregnant dark, as if whispered close beside him by some unexpected other.

A world unto himself he walks.

Mortality Bridge

* * *

As he passes on into the unconstellated night there grows around him a persistent murmur. The cumulation of untold millions in torment giving voice to their despair, wailing their pain, howling their rage, sobbing their unalloyed separation from all the sanguine world. A ceaseless threnody of anguish that constitutes a white noise of the suffering world, the hubbub of Hell. Its collective growl and purr the endless operation of a factory of misery, churning mindless yet somehow alive. It will be with him always here, and he will never get used to it.

Bring up chorus as the Greek approaches stage front.

Voices he hears voices.

"Oh hey thanks for leaving the gate open, asshole."

"What's he got in his hand?"

"They let him in with something?"

All is so amazing dark.

"Shit, they let him in with clothes."

Dimly as he walks he starts to sense their outlines in the faint infected light. The total darkness giving way to intermittent sickly orange light from somewhere high and far away. Beyond him in the blind world waiting is a sound of shifting figures, murmured voices flattened by enormous open space. How do they see him in this fetid gloom?

"Whose ass you be kissin fuh to get in here like this, mon?"

The ground crunches and crackles beneath him as he walks.

"You deef, son?" another voice calls. "Boy done ast how come you rate."

"Now Judge mon. Ah tell you bout callin me boy, hey."

"You kin tell me all you wont, porch monkey. I'm still gonna—"

"Ah don take yuh shit no more Judge, hey. You don't be remembrin how long it take yuh to pull yuhself back together after Gombe take you apart like fresh bread mon? How much it hurt? Yuh scream like the woman, Judge. It sound like the old work whistle an yuh know it true. Yeh an it take you longer ta heal every time too."

"Fuck you nigger. I hung more a you Ubanges than Carter's got pills, an I taken enough a yo big fat lip to—"

A sudden scream pierces the gloom. Terrified, highpitched, cracking. It does in fact sound very like a work whistle. It goes on longer than any living being could possibly scream.

Niko heads off to one side, aware that those ahead of him have been down here so long their eyes can detect him, aware too that down here the dark at times will be his friend. His instinct is to see why the man is screaming. To help someone in pain. But this is not the country for Samaritans and the dead lie well beyond his aid.

The screaming stops.

"Always save the troat fuh last," comes Gombe's voice. "Here yuh go mon. Catch." Something lands close by with a soggy sound of wet mop slapping concrete. "Now yuh tell old Gombe," the voice says, closer now, "who are yuh that come here before yuh time?"

So much for stealth. Niko takes a long deep breath, releases it slowly. Readies himself for the violence he hears in the man's tone.

Again pale orange smears the distant starless air. Niko makes out human shapes again, dozens of them, closer than he'd realized. The closest is dreadlocked and only a few yards away.

"He's wearing shoes," an Englishwoman says.

Someone screams at him in Cantonese.

"Is that a guitar?" a husky voice.

Gombe laughs long and loud. The orange light fades and the shapes coalesce with the heated dark. "Yuh don belong here fuh certain. What happen mon? Yuh dig yuh swimmin pool too deep?"

Laughter all around him not quite sane.

"On yuh way to a gig maybe? They be trowin a righteous party all the time down along dat way I hear. Righteous party fuh true."

"That's right," says Niko, his own voice flat and thin and airless. "I'm on my way to a gig." He's stopped walking now.

"Sneakers an a coat mon." Gombe laughs. "Yuh from California fuh certain."

Niko's face heats. You have got to be fucking kidding me.

"Yuh long way from home ma friend." Gombe is getting closer. Niko hears the man's footsteps crunching on the unseen ground.

"Maybe Gombe jus take yuh shoes an send yuh on yuh way. Yuh play yuh gig barefoot like de bluesman hah?" Gombe laughs.

Once more orange light smears the distance like a comet's ghost and now Niko sees Gombe there before him. The man's skin glistens with crawling shapes. He is covered head to foot with enormous roaches. Their crawling traffic on his naked body is unceasing, even about his face, but Gombe pays no mind. Now Niko hears the aggregate rustle of millions of jointed cockroach legs picking their filthy way, millions of fat and glossy cockroach bodies brushing, millions of brown thin wings beating. Gombe steps forward and the ground crunches underneath his naked feet. Niko's mouth tightens with nausea as he realizes that for some time now he has been walking on a living carpet of the filthy creatures.

Gombe sees his face and laughs. An enormous cockroach crawls across one eye. "What the matter mon? Yuh don like how Gombe dress? Maybe soon yuh and him have the same tailor huh. Or maybe yuh give old Gombe yuh shoes an he let yuh go with the res."

"I'm sorry," Niko says and hears his voice's tension, "but I think I'm gonna need them more than you."

Gombe grins. "Now what yuh be needin fuh to wear runnin shoes here mon?"

"Watch," says Niko. And runs. The rhythmic crush beneath him is sickening, the rapid crunch behind him spurs him on. Within a hundred yards the yelling pursuit begins to fall away, which is good because although Niko is in great shape he is no track star and certainly no spring chicken. The crushing beneath him lessens as well, gives way to hard pounding on flat stone. Niko slows to a stop, breathing heavily. Why aren't they pursuing? Could they who do not breathe grow winded?

He feels a tickling on his ankles as he bends panting with hands on knees, a tickling climbing his shoes and calves. Suddenly he drops the hardcase and scrunches up his pantlegs and compulsively slaps at his ankles and shins and calves, goes on to his thighs, his rear, his stomach. Takes off his coat and snaps it before him like a rug. Hears soft bodies patter onto stone. Another shudder convulses him, and he hurries on his harried way.

* * *

NIKO WALKS DISCONSOLATE along the midnight plain. Soon the flat ground becomes cracked and broken like the parched skin of the Bonneville salt flats. Earthquake fissures run dark and jagged like frozen lightning shadows. Niko has encountered not another soul although he hears their lamentations in the distance. It's a lot less crowded here than one would think. Then again it's goddamn huge and he is only on the outskirts. How big, how long his traveling to come? This geography is not physical or mappable. Cartographers of this sullen abyss might light black candle and cast bone and carve rune and paint in chicken blood on parchment skin and still not fix it for the eye to read because it is not fixed. There ought to be a word for such a notion, for the cartography of Hell.

Hadeography.

From far off comes a freight train rumble. Niko peers across the dolorous distance and faintly sees a giant living thing glide stately on the cracked and broken ground. No, not living. And not gliding either. Sinuously twisting, bottomlit and lifting itself up at points like a woman in a hoopskirt stepping high across a puddle, touching down again capriciously, a tornado heaves across the tortured landscape toward him. The gloom alive with static sparkings like a plague of fireflies. The churning funnel owns the landscape like an Old Testament god, vengeful and malign and bent on wrath and thunder. The locomotive roar of its approach grows deafening as it stoops and gathers writhing clots of feckless damned to bear them up and dance them doll-like in the air around its undulating body in a hundred mile an hour waltz. Their naked skin sandblasted. Fleshy layers flense to raw and glistening muscle and white tendon band, gouting arteries spray particolored tendrils that whipstain the massive shaft before dispersing. Screaming faces filed down to glossy bone. The twister touches down again to amble toward another clump of running damned, leaving in its quiet wake a stripped debris of gleaming bone and conscious jelly.

Niko doesn't even think of running from the whirlwind twisting there before him. He only watches in mortal dread as the vortex lifts to hopscotch over his windswept head and pass mercurial above him. The voice of the whirlwind a leviathan moan. It augers down again behind him to gyre like a mindless deadly battling top. The wind of its periphery whips him and he covers his eyes as sand stings his exposed skin like nettles. Then the wind abates to scour elsewhere on the naked dark.

Niko realizes he has fallen to his knees as if in supplication to some oblivious god. He rises, lucky or blessed or perhaps just insignificant, and walks on. He passes piles of glossy polished bones that clack like windchimes in the remnant breeze. The sockets of sandblasted skulls contain a residue of pureed eye and muscle pulp. The bones appear to writhe with pink maggots until Niko sees that ligaments and tendons and muscle tissues are slowly regrowing, stretching over tortured frames while polished skullteeth chatter as if cold. Purple filigrees of veins spread thickening webs. The twister's murdered are not dead but are to slowly reassemble to endure new torments that await them when again they are made whole.

The mashed grape eyes of one such skull inflate to fill sandblasted sockets once again. Eyes that track him in their polished frames as Niko navigates the endless gloom. And though these dead are flayed to glossy skeletons he feels certain they are conscious all the while. That their reconstitution is a deep and undiluted pain in every lazarus nerve and cell.

Again pale orange smears the abyss. He decides to head toward the source of the intermittent light.

Enfleshing skeletons rise quaking against the light that glowers through the gaps between their picket ribs and glistens on wet marrow and raw meat. They twitch and shudder and convulse and jerk, uncertain as yearlings in their newmade frames. As they stand they slowly turn to stare at him like vivitropic flowers.

IX

LIFE BY THE DROP

HALF AN HOUR LATER NIKO encounters his first demon.

The ground shudders beneath his feet, followed by a loud deep boom of something massive smashing on the broken plain. In the distance large square silhouettes are scattered about. Some kind of structures. Temples? Houses? Hard to determine size and distance because there is so little light and because the plain he walks is vast and featureless and without horizon.

A low shape undulates toward him. Niko turns to avoid it and it swerves to meet him, traveling close to the ground in jerky flopping motions like some enormous writhing maggot. Fifty yards away and Niko sees it is in fact a human being, prone and dragging itself toward him with its pale arms. Twenty yards and the shape is a woman, naked and fat and oozing a doubled sluglike trail of her own blood from stumps of amputated legs.

Niko stops walking and she raises on her arms. "Por favor." She shifts her weight to one arm to beckon with the other. "Por favor."

Niko steps toward her, the question How can I help? already breath in his mouth. But she is dead and damned and consigned to torment. Relief from what has been willed is beyond action or even consideration. How many damned down here, what private universes of suffering? Millions certainly. Billions probably. Even to alleviate their torment would consume the balance of his mortal years and derail him from his mission. Harden your heart, Niko. You cannot save them. They are already lost. Harden your heart.

That shouldn't be too difficult for you, buddy pal, whispers another facet of himself, the demon voice in the Greek chorus of his self-deprecating soul.

The legless woman regards him now with her head atop her upcurved back. The shocking termination of her thighs. Some carved sphinx half buried in the hardpan of the plain, artifact of a civilization lost and alien and cruel. Her pleading face. Her pain-dulled eyes. Her outstretched hand. Already sprouting from her ragged stumps are tiny buds of legs to be.

Orange light throbs again to gleam her doubled trail of blood, which leads toward one of the distant blockish shapes.

I'm sorry, Niko says. I'm sorry. And hurries past ashamed and afraid. Behind him come her spanish imprecations. Niko feels her gaze between his shoulderblades. Don't look back. Don't look back.

SCATTERED ON THE lambent plain are granite blocks. Ten feet square and smoothwalled, their shadows moving in the intermittent airborne orange light that waxes, lengthens, flickers, dies. The spanish woman's driedblood trail abruptly stops beneath the bottom edge of one such block.

Warily Niko touches the rough hewn granite. A fissure jags the surface. The hard ground around it fissured too. Niko lowers his hand and steps back. A block like this would have to weigh what? Fifty, sixty tons? Niko leans away from the block and cranes up at the cavernous expanse of black that is not night. He frowns and quells a welling urge to blindly run. Instead he walks among the widely scattered cubes toward the source of the orange light. No nightchirps of crickets here, no hiss of wind in leaves. No freeway surf boom, no distant music or conversation. What he will hear down here is screams and moans and cracking whips. What human laughter he will hear is maniacal and leached of pleasure. The sounds that come across the plain are oddly flattened. The space is vast and the horizon unattainable, but Niko cannot shake his sense of being inside something, the certainty of living rock above his head. The panic-tinctured claustrophobia of being underground.

Now a man's voice weakly calls out to him. Hey. Hey. Hey. Dull repetition as if uttered by rote. Hard to fix direction. Hey. Hey. Coming from his...left? Yes, from the block of granite nearest him. From its base.

Niko has decided to ignore the voice when it begins to call his name, Niko Niko Niko, with an urgency quite different from its leaden repetition. Gooseflesh sweeps his back and arms and his scalp grows tight. Your name is something you don't want to hear called out down here. Unaccountable shudders in the mortal world are caused when someone says your name in Hell.

Niko turns toward the granite block. Emerging impossible from beneath the bottom and flush with the flat hard ground is a man's head and neck and right arm. The man lies facedown where he's been smashed flat. It's too dark to discern more detail.

Niko stops before the man. "How do you know my name?"

The chanting stops. Then once more, Niko, in a whisper all relief. A thin weak voice with little air behind it. No surprise when tons of granite sit on top of lungs pressed flat as burst balloons. "You don't. Recognize me? I'm crushed."

"I can barely see you." Niko glances around, half expecting some trick, some ambush or cruel joke.

"It's Sam."

"Sam?"

"Sam Gamundi. Samwise."

"Samwise?" Niko can't believe what he's just heard. "Sam?" And hears himself ask a question that must, in this place, be the most hackneyed of clichés. "What are you doing down here?"

"Trying to. Dig my way out. I've made a start. Already." But then Sam senses Niko's larger question. "I don't know. No one tells us. Anything and. There's no way to. Find out."

Pale orange flares and Niko sees that Sam indeed has made a start. Beneath the free right arm a small depression near his free shoulder has been scraped out with his fingernails and presumably leads beneath his flattened chest.

Niko frowns. The ground here is like rock. How long would it take to—

He gasps at sight of Sam's face. Hydrostatic pressure from the impacting granite block burst cells and arteries and veins toward the free end of Sam's body like stepping on half a waterfilled balloon. One of Sam's eyes has popped partway from the socket. The other is beet red. Blood has burst from his ears and nostrils and mouth, from beneath fingernails scraped down to nubs.

Mercifully the orange light fades. "I'm luckier. Than most. I have something. To dig with." Sam waves his free arm feebly. "Most others have to. Wait until. The rock wears away. Before they can. Get out."

"Until it wears away?"

"Yeah. We're gonna be. Down here forever. You learn to. Think longterm. You must not. Have been here. Very long."

"I only just—"

"Well that's the thing. It takes a while. To adjust. Hey are those. Shoes?" The head turns slightly. "And clothes. They let you in. With clothes? And. Shit is that. Your guitar? Son of a bitch. You mean you get. VIP treatment. Even here?"

"It's not like that, Sam. I'm on a kind of mission. I'll do whatever I can to help you but—"

"Son of a bitch. You're not dead."

Niko slowly shakes his head.

"Son of a bitch. You always were. The luckiest guy. I ever met. In my life. I followed your career. Since we were. In school. Had all your albums. Used to tell people. I knew you. Way back when. Told em even then. I knew you were. Going to be. Famous. Always carrying that. Little guitar around like. Linus' blanket. Son of a bitch. How in the world. Did you get down here. And you not dead?"

"Um. I took a cab."

Oddly enough Sam accepts this with a slight nod. But then Sam has probably learned to accept an awful lot.

"What can I do, Sam?"

"For starters you can. Get me out. From under this. Damn thing."

Niko appraises the block. "I don't see how. There's no way in hell—uh, there's no way to move this block."

"Don't move it. Dig me out. From under it. I'm pretty much. Healed under here. But I can only. Do so much. With one arm."

Niko squats, sighs, lets go of the guitar case. "Sam. I don't—that would take a long time, and I don't—"

"See the block. Closest to us. Over there?" The free arm points.

"I see it."

"On top of it there's. A tool that. Got dropped there. Bring that back. And you can. Dig me out. With it."

"A tool."

"Uh huh."

"You want me to climb on top of that block and bring back a tool that got dropped there and dig you out."

"You got it."

Niko sighs again. "Sam."

"Listen Niko. You're mortal. Down here. You'll need sleep. You'll need food. Whatever your mission is. You aren't gonna get. Far without food. Or sleep. And you'll get filleted. Like a chicken. If you get caught. Sleeping anywhere. In this joint. I can help you. I don't know. What you're doing here. But this place is really. Really big. I can help you get. Where you're going."

Niko shakes his head. Not negation but resignation. "All right, Sam. Back in a few minutes."

"That's the ticket."

For some reason Niko takes off his coat and sets it neatly on top of his hardcase. He starts away, rolling his eyes at the unseen canopy of rock and still shaking his head.

"Niko."

He stops. "Yeah?"

"Try to be in. Conspicuous. These blocks didn't just. Grow here. You know?"

Niko thinks he does know, but he merely nods and sets out.

SAM GAMUNDI. SAMWISE, for Christ's sake. Of all the people to run into down here, the last I would have expected. When was the last time I saw him? High school? Yeah, he came back for a week or so and stayed with me and my family after he'd moved away with his mom. And even then I hadn't seen him since…eighth grade? First time I ever got drunk was with Sam. Skipping school and getting into his mom's gin. Jesus, a gin drunk at fourteen. Watered the bottle down so she wouldn't know we'd been at it. Caught us anyway. Caught Sam that is. He never narked on me. What did she do to him? Can't remember.

Dark as hell here. To coin a phrase. Not much to trip over at least. I hope.

First time I smoked pot was with Sam too. Hell we were trouble, weren't we? Poor Mom and Dad. That time they picked us up from the movies in that old white Ford and me and Sam so stoned we would've giggled if you hit us with a shovel. Sam had somehow got his shoelaces knotted together and couldn't get them untied. Tried to karate chop them and knocked his feet out from under him and landed on his head on the sidewalk just as Mom and Dad pulled up and I laughed so hard I banged my head on the roof getting into the car. Which only got us laughing harder.

I used to wonder what happened to you, sitting tuning my guitar or reflecting on someone else's story from their youth or just daydreaming on the tour bus during those long stretches of paved America between dates. Were you still alive then Sam? How did you finally die I wonder? Would it breach some etiquette here to ask you? And would you tell me if I did?

That week you came back to visit me at my parents' house. You'd been Saved. Some Baptist summer camp you'd been to had gotten to you in some lonely fearful hour. You were worried about my life and my soul. The way I was carrying on. Pot speed booze girls coke smokes and never never never any sleep. I called you holier than thou. Saint Samwise. That was a long week huh? That party my band played. Howyadoin, we're The Spanish Flies. And me getting drunk and scoffing at your thinly hidden disdain. At some point I decided to throw all that contempt back in your judgemental face, only I threw it out through my guitar. A pawnshop Les Paul that'd be worth a pretty penny now I'm sure. And you heard that volleyed contempt all right but you stayed on because I could see you couldn't believe what was coming out of those beatup Fender amps.

To this day I sit amazed six wires on a piece of wood can make a hundred thousand people crazy. That gig got dark and scary, the whole band picking up the vibe and magnifying it, and everybody drunk or stoned or tripping or just plain fuckedup somewhichway. And you better believe they grooved on it, St. Samwise, because they tore that joint apart, throwing bottles and tearing stuffing out of the couch and beating the hell out of each other. You said I was possessed and you ran off while feedback howled up to the bleeding edge and I surfed it all the way and felt maybe just a little bit of bad I'd run you off. But mostly it felt good to be the voice of that crowd's anger. Good to drive you off in your sanctimony, good to drive those people wild enough to turn on themselves like dogs, good to push the amplifiers to the limit, good to push. And when you walked into Mom and Dad's kitchen hours later, having walked all that way home, you suffering martyr, I remember looking up still drunk and hunched over a cup of reheated coffee and seeing both your umbrage and your concern, and Sam I think that was the moment I realized something writhed inside me with an appetite for self destruction. And perhaps we kept our distance after that night not because of your unswervable faith but because of the dark mirror you had held before me. And maybe you backpedaled with equal horror from the pleasure you saw me take in that reflection's corrupt and ruinous bent. I had a demon inside me and I hated him but loved him too. Or maybe I just felt I needed him.

Your black bible and your suffering jesus. My black Les Paul and my suffering blues. You find salvation your way, I will find it mine.

Only—what hope of redemption or salvation or even some small reprieve is there for anybody if our own St. Samwise lies crushed and suffering beneath a granite slab on the outskirts of what deranged god's mad Hell?

Ah, Sam.

NIKO'S FINGERS JUST clear the top edge of the granite block when he jumps. He raises himself up and clears the edge. He climbs up and rolls onto his back and stares up at the solid blackness and then scrambles to his feet. He looks around the surface of the smooth granite cube, looking for a...tool...that got dropped there.

It's so damned dark. Then again, the cube is only ten feet square, and anything that would help dig Sam out from under his own particular Lego block from Hell ought to be fairly easy to—

He steps on a bump and bends to find a metal rod. He picks it up. It must weigh fifty pounds. About eight feet long. Projections on the bottom end. Some kind of shovel? He turns the rod over and regards the arrowheaded trident splayed above his head.

Pitchfork.

IT RINGS DULL and steady as it drags behind him on the hard flat plain. Niko is trying not to think about what the pitchfork implies when behind and well above him he hears something flapping. He turns and sees motion just as whatever flies above him yells Bombs awaaay! in a guttural delighted voice like whirring blades chopping meat. Then twin descending cartoon whistles as of plummeting bombs.

A large gray square occults the sky.

Shit oh dear. Niko bolts, realizes they may have taken his running into account, and cuts left. He runs as fast as he can, left arm pumping and the trident jouncing along. Behind him comes a deep slam he feels in his chest and an earthquake tremor that shudders through his feet. Niko glances back at a granite block that wasn't there a moment ago.

From the sky come curses. There are two voices up there. Niko has a moment to take in jaundiced lantern cateyes and mottled membranous leather wings and impossible combteeth fangs that bristle as the demons grin wide enough to split their heads. Dangling legs that end in talons. Upcurved warty penises the size of Niko's arm.

One of them yells Booooo.

It isn't easy running fulltilt with a fifty pound pitchfork. It's easier when you think something the size of a minivan is about to plummet down from the Great Unseen and flatten you like a fruit rollup. Niko runs.

Sam is waiting—no shit—when Niko returns. "Thought they got you," he says as Niko draws up panting.

Niko drops the pitchfork and puts his hands on his knees until he catches his breath. "Can I expect much more of that?"

"If you were. One of us. I'd say. Definitely. Safe bet you could. Expect more of that. Forever. But with you still alive?" Sam turns his free palm up. "Reckon I don't know. The rules there. Pardner."

Niko grins albeit grimly. Sam had always done a creditable John Wayne. "Found your toadsticker." He holds out the pronged iron rod.

"You are. The man."

"How do you plan to get out from under there? Dig?"

"Thought you might."

"Sam. Look." Niko looks around and then squats down, feeling absurd. I'm in Hell! I'm talking to a dead guy! And he's squashed under a fifty ton block! "We were friends, Sam, a long time ago."

"Setting me up. For the brushoff. Mister Rock Star?"

"If I were dead and stuck down here forever with you I wouldn't think twice, Sam. But the clock is ticking and the longer I hang around the less my chances are, and this ground is hard as rock and it'd take days to dig you out of there."

"Half an hour."

Niko scrutinizes the unnerving spaceless juncture of granite and ground from which part of Sam emerges like some inflatable Sam doll flattened there, the rough depression beneath him meticulously scraped for how many patient painful years like a dribble of water carving out a canyon. Half an hour? "No way."

"Half an hour, Niko. I swear to. Well, I swear. Look, I've dug down to. About my belly button. My arm won't go. Any lower because. My back won't bend. It's just my hips. And my legs. Taking the weight. Under here. If you use that. Pitchfork. To jab out a. Shallow trench about. Down to my knees. I think you can. Work it in. From an angle. And lever me out."

Niko stares. "Are you out of your fucking mind? I'll probably stab you as much as the ground. And do you know what it'll do to you if I lever you out of there?"

Sam grins. "What, you think it can. Get any worse?" He pats the granite looming over him. "Come on, Niko. I can't bleed to death. I can only bleed. And you're not. Gonna kill me. Cause I'm already dead. And if it hurts me. Well. Death's a bitch huh? Half an hour and. If I'm not out. You can go your. Merry way and.

I'll still be grateful. For you knocking. A hundred years off. My downtime here."

Niko eyes the iron rod. He stands slowly and reverses it until the business end is pointed toward Sam. "You always did talk me into the most unbelievable shit."

In the dimness Niko can't tell if Sam's expression is deadpan or earnest. "You ain't seen nothin yet. Pilgrim."

IT TAKES CLOSER to an hour, every second of it nauseating.

The pronged rod is really more trident than pitchfork. Niko sets to work tentatively, pushing the prongs along the depression begun by Sam and jabbing at the hard ground. Soon he sees his trepidation will get him nowhere. Propped on his free arm Sam lifts up to make a space between himself and the compacted ground. There's still only a few inches' clearance and it's hard for Niko to get leverage. On one knee he pulls the trident back and shoves it forward again. The shock of it striking jolts his hands. Sam hisses and grimaces.

Niko hesitates. "Did I hit you?"

"Just ignore me. Okay? I've developed. A high tolerance."

"Okay." Niko jabs again. Again Sam winces. They continue like this, Niko jabbing and Sam making pained faces and even whimpering once, until Sam suggests Niko scoop out the dirt he has scraped loose. Niko wipes sweat from his brow and reaches under Sam. His position necessarily close and uncomfortably intimate. Sam's face caked with old blood. One eye nearly bugging out of his head, both cobwebbed with burst capillaries. Smell of rot.

What Niko's hand encounters in the cramped hot damp space beneath Sam's flattened body does not feel recognizably human. He scoops dirt back toward himself and his hand emerges bloody. "Jesu—"

"Don't."

Niko stares amazed at the fear in Sam's cry.

"No holy names man. Not here. They'll be on you. Like a cheap suit. And they'll make you. Sorry you even know. How to talk."

"Okay."

"I know it doesn't. Mean anything. When you say it. We all got into. The habit up there. But it means something. Down here. Trust me. And they do not. Like it."

"Okay." And recommences jabbing with the trident.

Before long Sam screams with every trident stroke, but whenever Niko hesitates Sam begs him to keep going. The head of the trident caked with blood and dirt and gore. Niko puts his hand beside Sam's ruined face and reaches under the block and scoops out tacky dirt and something moist and filthy. He brushes off the dirt and the object flops in his hand. Sam's penis. Niko stares stupidly at it and then realizes what it is and yells and jumps backward, flinging it away as if it is a snake poised to strike him. He turns and spews his last earthly meal upon the hard flat ground. When he's finished heaving and he straightens and turns to Sam to say he's sorry but he just can't do it, he can't do this to another human being dead or damned or friend or stranger, and Sam sees it in his face and interrupts to tell him that it hurts but not that bad, and besides the pain is easier to take when you know it isn't mortal. That no wound here is mortal. If you didn't heal they couldn't keep on torturing you.

It doesn't make Niko feel any better but it does let him go on. Soon he's jabbing the trident in as far as it will go, and Sam tells Niko to try using it to pry him out.

There's only one way to do it and Niko doesn't protest. He pushes the trident until it grates against Sam's flattened hipbone and then wedges the iron rod where the bottom of the block meets the lip of the depression and begins to pull. Easily at first, then harder. Sam pulls himself with his free arm, screaming but refusing to let Niko ease up. The trident tip scrapes bone and the rod slides back toward him. Either Sam has moved forward or the trident has ripped across his flesh. Or both.

Niko wedges the trident and pries again. Sam is definitely coming loose. His crushed arm flops into the depression. Sam reaches with his good arm to drag the crushed one free of the block and it flops onto the plain like the boneless limb of a freshbaked gingerbread man. Sam oozes from his stone prison like something excreted. Niko drops the trident and grabs Sam around his chest to pull the rest of him free. Sam's chest is soft and full of lumps and it gives in the wrong places. Niko feels as if he's hugging a loose and lumpy sack of flour. Both men yell as Sam pulls free, jellied legs dragging behind him and raw exposed muscle and bone and a loop of intestine coming out his ass and glistening in the pale orange light.

Niko is about to blow his groceries again and he sets Sam down. Sam clings to him a lingering moment with his only working arm, drowning man to driftwood, then lets go to flop onto the ground with a soft resilience that makes Niko tighten his throat and look away. His old friend's body so distorted it inspires horror more than empathy or even dread. Sam's been trapped long enough to heal but his organs and bones have grown back flat.

Unable to lift his head Sam stares up at the sky. "How do I look?"

"Like you crawled out from under a rock. What now, Sam?"

"Now we get out of here."

"Sam, you can't walk."

Sam merely stares up at him. Of course he can't walk, his legs are flabby tentacles. Blood burst from his skin and even toenails when the block landed on him, blood and shit spurted from his bowels along with loops of intestine and other unidentifiable stuff. His pelvis and ribcage are crushed and every organ that wasn't shredded by bone had to have hemorrhaged. The pain alone would have killed Sam if he weren't already dead. His brain had probably hemorrhaged like sat-on macaroni. It's obvious as the block beside them that Sam isn't going anywhere anytime soon unless somebody carries him, and the only person likely to do that for a long long time is Niko. The blunt truth of it hangs there between them like an odor.

Sam looks up at him. "I'd do the same for you."

"I know you would." Sam would, too. He was the guy who made the news by charging a machine gun nest with a grenade in hand and pulling the pin to lob it in through sheer inertia long after he'd been shot dead, the guy who dives in the frozen river to retrieve the fallen baby and hands it up to the mother before submerging one last time. Posthumous decoration was invented for men like Sam.

"Can I ask you something?"

"Fire away."

"How'd you die?"

Absurdly and despite his horrific appearance Sam looks embarrassed. "Tried to break up a fight in a bar. Don't know what it was about. Guy had a knife and the other one didn't. I didn't think it was fair, that's all. I was—well, what difference does it make, here I am. Oh well, huh." Sam snorts. "That's probably what they put on my tombstone. Oh well."

Niko's thinking how much he doesn't want to do this as he puts on his coat and bends to pick up Sam.

"So how come you're down here in the Park?"

"That's what they call it?"

"Yeah. Like an amusement park, only for torturing people. An abusement park."

Niko's wearing Sam like a knapsack. He snorts.

"Seen anyone else you knew?" Sam's carrying Niko's guitar case.

"I really just got here a few hours ago. And I can't see a damned thing."

"I guess you get used to it. The dark I mean. I don't think you ever get used to the rest of it. I think that's the whole idea."

Niko carries the trident.

"Why are you down here, Sam? You were a good person."

"Well thanks. It's a mystery to me. Nobody tells you. You just wake up here and they start in on you. I had plenty of time under that block to go over my whole life front to back and I couldn't come up with anything. Except maybe that I was a good guy but I wasn't great, you know? Not a hero or a saint or anything like that. Maybe that's what you have to be to make the cut."

"Then I imagine there are an awful lot of people here."

"Well, yeah."

Sam's blood is soaking through Niko's coat.

"I've never seen a living person down here. There can't have been very many, huh?"

"Inanna came to visit her sister. Gilgamesh came to conquer death. Odysseus—well, he summoned the shades of Tiresias and Agamemnon from the mouth of Hades more than really descending. Theseus tried to kidnap Persephone and was tormented until Hercules rescued him when he came down to bring Cerberus to

King Eurystheus. Virgil wrote about Aeneas coming down to find his father and then guided Dante when he got the nickel tour. Most of the medieval visits weren't true descents but visions. Oh, and a lot of virtuous pagans like Adam and Eve and Moses were rescued by Jesus after his cruci—"

The ground trembles and a roaring rolls across the lidded sky.

"Shit. Now you've done it."

"What—oh."

"Oh, he says. Man, go faster if you can. They're gonna be on us like flies on shit." Sam peers in all directions, one eye popping, both eyes blooded.

"Sorry. I forgot."

"Oh well."

Niko picks up his pace and Sam slaps against his back. Mangled Gumby or not Sam still weighs a grown man's weight.

"He was already dead though so he probably doesn't count."

"Who?" Niko sounds a little breathless.

"You know. Son of He Whose Name Must Not be Said. He supposedly did it between the Crucifixion and the Resurrection. The Harrowing of Hell, Catholics call it. Between Good Friday and Easter Sunday."

"Some weekend."

"Funny, when you talk about all the mortals who've come down here, you forgot one I'd have thought you'd mention first."

"Who's that, Sam?"

"Orpheus. He always reminded me of you. For one thing he was Greek—"

"Thracian. Son of Calliope and Œagrus."

"And he played the lyre, which I guess is some kind of harp."

"Invented by Hermes. Nero played it. Most people think he fiddled."

"But Orpheus was like a force of nature. You know, he'd play, birds would harmonize, lions and lambs would crouch down to listen, rivers changed course to be nearer to the sound. Dogs and cats were pals. All that big mythic type stuff. Didn't he also save Odysseus' ship by drowning out the Sirens with his playing?"

"The Argo. Looking for the Golden Fleece with Jason."

Niko's stride has become determined, his heels pound metronomically.

"Somewhere along the line Orpheus fell in love with the maiden Eurydice—"

"After the Argosy."

"The myth doesn't say much about her, does it? I guess she's what Hollywood calls the love interest."

"She was a nymph."

"Like I said. So Orpheus and Eurydice get married. The wedding's barely over and what happens? Eurydice goes walking in a meadow with her bridesmaids, who knows why, and she gets bit on the ankle by a viper and dies instantly. Say, could you not grab my leg so hard?"

"Is there some point to all this?"

"So Orpheus' wife of about five minutes dies of a snakebite and Orpheus goes out of his mind with grief. He grabs up his lyre and goes to some cave—"

"Tænarus, in Lacoön."

"—and he walks down until he reaches Pluto and Persephone, the King and Queen of the Underworld. And he plays his lyre for them and sings his grief at the loss of Eurydice. Say, doesn't this guitar case get kind of heavy after a while?"

"Fuck you, Sam."

"He tells them Look, everyone comes back to you guys sooner or later anyhow. Our life is only loaned to us, at the end of it you get us no matter what, right? So what's the difference if you let me have her now? It's just a loan. Lend her to me and let her live out her natural lifespan with me and then you'll have her again forever. He doesn't even try to beat the rap the way they do in all those deal with the devil stories, because the Greeks didn't have a heaven and hell. Just an underworld where everyone ends up. Nowadays who knows what old Orpheus would do?"

"Might as well finish it."

"Okay, well, Pluto and Persephone can hardly turn him down, can they? This guy's music defeated the Sirens. So Orpheus plays his lyre and all of Hades pretty much grinds to a halt. Pluto and Persephone are like, enough already, you're killing us here. They get Eurydice from the newly arrived souls—maybe she was in a line for processing or something, I don't know. But they give her back to Orpheus and they tell him he can take her back up to the world of men. But there's a catch."

"Don't look back."

"Don't look back. Eurydice can follow Niko—sorry, follow Orpheus—back up to the world, and he can hold her hand and lead her through the cave and back to the daylight. But if he looks back the way they've come the whole deal's off."

Niko watches his own feet plod the treadmill ground.

"So they come back up through Hades, which couldn't have been much fun. They're holding hands and walking near the end of the tunnel and Orpheus sees a light ahead. He steps into it and—"

"He stepped into it and looked back to tell Eurydice how happy he was to be back in the world with her. But she was still in the shadows and the second he looked back her hand pulled away. She let go. He tried to hold onto her but he'd looked back and she'd become a shade again and she was slipping back into the dark."

"And he tried to follow her, didn't he?"

"The gods wouldn't let him go back a second time."

"Once in a lifetime opportunity I guess."

Niko stops walking. They are near another of the granite blocks. "I have to stop, Sam. I need a couple minutes."

"Sure. I'm not very light, am I?"

"Heavier by the word."

Niko kneels and drops the trident and Sam lets go the guitar case and then Niko lowers Sam from his back. Sam peels away with a sound like getting up barebacked from a vinyl chair. Niko is sweating and breathless.

"I always thought that story was mean," says Sam.

Niko laughs a single syllable. "Yeah."

"I always wondered why he never told the gods fuck you and went back anyhow."

"Maybe he was more broken than angry. Maybe he realized he'd just fuck it up again. Maybe he knew it would all come around again one day. Maybe he swore he'd change the ending if it did. It's an old story really. It's been told a lot of times a lot of ways."

They're quiet a few minutes.

"The first time I heard Notes on Her Sleeping," Sam says. "I'll never forget it. It broke my heart. I was a first-year grad student sharing an apartment with two other guys. But that day I was alone and enjoying no one else being around. Just sitting on my ratty couch in my shoebox apartment and listening to the radio. You don't know what paradise is till it's way too late. So this song comes on and a minute into it I just know it's you. I had your first two albums, with Perish Blues and Stagger Lee. I liked them but you never got much airplay till that song. It was the first time I heard someone say your name on the radio. I was so proud of you. This was like nothing I ever heard out of you. Really sweet and just so sad. And I just sat there alone and cried. I guess people tell you things like that all the time."

"Not quite like that."

"Well. Bridge was one of my favorite albums. It would've been even if I didn't know you. I mean that."

"Thanks, Sam."

"I just wanted you to know. I'm not just saying it."

"Thanks."

"I hope the ending changes this time round. I hope you get her back."

Niko says nothing. What is there to say?

Pale orange throbs the sky.

Sam says Oh shit.

Niko turns and looks out where Sam is looking but sees nothing. "What?"

Sam's good hand points toward what he sees with his dark-adapted eye. "Our friends are back."

"Shit." Niko puts his coat on and feels the pack of cigarillos in a pocket. He bends to Sam.

Who shakes his head. "Never mind, Niko. Grab your case and haulass over to that block. Stay up against the side and it'll be harder for them to get you. Their aim's good but I doubt it's that good."

"But—"

"Go on. You won't make it if you have to carry me. If they miss you, haul back over here. I promise I won't go anywhere."

Niko hesitates. He wants to say he knows old phrases and word-keys and charms. But Sam's right and now is not a time to learn that ancient keys are useless. He picks up his guitar case. "Back in a few."

"They'll have to go back for another block after they drop this one. Come back right after they drop."

"Okay."

"Luck, Niko."

Niko runs.

A hundred yards later and with fifty yards to go he hears demoniac laughter above and behind him and he puts on a burst of speed. The guitar case is a liability. He considers dropping it to recover later but suppose they take it? Suppose a seventy ton block lands on it? What good will all his journeying do him then?

Niko reaches the block and presses his back against a side and brings the case in close.

One demon yells Tim-berrrr! and the other whistles a long descending note like the swan song of a diving bomb. They let go the block they hold impossibly aloft and Niko sees a patch of sky swell toward him like a gaping maw. His face tightens and it's a great effort not to close his eyes and turn away.

The granite block hits. One edge strikes the top of the block Niko presses against. The bottom edge hits ground and the block tumbles away. The sound is deafening. And more than sound is the concussive push inside his chest. Niko's knees buckle. Granite shrapnel stings his cheek. By the time his knees touch the plain all is as impossibly still and quiet as it was before the block was dropped. Niko is afraid to move.

"Get him?" Purring voice from on high.

"Think so." Gruff voice. "Did you see? Monkey son had my poker."

"We'll get—" This last fades into incomprehensibility as they fly away.

Niko doesn't realize he's been holding his breath until he lets it out. His heart is playing thirtysecond notes. He relaxes against the protective block and relishes the relief he knows is fleeting.

He hears faint noise. A dim and distant screaming coming from behind him. He frowns and turns but there is only solid granite. He sets his ear against it. Yes, faintly through the stone: screaming.

* * *

How good it feels to see Sam's body in the distance on the plain. Niko waves and Sam waves back. Niko picks up his pace. The guitar case feels good in his hand. For the first time since this whole affair began he feels not merely purposeful but confident. He's gonna beat this thing, he really is. He's high on epinephrine of course but that's okay. Believing in yourself is half the battle. Hasn't he told a couple dozen interviewers that?

Sam's still waving. Niko grins. Glad to see me back, huh, Sam? Didn't think I'd make it. Or maybe you thought I wouldn't come back for you if I did.

Niko frowns. Isn't that why Sam is waving?

He stops and looks behind him just as they flap overhead, frightening humanoid bats they seem in the dim vast trembling air, holding between them a huge chunk broken from the block that nearly crushed him. Reflexively he ducks and ludicrously clamps his arms around his head as if that will protect him from the piledriver blow of falling granite. But they pass low overhead and shriek and laugh. All in a day's work. One of them pisses with an armsized penis and the urine scatters in the windless air and splashes Niko's jacket and his guitar case and his hair, and where it splashes hisses and smokes and burns. Reek of sewage and spoiled milk. Niko runs again, runs fullout, runs for—

"Sam!"

They're over Sam now, flapping rapidly to hover, stretching out the moment.

"Pilot to bombardier, pilot to bombardier," one demon calls. "Bomb bay open."

"Bombardier to pilot, bombardier to pilot, roger that. Bombs away."

The slab descends like an outcast angel. Niko runs, uselessly runs. Just before the impact he sees something he will not grasp the meaning of till later. Right now he just records it. The slab hurtling down. Sam's arm up as if to ward it off. Fingers not outspread but in a fist, no not a fist but clenched with just the middle finger out and stabbing upward like a steeple.

* * *

HE'S STILL STARING at the chunk of granite flat against the ground when they land in front of him. They're eight or nine feet tall, muscular and clawed at hand and foot. One has the elongated head of a skinless rat, the other is a grinning nightmare from a parapet of Notre Dame. Both have needle teeth and amber eyes with knife edge pupils. Rat Face has a Buddha's potbelly. Those absurd Beardsley penises waver clublike as they move.

Rat Face wraps his mottled and membranous wings around himself like a cloak and hunches his head down to peer at Niko with one wide and leering eye. He moves toward Niko in a loopy caricatured sashay. He stops ten feet away and surveys Niko with that cartoonish eye. In a burlesque Hungarian accent he says, "Vee are cheeldren of de night. Donnn't be afraid."

Behind him Notre Dame leans on his trident like a Roman centurion on his spear and cracks up laughing.

Rat Face circles Niko, keeping a shoulder toward him and staying hunched into his cape of wings. Niko circles with him.

"Vee vant to know how is it you haff come by...mortal things."

"I'm mortal."

At this Rat Face straightens and drops the Lugosi act. His wings curl back behind him and then furl to rest there quivering. His claws come up with fingers spread in a gesture of melodramatic surprise. "Mortal?" His ridiculous penis wilts and drools a thin yellowish pus.

"Come on, Maurice," calls Notre Dame, still laughing. "Gack him and let's go."

"He says he's mortal."

Notre Dame stops laughing. "What's he doing in the Park if he ain't a guest?"

Rat Face draws up to his full towering height. "What you doing in the Park if you ain't a guest?"

"I want to be taken down."

"Taken down?"

"I command it."

"You command it?" Rat Face gives a sawmill grin. "Mortal boy I'm gonna peel you like a roasted pepper."

"You have no jurisdiction over me. Your business is tormenting the damned." Niko moves his right hand as if writing in the air. "I abjure thee by all the ancient names—"

Rat Face hollers Shit and backs off and spreads his wings to their full and sail-like width. "This monkey son knows the old keys."

"I'm wingin out," says Notre Dame. He turns and leaps into the air.

Rat Face turns to regard Niko once more with a look of seething hatred.

"Take me down," says Niko. "This has been willed where what is willed must—"

Rat Face stabs clawed fingers inches into his own tapered ears and shouts La la la la. And so singing jumps and flaps away.

Niko stops the incantation and watches them dwindle as they fly toward where the intermittent orange light originates.

NIKO WALKS AROUND the dropped stone fragment. From one edge a huge fan of blood has sprayed the ground. Niko glimpses motion at the base of the stone in the bloody patch's midst and hurries to it. Unbelievably Sam's hand sticks out beneath the stone. It is grossly swollen and once more blood has spurted from the fingernails. The fingers twitch as Niko approaches, wriggle frantically as he bends toward them.

Niko clasps Sam's hand. The blood-drenched fingers clench.

"Sam."

The grip tightens.

"Can you hear me Sam?"

Relaxes and tightens again.

"One for yes, two for no, okay?"

One squeeze.

"I'm sorry, Sam."

One.

"I can't get you out this time. I've got to go."

Two.

Niko glances about at the air, at the quiescent plain. Spies an object. "Hold on a second, Sam. I'll be right back."

Two.

"I'm coming right back, I promise. I'm just going to get something."

A hard squeeze and a release.

Five feet away is the trident Niko used to dig Sam from his former prison, a freedom Sam enjoyed for what, an hour? Niko drags the trident back.

Sam's fingers drum with exaggerated impatience as Niko bends down again and says Aw Sam. He touches the hand and the bloody fingers slide around his.

"This is the best I can do. Here." He sets Sam's fingers on the head of the trident and traces their contours so that Sam knows what he's holding. "It's not much but it ought to speed things up. Better than fingernails anyway."

One squeeze.

"All right Sam. I have to go."

Two.

"Come on Sam. Don't make this harder on me."

The hand bears down.

"Sam. You have to let me go."

The hand holds tight and then lets go.

Niko straightens. "Good luck, Sam."

The hand gives a thumbsup and Niko barks a sort of crying laugh. He says Okay and turns away. Even as he picks up his case the hand behind him grasps the trident and begins to dig.

X

LAST FAIR DEAL
GONE DOWN

N IKO STUBS A TOE AND jerks awake. He slept? Walking? How far has he come, how long did he sleep?

He looks around and wonders if he isn't still asleep and wandering the province of a nightmare. The plain has grown more crowded and the crowd is more tormented. The air around him throbs with cries and sobs of voices flattened by the diseased wind.

The catalog of woe he's seen thus far has now become a circus of debasement. To Niko's right a raised wood platform twelve feet high and several miles long swarms with legions of the naked dead. Mostly men but a scattering of women. Surrounding the platform a picket of wooden spikes impales the damned. Speared like cocktail sausages atop each other and writhing like babies. Convulsive shudders, feeble grasping, useless mewling. Hopeless eyes track Niko as he walks their skewered picket.

Alternating with the spikes are taller, rough-hewn logs driven firm into the plain and slathered with black grease.

A demon with black horns, one jaggedly broken, towers above the platform's milling dead. Grinning and hermaphroditic, pendulous baglike breasts and clublike penis. "Who's next then?" Its voice oddly effeminate. It grabs a pale fat man with doughy skin and a bald spot large enough to make him look tonsured like a monk and hoists him by the throat. "Have a seat, my sweet meat pie." The demon slobberingly kisses Tonsured Monk then hoists him over the platform's edge. The man holds to the demon's arm, his hands barely encircling the thick black wrist. His face gleams with the demon's spittle. His struggles listless as he's set onto a greased pole above a spike. Perhaps because the dead are fatalistic. Perhaps because the dead are dead. When he's pushed against the slippery pole he lets go the demon's wrist and wraps his arms and legs around it. He begins a slow slide down toward the ragged spikepoint just below his buttocks. He clutches and digs and undulates and scrapes splinters into his forearms and thighs but lowers nonetheless until the spike tip spears his naked anus.

On the ground a demon with a feathered head and blackbird wings inspects the picket of alternating poles and pikes. Casually it bangs a massive club against the shaft of one pike topped by a frail old man impaled and hanging motionless. The pikeshaft quivers and the old man gives a soft grunt that is worse than any scream.

The birdhead demon doesn't even glance at him but continues down the spitted line, whacking skewers like a child with a branch against a picket fence. He trails a wake of cries and moans. "Well well well," he calls. Whack whack whack. "And how are we fine pederasts today?" Whack whack whack. "Like being up on a pedestal do we?" Whack. "Want the kiddies to look up to us, yes?" Whack whack whack whack. "What's the matter, meat pie? Got a stick up your ass?"

One man has managed to pull himself partway off his spike. The wood beneath him slathered with gleaming gore. Below that struggle half a dozen spitted damned. The broadshouldered man is powerfully built, Nordic with pale skin and long cornyellow hair. Thick legs braced against the thick greased pole in front of him and arms encircling. Incrementally he jacks himself up like a logger up a tree. One inch at a time and every fraction of it agony. Yellow Hair pulls himself off the spike—to escape to where, Niko can't imagine—but just as his face flushes with a ghost of triumph the gigantic keening hermaphroditic demon jumps up from the plat-form and lands both birdlike feet atop his shoulders and drives him down until his naked ass impacts the dead impaled below him. A yard of gory spike protrudes now from his larynx. The demon grins and bends and kisses Yellow Hair's forehead and then sucks the tip of the spike and jumps back to the platform with a farewell push. Yellow Hair screams an obstructed gargling shredding scream. He screams until cords stand cobralike from his neck, until the corners of his mouth tear back toward his jaw and his head flops backward on the ripped hinge until the back of it touches the nape of his neck and still his scream trumps wetly from his fleshy windpipe, ululated by the flopping meat of tongue. And still he screams.

Niko turns from the platform.

A line of several dozen children is being led by a demon Niko's height but proportioned like a dwarf. This demon has a long raven beak and bloodred eyes set in a narrow wedge of head. Raven pulls the naked crying children merrily along, then stops abruptly. The children bump and scream.

"Shuddup ya babies," Raven yells. "Whassamadda widjoo? You wanna find you twin, doncha? The one you murdered inside mommy?"

The children blubber louder and the demon puts his hands on his bladed hips and looks disgusted. "Crybabies make me sick." To prove it he opens his beak and spews a chunky yellow bile that hisses where it strikes the children. The children in front jump back and all begin to scream fullout. But they remain standing in a perfectly straight line.

"Maybe you twins is over there." Raven indicates the lengthy barricade of spitted damned. "Maybe you mommies and daddies is over there. Let's go see." He raises a metal whistle from a leather lanyard round his neck and puts it to his dripping beak and blows it even though he has no lips. "Ready, march. Hup two, hup two, hup two."

Raven pulls the children along and Niko sees now that a rod runs through their bellies to connect them in a single line. A shish-kebab of little boys and girls. Raven tugs the rod to urge along the naked children who must either march in step or jostle one another and increase their pain. The demon slows and speeds up and stops altogether and jerks randomly on the rod, all the while exhorting them like some gungho camp counselor. "Cmon cmon. Calvin, getchoo thumb outta you mouth or I make you eat it again. Mei Lin, izzat you daddy over there? Whaddayoo mean you dunno? What iffiz eyes was inniz head, wouldjoo recognize him then? Oh stop you bawling. Trina wouldn't cry if she saw her daddy, wouldja Trina? Whatsat? It's not you daddy? Well wave to him anyway you little fetus eater." And pulls them along toward the next stop on their eternal and demented tour.

Niko's face heats with the shame of his inability to help. Even children then. No one is spared, no one is spared.

Now he sees a crowd of meandering adults carrying their frowning perplexed and severed heads before them like Diogenes with a jackolantern. They bump into one another and stumble and fall over themselves and drop their heads. The bodies grope blindly about, watched by their own helpless rocking heads that cannot call instructions because they have no lungs. Eventually bodies encounter heads and lift them up and an obscene charade ensues as rightful heads and bodies try to reunite.

Niko wants to ask the demons about the tormented. Ask the damned about their deeds. He wants to know the reasons for such punishments, for like everyone who wants to believe there is somewhere a cosmic balance sheet dispensing justice Niko can accept the meting of the cruelest torment if the punishment fits the crime. But though he knows old phrases and keys and abjurations, dark geographies inlaid along a chromosomal tunnel untold generations long, unlike Dante Niko has no Sherpa to conduct his harrowing and much of what he meets with here will remain a mystery.

The undiscovered country. I have awakened inside Bosch's sleep.

MILES LATER THE platform and its suffering scarecrows yields to a vast and lightening plain bestrewn with casual atrocities and manifest ironies. A molten glow in the distance eventually becomes an enormous banked bonfire attended by demons who stir the sluggish coals with their tridents. The demons squat before the bonfire like cowhands at the end of a long day, heating their irons and joking and laughing and punching each other on the arm until they withdraw their makeshift brands and lazily press the whitehot points against the carefully exposed wet muscle of thousands of flensed men nailed to the plain with iron spikes. When muscle takes the kiss of hissing brand the sickly air becomes a cauldron of screams.

A wooden rack stands by each man and on each rack is fixed the outspread leather of his tanning skin stretched taut and drumming in the fire's breeze. A barbecue smell hangs on the air. A constant snow of ash descends.

Several demons sit on thickframed chairs and read thick books by the glow of tall white candelabra oddly necessary in the angry shifting light. The bonfire's constant crackle an enormous beast charging through a dry and brittle forest. Even a hundred yards away Niko's forehead grows wet from the heat.

He means to give the bonfire a wide berth but a voice behind him stops him in his tracks. "Guten Abend, Herr Doktor. Sind Sie deutsch?"

Niko turns to see a demon standing near him, black and saillike wings outspread and drumming in the bonfire's wind. She would look carved from onyx if not for her pendulous breasts.

"£um Beide, nein," he replies. "Kein doktor bin ich, auch kein deutscher."

The demon looks surprised. "Nein? Sind sie nicht Herr Doktor Faust aus Heidelberg?"

"Nope," says Niko, "I'm a musician. An American."

"Ah, the mortal. We heard about you."

"News travels fast."

She grins. "You know what they say about idle hands." Her dagger teeth are obsidian as the rest of her. Her eyes are black and have no color but what they reflect.

"Why did you think—" and realizes as he says the next three words that he has just spoken that language "—I was German?"

"Most everybody in this section is." She indicates men staked beside their drumhead skins. "The guests, I mean."

"Why are these men here?"

"Well. They were bad."

"But why this torture? What was their crime?"

"I'll show you." She indicates the bonfire.

Niko hesitates. "I'm really trying to get to the center. Can you tell me—"

"It's an infinite plain, bucko. Ain't no center."

"There's a head office I'm sure. Somewhere the boss parks his ass."

"Hey hey." She lowers her trident meaningfully. "Do I show up where you work and piss on the french fry cooker?"

"Never mind. Sorry I asked. Have a nice day." He starts away.

Onyx frowns, one long claw laconically scratching a breast. "Make you a deal."

"I've had it down to here with deals."

She cocks her head uncertainly. "A trade then. Play some music for us and I'll tell you how to reach the—" she grins frighteningly "—head office."

Niko considers. "One song."

She grins. "You have dealt with us before." She holds up three knobby dangerous fingers. "Three."

"Two."

She claps her hands. "Done." Her dark wings flap and furl and rustle when she moves toward the bonfire. "Ahh. Nothing like hot air under your wings. How you mortals stand not being able to fly is beyond me."

"We fly."

"What, in airplanes?" Her wings convulse. "Never get me up in one of those things." She shoves three inches of clawed finger into her fierce broad nose and swabs it and yanks it out and then examines the lump that quivers there. She flicks it away and it hits the ground and squacks and scampers off. She puts her finger in her mouth and turns toward the bonfire. "Walk this way, mortal man."

"If I could walk that way."

"Don't start with me."

THE CHAIRS ON which the clustered demons sit are made of bones removed from the staked men, who cry out every time a demon sits or stands or shifts about. The demons make a point of sitting or standing or shifting about a lot. Onxy tells him that the men staked here are nazis. "They feel everything we do to them, even after we take them apart." She pulls a wad of green mucus from her catslit eye and stretches it like taffy and loops it round her palms. "We have a lot of latitude with the guests. And we're very efficient you know. No part of the nazi is wasted." She forms the band of mucus into a catscradle. "Thumbsies?"

Niko ignores her and sets his guitar case on the shadow-crawling ground.

A demon reading on a thighbone chair uses a strip of blond scalp to mark his place in the skinbound bloodlettered volume of Mein Kampf he peruses by the light of humanfat candles glowing in an armbone candelabrum. The demon tosses the book into the crackling bonfire and in the distance someone screams in pleading German.

Another demon kicking spiked heels against the legs of his bonechair offers Niko a deepfried pork rind from an upended skull cookie jar with clacking jaws.

Niko fights to ignore the pure dementia of his surroundings as he thumbs the latches on the hardcase. The demons stare as he draws the Dobro from the plush like some implement of ritual. The rounded body of the steel guitar throws firelight back upon the curious gazes of the gathered demons as he shrugs into the strap and bends to the case and opens the storage compartment and takes out a three inch length of burnished steel pipe that he slides onto his bare ringfinger.

The demon munching pork rinds stills his kicking legs and crunching teeth. "Oooh. Pretty."

Niko realizes the pork rinds aren't made of pork.

Onyx touches Niko's arm. Her deadly fingers feverish hot. "Chair?"

Surprised by the hospitality Niko starts toward the proffered thighbone chair, then stops. The demons grin and wait. The skinless nazis beyond the bonfire struggle and moan.

Niko nods toward a flattish rock a few feet away. "I'll just sit there."

"Aww," says Pork Rind. "He no fun."

Niko sits upon the rock and strums an open chord. He twists the Dobro's E-string key while he tunes it against the D. He frowns and adjusts the D. Around him grotesque figures gather waiting. The bonfire pops as Niko studies metal lines and curves distorting flames and nightmare faces.

Demons nudge each other as the mortal bends to play. Waylaid deep within the old world's bones he strums his steelbodied guitar on a warm flat rock before flensed genocides and congregated demons, and he plays slow somber blues and thinks about life's shitty sense of humor. The area around the bonfire oddly quiet as he slowly rocks with his eyes shut and his mouth a little open and his voice emerging as the everbending cry of metal slide against the Dobro's strings. The fire's crackle loud. The demons still and silent as they listen. The staked and skinless Germans given brief and miraculous surcease from their affliction, the only such reprieve they will receive for all of time to come.

Niko bends a final trio of a slow atonal upswing stranger by far than any cry ever released in this forsaken place and aching to resolve. But resolve it finally does, a tight harmonic fit that fades into the heated air.

He mutes the strings and opens his eyes. And starts at the disfigured assemblage before him. In shifting monochrome chiaroscuro they stand eager and quiet and staring. Firelight on leather and fur and scales. Drumhead wings rustle like sheets hung in a gale. They have flocked from all around in the short time of Niko's playing and now they stand or sit or squat or perch attentive and oddly respectful as Niko looks up from the Dobro and sees them hearing him. He has been so lost in the familiar world of his music that he has in the brief span of his fretting forgotten the ruined world he's really in and what he is rehearsing for. That lostness, that going away, that letting go is why he's always played in the first place. Because even more than drinking whiskey or shooting smack or making love, music is the only place where he can go and not be there anymore. With those other means of going away forbidden to him ever since the Deal, music really has become his one permitted drug.

"Fuck," says a demon near the front, a shortbeaked nightmare with an ornate silverhandled florentine dagger in its human-leather belt.

Onyx elbows Florentine in the head without looking. Her thornlike elbow spike impales the demon's skull. The demon doesn't even flinch as Onyx yanks her elbow from his head and wipes a blood tear from her glossy marble cheek upon a sculpted talon. Contoured in the bonfire's light she looks like something made of space itself. The wells of her eyes find Niko's. "Uno mas."

Hubbub among her colleagues. "We could get in trouble," one of them says.

Onyx jerks her head and two demons detach themselves from the boneless and eviscerated soul they're doubleteaming. They grab the trepidant protester by his feathered arms and naked chicken legs and swing him in big arcs while the others call out Ooone twooo threeee. At which they let him go to arc high up and crash headfirst atop the bonfire. Sparking ashes lead brief escaping lives and a brighter patch of glowering heat within the burning hill is exposed. The nazis resume their wails as the pitched demon claws through their charring ember parts to the bottom of the bonfire and scampers from the halloween coals and brushes embers from his smoking feathers without another word.

"Song," a demon orders from the rear.

A castanet clattering of clapped beaks sounds approval. Other demons stamp their tridents on the hard ground. Bird- and batlike wings spread wide and fan. Near the fire two demons caper and cavort. One uses a found fingerbone to play a rack of whitepicked ribs like a washboard. The other has a line of half a dozen silent screaming skulls thrust onto his priapic cock.

Niko looks back down at the guitar and wipes filthy hands on grimy jeans. Come on, son, you've played worse gigs than this. That Kiwanis dance when you were hurting bad.

Niko noodles and tunes and gazes at the twisted assemblage. What do you call a group of demons? A gaggle? A herd? A murder? If they were angels they would be a host.

Of their own accord his arms embrace the Dobro and he strums a big fat wall of texas shuffle with a strong and syncopated upstroke, brazen and uptempo. Niko's playing has caught a whiff of the demons' bacchanalia and handed it back to them and they obligingly stomp and cavort and whirl in one big feedback loop.

And like a feedback loop the music starts to howl. Something dark has always lived in Niko's music, something he's spent decades mastering if not overcoming. But down here darkness is a force of nature and the demon he has nurtured and despised within himself might very well be given flesh. Might tap him on the shoulder and address him by his name.

These demons have a nose for Niko's darkness and they make it all their own. As he plays they dance and jump and shudder and convulse and shriek. One screams in abhorrent and inhuman languages and yanks his forked and footlong tongue with both reptilian hands. One sprays crackling acid semen on a row of screaming skinless nazis as he's masturbated by a giggling other. One claws at her own face with razor talons. Seeing her two others leave behind the pile of gutted corpses they are rolling in like happy puppies and hurry to her so that they can lick the flowing ichor from her pitted cheeks. Whooping demons wrestle in the bonfire like children in a sandbox. Their wingbeats fan the smolder to a burnished gold. The music's beat is taken up with thighbones rapping everstartled skulls and fingerbones scratch rib accompaniment.

The hub of this debauchery sits rooted on his pedestal with his right foot tapping and his right hand doing most of the work. He senses the circus of depravity that gyres and shudders about him to the beat of his own music and yet is apart from it. But Niko does share one thing with these dancing demons and these suffering genocides: all of them are lost, they are lost, they are lost.

So lost are they are now within their saturnalia that none notices the small shadow cast by no light against no figure, a long thin shadow that pools into their midst like oil. That swells and rises and shapes itself like a djinn from a bottle into a corpulent mass of ebon flesh that towers quivering above the manic congregation until it is a vast and naked carnival of bloat that clenches carsized fists above its round and hairless boulder of a head that shakes from side to side and swings huge jowls like turkey wattles above the hillocks of its breasts. This black flesh mountain bellows like a warhead's detonation and abruptly now the revels cease.

Niko's mind rejects the impossible thing before him. Demons he has been able to accept. Intimidating and disgusting as they are, they're still humanoid. Convincing costumes. But this. This conflation of gluttony cannot possibly exist. It should suffocate under its own pestilent obesity. The sagging acres of inky skin, the runnels and valleys and craters and folds, look more like lavaflow than flesh. This is not a creature. It is geologic, tectonic, it should have its own gravity and perhaps a moon or two.

And indeed it does have satellites, for demons wheel about it like lured moths around a spotlight that absorbs illumination rather than emits it. They rend their flesh and cry out and abase themselves, their wings spasmodic as they offer gouged or torn and dripping offerings of themselves to this alien deity.

The black cathedral of glut has eyes for none of them. Rearing monolithic above Niko it inclines its baldmountain head and looks down on him with eyes as black as any sunless cavern underneath the ocean floor. What face there is below those seacave eyes is half eclipsed by the black planet of its pulsing belly.

An irontree hand swings up to point at Niko. YOU. The pronoun is a booming surf.

Niko cowers and his sphincter clutches. The rotting mistral of the titan's breath breaks over him. Reek of sewage and spoiled milk. "Muh, me?" His voice ridiculously small and ineffectual.

YOU ARE THE MUSICIAN.

"I, uh, yeah, I—"

WHO HAS ALLOWED YOU TO DEFILE THIS PLACE?

"Defile?" Niko feels stupid and afraid. Supernatural cars and sadistic demons and giant threeheaded dogs he's dealt with pretty okay considering. But this continent of menace has caught him by surprise and it's huge and powerful and really pissed off.

WHO HAS ALLOWED YOU TO DEFILE THIS PLACE?

"Who let me play?"

WHO HAS ALLOWED YOU—

"To defile the place, okay." Niko glances at prostrate demons everywhere, faces shielded from the dread black light of titan gaze, wings tight to their bodies and claws opened above their heads in abject supplication. The bonfire coruscates upon the ripped and bleeding figures of the nazis staring walleyed at this gargantuan apparition. "Uhhh." Niko feels an odd pang of guilt as he spies her, midnight black among the cowering demons. He begins to raise a traitorous finger to single her out but checks himself. Onyx has done him no harm and in fact was going to help him in exchange for the diversion of his playing several songs. Niko rests his hands upon the metal body of his guitar. The slide still on his finger glimmers firelight. "No one. I was only—"

"Me!" Onyx rises trembling to her spiky knees. As the black spotlight of the giant's attention turns to her the demons cowering around her scatter like fish darting from a stone dropped in their midst. "Great Moloch it was me!" Her obsidian claws clutch her naked scalp and dig in deep. "This mortal man was moving among us, I am not worthy to speak to you, he was moving among us and I only sought a new torment, I worship you, this mortal and I struck a deal—"

Faster than Niko would have believed possible the giant's hand plummets like a crashing jet to pulp the demon Onyx under his massive thumb and swab her across the ground like a bilefilled bug.

Niko feels his bladder let go.

The giant straightens and licks gore off his thumb with a thousand pounds of mottled gray tongue. He cocks his head at Niko with an expression absurdly reminiscent of Victor the RCA dog. MORTAL MAN WHAT BRINGS YOU HERE BEFORE YOUR FINAL DAY?

This is more familiar ground at least. "Up there in the mortal life," recites Niko, "my wife of common law was taken from me before she reached the fullness of her days."

AND YOU HAVE STRUCK A DEAL WITH THIS. The giant indicates the jellied smear of Onyx on the ground.

"I have." Niko's teeth are chattering from pure fear. "In exchange for two songs I have just played she was to tell me how to get to—" Niko hesitates over the euphemism "—to the, the head office." His knees are shaking.

IN THIS PLACE A DEAL WITH SUCH A ONE IS BINDING AND IS LAW. THOUGH SHE IS NO MORE THE BURDEN OF HER TELLING FALLS ON ME AND I MUST HONOR IT. BUT KNOW BEFORE I TELL YOU THAT I HAVE HEARD YOUR MUSIC AND RECOGNIZE YOU FOR WHAT YOU ARE. YOU HAVE BEEN HERE BEFORE.

"Me?" Niko shakes his head. "Oh no no. No. Much here is strangely familiar to me but—"

Mortality Bridge

BENEATH YOUR MORTAL GUISE YOU WEAR A SPIRIT OLDER STILL. THE MASK OF CRAWLING MEAT DENIES THE TRUE ETERNAL FACE BENEATH. I SPEAK NOW PAST YOUR MASK TO TELL YOU THAT YOUR QUEST IS AND ALWAYS HAS BEEN AND ALWAYS WILL BE FOR NOUGHT.

"I don't understand."

I DO NOT SPEAK TO YOU. FROM MY MASTER I AM COME TO TELL THE WEARER OF YOUR FLESH THAT HE IS WEARY OF THIS REENACTMENT. I REMIND THE HOST OF YOUR FACADE THAT IN THIS PLACE WHERE WORD IS LAW AND BLOODSIGNED DEALS ARE GRAVEN ON CREATION'S BONE, YOU HAVE GIVEN US YOUR WORD AND SIGNED YOUR NAME. IN THIS YOU AND MY MASTER ARE WED, FOR YOU MUST HONOR AND OBEY.

"These are your words?"

THEY ARE MY MASTER'S.

Niko bites his lip and thinks. "You haven't come to stop me?"

I AM COME TO STOP YOUR DESECRATION OF THIS HOLY PLACE.

"But not my—my quest."

I AM BOUND BY YOUR BARGAIN WITH SHE WHOM I DESTROYED. He wipes his thumb on his obscene and dimpling hip. I MUST TELL YOU THE WAY TO...THE HEAD OFFICE. At this last the titan smiles for the first time and a shrieking horror of vertiginous death assails all Niko's being with the writhing soil of the rotting grave that is not oblivion or peace or even surcease from our earthly pain and sorrow for in every cell there is evolved revolt against the undeniable corrupt majesty of inimical death, a horror of annihilation shaped not by the senses but from deep within the gene, a viper nestled in twined strands of DNA. What corruption awaits us all.

Niko forces his gaze from that graveyard smile and the allconsuming feeling slowly fades. The titan raises a huge flabby arm to point across the endless plain. THE BATTLEMENTS OF APATHY ARE THE SOURCE OF THE LIGHTS THAT BURN ACROSS THE PLAIN. THERE FIND THE MONSTER GERYON AND CALL HIM BY HIS NAME. ORDER HIM TO TAKE YOU DOWN, SAYING TO HIM THIS HAS BEEN WILLED WHERE WHAT IS WILLED MUST BE. THEN MAKE YOUR LIGHTWARD WAY ACROSS THE REACH ON WHICH HE LEAVES YOU.

"That's all?"

NOTHING MORE. That vast entropic grin again. AND NOTHING LESS. Niko suspects for all his pending wrath the titan is amused by him and enjoying all this drama greatly.

He stands with his guitar and feels the rising bravado that strikes him at the oddest times. "Well. I'll just be on my way then. Thanks." He waves. "See you."

EACH AND EVERY TIME. And in Greek the titan says GOOD TRAVELING, ORFEO.

"And you Moloch."

The titan pauses. IT'S A HORDE.

"Excuse me?"

A GROUP OF DEMONS. COLLECTIVELY A HORDE.

Then the titan simply is no longer there and Niko is knocked off his feet by air that rushes in to fill the space the vast abomination occupied. He picks himself up and absurdly dusts himself off. His hand brushes the damp patch on the crotch of his jeans and shame heats his face.

He stops in the midst of putting the Dobro back in the case as he remembers the titan's parting wish in Greek and his own unthinking reply. As he had understood Onyx's German. He frowns. Old locked doors are opening in his mind and in his heart this long and godforsaken day. BENEATH YOUR MORTAL GUISE YOU WEAR A SPIRIT OLDER STILL.

Around him the demons slowly regain their feet or hooves or paws or talons. Some glance fearfully at the gleaming purple wipe that's all that's left of Onyx. None look at Niko the Troublemaker as they resume the work they have performed for all the generations of mankind at least.

Screams and German curses once more fill the oven air.

A slickheaded demon beside an excoriated nazi holds a bright plastic sandpail and a cheery red plastic shovel. The demon uses two sharp claws to carefully separate two of the man's facial muscles, which are as clearly defined as those on a colored medical diagram, and then shovels fine blond sand into the breach. He shoves the shovel back into the pail and begins to pat the man's face in an oddly motherly fashion and he smiles as the man begins to scream.

Niko turns from the bonfire and gazes out into the black and starless air. Soon a streak of burning orange flares and shadows stretch from standing objects on the plain. A distant cry from high up in the direction of the flare is carried across the flat ground.

Toward that source of light then. Once more Niko sets out on his ragged way. As he nears one of the staked men he hears a soft and pleading voice. Mein herr. Mein herr.

Niko looks down at a naked German staked spreadeagled and facedown. Iron spikes pin the twitching spiders of his fractured hands to ground. His skin meticulously flensed in perfect alternating one inch strips from head to toe. The inchwide strips of remaining skin embroidered with yellow stars of david, strings of numbers, pink triangles, barcodes. The space between the naked muscles packed with sand.

"Entschuldigen sie mich. Mein herr?" the man says in a whisper more awful than any scream. "Danke shon. Fiir die musik, ihre musik." His head is turned to the side and his bisected lips move carefully. "Danke shön, gnedige herr. Fielen danke."

XI

BEEN DOWN
SO LONG

I N THE DISTANCE THERE APPEARS to be a stadium or
coliseum Niko's path will near but not quite intersect. The
enormous structure brick red in the murky light. A roar perhaps
a hundred thousand voices strong carries from it even miles away.

To Niko's right lie toppled statues, informed giants with undifferentiated features, stone eyes open and forever staring sidewise
at the broad expanse. All have fallen from their pedestals, some
to fracture, some to break, some to shatter into scattered rubble. Hard about them on the flat stone plain are radiating cracks,
jagged epitaphs engraved by their demise. Blood seeps from the
statues' cracks.

Distant ratcheting like rattling engine valves. A mile or more
away a group of demons standing high atop a recumbent head of
granite performs a kind of sculptural lobotomy with jackhammers
against the stone temple. It looks like what a migraine feels like.

Another flare of orange lights the sky. This time the accom-
panying scream is more pronounced and grows still louder as the

sparking comet streaks from what looks like a huge wall several miles away. It's hard to judge the distance. There is no true horizon for the earth here does not curve. Only vanishing points on an infinite unvarying plane.

Yet there where the flares streak from, where the massive wall holds sway, it seems there is an oddly close horizon. As if the earth beyond were sheared away. Five miles? Ten? There are a lot of objects in between, moving creatures, stationary structures. It also looks more crowded out there toward the wall. What's the draw? Well he'll know soon enough.

Niko trips on scattered statue chunks and catches himself. His jeans have dried but he is conscious of the smell of urine clinging to him, of Sam's gore tacky on his hands and arms, of stubble bristling at his neck and the underside of his chin, the saltrings of dried sweat and stiff patches of Sam's dried blood staining his shirt and coat, the swampy slickness of his cotton socks encased by hiking shoes. His tongue is dry and thick and reptilian. His parched throat makes a tiny click whenever he swallows. His eyes burn from arid kiln air, from vapors and from lack of sleep.

A group of demons with krylon spraypaint cans industriously tags a fallen statue that somehow conveys an air of quiet desperation. Little balls rattle when the demons shake the cans.

Niko steps on something soft that screams and jerks from underfoot. He leaps away from the disemboweled man he's stepped in and a demon looks up from the gutted body it is violating. It rises tall and slim and muscular and frightening and beautiful before Niko and looks down at him in wonder with catlike eyes of startling cerulean. Pendant cock slurried with shit and gobbeted blood. Chest slick and breathing hard from foul exertions. It surveys Niko head to toe and grins and licks the length of its chin with a pointed black tongue caked with gore. It raises an oddly elegant talon and waggles the tapering slim fingers.

Niko tries not to look down at the spasming husk at the demon's feet.

The demon's hand lowers. "Your name." Its voice a beautiful contralto.

"That word is mine to keep or give."

— 134 —

The demon's laugh does something to Niko's spine. "Credo in un deus crudelis." It mockingly blesses him like a priest, tracing the sign of the cross hand sinister, bottom to top, right to left.

Thunder shudders from above and Niko glances up. The charcoal sky convulses with a swarm of bats, black scraps that flex like epileptic birds across the hot abyss.

"You have no quarrel with me. I'm mortal."

"And you think that opens every door? Spreads the legs of every whore? Unlocks each and every lock? Makes my cock hard as a rock?"

Niko tries to break in but the demon speaks nonstop and does not pause for breath. "Pulls the cork from every bottle? Melts the king's wax like a griddle? Breaks the vows of silent monks? Pries the lid from every box?"

Babbling doggerel it advances. Niko steps backward in kind and raises a placating hand, the guitar case moving forward as a shield. "Come on now. I'm still alive, I haven't been Judged, you have no power over me here."

"Biggest ass gets softest seat? Living flesh gets choicest meat? Smoothest tongue gets softest thigh? Sharpest glance catch brightest eye?" A graceful and accusing finger points at him and he retreats as if pushed.

"My business is with one who would destroy you should you hamper me," Niko recites. He looks around for a place to run to or a weapon or even another demon to enlist against this one, for they seem to fear the wrath of their superiors.

"Quoted word should make me quake? Stolen fire make me bake? Demon nose whiffs mortal dung. Shit must spew from borrowed tongue."

The backs of Niko's knees touch something hard and warm. Another demon crouched on hands and knees and grinning up at him. The doggerel-spewing demon grins and pushes Niko backward. Niko lets go the guitar case and tucks and rolls to come up in a doubtless futile fighting stance.

The demon he has fallen over straightens up and dusts itself off, still grinning at Niko as it guffaws in a big loud stupid voice, literally saying Haw haw haw haw. He's wide and burly and covered with piercings, studs and bars and metal rings.

The demons highfive each other and their palms strike sparks. Absurd embarrassment heats Niko's cheeks. He has quite literally fallen for the oldest schoolyard bully trick in the book.

"Oh you wacky funmasters," Niko says.

"Haw haw haw." Pierce slaps his thigh hard enough to kill a small animal. "That's the spirit."

"Not the spirit but the flesh. Mortal meat pie, him no guest."

"Naww." A stubfingered hand goes to the flat broad face in caricatured astonishment.

Doggerel nods. "This widdle meat pie, him go hunting. This widdle meat pie, him not home. This widdle meat pie, him got mojo. This widdle meat pie, leave alone."

Pierce looks Niko up and down. "No molesta?" He sounds disappointed.

"This widdle meat pie, him go wee wee wee all the way home."

Pierce slumps and Doggerel drapes an arm partway around the massive demon's shoulders. Doggerel's arms are long but Pierce's shoulders are much broader. "Not to worry, never fear. Us will leave this meat pie here. Let him go his meat pie way. We see him again someday."

And paying Niko no more heed they walk away. Niko watches them go, unaware of his incredulous expression. He shakes his head and picks up his guitar case and continues on his dire way.

THE STATUE GARDEN now consists of lifesized sculptures of mounted generals and declaiming politicians, the kind of statues found in parks or civic centers the world over. Except here they are not lone monuments to fallen leaders but thousands on thousands of stone figures crowded on the plain like forgotten figures in some giant child's toy army. A general of Pharaoh's army clutches his staff of command and inspects troops only his stone eyes can see. A Grecian senator in draped double chiton clutches a scroll and raises a fist. A Civil War general on horseback stares out across the plain with gloved fist on West Point saber. An Arab chieftain looks up to Allah with upturned palms. Their alabaster ranks are all in different stages of erosion, some merely blemished as if suffering a century's urban acid rain, others deeply corroded and runnelled. One statue of a furclad Hun on horseback is so dissolved his helmet is cleaved in two and his features smoothed to disturbing anonymity. His mount's ears have worn away and one hoof eaten to the base. Many statues have toppled like defeated chessmen as their foundation dissolved by whatever slowly eats their quarried flesh.

Threading through them Niko catches a fleeting glimpse out of the corner of his eye. He turns to look but it is gone. Only the vast array of frozen figures. Niko continues on his ordained way, a strange pressure between his shoulderblades. He cannot shake the feeling the statues are watching him.

After navigating the marble orchard for an hour Niko realizes that the area is littered with motley pigeons. They peck the ground and scatter in waves at his approach. Though they are stupid useless birds he keeps an eye on them. On a sidewalk or in a park he would not give mere pigeons a second thought. Here where all is sinister and strange no thing is mere.

But the pigeons waddle aimlessly and peck at nothing and stare at nothing and ruffle their feathers at nothing and crap on statues—

Niko stops.

A pigeon roosts atop the combat helmet of an American twostar general in field uniform holding stone binoculars in one hand near his leg, the other hand a fist. The pigeon shits on the general's head.

Niko approaches the statue and the pigeon flaps threateningly, then flies.

The general's face is worn and pitted. A deep gouge has eaten into the bridge of his nose as if someone gave up sawing it off. Below one marble eye a shallow runnel grooves the pitted cheek, steady track of geologic tears. The eyes are blind as a bust of Homer but Niko feels they see him nonetheless. Where the pigeon roosted a fresh white splash of pigeonshit bubbles and crackles as acidic excrement eats into living stone.

Niko reaches out toward the sculpted face and hears an unmistakable faint moan. He snatches back his hand. The fear that speeds his heart is quickly replaced by pity for the soul imprisoned in corroded stone before him. The man now monument to himself, frozen at the apex of his glory and feeling every atom of his slow decay.

Niko turns to gaze at acre after acre of corroded statues. One nearby pedestal supports nothing but a pair of sandaled feet, all else worn away by millennia of intermittent pigeonshit.

Niko hurries through their prolonged agony.

"Excuse me, sir? There has been some kind of mistake. I would like to see someone in charge."

Niko has come to an astonishingly long line of the damned standing patiently in a roped off queue that twists and turns and doubles back like the worst imaginable wait for the most popular attraction at Disneyland. He's a mile closer to the wall now and the numbers of the dead are growing. Demons with pitchforks—may as well call them that even if they are tridents—herd new batches of the sheeplike damned to the end of the line, which shuffles forward constantly but doesn't quite keep pace with new arrivals at its everlengthening end. Throughout its snaking length are arguments, shoving matches, fights.

"Sir? Are you hearing me?" The voice is Slavic, faintly adenoidal. "I wish to see someone in authority." Near the end of the line a tall thin sickly man with springy darkbrown hair and large intense brown eyes is waving his arms for a demon's attention.

Which of course he gets. The demon closest to the clamoring man turns its twin heads away from the group it's prodding and gives the man the once-over. ""A mistake?"" the demons ask. They look at each other. Its right hand passes the trident to the left hand and then thoughtfully scratches its left head's left cheek. "What kind of mistake?" asks the right head, which Niko privately names Dexter.

"I am not supposed to be here."

The damned around him laugh. There's a polyglot murmur as others translate for the dead and then a second wave of laughter follows.

Sickly ignores them but he cannot hide the flush that darkens his pale face. Niko looks on wonderingly as the delicate man defiantly raises his chin.

"Hey hey," says a swarthy little man with a thin moustache. "Issa fonny ting, Ima nah supposta be here too."

Around him comes more laughter followed by a chorus of sis, ouis, das, hais, jas, and fuckin A's.

"Okay look," the left hand, Sinister, tells Sickly. "Did you wait in line for your ticket?"

"Of course."

"Number called?" says Dexter.

"Naturally."

"Naturally," says Sinister. "Go to your designated line?"

"Yes."

"Get your ticket stamped?"

"Yes."

"Get a receipt?"

"At the next line they tell me go back to the previous line and get a receipt. Then in the next line I wait again for my receipt to be stamped."

Sinister's hand picks Dexter's nose and then puts the jellied finger in Sinister's wide mouth. "And of course," says Dexter, "you took your stamped receipt to the Receipt Processing Window."

"Yes, and there I exchange my stamped receipt for a Personal Information Form."

"Excellent," says Sinister.

"Then I stand in the Pencils line to get a pencil."

"We're just whizzing right along here, aren't we," says Dexter.

His other half smirks. "I'm getting a nosebleed."

Dexter ignores him. "So with your official number two pencil and your PIF in its handtruck you waited your turn in the Forms Completion Room."

Sickly grows sheepish. "I am completing it before a space becomes available."

Dexter scowls. "You filled out all seven thousand six hundred fiftysix pages of your Personal Information Form—"

"—staying within the margins—"

"—no erasures, emendations, errors of spelling punctuation or grammar—"

"—bubbles completely filled in, no streaks smudges stippling or stray marks?"

"Well, I would have completed the form but the pencil is breaking."

"Ah," from Dexter.

"His pencil broke."

"It happens."

"What can you do."

"Nothing to do but wait in the Pencils line again."

"Management really ought to get better pencils. If they don't break they wear out."

"Well I'm not going to be the one to suggest that Management change pencils."

"Me neither."

Sinister looks at Sickly. "I assume you got another one."

"Don't assume," says Dexter. "You know what they say about when you assume."

"No, what?"

"You make an ass of you and me."

"Really. You and me?"

Sickly plods on. "A year I wait again in the Pencil line—"

"A year," says Sinister. "They're really quite the welloiled machine these days."

"It's those Disney engineers. They get the trains running on time. You were saying, meat pie?"

Sickly is looking more and more flummoxed. "After I am waiting a year in the Pencil line they tell me I must to go to the Replacement Pencil Requisition Desk. And finally I get to that and they give me a hundred page form to complete if I am to get another pencil."

Sinister shrugs onesidedly. "Well they can't just hand out pencils indiscridedly."

"Think of the chaos," says Dexter. "There are people in those lines who'd kill you for a pencil."

"If you weren't already dead," says Sinister. "But at least you completed your Replacement Pencil Requisition Form."

"I certainly did not."

Dexter is aghast. "You didn't?"

Sickly's jaw is clenched so tight he can barely speak. "I. Had. Nothing. To. Write. With."

"Well," says Sinister, "you should have asked for a pencil at the Pencil Window."

"They don't let me have one! They send me to the Replacement Pencil Requisition Desk!"

"That's just for a replacement pencil for filling out your PIF," says Dexter.

"Skilcraft Number Two Medium Soft Point," adds Sinister.

Dexter nods. "But the Replacement Pencil Requisition Form can be filled out with any old thing."

Sickly looks as if he's going to cry. Sinister clucks and shakes his head. "Poor little meat pie. All that time wasted."

"If he'd only learned his way around the system."

"Some people just can't be bothered."

"Guess they don't think the rules apply to them."

"Why make life any easier for some poor flunky who's only doing his thankless job?"

"For want of a nail."

"Or a pencil."

"Sad really."

"Yes, sad."

Sickly's dam breaks. "I did not go back in the line for a fucking pencil, you—you stupid freak! The broken one, I am sharpening it with my teeth."

The demon draws himself erect. "My brother's just as he was made, sir," Sinister says.

"He was talking to you," says Dexter.

"Nonsense." Sinister narrows his eyes at Sickly. "I am curious, though."

"I'll say," says Dexter.

"When your pencil broke that first time, I imagine it made a... stray mark?"

"A stray mark you certainly didn't attempt to...erase?"

"Naturally I am obtaining another PIF. I am in this line now."

Sinister nods. "Adjustments and Closures."

"Last line, by the way," adds Dexter.

"Well why would I be in this line if I am not getting the forms taken care of properly?"

Sinister shrugs. "You could be cutting."

"Oh this is—why would I do that? People who cut in line are torn apart by this, this mob. And no one will process me without the proper forms anyway."

"Terrible isn't it?" says Dexter. "You'd think people would learn their lesson."

"All right, maybe you aren't cutting," says Sinister. "Maybe you're just ignorant of proper procedures."

Sickly looks insulted. "I am a master of proper procedures. In my earthly life I have earned a law degree and am employed at Workers' Accident Insurance Institute of the Kingdom of Bohemia for fourteen years."

Dexter slaps his own forehead. "Hear that? Meat pie here's an insurance lawyer. I love this guy. I could kiss this guy." He cranes forward to do just that but Sinister looks disgusted and puts his chin on his fist and watches his other head attempt to close the distance to Sickly.

"We don't go anywhere till I say," says Sinister.

"Just because you're older."

"Yeah but Mom always liked you best."

The demon reaches up and from out of nowhere produces a clipboard with a thick sheaf of printed fanfold paper attached. "Name?"

Sickly gives his name. Niko is startled to recognize it.

The demon opens up the stack and the heads bob up and down and mutter as they read. Suddenly they both grin unpleasantly.

"You thinking what I'm thinking?" says Sinister.

"Not if I'm thinking at all. But sure, why not."

They turn to Sickly and Sinister says, "Well, France old buddy—"

"Franz," says Sickly.

"Whatever," says Dexter. "I'm afraid you aren't on the Exemptions list."

Before Franz can reply the demon leans forward. Sinister lowers his voice while Dexter glances around melodramatically with narrowed eyes. "But I'll tell you what. Seeing as how we're colleagues and all—"

Now Sinister looks around conspiratorially while Dexter picks up smoothly: "—and seeing as how it only took you since nineteen fiftytwo to make it to the last line in the bunch—"

"—I'm gonna make a command decision and take it upon my selves to pull you out of this line and put you up at the very front."

"How's that by you?" Both heads regard Franz enthusiastically. Franz brightens. "Oh that—that would be capital."

The demon looks at himselves. "Capital he says."

"Oh wouldn't it be evah so?" Dexter pretends to swoon while his left half slides the clasp on the chain holding it to the post and lifts the chain to let Franz out. From behind the pale thin man come astonished looks and multilingual curses. Dexter/Sinister tut tuts the crowd and raises his pitchfork. "Now now," says Sinister.

"Okay, Fritz," says Dexter. "Let's go."

"Franz."

"Whatever," says Sinister.

Niko steps forward tentatively. "Uh, excuse me."

The demon eyes him and does a quadruple take. Sinister scowls and Dexter glances at his brother. "Qu'est-ce que c'est, mon fil?"

"L'homme." Sinister points at Niko. "C'est l'homme mortel."

"Sacre merde. He must be the musician that Onyx got obliviated over."

"Well she let him play Deutschland Uber Alles or something."

"It's never anything but trouble when one of them comes down here."

"How many's it been now?"

"Not counting spiritual visitations?"

"The ravings of celibate monks and the hallucinations of oppressed Catholics hardly signify, I should think."

"Maybe forty."

"That many?"

"We should sell tickets."

"Sporty jacket though."

"Nice shoes too."

"What do you think is in the big violin case?"

"A big violin?"

"You know there's a pool going on him?"

"Sure. I've got a fiver riding on him. Thousand to one but what the hell."

"You bet for him? Where was I."

"Hitting on some babe in line."

"I never. I am a consummate professional."

"Of course you are. I meant to say you were acting in your capacity as punishment liaison with one of the guests."

"Just for that I'm putting five against him."

"Your money, pal."

""So what can you do for me?""

It's a moment before Niko realizes the question has been directed at him. "I'd like to follow you."

"He'd like to follow us."

"Ooh, we're attracting followers."

"I always say there's two kinds of people in this world."

"Followers and leaders."

"I know which one I am."

"Follow us where?"

Again Niko lags. "To, um, the front of the line."

The demon exchanges a look. "I suppose you'd like to be put right behind Frances here."

"Franz."

""Whatever.""

"No, I'm going to the Battlements, and I'd—"

"The Battlements. Tourist boy wants to go to the Battlements."

"And him without a camera."

"Why you want down there, organ bucket?"

"It's a long story."

"Old story too from what I hear."

"Guess we shouldn't ask him to play us a song."

"Maybe if it's depressing."

"Know any depressing songs, bloodbag?"

"A shitload."

"Shitload he says. Can you play and walk at the same time, wormfood?"

"Yeah."

"Then here's the deal—"

"Watch it, there, hermano. Spoken deals with these things are binding as gravity."

"What, you think I'm an amateur?"

"Just covering our ass."

"The deal is, you play us some seriously depressing music and you can tag along. Got it?"

"Got it."

"Play anything happy or bouncy—"

"—or even a little bit uplifting—"

"—so much as one single note that doesn't make me want to open a vein—"

"—and I'll make you eat your own heart—"

"—with a side of fries."

"Deal?"

"Deal."

"My, he didn't even hesitate."

"Sure of himself, isn't he?"

"Come on then maggot chow, it's troubadour time."

"There's just one thing," says Niko.

"A catch."

"Always is with monkey spawn. What is it?"

"I can't play my guitar and carry the case at the same time."

"Well don't look at me."

"Or me."

"I will be happy to carry your case, sir," Franz says, "if it will allow us to proceed on our way."

"Impatient all of a sudden, isn't he?"

"Well his end's in sight."

The demon cackles in unison.

Niko opens the case and removes Dobro, slide, pick, and shoulder strap. He holds the case out to Franz and says Thank you.

"It is my pleasure."

They walk side by side, the demon bringing up the rear. Niko tunes the Dobro. Franz's intense and birdlike gaze flicks everywhere as Niko begins to play long upbending chords.

"I am familiar with the decadent American jazz," says Franz after a few minutes. "But this is different I think."

"It's called blues," says Niko.

"Ah. The rural music of the oppressed American Negro. I am hearing of it but have not heard it myself."

"Then shut up, Fats—"

"—and you might hear some now."

"Franz."

"Whatever."

Franz stumbles as he's prodded from behind.

Niko plays. Not thinking about it much, not even worried about the demon's threats. If he doesn't know how to play music without a note of happiness, he's never played a note at all.

Niko is reluctant to strike up a conversation with the naked soul beside him. Whatever hope the man holds for reaching the front of the Ouroboros line, he is doomed to an eternity of suffering and deprivation and to get to know him will only lead to helpless pity and frustration at the man's suffering. Yet that reluctance also bothers him. As below so above, is that it, buddy pal? Mitigate your pain by backing off from feeling altogether. What kind of life is that? We all lose friends and relatives and lovers. Everything goes away. People die. Those two words encompass all the tragedy of the living world. At the core of life there lies a coiled waiting horror that is death. Niko's always felt it slumbering there. All his life he's drowned it drugged it lulled it with his music. And looking back now understands he saw it wake a little bit with every cigarette or shot or measured spoon or needleprick, felt it tremble closer with each shuddering climax, heard its lungless breath in every anguished note he ever played.

He mutes the guitar strings.

"Boy howdy. That was—"

"—depressing."

"Play another one."

Niko snorts. "You guys are gluttons for punishment."

"Shit. Have you seen the gluttons yet, meat pie?"

"If he's going over the Ledge he will."

"Over the Ledge?" Niko drops back even with the demons.

"Now now," Dexter says. "You'll find out about the Ledge soon enough. We have a little wager on you—"

"—and we don't want to influence the outcome," Sinister finishes. Dexter yawns as Sinister talks and Sinister absently sticks his finger in his brother's gaping fanged mouth. Dexter stops midyawn and snaps at the finger and narrowly misses biting it clean off.

The demon prods Niko and Franz and resumes walking beside the line, which has also started shuffling forward again. "You." Dexter prongs Niko with the trident. "You want to know who's being punished for what. What do you think these people are guilty of?"

Niko glances at Franz.

"It is all right," says the softspoken Czech. "I am curious if their assessment of my, my sins agrees with my own." A hint of amusement in the large brown eyes.

"From what I've gathered," Niko says, "I'd say these people were bureaucrats."

Dexter grins and even Sinister looks pleased. "Hand the man a Kewpie doll," says Dexter. "But bureaucracy ain't no sin. So why are they being punished?"

Niko frowns. He thinks about the protocol of lines and forms, Franz's eagerness to comply and to assure the demons that he knows the system.

"Maybe they liked making people comply with procedure even when there was a shortcut. Or maybe they liked using the system to thwart people."

Dexter nods. "Now that's a complicated sin. On the one hand it's a kind of tyranny, because they're wielding power unjustly. On the other hand it's irresponsibility, because a bureaucrat uses dogma to avoid using his will to decide."

"Irresponsibility is a sin?" says Niko.

Franz surprises them all by saying, "To consciously refuse to exercise free will by hiding it within a bureaucratic system is to demean the very quality that renders Man special in the eyes of his creator."

"Or so the dogma goes," says Sinister.

"So you're punishing them forever for being weakwilled?"

"For squandering. If a lion doesn't use its teeth it gets punished by starving to death."

"Look at your own name for yourselves—"

"—homo sapiens—"

"—thinking man—"

"—and then look at these fine examples—"

"—oxymorons if ever there breathed any—"

"—human beings who relegated their forebrains to a handbook."

"I believe I begin to understand," says Franz.

"You only think you do, Hans old buddy," says Sinister.

"Franz."

"Whatever. You haven't been punished as a hypocrite yet."

"I am to be punished as a hypocrite?" Now Franz looks genuinely fearful.

"You're telling tales out of school," Dexter tells his brother.

Sinister shrugs. "I yield to your greater experience."

"Stick around, kid, and I'll tell you about when they invented rocks."

Dexter's quip prompts Niko to ask where demons come from.

Dexter smiles toothily. "You ever own a cat?"

"I'm a dog person. Mostly."

"I have owned a cat," says Franz.

"It ever die?"

"Yes." Franz raises an eyebrow. "Once."

"Well then—"

"—it's probably around here somewhere." The demon waves to indicate the corrupt vast cavern around them.

"I don't get it."

"Music boy don't get it," says Dexter.

"Insurance boy do."

"Tell him, insurance boy."

Franz indicates the demon before them. "They are the souls of cats."

Niko stares at the twinheaded demon. They blink, blink, nod solemnly, nod solemnly, and sing in unison but not in harmony, ""We are Siamese, if you please.""

"I have long suspected something similar," says Franz.

FRANZ GROWS MORE excited as the head of the line grows near. It would be amusing to watch the mildmannered thoughtful man becoming manic if Niko didn't pity him. What does he think is waiting for him up ahead, paradise?

And what do you think is waiting for you farther on, buddy pal?

Table that discussion. Just play.

Aching blues scores the plain of Hell.

Franz's eyes are bright as their motley group walks along the shuffling outside of the massive line. "I wonder how long would be this queue if one were to unfold it in a straight line?"

"Exactly as long as it is now, moron," says Sinister. "Guess Mensa isn't knocking down your door."

They pass and pass the trudging dead.

For his part Niko has eyes mostly for what the demon called the Ledge. It appears to be a cliff edge that extends to his left and right as far as he can see. Faint glimmerings that might be water lead toward the false horizon of the Ledge. A river? To become a waterfall spilling off the edge and emptying into someplace worse? Who knows what lies beyond the precipice. The twin demon does but Niko is reluctant to ask what he will find below.

On the Ledge itself, the Battlements. Hewn into the cliffside they hunch in glowering light like an argus remnant of some fallen Troy. Running several miles along the Ledge's stark cutoff the parapets and crenellations of the Battlements lend a faint medieval air to an architecture oddly streamlined and industrial.

A stubble of the flocking dead is thick upon the plain before the Battlements. Once in Buenos Aires Niko played a festival two hundred fifty thousand strong. It would have disappeared within that distant throng.

Franz walks ahead of him talking animatedly and gesturing often to the head of the line, which Niko now sees is a roped off section at a huge rock outcropping guarded by half a dozen demons. Niko frowns but keeps on playing.

Dexter/Sinister watches the line ahead and looks back the other way at Franz, nodding nodding at the man's questions and comments. Franz is oblivious to the amused look on the demon's lefthand face.

Niko catches up to Franz. He plays mean old twelvebar blues for a couple measures and even sings a few verses in his gravelly voice aged like whiskey by whiskey. The demon is watching him now and so is Franz. Niko fingers and chords and nods along.

"You do not really sound like a Negro I think, but there is much pain in your voice."

"How many Negroes have you met?"

"Admittedly few. They are not so many in Prague and Vienna." Niko studies the neck of his guitar. "I've read your work."

"You, you have?"

Niko nods. "You became very well-known after you...you know."

"There is no need for delicacy, Mr...?"

And smiles down at his guitar. "Popoudopolos. Call me Niko."

"Mr. Niko. You are Greek?"

"American. Greek descent."

"Mr. Niko, I am living with my—I believe in English you say consumption—for many years. It is what finally took me from my home." The thin man looks about the redlit plain, his ascetic face pained by distant memory. "I am here longer than I am alive on earth I think."

"Yes."

"So Max did not burn my work as he promised." He laughs. "I think perhaps I knew he would not, you know."

"You're very famous now."

"Really. Oh really." He starts to say more, perhaps to ask about the other immortality he has gained through the redemption of his pen, but now the demon steps between them and glares and glares down at Niko.

"Don't think we don't know what you're trying to do," says Sinister.

Niko isn't quite sure which one to stare at and his gaze goes back and forth.

"It's really kind of cruel when you think about it," Dexter says. "We're going to hand him over anyhow—"

"—and you jacking him up is only going to make him fall that much harder—"

"—and our deal's off when we reach the front of the line anyway—"

"—so keep your damned mouth shut and in another hundred yards you're out of here—"

"—capiche?"

"Si, prego." Niko stares at the demon and realizes it is impossible to stare them down and so he looks away. Hurting minor chords carry on the bruised air. "He was a good man I think."

Dexter spits while Sinister says, "If I fired a shotgun into that line I'd hit ten good men."

"I've seen him do it."

"We got good men like a barn's got rats."

"Place is crawling with em."

"We oughta put up signs."

"Do Not Feed the Rats."

"Get it?"

"Got it."

""Good.""

They turn away, and the three or four of them finish their small journey together.

A DEMON NEAR the head of the line holds a length of fanfold paper feeding from a tall cardboard box at his hooves. The dead call out their names and the demon, tigerstriped in black and red with an anteater snout and teeth splayed like a falling picket fence, searches through the fanfold stack until he finds each name and when he does he checks it off with a pencil and the damned soul is allowed to pass from the line in which he has spent years.

Dexter/Sinister halts before Tigerstripe. "Zeke," says Dexter, "I'm passing one through. My authorization. He's under K."

The demon shrugs. "Your funeral."

Franz steps eagerly away but Niko calls his name and points to the hardcase in Franz's hand. "Oh yes of course," Franz says. "It would not do for me to walk away with it, would it?" He returns the case to Niko. "Thank you so much for your music. It is so long since I hear anything of beauty even if that is perhaps an odd word to describe what it is you play. I mean no offense."

"None taken. It was my pleasure." Niko's gaze meets Franz's. "See you."

"Yes, twentythree skidoo, as you Americans say." Franz waves and turns away with his stamped and authorized papers, heading around the rock outcropping and out of sight.

Niko watches him go. He glances at Dexter/Sinister, then puts the Dobro in its case.

"Beautiful, Fonz said."

"It sounded depressing to me."

"How can it be beautiful and depressing?"

"I dunno. Ask the meat pie."

"Hey meat pie."

Niko doesn't look up. "I thought our deal was finished."

"We think you may have cheated."

Niko shrugs. "I did what I said I'd do." Behind him Tigerstripe has resumed calling out name after name from the fanfold list. "You both agreed it was depressing."

"Yeah but it didn't make me feel bad—"

"—In fact, it made me feel kind of good—"

"—Which is bad."

Niko stands with the hardcase. "Well that's your problem."

The demon looks at one another. "How can something depressing feel good?"

Niko smirks. "Ever read Russian literature?" Without waiting for reply he starts away.

"This can't go unresolved—"

"—uncompensated—"

"—unrewarded."

"Want to see what happens to Fritz?"

Niko stops. He knows better. Knows it will be terrible. Franz seemed a gentle and kind man with a keen mind and a wry sensibility. But Niko does want to see what happens to him.

He turns to face the demon. "Franz," he says.

THE LANDSCAPE ON the other side of the enormous rock outcropping is completely different. Rounding the rock with the demon beside him Niko pulls up short as he sees an enormous dark lake that cannot possibly be here. It should have been readily visible to the shuffling line but it had not been. The Ledge and Battlements are nowhere in sight. In the murky distance rises a low mountain range that ought to be a flat and featureless plain. It's disorienting.

On the near shore of the placid lake is a low dais of black stone that overhangs the lake. A palmwide groove runs down its center. The ground around the dais is soaked with blood. The tiny waves that lap the shore leave dark red stains. The lake is a lake of blood. This then is the source of the dark river coursing toward the Battlements.

The plural demon nods both heads to indicate Franz, who leaves a cheap folding table with his stamped forms in hand and approaches the dais with a demon walking to either side of him. The demons smile as Franz chatters excitedly all the way up to the dais. Franz stands where they indicate and fidgets as a third demon approaches with a graywhite softball-sized object in both hands. Franz frowns but holds his ground, more curious than afraid it seems.

The demon to Franz's left points at the starless sky. Franz looks up and as he stands there craning skyward the demon to his right reaches out with a baling hook and unzips Franz from crotch to throat.

Franz's face fills with surprise and then with agony. He stares in pain and disbelief as his entrails spill onto the dais. He feebly grabs for them then sways. The demons catch him and lower him to the freshly wetted stone. Franz's blood flows down the groove and into the lake.

The third demon gently sets the softball-sized object into Franz's chest cavity and begins sewing him up with a large curved suturing needle while the other two hold his struggling arms and legs.

Niko glares pure venom at the twinheaded demon beside him.

Sinister grins and mimes pushing an object into a body while Dexter pretends to sew it shut. "Wasp nest," says Sinister.

The suturing is quickly finished and the demons hoist Franz to his feet. Franz is white and wildeyed.

The third demon pats Franz on the shoulder and then punches him in the stomach. Franz gapes like a landed fish. His face wears a horror Niko's never seen, and he begins to scream as the outraged wasps sewn up inside him swarm.

The demons on the dais laugh and shove Franz off. He falls and rolls and howls and claws at his crude stitches.

Dexter/Sinister laughs and points and wipes tears from his eyes. "I think Franz has anz in his panz."

"Vive le Franz! Vive le Franz!"

A roar fills Niko's ears and a white heat fills his belly that could spill over and become anything, take any form at all. He turns and hurries away.

* * *

ON THE OTHER side of the rock outcropping the lake of blood cannot be seen again. Only the evercrawling line, the names called from the bottomless list, the neverending plain. See them shuffling in their slaughterhouse line, crawling out there on the plain like mewling wounded babies, scraping under granite blocks like entombed cadavers falsely dead, gathered sheeplike at the Ledge. How many have lived and died since humanity began? One hundred billion? How many of that number tortured in this loathsome place? Sandgrains on a bloodwashed beach. Souls every one, all doomed, all damned, all lost. Judged and found wanting and consigned and then forgotten by what dread remorseless will. You cannot save them. Cannot even save yourself. For without even believing in a soul you bartered it away decades ago and cast its lot with every pathetic pilgrim you will see in this forsaken place. As always you have bartered. As your story says you always will.

But Jemma. Perhaps not doomed. Not damned. Not lost.

DEEP IN ANGRY reverie he stalks toward the thick dark river winding toward the Battlements on the Ledge and does not hear the naked footfalls running at him from behind or sense the knotted fist until it hits the back of his head. He hears but does not feel his head hit ground.

XII

ALL ALONG THE
WATCHTOWER

H E JOLTS AWAKE AT SCREAMING overhead. Two
sparking orange flares arc out from the Battlements. Niko
blinks and shakes his head. There's only one flare but his vision
is doubled. The screaming flare grows nearer. Niko rolls onto his
knees and vomits. Catherine wheels spin burning behind his eyes.
The scream claws through his brain. The blazing comet's coming
awfully close.

Niko rolls onto his back and shuts his eyes. Let it hit me, I don't
care. Let it end the whole charade. The ground is evertilting like
the downside of a fullon drunk.

The scream cuts off as the burning object slams onto the plain
hard and close enough to send a shudder through the ground. Niko
tries to lift his head to look but soft things tear inside his skull.
His feeble fingers trace the contours of a large hard swelling at the
base of his skull. His hand moves like it's remote controlled and
the batteries on the control unit are failing. His fingertips are moist
and warm.

He gives his hand the day off and it relaxes behind him. He looks like a man lying pleasantly on the ground communing with the night sky.

He shuts his eyes again and moans. Concentrates on warm wind playing on his skin and then realizes that skin is entirely what it's playing on. His clothes are gone. Shirt jeans jacket shoes filthy socks and even underwear.

His right hand flops onto his chest and spiders to his throat. The locket's still there. Clothes are much more valuable here than jewelry.

Guitar?

He manages to raise his head. Smoking lump on the ground there. Sweet smell of cooking bacon. Nope. No guitar. Guitar go bye bye.

Get up. Get up.

Okay. All right. I'll get up in exactly one minute. Just gonna rest my eyes first.

AND STARTLES AWAKE. He pats his naked body. Everything seems to be there. Except his clothes of course, yuk yuk. Feels like history's worst hangover. Which is okay right now because that's twice as good as he felt a few minutes ago and the pain means that he isn't dead.

Doesn't it? I mean, a blow to the head and then darkness and then you wake up hurting and naked in Hell. You don't gotta be Einstein to figure that out, buddy pal.

Can we sit up? An experiment will satisfy this question, Doctor.

Niko flops to one side and raises up on one elbow. *At this point on our evolutionary chart the primordial sludge attains a rudimentary awareness of the outside world.* He pauses and breathes hard until the Bastille Day in his head subsides. Okay. On our feet now. One. Two. Two and a half.

Three.

He's on his feet and turning about when he realizes he's about to be sick. *Now the primate has discovered upright posture and his hands are free to manipulate tools and so begin the conquest of his world.* He gets back on his hands and knees and comes awake standing and staring out across the plain at nothing. Blinks and shakes his head and rubs his eyes. Touches the spongy knot on the back of his head. Looks stupidly at the dried blood on his fingertips nearly black in this furnace light.

Something like a skinny pig with unnervingly human eyes is licking up his vomit a few feet away. Niko doesn't even have the energy to yell shoo so he ignores it though its smacks and slurps and wet splatches threaten to make him sick again. Which would likely be just fine with Mr. Pork Lean.

A bundle of smoking rags lies on the ground ten feet away. Niko takes a step toward it and when he doesn't fall down dead he takes a couple more.

The ragbundle is the charred body of a man. Cracked black skin above crackled fat. Clumps of burned hair mottle a seared scalp punctuated by white bone. Cloying smell of fried pork and burned hair. Niko's stomach clenches and he turns away. After a moment he turns back.

A few miles away are the Battlements. Several miles of long straight wall built on the endless line of the Ledge itself. The river of blood terminates there at a broad arch leading through the Battlement wall. An enormous congregation of the dead is gathered there, corralled by the river and the wall itself. On either bank of the river of blood the damned condense along the base of the wall. Niko tries to spot anyone wearing clothes or carrying a guitar but the light is too dim, the distance too great, his vision too blurred, the damned too many.

The smoldering figure at his feet gives forth a groan and opens singed and lashless lids. Pale blue eyes are filled to bursting with pain.

"Can. Can I do. Anything?" Niko croaks.

The charred head shifts an inch. A single word grates from the ruined throat. Niko thinks the word was time.

THE TWO MILES to the Battlements are the longest Niko's ever walked. Every step an act of will. His ears are ringing and his vision sometimes blurs but seems to be improving. He's hungry and parched and his throat tastes of sour vomit. A drink of water would fix everything right now he's pretty sure. Yes sir a good old-fashioned sweaty glass of tinkling icewater with a twisty slice of sunshiny lemon would take care of just about all his worldly and spiritual needs. Can't you just taste it? Wouldn't it just make your mouth water if you had any saliva left?

Niko's having trouble concentrating. The ground is hot beneath his bare feet. Walking naked in the open feels just wrong. Now there's nothing to prevent him being mistaken for just another of the damned. It figures this would happen at the very time he's most unable to deal with it.

And what about his guitar? He can live without the clothes. He can probably even manage without the shoes, though his cityboy feet are hardly primed to pound along the grit and filth and bone upon a baking plain. But what are you supposed to do without your axe, champ? How you gonna rescue the fair maiden now, Parsival? Maybe you can talk the head honcho into a round of scissors paper stone. Best two out of three, be a sport.

His big toe stubs a rock and he cries out and stumbles. Niko glances down and sees that it is not a rock at all but a blackened lump he would not recognize as a charred human being had he not just spoken with a similar creature. He apologizes to the lump and wipes his toe upon the ground. He realizes the surrounding plain is dotted with similar lumps of charred remains in various stages of reconstitution, some writhing or crawling about, some with speech regained but able only to scream, many just shapeless burned lumps waiting to resume their former shape to meet whatever punishment awaits them next.

A woman runs screaming past him and looks fearfully over her shoulder. An obese tumescent creature runs drooling after her, footwide tongue flopping to its jiggling belly like an obscene and slathering necktie. Its long translucent fingers tremble toward her as the pair runs by. Niko barely registers them. Just one damned thing after another. A tiny voice inside him, that little demon all his own he lived with all those years, is prodding him again. Why bother? it asks reasonably. What's the point now? You're barefoot and dick-naked, buddy pal, and your one bartering tool is as missing as a conscience in a cathouse. It's not like any of this was gonna work anyhow, wetbrain. You've been a lame horse from the getgo. Pack it on up, move it on out, bring it on home. Go back to the world and grieve and live the rest of your augmented life and honor the bargain you made. I gotta admit you gave it a great try. Who else could've gotten this far? But now's the time to let it go. She's gone. She's dead, asshole. The only way you're gonna see her again is by getting your stupid ass killed down here and joining her.

Niko slaps imaginary duct tape over his demon's lulling mouth. Fuck you. I'll get there or I won't. But I'll have to be stopped because I will not stop so long as I can move. One step at a time, like the bumper stickers say.

Another fireball launches from the Battlements and screaming streaks to light the plain, shifting shadows from the grubbing creatures scavenging. The river of blood glints darkly in the moving light on high. Rio Rojo.

Footsteps pound toward him from behind. Despite his aching head he turns, paranoid from his last encounter. Two hundred yards away and running toward him is a teenaged girl. Ghostly pale and whippet thin. Her hair streams back and bloody footprints dot the plain behind her as she sprints. "Run," she yells at Niko. "Run."

Niko frowns. "There's nothing chasing you," he calls back. His head pounds harder from his shouting.

She's a hundred yards away now and still running. Niko peers across the dimlit plain. There's movement everywhere but so much of it is indecipherable against the unimaginably huge and perspectiveless plain.

The girl is running by him now. He turns to watch her pass. Athletic and trim and not an ounce of fat. Her breasts do not bob and her buttocks do not jiggle. The soles of her feet gleam with her blood.

To the far right is another running figure whose path will intersect the girl's close to the fortress on the Ledge. Niko squints. Something's chasing this runner, something low to the ground and wagging forward with deceptive speed. It closes on the distant runner. The thing is wide and long, waisthigh and dark. It edges up and stretches forward and passes the runner, and when it passes the runner is no longer there.

The running girl cries out. The long dark shape now stands between her and the Battlements, and she veers.

Behind Niko comes fast rhythmic clacking like a nail caught in a tire. He turns to see one of the long dark creatures running fulltilt toward him, twentyfive feet long and ten wide, many-legged and sidewinding but fast as a man on a bike. Mottled craggy hide and eyeless head shaped like a crescent held low to the ground like a vacuum attachment. The creature is some kind of living woodchipper.

Niko turns and runs like a cheetah with its ass on fire. Instincts old as mammals themselves scream at him to climb a tree and become very still and small. There's not so much as a blade of grass in sight, only flat hard ground he cannot dig. His heart jackhammers and his head feels like it's going to burst and he cannot possibly maintain this speed for long.

Another flare streaks from the Battlements.

He can hear the goddamned thing behind him now. The figure burning in the sky lights up the plain below and Niko risks a backward look. Big mistake. The mulchosaur is about five hundred yards away and gaining.

Niko puts on speed. He feels energy drain from him like an unplugged barrel. In the orange flare of light he sees two hundred yards ahead the slithering figure of the mulchosaur that ate the running man. Niko heads toward it. The way they're built he thinks they're blind and wonders if they can't stop running. Perhaps they simply prowl the plain before the Battlements and vacuum up whatever fallen burned souls they encounter. In his bruised and addled mind an insane notion forms.

The overhead light grows brighter as the flaming soul arcs down. Niko's bare feet pound among the immolated dead who salt the ashen plain, scatter bones and ashes, stub on crackled flesh, step once on a protruding knob of bone.

The mulchosaur ahead is by far the closer of the two, which is good because this one isn't running after Niko. Its path runs perpendicular to his own. Niko veers to intercept.

A stitch prongs Niko's side. His thighs and chest are burning. His calves are still knotted from having run hours before, just inside the gate. He wheezes. His cock slaps his thighs as he runs. A demented corner of his mind wants to laugh.

The mulchosaur ahead of him slows down and makes an oddly trainlike chuffing. Maybe Niko's wrong about the eyes.

Niko dares not look to see how close the mulchosaur behind him is. Its close clacking is alarm enough.

The overhead flare has grown quite bright and the mulchosaur in front of Niko lifts its crescent head and gamely tries to catch the falling flare of burning soul. It doesn't make it and the human meteor slams the side of its broad head. Sparks explode and the mulshosaurus rolls like a trailer on a freeway coming off the hitch.

The mulchosaur writhes and kicks manifold short legs as it struggles to right itself, stopped for perhaps the first time in its existence. Its chuffing noise has gained a keening overtone. Niko runs toward it. The clacking sound behind him is a pressure on his naked back. Niko is flagging and nearly blind with fear. He wills his legs to run, his arms to pump, his chest to breathe.

The mulchosaur in front of him ripples like a gardenhose and flips upright. It does not run but lowers its scoop head to the smoking body that slammed into it. It seems uncertain or maybe stunned from the blow. Maybe it's not used to having meals delivered.

The rapid clacking is now on Niko's heels. Niko ignores the screaming in his monkey brain and runs straight at the confused mulchosaur and jumps up and runs across its back. Rough alligator hide beneath his naked feet and reek of spoiled food. Two running steps and he jumps off and stumbles and falls and lies there watching as the mulchosaur chasing him plows into the one he just ran across. A sound like silverware in a Disposall. The wounded mulchosaur keens and whips around and clamps its everbiting jaws on its attacker.

Niko fights to stand but cannot move or even breathe. Smell of shit and rotten meat. Get up. Get up.

His insides unclench and he takes in a wheezing breath and lumbers to his lacerated feet. The mulchosaurs are rolling on the ground, jaws locked on each other's hide like dogs, bodies lashing and legs kicking. He can hear their meat tear off the bone.

Grand as it would be to stay watch the battle royal Niko doesn't even want to be in the same time zone when one of these puppies wins and starts directing its attention elsewhere. Niko turns and beats a raggedy retreat.

NIKO's RUNNING ON fumes. Both feet are cut and scraped and blistered and his right heel throbs where he has bruised it on a protruding bone. His feet are literally dragging and every step is like walking in a swimming pool full of broken glass.

Now that being eaten is no longer an immediate concern the Taiko drummers in his head are back for an encore and he thinks he might be sick again. The blurred vision seems to have gone though. Boy howdy.

Dry tongue swabs cracked lips. His armpits and groin are chafed where sweat has dried to salt and rubbed. Niko doubts he has enough fluid left to sweat.

He trudges like a zombie toward the Battlements, indistinguishable from the damned.

Sometime later Niko comes back to himself as if breaking from a daydream to find himself surrounded by the naked dead not two hundred yards from the Battlement wall. They converge on this place like ants around a sugarcube, a continual fatalistic march that files beneath the massive wall toward the river of blood that gouts in a continual loud hiss through the broad arch in the Battlement wall and over the Ledge like a severed artery of the world itself. The dead press close among each other unconcerned about their nakedness, faces sullen and lethargy all that lives within their eyes.

Their bodies are a cornucopia of affliction. Most of the damned are missing fingers, hands, arms, toes, feet, legs, eyes, breasts, penises. A woman slit from pubic bone to sternum and gutted like a fish clutches looped and trailing organs to her bleeding wound. A length of gray intestine drags the dirty ground. The legless drag themselves along. The footless lurch on filthy bleeding stilts of truncated legs. The onelegged hop like strange plucked birds. One woman clamps her severed arm beneath the one remaining. One man hunches forward like an inchworm on his everbleeding stumps of wrenchedoff arms and legs. A teenaged boy seems to be walking on his hands until Niko sees that his arms and legs have been severed and reattached in each other's place and the joints bent backward like an ostrich. One man waggles an obscene tail of someone else's severed arm whose hand has been inserted in his anus. Cockroaches continually crawl from one woman's vagina. A fat and diarrhetic woman walks with a thin man bent behind her, face against her jiggling buttocks, lips sewn to her rectum.

Many of the trudging dead are cut and always bleeding. Some are diseased and covered with festering boils, buboes, blisters, scabs, hives, chancres, shingles, gangrenous wounds, burning rashes, melanomas, leprosy, warts, elephantiasis, suppurating burns. One man's hairless body is covered head to foot with an elaborate maze of scars. Another woman is tattooed with moving screaming faces that cannibalize themselves by eating at her flesh. Most are gaunt as concentration camp inmates, skin stretched paperthin on fragile frames of jutting bone. One armless woman walks upon the hilts of knives embedded in her feet and screams with every step. Behind her a flensed man gleams with staples stamped into his exposed muscles. Another poor soul seems to have been turned inside-out, veins and organs pulsing on the outside, exposed eyes turned inward, filthy with dirt and bleeding from torn snags. One man's eyes are pulped meat on his cheeks from the eternal pecking of a crow embedded in his forehead.

The river of dead washes around a pale enormous person beside the flaring base of the Battlement wall, a figure so obese it is impossible to tell whether it is a man or a woman. Doughy folds of fat quiver like thick gelatin as the sagging face strains with the effort to drag itself forward like some gargantuan nocturnal fungus.

The closest thing Niko sees to a single soul helping out another is a line of corpsewhite figures each with right hand on the shoulder of the one in front. Strangely hunched and jostling one another as they shuffle forward. One looks straight at Niko who stares back at raw and empty sockets. The man looks away and the blind continue leading themselves.

The sweatshop air is filled with oddly monklike murmurings of lamentation, an eerily lulling accumulation of moans and sobs.

What keeps Niko going now is the knowledge that in the face of those he sees around him his thirst is merely thirst, his hunger simply hunger, his aches a reminder he is still alive. His pain is of a very different sort than theirs and theirs will never end.

The Battlement wall is a dozen feet high, angled turrets and squared merlons carved from the living rock of the Ledge itself. It will always be a work in progress, for Niko passing the Battlement's beginnings sees thousands of squatting workers grading the plain and continuing the carving of the fortress wall along the stark line of the Ledge. Their only tools are metal spoons.

Scrutinizing demons pace behind the workers and bash the indolent against their insufficient works until their brains spill out across the rock, then hurl them down to lie like savaged ragdolls until they are recovered enough to pick up their spoon and resume their neverending labor.

One demon holds a worker by his throat in one hand and inspects a spoon in the other. The spoon has been worn down to a slim wedge. "How can you get a new spoon when there's metal left on this one? You can't have a new spoon until you've worn the old spoon out." He jabs the worndown spoon into the dangling man's eye and throws him back to work. With horrifying calmness the man pulls the spoon haft from his eye like a stopper and ignores the ichor that spills to his face as he patiently returns to scrape again forever.

High up on the crenellation huge stone gargoyles hunch. Beneath their frozen grins and leers the ceaseless stream of naked dead flows toward the rushing river of congealing blood. The ground continues for a dozen yards beyond the near end of the arch set into the Battlement wall to form a small pathway that follows the red river through the wall on this side, presumably ending at a sheer dropoff of the Ledge. The dead stream toward it in such numbers that those close to the edge continually spill into the coagulant river and are swept along to pour out on the other side, a bloodfall spilling into some abyss like tubercular spittle.

Someone in the nightmare march ahead stands out from all the others. Niko stares at it for several seconds before he understands that the figure is distinguished from the other sheeplike dead because it's wearing clothes.

* * *

Niko pushes and worms his way through the dense crowd toward the lone clothed figure. It's his coat all right. Also his jeans. Who else's would they be? No sign of his guitar. There is no avoiding touching the dead around him. They press like mindless cattle heedless of their nakedness, of their stink and affliction. Their flesh rubs cold against him. Niko is brushed by pustulant sores and diseased limbs and bleeding wounds and excrement. He is groped and prodded and pushed and hit. An unidentifiable amalgam squishes beneath his bare feet as centuries of accumulated filth work into his cuts and well up between his toes to dry and cake. He moves amid the vesper moaning, the steady lament sung by the streaming chorus of the damned. Their voiced despair sounds oddly orchestrated, as if the trudging throng are opera players singing to an unseen host upon a boundless stage, a choir murmuring a requiem conducted by some unseen hand.

Some among the shambling dead sense Niko's living warmth and seek it out as if by leeching from him they will gain some flavor or forgotten grain of life itself. They reach to feel the press of living flesh and Niko struggling through the prison of their mutilated flesh cannot avoid their terrible caress. He keeps a hand up near his face to ward away their jealous hands and presses toward his clothed objective. Around him voices break the mass eternal to beseech the mortal visitor in every tongue in which a cry of pain was ever uttered. Whatever pity Niko feels toward the suffering legions is blighted by disgust now that he shares in their corruption. He feels the stirring of an old selfloathing. So your compassion is just luxury then. Well and good to sorrow for the distant sufferers until their tragedy afflicts you.

The wearer of his clothes is only thirty feet ahead now but Niko has to close the gap through human quicksand. The jacketed figure strangely unmolested. Niko would have thought the damned would fight like dogs to take away the stolen clothing not so much because they need it as because they long for evidence of earthly life, mementos vivi.

Cold fingers clasp his ankle. He tries to pull his leg away and something drags. He looks down to see in flitting spaces between the teeming dead a small and beautiful little girl not more than ten years old who hugs his leg and gazes up at him with wide brown eyes set in a milkwhite face framed by long straight raven hair.

Startled by a sight of beauty Niko stops. He slaps away a blindly groping hand and bends down to the little girl. To ask her what? Are you lost little girl? Where's your mommy? Do you know where you live? Can I help you? It's likely she's been down here longer than Niko's been alive. But she's a little girl. Unmangled and whole and clutching at his leg, and despite whatever abominations her odd calm eyes have seen her face remains unsullied as a newly minted doll. No sane and mortal eye could look upon her and not wonder how a god could so renounce its own.

So Niko bends to her, about to ask he knows not what, but feels his breath grow still and give no voice to wonder as he looks into her eyes, her calm gaze patient as the rock around them and as ancient, that roots him to this spot as sure as any certain love or venom. Looking into the little girl's eyes Niko feels a flush throughout his body. Her cool dry hand against his leg.

Still holding his gaze the little girl slowly leans to set her cheek beside her hand against his naked leg. Her dark skin smooth and cold as the shell of a nut. Her eyes unwavering as she turns her head to kiss his thigh. His heartbeat louder than the din around him. The little girl closes her eyes and opens her mouth and Niko feels her cold dry tongue against his thigh. Pressure of her teeth upon his skin. Distant nip of pain. And then white blindness as her mouth clamps on his thigh. He arches his back and shudders and cries out. It uncoils from the pit of his stomach and locks his muscles, it's centered around the little girl's mouth fastened to his thigh, her mouth now hot and cool cheek warming and face growing flushed, her lips reddening as red overflows to run down her chin and trickle down his leg, his lifeblood coursing like magma in the cold stone tunnels of her empty veins. Niko knows she'll take it all, drain the burning life from him in trade for the few hours' warmth it will provide her, surcease from the mausoleum of her flesh. She'll kill him and he knows it and he knows that it will feel so good if he'll surrender to it, so good if he will let her take him from his anguish.

Something punches the side of the little girl's head. She breaks her kiss without a sound and blood sprays from her mouth and from his leg. Some desperate inner voice protests the disconnection like a distant caller on a phone not wanting to be hung up on. Unaccountably he feels an overpowering desire for a taste of whiskey.

Niko glimpses cold and spiteful laughter in those ancient child eyes and then the little girl is lost among a forest of legs. Whatever struck her and tore her loose is gone as well. Niko in his rapture had no certain sight of it. Leathery tendriled fast and gone.

Niko compresses the wound on his thigh. It's bleeding but not gouting. At least she didn't open up an artery. He feels embarrassed and foolish as he limps along. His leg is warm and tacky with blood along its inner length. Her saliva must contain some kind of anesthetic and anticoagulant. Like a tick.

A fresh wave of revulsion sweeps him. Now more than ever he wants his clothes, wants to mark himself apart from these poor lost defiled souls, to have a barrier however thin between himself and them.

He takes his hand off of his wound and stands on tiptoe and cranes about and feels fresh blood flow down his naked leg. Much more bleeding and he won't have to worry about dying of thirst. The man with his clothes is lost from sight. Niko frowns. Where could he have gone? He was only ten yards ahead, he couldn't have already made it to the river.

Niko stands as high as he can and then jumps up and down, feeling foolish but needing whatever vantage he can gain. With each leap his quadriceps feels as if it's being ripsawed where it was bitten. The wound gleams nearly black in the faint reddish light.

Niko stops jumping when an enormous muscled arm lowers and grabs the woman beside him by her long and filthy hair and snatches her up. The dead around him pay no mind but Niko's gaze follows the woman until he sees the thing that clutches her. One of the carved stone gargoyles sitting on a Battlement embrasure. The gargoyles are alive. Made of stone and yet alive and moving. The other gargoyles look on eagerly as a granite muscled arm cocks back to bring the woman near a tapering stone ear where she dangles like a living earring and does not struggle or protest or even set a hand upon the quarried fingers holding her by the hair to mitigate her pain. Her face shows nothing at all.

The gargoyle holding her has a face like a caricatured nightmare bat. He glances at the gargoyle to his right who has blunt square teeth in a round face with a snout like a pig. Pignose draws a tremendous deep breath and holds it and nods at Batface. The gargoyle to Batface's left grins to show stone teeth below an elongated snout in a head with curling horns like a ram. In a voice like a tuba he shouts Pull.

Batface lets fly and the woman spins end over end out into space. Pignose stands with stone cheeks bulging like a trumpet player blowing. He grabs a finial protruding upward from a merlon and leans out over the oblivious damned. He opens his mouth obscenely wide and vomits an enormous stream of burning stinking napalm that jets out like a flamethrower and the tumbling woman ignites and screams and streaks across the sky trailing sparks.

"Ooooh," says Ramhorn in his foghorn voice.

The others cheer while Pignose wipes his blockteethed mouth with the back of one scaly arm and bows with mock humility.

This then is what has intermittently lit the plain all this time.

Batface's stone arm lowers again and clutches like a penny arcade crane. Stone muscles bunch as the granite arm lifts its prize into the air. Not a naked prize like all the others. This prize is wearing filthy jeans and a torn black T-shirt and a light jacket.

"Son of a bitch." Niko hears his own voice yell against the choral tide. The heedless dead part round him.

The gargoyles pass the oddity among themselves and sniff at his clothes like dogs and frown and scratch themselves and poke and prod the man who is not complaisant like his confederates among the dead but screams and even takes a swat at one of the gargoyles leering at him. The fist hits stone and the man howls louder. The gargoyles laugh. Even though this is the man who struck and robbed him Niko can't help but admire his defiance. But admirable or not the son of a bitch is wearing Niko's clothes.

Niko cups his hands by his mouth and shouts a name. He shouts it louder, trying to be heard above the crowd and constant hiss of bloodfall. Shouts a third time, and above him the conversation and laughter die. Niko finds himself the subject of huge-eyed scrutiny. A great scythe-nailed stone hand lowers and clenches Niko's bloodmatted hair and lifts. Oh what has he done. Niko presses down on the giant fingers so that his weight is supported more by his hands than by his hair but it still hurts a lot. An enormous batlike face swims into view. Niko shouts the name once more and Batface frowns. He looks at Pignose on his right who's using a woman's sharpened thighbone to clean his granite nails and looking mildly bored by the woman's piercing screams. The man wearing Niko's clothes has gone limp.

"Hey," calls Batface, shaking Niko like a kitten. "This one knows Gery."

Pignose doesn't even glance at Niko. "No kidding."

"Yep. Knows his true name."

This gets Pignose's attention. The gargoyle flicks the remnant woman over the far side of the wall and she screams as she falls out of sight. Pignose rises to his hooves to stride across the parapet, stone wings flaring in the breeze of his motion. He bends to examine Niko. "Never saw it before." The breath that washes over Niko's face would blister paint.

"Should I toss it back?"

Stone wings ripple as Pignose shrugs. "Might as well light it up. Why's the other one wearing clothes?"

"Who knows. Different jurisdiction?"

"Well they'll burn good anyhow. Oh what's this one yelling now? I can't make it out."

"Hold on." Batface shakes Niko again and Niko yells louder. "Clearer, how bout," the gargoyle requests.

"Fly me down," yells Niko.

Pignose leans toward Niko until his head fills Niko's vision. He grins and Niko becomes quite aware of the human gore slathered on the gargoyle's granite teeth. "Tell you what," Pignose says. "Since you've had the bad manners to yell somebody's true name to everyone here, I'll fly you all the way to the far wall." The pigsnouted head turns right. "Asmodeus. You still got that slingshot?" And turns back. "Now what is it going on about?"

"It says," says Batface, "This has been willed where what is willed must be."

Pignose's granite eyes narrow. "Oh for crying in the sink."

"Look, what's this all about?" says Batface. "Do I toss it back or do we make it a crispy critter? My arm's getting tired."

The others laugh and Ramhorn calls him a pussy.

"It's a bad angle," Batface insists, and they laugh again.

Pignose purses stone lips at Niko. "Go ahead and put it down. That this has been willed stuff is one of the old keys. It's mortal."

"Mortal." Batface holds Niko before him and frowns as he inspects him like a new kind of Ken doll. "No fooling." Shaking his head he sets Niko on the parapet.

Niko starts to say something to Pignose but the gargoyle holds a finger up for him to wait and turns his attention to the man wearing Niko's clothes who has apparently passed out from the pain of trying to tear his hair out of his scalp to free himself. Now Pignose nods at Batface who draws the limp clothed figure back while Pignose takes a deep breath—

Again Niko shouts Stop, stop.

Batface lowers the man and inclines his monstrous head at Niko. "It's really starting to get on my nerves."

Pignose glares at Niko, cheeks bulging enormously. He lowers his head and spews his noxious fiery breath. Screams renew from the dead below and an awful smoke and bacon smell wafts up.

Pignose wipes his gleaming chin. "What is it now?"

Niko points. "Those are my clothes. He stole them from me."

"Do I look like a cop to you, meat pie? I don't give a fat rat's ass if they're the Pope's pajamas."

"Please, I'd like them back."

"Ooh, please it says," Ramhorn says to Pignose. They curtsy and bow to one another like courtiers and then Pignose grins unpleasantly at Niko. "What are you willing to do to get them back?"

Niko hesitates.

"Guess he don't want em that bad," says Batface, dangling the unconscious dead man.

"What do you want me to do?" calls Niko.

The gargoyles frown thoughtfully and glance among themselves and shrug. Then they grin and set the clothed man down on the parapet. "Wake him up," Pignose tells Batface.

Pignose turns to Niko and smiles. "You're going to fight him for your clothes."

THE FAR SIDE of the Battlements is a sudden raw dropoff that could be two hundred feet or two hundred miles, Niko can't tell as he gazes over the edge because a pure and famished darkness swallows the face of the cliff below a hundred feet. To his left the warm red river vomits from the arch to become a spraying frothing bloodfall that disperses into fine red mist to rain upon whatever horror lies below, ferrying its tumbling voiceless cargo to some lower deeper fate.

A ramp is carved into the Ledge. It begins on the near side of the arch and angles down until it disappears into the bleeding dark. A sick parade of thoughtless dead marches downward without end, so many dead no floor of ramp itself is visible, so many that they spill over the edge of the ramp and tumble down the sheer face of the Ledge. Ravenous darkness swallows the ramp as it descends. The blind abyss is filled with screams and earthen rumblings and a distant thunder, the deep arrhythmic grinding of a factory of despair.

The Battlement wall is twelve feet thick and solid rock so far as Niko sees. He takes his time because it's about to become his arena as he fights a dead man for his clothes. The dead man is awake again and naked now. Niko's clothes are draped across an embrasure near the waiting gargoyles. Jacket shirt pants and even underwear but not his shoes and socks. Niko insisted the clothes be removed so he can meet his opponent on equal ground. And why fight to get them back if they're torn to uselessness by the fight itself?

Niko stretches out and gazes down the far side of the wall, covertly sizing up his opponent. The man is not some kind of bruiser. He's tall and bony and welldefined, which is even worse. Tall and bony guys are hard to fight. For one thing they've got range. It hurts to block them. It hurts to hit them. It hurts a lot when they hit you. Then there's the fact that Niko can't kill the man because the man is already dead.

Bony just stares at Niko without expression as Niko stretches out. Pale blue eyes and thinning brown hair. Scalp encrusted with blood where he tried to pull his hair out to escape Batface's clutch.

Smoker's teeth in yellowed disarray. He doesn't look afraid or worried or eager. He probably just doesn't care. After all he's been through down here this is probably a resort massage.

Niko's heart is pumping madly and his palms are sweaty and he's breathing way too fast. The man's indifference is more worrisome than if he were chomping at the bit. Niko makes himself take long deep breaths. His thirst is unbelievable. He feels his very skin demanding water. Even his eyes feel dry.

The gargoyles lean against the merlons and wager on the outcome. Niko's not sure he wants to know who's favored or the odds.

The gargoyles are becoming impatient. Before they can yell at him Niko straightens from his hurdler's stretch and gives Pignose the nod and says Let's dance.

"Bout time." Leaning against the wall Pignose folds his burly arms. "No rules, boys. Come out swinging till ya can't swings no more."

Ramhorn mimes pulling a bell cord. "Ding ding," he says basso profundo.

Bony walks calmly to the middle of the parapet and looks Niko in the eye and extends a hand. "No hahd feelins, mite," he says in a thick Australian accent.

Niko takes the hand to shake and Bony yanks him in and unloads a left hook to the side of Niko's head. Or where Niko's head would have been if he hadn't gone with the pull and ducked. Niko continues the motion and pushes up on Bony's hand to raise the Aussie's arm and glide under it and turn away from him as he does. He straightens quickly and turns the arm to lock it and bend Bony over and then comes down hard on the upturned elbow joint with his own elbow. Bony yells but the joint doesn't break so Niko tries again. As he comes down Bony lets off a kick to Niko's shin that glances off but doesn't exactly tickle and then Bony jerks free.

They square off.

Bony stands a little hunched with hands up to protect his face and upper body, left shoulder leading. A boxing stance. Niko's armbar has hurt Bony's elbow but not enough. He's probably acquired a stratospheric tolerance for pain.

Bony sees the way Niko's sizing him up and he grins pure enjoyment. "Yer a goer then eh? Cmon then. Cmon."

Niko waits in his stance. Bony's a boxer, he's Australian, and there's something oldfashioned about him. Niko's willing to bet he never saw martial arts in his life or since. Which means there's a lot he won't be expecting.

Niko assumes a boxer's stance.

Bony nods. "That's it mite. Now cmin eer an get slapped loyk a gull." Bony begins to circle, still grinning as he bobs and weaves and feints and jabs. He's out of range, just trying to intimidate. He fights flatfooted, European style. As Bony circles he begins to spiral in toward Niko, slow and subtle but the taunting jabs are getting closer. Niko hasn't bothered to block any yet.

"Not much chance a gettin the sun in yer eyes, eh?" Bony feints and bobs right. "You look loyk ya been out in the sun ricently. Eh? That royt?"

And Niko realizes Bony hates him for his mortality.

Bony jabs again and rushes in to unload a right cross. Niko stops him cold with a sidekick to the knee. It hurts like hell because the sole of Niko's foot is so cut up from running from the mulchosaur. He tries to follow through with a backfist to the head but Bony sidesteps and dances back. Niko's kick had been an inch too high. Probably charliehorsed Bony's quad pretty good but Niko doubts a charliehorse is going to send the Aussie running home to momma.

The Aussie looks surprised at the kick and perhaps as well at the way Niko moves. "So that's how you ply, eh? Leave it to a Yank ta kick loyk a sheila." He spits into his hands. "Bloody septics."

On the last word Niko fakes a backfist to the head and Bony's guard comes up. Niko leg-sweeps Bony's front leg out from under him and Bony lands hard on his naked tailbone and Niko drives down a left punch. Bony rolls enough to take it on the shoulder and grabs Niko's arm and pulls him down with him. Now it's a grappling match and technique is out the window. Gouge and scratch and bite. They might as well be two cats tied together in a bag going over a waterfall. They roll around on the parapet for ten seconds before Niko gets away, bleeding from a cheek and an earlobe and from his forehead where he butted the Australian in the mouth. An eye got gouged in the fray and he's bruised where Bony grabbed his balls and tried to pop them like grapes. His shoulder wound and the bite on his thigh have opened up again. Bony's bleeding from the forehead and chest and lip. Left eyelid swollen and two fingers broken.

They face each other once again. Both men panting. Bony wipes his split lip with a forearm. "That'll get the old pump wuhhkin, eh?" And he jumps in to do it again.

Niko sidesteps and roundkicks Bony in the solar plexus. He hits him with his big toe instead of the ball of his foot and goddamn if he doesn't sprain it on the son of a bitch's skinny chest. But at least Bony says Whuh and doubles over.

Niko dances in to finish Bony off but his bleeding feet skid on the stone. Bony mulekicks at Niko's groin and catches the fresh bite gouge on his thigh. It feels like a branding iron. Niko yells as he falls. He rolls and comes up in a fighting stance and then the leg collapses under him. He tucks tight as Bony stumbles to him and tries to stomp him. Niko's leg piledrives Bony's shin.

"Oh that smaahts," the Aussie yells. His savage grin remains.

Niko stays down. The stone is warm against his naked ass. Bony can't get in on Niko while he's made himself a little fortress like a turtle. But like a turtle he is roadkill if he tries to pick up and go anywhere. Stalemate.

It's been about thirty seconds since they started in on each other. Plenty of time to cause a lot of damage in an unprotected fight. Niko now sees he's at a serious disadvantage here. Maybe Bony was a Boy Scout Leader in his earthly life, though Niko doubts it because the son of a bitch is enjoying this way too much, but since then the Australian has experienced decades of true and utter ruthlessness. He's lost the governors that hamper most people. He has no instinct for selfpreservation because he's already dead. And Niko's holding back that little bit that's going to let the Aussie beat him.

Bony makes a third attempt to kick Niko while he's down. Niko tries again to kick Bony's kneecaps. The gargoyles decide things have gotten boring and it won't improperly influence the wager to let the mortal get back up so the boys can finish up their little dance.

The moment Niko's on his bleeding feet the Aussie goes for broke. Jab and jab then slide up jab and here comes a right with murder in its eye. Niko kicks him in the side and feels a rib break beneath his heel. Bony flies back and hits a merlon. Niko catches him on the rebound and takes him down and slams him facefirst onto the bare rock parapet and smashes his nose like a stewed tomato. The Aussie bucks once and then lies still. For a moment Niko's sure he's killed the man and then remembers that's not possible. For insurance Niko folds the Aussie's right leg until the heel is against the buttock and then sits down on the upturned instep.

"Finish it," says Pignose from his makeshift throne of an embrasure.

"How the fuck am I supposed to do that?" The Australian suddenly struggles beneath him. Niko keeps pressure on the leg. "I can't kill him."

"Make him say uncle."

"Are you—" Niko frowns. He supposes one word's just as good as the next. He glances at the man beneath him. One skinny arm is struggling feebly to find purchase. Fuck it.

"Say uncle," Niko says.

"Oh uddy ay."

"What's he saying?" complains Batface.

"He says no bloody way," says Niko.

They sit there a moment in a strange tableau. Wrestlers on a Grecian urn.

"Ood thot, ite."

"Thanks," says Niko. "You got me some good ones yourself."

"Orry out ya glothes. Oodnt elp oyself."

"Way it goes," says Niko.

"Look, I want subtitles or something," says Ramhorn.

"He said he's sorry about my clothes. He couldn't help himself." The gargoyles laugh.

"Well isn't that sweet," says Ramhorn. "Maybe if you let him go you two can kiss and make up."

"I don't think so," says Niko.

"Ont tink oh," the Australian agrees.

"Over the side with him then," says Batface.

"That side," adds Pignose, nodding at far side of the Ledge.

Niko leans close to the Australian. The naked contact is unnervingly intimate. "Give. There's no shame."

"Uck oo, ank."

Niko sighs. "Where's my guitar? And my shoes?"

A pause. Beneath him the Australian hawks and spits out teeth and blood. "Lemme ub an I'll tell ya."

"I don't think so, Cisco." Niko glances up. The squareteethed edge of the parapet is only a few feet away. One sudden rush will heave the Aussie over the side like last week's garbage. Harder without clothes to grab onto though. Niko must have missed the class where they showed how to fight naked against people who are already dead.

"Loyk to thang ya for the divuhsion. Bit of a chinge from the old ruh-tyne, yknow."

Pignose strides over to them and glowers down. "If you don't throw him I don't collect." His textured stone wings spread. "And if I don't collect, you don't get your ride."

"Go on, mite. Oyve had my fud an ya bead me fair an zguare. Oy got nothin left to lose unda thize bastids."

Pignose casually reaches down a massive hand and grinds the Aussie's mashed nose against the parapet. The Australian screams.

Niko takes a deep breath. All right. He bends the Aussie's right arm sharply up between the protruding shoulderblades and lifts. The downed man rises as if levitating. Niko moves the arm forward and drunkwalks the Australian toward an embrasure. Smooth, steady, don't stop. Remember you won't be killing somebody.

It's still not easy to find it within himself to hurl someone over the edge of a cliff.

He relaxes just a bit on the arm and the Australian immediately comes nearly upright and Niko yanks down and lifts to throw him overboard and son of a bitch if the Australian doesn't whip around as he hits the embrasure and grab Niko by the both forearms to pull him over the side along with him. Niko drops to the parapet but he scrapes forward until his bleeding shoulder hits an embrasure and he's wedged against the inside wall. The Australian is leaning out from the Battlement with both legs braced against the outside wall, deathgripping Niko's arms and pulling for all he's worth. Niko braces a leg against the embrasure and manages to keep the Australian from pulling him over the edge, but he has no leverage to force the man back. He can't hold this position very long.

The two men look at one another across the width of stone. The man's pale eyes are bloodied and his lip is gashed and he's missing front teeth. His nose is a swollen shapeless ruin dripping blood. And he's grinning.

Niko's arms feel as if they're wrenching from their sockets. His face is hot and his head throbs as if he's about to blow an artery.

"Let go."

"Not on your loyf, mite." The Australian strains at Niko's arms like an angry dog on a leash, each leg on a merlon and holding onto Niko in the gap between. He's standing sideways above an unfathomable space of writhing darkness, the hiss of the bloodfall loud below. He's a son of a bitch but he's a brave son of a bitch.

Niko strains his arms inward to make a narrow X and slowly draws big outward circles, turning his wrists up as he does. For a moment it looks as if he's making a handshadow of a bat as he follows the direction of the grabbing thumb in a slow elaborate shrug. He tucks his elbows toward his ribcage and brings his hands back toward his own shoulders. The Australian now holds on by little more than thumb and forefinger and it's not enough. For the first time Niko sees something like alarm on the man's face. He feels the grip weakening and he pushes his elbows forward to increase the angle.

Now the Australian's grin holds a different edge. He concedes with a nod and never takes his eyes off Niko. "See ya in ell, mite," he shouts above the torrent.

Niko moves his elbows outward and the grip slides off and the Australian falls away. He kicks out from the wall, upturned like a man backswimming toward the misty bloodfall far below, and silently he stares at Niko until he's swallowed by the deeper darkness far below.

Niko turns and slides down to lie against the wall and rubs his burning forearms and looks at Pignose holding an upturned claw out to the rest of the gargoyles. No one else seems to have bet in Niko's favor.

"O ye of little faith," Niko mutters, and then he's still for a good long while.

* * *

"PULL."

Niko wakes to orange light. A weight of stone looms somewhere high above him. He can feel its pressure overhead. Yet he also feels a fragile sense of lying on a slender rampart jutting out into an immense open space. Vertigo assails him and he shuts his eyes. The back of his head is pounding and he's covered with scabs and dried blood. His knuckles are bruised and swollen and his big toe feels broken. His testicles are lead weights. His arm and leg muscles burn. A tic in his cheek and his thigh. His gums are swollen and his tongue is thick and his breath feels like shimmering waves of heat should be rising from his mouth. His heel is bruised and his feet are cut so badly he's afraid to stand. How good it is to shut his eyes and sink into the primal mud of sleep. To feel himself drift away from himself.

A tongue not human speaks his true name in a language dead to all but archeologists poring over earthen ruins. The single word a hook to reel him struggling back into the hopeless world.

Niko opens his eyes to see a huge and alien face peer down at him with eyes of purest aqua. Pupils shaped like plus signs. The eyes blink and Niko startles even more awake.

"Here." An enormous hand offers Niko's neatly folded clothes. Niko accepts them dumbly and stares at the proffered hand. A mass of writhing digits too slim and articulated to be called fingers. The skin seems made of smooth and glossy marble with a faint intaglio of slightly darker veins.

Feeling half in dream he sets his clothes upon his naked lap and looks up at the looming face before him. Violently carved yet in its lineaments there lives a kind of beauty. Ruinous terrible and cruel but beauty all the same. What emotion it contains embedded in its frozen features.

The monster is bald as a cueball. Faint blue veins roadmap its scalp. Ivory horns curve like baroque newels. And in the rough hewn setting of the monster's face the adamantine of its eyes. Cold stone eyes of some dead blind idol carved and revered and then marooned by aliens who abandoned their world in some forgotten exodus. To look at them is to lose sight of their dreadful housing. The plus sign pupils give no hint of soul behind them.

Looking at the monster's aqua eyes he feels a sudden oceanic pull.

The monster Geryon kneels until he's only double Niko's height. "Do I know you?" His voice is startling normal but those unnerving pupils throw back nothing Niko can read.

"I don't think so."

"I understand you know my true name."

Niko nods. He tries to stand and finds he hurts too much and lacks the strength. Geryon holds out an everchanging hand. Reluctantly Niko clutches it and is surprised to find he touches cold unliving stone as Geryon easily hoists him to his feet. Niko's head swims and he drops his bundled clothes and sways forward. Geryon catches him up and sets him like an infant on an embrasure and supports his back with one hand until Niko nods that he's not going to fall off.

The monster steps back but watches him carefully. "I understand you want a favor."

Niko nods. It hurts. "You're very understanding."

From down below a funhouse whipcrack snaps before a ragged scream.

"I understand you would like a ride down," the monster continues, oblivious to the noise and Niko's sarcasm.

"Yeah."

That aqua scrutiny. Niko cannot meet that unremitting gaze for long.

"You are in a great hurry to be in a world of pain."

Niko shrugs. "Oh well." Heated wind rushing up from the abyss ruffles his hair.

Geryon stares. The gargoyles have returned to their horrific human pigeonshoot and crouch now upon the crenellation with their granite backs to Geryon and Niko. "I cannot willingly do this," the monster finally says.

Niko forces himself to stand and holds on to a merlon for support. Oh man. "Then I'll walk."

"You would never make it."

"I've come this far."

"Yes."

They regard one another. Finally Niko sighs and breaks the stare. His eyes throb as if he's looked away from a bright light. He slowly bends to pick up his clothes. Pain lights up his hamstring so he squats instead. The cuts on his arches spread and tears spring to his eyes. Putting on his clothes may truly kill him. He fishes out his underwear and turns them inside out and feeling like an invalid steps into them. Tries not to think that they were recently worn by a dead man he just threw off a cliff. Glances at his ragged shirt and shakes his head. Hisses as the fabric rasps the shoulder that scraped the merlon in the fight.

The jeans are stiff and ripe with blood and dirt and shit and sweat and piss, but damn if there isn't a single tear in them. He struggles into the pants and tries not to cry when the denim slides across his bite wound.

Buckling his belt Niko becomes aware of the monster looking on in what he thinks is amusement. "What?"

"You tucked your shirt in."

Niko stares down. So he has. "Well. You never know who you'll run into. Maybe my elementary school principal is down here." He buckles his belt and painfully shrugs into his torn and filthy jacket.

"Mr. Wilson. He is."

Niko stops with the jacket halfway on and stares at Geryon who stares back without returning a thing. Niko shrugs and works his arms the rest of the way through the jacket and shoots his hands through the cuffs and pats the pockets. Son of a bitch. He fishes out the Swisher Sweets and sees the cabbie also tucked a box of whitehead lucifer matches into the pack. He tamps the battered half full pack against his unbitten thigh while gazing around the Battlements. Ramhorn rears back holding a bald old man by the torso. Pignose shouts Pull and the poor soul flies away.

Niko looks away from the dwindling strangled scream and offers the pack of cigarillos to Geryon. "Smoke?"

Sudden orange light stains spooncarved stone and turns the aqua eyes a filmy yellow. Geryon reaches toward the pack but stops. "We are not supposed to."

Niko shakes the pack. "Live a little."

"Well." The monster plucks a cigarillo from the pack.

Niko taps out one for himself. He pops a match alight against his thumbnail and as it lights the matchhead grinds onto the nail. As it spits and smokes there Niko calmly wipes it off against his jeans. He holds his hand up and stares at the burnmark on his thumbnail. Coals to Newcastle. "You ever have one of those days?" he asks the creature before him. He's not sure whether to laugh or cry. The unlit cigarillo trembles in his hand. Silently the monster takes it from his fingers as if Niko is a child and puts both cigarillos in his hard gash of a mouth, and when he pulls them put again they're lit. He hands one to Niko and returns the other to his lipless slit. It's like a toothpick in that enormous head.

Niko leans back against the wall and takes a long deep drag. His eyes water and his head throbs and he feels bitterness at the back of his palate and rasping in his throat and harshness in his lungs. It's wonderful. The nicotine goes straight to work, do not pass GO. Niko once read that every cigarette subtracts ten minutes from a smoker's life. Yeah well this is the most pleasant little suicide Niko's ever committed, and certainly the best feeling he's had since he stepped through the gate. On his deathbed he doubts he'll want these ten minutes back.

Geryon smokes his cigarillo down to the nub in one enormous pull. No smoke emerges from his mouth or beakish nose when he exhales. If he exhales.

A few minutes later Niko flicks the burning butt onto the walk and goes to grind it out but stops when he remembers he is barefoot as a hick. The soles of his feet are shredded wheat. That's gonna be awfully inconvenient.

Geryon eyes the smoldering butt and says nothing.

Niko forces himself to take his weight from the wall. Sparkling fish swim in his vision. "Okay. Gotta go. Gotta gig."

"A moment. I forget that you have barely arrived here."

"Feels like I've been here all my life."

Something in the monster's face intensifies the violence intrinsic to its form. His great stone wings rustle. "I mean only to say I forget that you are not accustomed to how we go about our business here." He sets a pale blue writhing hand against his massive chest. "We are servants. Our roles are narrowly defined." He counts off on his varying wormy fingerbunch. "We carry out the punishment of the damned. We prevent escape. We maintain order." The fingerbunches lower. "Your presence here upsets a balance. We have few rules for dealing with mortals who come here. But we do have protocols. We are not to unwarrantedly molest mortals on their journey in. But when those mortals try to leave—" A monstrous shrug. "Well, you know their stories as well as I do. The Park is easy to get into and very difficult to leave. Like marriage, the pundits tell me."

Niko registers the monster's eloquence only dimly. The mellifluous voice has gone hollow and distant and without content. Niko nods but he is fading out. Like a junky. "This is all very interesting," he hears himself say, "but I really need to be going." He steps away and wonders absently how many steps he'll get before he passes out.

But Geryon holds up a muscled arm. "What I am telling you is that I cannot willingly carry you down. I can only follow orders."

Niko frowns. Brings a hand to his face to rub the aching flesh. Knows the monster's trying to tell him something but feels thick and slow and stupid and can't mine meaning from the words. Can barely link the words together as coherent information.

A recent memory surfaces and the voice of a titan sounds in his mind. FIND THE MONSTER GERYON AND CALL HIM BY HIS NAME. ORDER HIM TO TAKE YOU DOWN WHERE WHAT IS WILLED MUST BE.

Oh. He gets it now. He cocks his head at the cubist face of the monster standing patient and immense and inscrutable before him. Pearlescent depths of aqua eyes. Those frightening alien pupils. He could pulp me like a rotten prune. How much to trust a monster such as this? What choice do I have? He senses that the monster wants to help him. What he cannot figure out is why. But ascribing human motivation to such a being is useless.

Niko draws a breath to clear his muddied mind and unearths one of the old keys. "Then Geryon," Niko says, translating as he goes and paraphrasing to fit his circumstance, "in the name of the power by which I go this sunken way across the floor of Hell, carry on your back my mortal flesh down to the lower depths, for I am not a spirit to move through air."

The monster nods thoughtfully. "Nicely put. You need the injunction, though."

"This has been willed where what is willed must be."

The great hands clap once and a sharp report cracks on the damaged air. A flash of spark illuminates the bluegreen stones of Geryon's eyes. The monster steps back and bows low. "I am," he says without a trace of irony, "your servant."

As he straightens, he surreptitiously scoops up Niko's spent cigarillo butt and pops it into his mouth like an afterdinner mint.

GERYON MOUNTS THE brink with each foot on a merlon and Niko on his back. The monster is an odd amalgamation, one foot clawed, the other hooved. The monster's back is much too wide to wrap his legs around. Instead he hangs on with his arms locked around Geryon's neck and tries to wedge himself between the muscled anchors of the monster's tightly folded wings. Along his clinging length the massive body's hard and cold as one expects unliving stone to be and that is the surprising thing. The monster smells oddly pleasant, musk and moss.

Despite the steady warm updraft Niko's hands are clammy where they monkeygrip the monster's neck. He no longer feels as if he's going to faint but rather too alert. The bulk of his inhuman ferry hides the greater portion of the view but this may be a mercy. Below is only swarming dead and falling blood and vast unmeasured deep.

Geryon's head turns backward like an owl's. "Ready?"

Niko jerks back as the swiveling horns nearly knock him off. "Don't do that."

Pale lids shutter aqua globes: Geryon blinks. "No reason to get excited." The great head rotates forward again and huge filigreed wings unfurl on either side of Niko. Their muscles flex beneath his ribs as they beat once to shudder the surrounding air. The dead world swims. Niko has an awful moment to realize that Geryon has duped him, that the creature is indeed the Monster of Fraud, that the beast is made of stone and therefore cannot fly. There must be some kind of way out of here apart from this.

The monster gathers itself and leaps into the dusky air.

* * *

AND FLIES.

A hole opens in the pit of Niko's stomach as the monster plummets. Outside in the cold distance the wind begins to howl past great and cupping wings. Now Niko lies prone upon the broad back and holds onto Geryon's shoulders and feels massive muscles flex beneath his chest in time to the beat of the wings.

They bank left and spiral down the darkening air. Beneath them the vast undifferentiated wall of cliff rises out of blackness to circle them and circle them. Slanting along its length like a scar runs the carved ramp down which listless souls trudge until they're swallowed by encroaching darkness well before the bottom can be seen. From the arch hewn into the Battlements above the ramp and to the right, red rain and bodies gout. Geryon's auger will not intersect the attenuating spray, which is just fine with his astonished passenger.

He sees a gleam from far below. A sea perhaps comprised of all the blood that rains onto the Lower Plain.

Niko is quite awake now, exhaustion and hunger and thirst forgotten in the moment. The beast to which he clings is unimaginable. The height from which he gapes is inconceivable. The number of the damned upon the ramp is incalculable. Wide as the ramp is, it is a mere thread against the vast face of the Ledge. There is such a nation of lost on their long march that bodies continually spill over the blunt edge along the ramp's length culled from the lethargic herd that pushes and stumbles ever downward falling like the myth of suicidal lemmings, falling for entire minutes, naked spinning starfish shapes that sometimes strike the obsidian cliff wall and spin out and strike again, a drawnout tumble down to who knows where.

Geryon's head swivels round again to check up on his passenger. He sees Niko staring at the everfalling bodies and tells him that they land atop a pile of their predecessors, and that those at bottom are crushed to shapeless pulp and never will escape. The mounded dead run the length of the ramp itself, piled higher directly beneath the apex of the ramp and gradually lowering until they meet the foot of the ramp where it empties on the Lower Plain.

Niko peers beyond the sculpted shoulder. Somewhere down there lies the shattered body of a brave and cruel Australian. Somewhere in that unknown space new torments lie. Afflicted in that empty sea of punishment are doubtless those whom he himself has met, known, liked, helped, wronged, loved, despised. Glowing dimly out in that anonymous expanse, a feather floating in a mason jar. Getting closer with each sinking leftward gyre through the starless air. Above them the Battlements hold sway, retching blood upon the parched and punished world below, falling on the unfathomed Lower Plain, quietly dyeing the mountainous piles of the mutilated dead, thickly flowing to feed the coagulated sea across the barren ground, raining hot and red in a fine red mist, descending general on the dead and their tormentors.

As the ramp rises ever rightward Niko hears a long lamenting growing from the multitude of unclad dead until his ears are filled with roaring on the naked dark.

His gaze snags on commotion within the chaos close at hand and he grips harder on the massive tendons underneath him. He shouts to no avail in the despairing din. He pounds the massive shoulder with his fist and once again the frightening beautiful head snaps round to face him with its soul-ensnaring eyes. Niko shouts again and points toward the seething ramp, toward the greater commotion within the squabbling damned, toward a figure naked save for hiking boots who is staving off the covetous crowd with swings and jabs of a black guitar case.

XIII

LITTLE WING

ARE WE THERE YET?"

"A great amount of heated air is rising from the lower plain. I am lifted by this updraft, and to descend I must spiral down in a kind of controlled stall. I can tuck my wings and drop if you prefer. It is a long way."

"No no no, thanks. I was mostly kidding anyhow."

"I should tell you I have no understanding of humor."

"I figured it out. You should have been a critic."

"I have met many here. May I ask you to move your instrument case a bit to the—oh that is much better."

"Thanks for getting my guitar back."

"I am for now your servant. Have you pried the hand loose yet?"

"I threw it off."

"It might poke someone's eye out when it lands."

"And you say you have no sense of humor."

"How do you find our Park?"

"You go into the Red Line and turn left."

"I do not understand."

"It doesn't matter."

"You hold all Hell in great disdain I think."

"How could I not?"

"This is my home."

"Then you're blind to what this place is. Or you just don't know any better."

"I am exactly as I should be for what and where I am. And I point out to you that screaming bodies fall around us as you speak yet you no longer even glance at them."

"If I let it get to me I'd go insane."

"Only the naive can afford such contempt."

"Is there some point to this discussion?"

"I will be silent if you prefer."

"ALL RIGHT, I can't take it anymore. Let's talk geography."

"If you wish."

"I wish. I don't have a very clear sense of this joint's structure."

"It is an infinite plain."

"But it's in an enclosed space."

"Yes."

"I don't get it. How could it be inside something and still be infinite?"

"I am not certain it can be gotten. Mortals do not comprehend the relationship between perception and expectation."

"I see what I expect to see?"

"In a sense. In five senses."

"Are you telling me that none of this is real? That I'm imagining it?"

"I am telling you that none of this is real but you are certainly not imagining it. And just as truly you are imagining it yet it is real."

"Look, I sure as hell couldn't have made this up. I mean look at the Ledge there. It extends as far as I can see in either direction."

"It always will."

"So the Ledge is infinite."

"More or less."

"An infinite ledge on an infinite plain."

"The Ledge was not always there. The entire Park was once a single flat and borderless surface. The Ledge is a tectonic upthrust fault."

"Say what?"

"There was an earthquake."

"An earthquake did this?"

"About two thousand years ago. We do not discuss it much."

"But—"

"We do not discuss it much."

"All right."

"What's it like having wings?"

"Do you mock me? I remind you that it is still a long way down."

"I'm completely serious."

"Well. I have never really thought about it. Does a fish think about water or a bird think about air? I have always had them. It is difficult to imagine not having them. That would be worse than naked. Crippled."

"Us poor mortals do all right crippled."

"You do not miss what you never had."

"You hold all mortals in great disdain I think."

"What you are would be pitiable if you were not so absurd. So limited."

"Tell me what we're missing then."

"It would be playing music to a deaf man."

"Beethoven's Ninth was composed by a deaf man."

"A good point. All right then musician. I will make you an offer."

"I've learned to be suspicious of your people's offers."

"Have we not always been good as our word?"

"It's your words that haven't always been so good."

"But it was your choice to listen to them or not. The price of free will is responsibility for your soul, you know."

"Thanks for sharing."

"Why not hear my offer? You wish to know how it feels to have wings. When we land I will show you a thing. I will give you an experience. It will not be dangerous or harmful, but I cannot describe it to you."

"Why not?"

"It lives in a place where language decays. It occurs before language begins. In exchange for your trust I will tell you that I would be obliterated for showing such a thing to a guest."

"Then why take the risk?"

"Because you are mortal and will forget."

"How do you know?"

"Because I have shown it to you before and you do not remember."

"Maybe I'll remember this time."

"Memory is the re-creation of experience. This experience is one your mortal senses are not equipped to retain. The very act of remembering the experience will falsify it, even destroy it—make it a thing unhappened. Think of it as a beautiful picture mounted on a slide made of something that dissolves when touched by light."

"You'll show me something beautiful here."

"You ask me what it feels like to have wings. I can only tell you the feeling with words. And words have neither feelings nor wings. Words are leaky vessels into which a cargo of meaning and emotion are placed, and when they leave you and reach the farther shore of another mind a considerable portion of that cargo has been lost at sea. Fallen overboard, gone to rot, consumed by vermin, decayed to a state unlike its original form."

"But isn't the cargo that survives all the more valuable for that very reason?"

"Yes exactly. Which is why it is a mercy perhaps that so much meaning and emotion are lost. Because you are so limited. Because you could not contain the whole of it."

"Our cups runneth over."

"Those of you who glimpse that broader apprehension of the world beyond the world of your perception and who endeavor all their sad short lives to convey it directly and completely to their fellow mortals—your Blakes, van Goghs, Stravinskys—were driven mad by the knowledge of the separation of one mind from another and by their own inadequacy to cross the gulf. Anything told is by definition insufficient."

"Words may be inadequate but they're all we've got."

"All that mortals have, you mean. And even then you are wrong. I have heard your music—oh yes—and you are wrong. You have all these different little boats named speech and writing and painting and sculpture and music and dance. They are none of them sea-worthy but you do have something of a fleet. And you have them precisely because your shores are so distant from each other."

"Tell me anyway. Tell me what it feels like to have wings."

"It feels like singing with your muscles."

"Poetic."

"Poetry afflicts me. Let me ask you something and perhaps you will better understand my difficulty giving your question a meaningful answer."

"Fire away."

"Tell me what it feels like to be mortal."

"Hell that's easy. It feels like not having wings."

XIV

DAZED AND
CONFUSED

L
OCOMOTIVE BREATH ROLLS OUT AHEAD of Niko
as he trudges on across the frozen plain. Biting wind has
turned his fingers, toes, and nose to wood. His feet are bound in
pitiful remnants of recovered underwear he tore and tied in lieu of
shoes when the plain gave way to this vast sheet of ice. Niko constantly alternates hands to carry the battered guitar case, his free
fist thrust into the pocket of his skimpy summer jacket as he leans
into the knifeblade wind.

He's trying to remember something. Something that happened
to him. Something he was shown. If he concentrates on what it was
perhaps it will help him make his way across this huge expanse of
ice on which his internal compass needle has gone awry.

Available light comes from the ice itself. Pale bluewhite like the
phosphorescent trails that bled from around his trailing fingertips
certain rare nights on Malibu Beach.

Niko trudges over bodies frozen screaming in the ice. Their stiff
hands claw skyward in the milky ice as if to rob him of whatever

ember gutters deep in his core. Niko has long since stopped staring down at them. One soul frozen and aware is an object of pity and compassion. A continent of frozen damned is as numbing as the cold of their estate. The truth is, if he had skates to hurry himself along he would glide without regret across their frozen moments and leave these transfixed wretches gaping upward at the lines that stretch like contrails across their reddish sky.

It is so cold. Each muscle is a slab of unkneaded clay, each step an effort of will. Niko tries to tell himself the biting cold is good and that as long as he can feel it he's okay. When he doesn't feel it anymore is when he'll be in trouble.

What is it he's forgotten? He tries to remember. To think back on when the monster left him on the Lower Plain.

GERYON HAD SET down on a huge rock outcropping. Inset on one rough slope of it were massive iron rings with battleship anchorchains attached, and manacled hand and foot to those was the eviscerated form of a blinded giant. Eyes pecked out and liver torn and eaten from his body. He lay mutilated and unmoving, and though there was no sign of life upon him Niko sensed a weary endurance, a geologic waiting. The patience of stones.

The shriek of a giant bird echoed across the plain.

Geryon bent down low and Niko climbed from off the monster's back.

"Do you know the word hubris?" Geryon said.

"Greek."

"Yes." The beast straightened and pointed one of many fingers at the bound form. "As is he. That is his crime."

"Being Greek?"

The finger lowered and the travestied face turned to Niko. "It might serve you to reflect on why I thought it appropriate to land here."

Niko surveyed the view from on high. The black wall of the Ledge filled one horizon, rising till it blended with the larger blackness, until it could not be seen as a wall at all but instead looked like empty Nothing, the border of the universe itself. Yet slanting down across its face there was the faintest rent, the angled notch of cliffside ramp sloping down to finally meet the Lower Plain, disgorging those who had survived the Olympian descent.

Foothills sloped against the base of the Ledge wall, undulating from the shore of a vast red lake at the base of the bloodfall and on into the far distance, lowering until they met the end of the cliffside path. These were the Meat Pie Mountains, a range composed of those who fell from the ramp and hit and broke and healed and remained trapped beneath an everpiling weight of falling souls who may be said to come to light or to rest but who would never truly come to either.

When Niko was a boy in St. Petersburg Florida his father found a line of sawdust along the length of the patio of their home, a sign of termite infestation. Niko and his brother Van had swept up enough sawdust to fill two grocery bags. Wondering about its odd red color Niko had looked at a handful under a magnifying glass and seen that cupped in his hand were the bodies of ants. The foundation of the house was literally crawling with them.

Looking at the mounds of vanquished masses fallen from the Ramp on their inexorable way to become citizens of the undiscovered country Niko had remembered grocery bags filled with the bodies of fire ants, tiny red bodies heaped thick enough to be mistaken for sawdust.

"I said I would show you a thing." Geryon's voice brought Niko back around. The monster had folded his wings tight to his broad back and now stood with the terrible spectacle of the shackled god a gruesome epic backdrop looming like some murdered Gulliver among sadistic Lilliputians. "Something that is to words as a cube is to a square. It will not harm you but you must willingly experience this thing."

Niko shrugged. "All right."

"You take this lightly."

"I'm not indifferent, I'm numb."

The monster studied him. "Your detachment is your armor I believe." He knelt before Niko like a bestial parent before its changeling human child. Those horrible plus sign pupils, the searing aqua of those eyes. "I have seen many here defend themselves like this. As they seek to turn away from all that they endure their thoughts fold inward like a spider in a flame. Their minds grow smooth." He reached toward Niko but stopped. "But there is no turning away. What is felt is past denying."

Unaccountably he felt afraid. "Why are you telling me this?"

"Because this place is based on feeling. To deny your heart here is to go insane. Your armor is the very weapon they will use against you."

"They."

The monster shrugged and Niko had the impression that the marble face would smile if it could. "We then. But you need to understand that this is not a cold unfeeling place. Look at the torments, the tormentors. That is passion."

"Look at the tormented."

"That is passion too. Passios is a Greek word."

"To suffer."

The monster seemed pleased. "This will be your language lesson for today. Two Greek words, hubris and passios. And now you must give me your permission to take your hand and show you what I will."

Niko held out his hand but Geryon drew back. "Permission must be stated."

"You have my permission then. What are you going to do?"

"Show you how I see the world." Cold fingerbundles covered Niko's mortal hand—

TRUDGING THE FROZEN waste Niko has arrived on the threshold of the moment he's been trying to remember. Touch of smooth marble on his skin. He remembers a deep shifting. A vastening. A sense of beholding the gulf that separates self from other, mind from mind. Of crossing the frontier to another soul. The deep-toned touch of tolling bells along his skin. Liquid voices of chanting monks. Taste of ozone air after lightning in the candleflame flicker of pilgrim souls constellating the plain. Tidal motion and pulsing air. The darkness smelled of amber. Dry perfume of entropy. Deafening beauty of decay. The lake of blood behind him breathing. The living pressure of the very air. All of Hell a living thing. Himself a cell within it acting out his rightful role. A small voice inside him said Remember this.

And even remembering as he labors on the frozen ocean Niko knows what memory he can conjure is a lie. Inadequate and pale. As if the mere word boat could somehow cross the ocean. Freezing air fills his wheezing lungs and Niko understands he'll never salvage a true memory of what the monster showed him. Easier to reconstruct an angel from its footprint in the sand.

—and then let go. The disconnection marooned him to the very world and trapped him in a cage of flesh, the prison of his insufficient senses.

Niko dropped down to his knees before the monster and cried out at his sudden loss. He had told himself not to forget and now he knew only that he could not remember. Could not say what he had lost beyond the sense of loss itself.

Geryon stood before the shackled giant like a priest before his fallen god and looked down at the mortal sobbing on the naked rock like a pilgrim arriving at his destination only to learn that all he has believed is false and that his journey's been for nought.

Niko can no longer feel his feet. He stalks upon their deadwood as if struggling on cauterized stumps. Every breath a painful draw on clotted bellows. Freezing to death. So this is what it's like. Bones grow cold then start to burn with a different kind of heat. Kindling. Sleepy warmth. Not like the way you float on heroin. That old nodding off. That was more personal. Rock me in the bosom of opiates. This is different. Cold's a vampire. Cold doesn't care. Need a stack of firewood. Big fireplace. Cognac in a snifter. Big cigar.

Niko stops. Niko you fucking moron.

He reaches into his coat pocket and pulls out a package of Swisher Sweets cigarillos and a box of lucifer matches.

Geryon had waited till the mortal man stopped crying. He watched the man collect himself and watched him slowly don his armor of control. Stone gargoyles face the world to guard the shrine within.

The mortal man regained his feet and wiped his eyes and nose on the sleeves of his torn jacket.

"You can't remember."

The mortal shook his head.

"You never will. But hold to it anyhow. Keep the idea of it. The sense of it."

"Why?" Niko's voice emerged clotted.

"It will see you in good stead."

Niko blew his nose. "What's that supposed to mean?"

Geryon shrugged. "What it says. I leave you a final gift now and then I take my leave of you again and until next time."

"I'm still recovering from the last gift thanks."

"Do not recover. Learn. More important than the memory you cannot retrieve is what happened to you after it. Remember that instead. This is my gift to you."

"What happened after it?" Niko wiped tears from beneath his eyes. "What, this?"

"Remember it." Stone wings spread to their full width and then furled tight. The monster pointed out across the plain. "Keep your back to the Ledge and keep walking that way. You will come to a reach of ice. If you survive the walk across it, well then. You will cross that bridge when you come to it." He lowered his hand and turned to Niko. "And now you must release me."

"A question first."

The great chest sighed but the monster waited.

"Why are you helping me?"

Geryon regarded him inscrutably a moment and then said, "We are ever willing to help a soul head deeper into Hell. But when you try to leave I will be baying at your back like all the others trying to flay your soul. Now let me go. You are ready to complete your little walk."

Niko formally released him with the old phrases and the monster turned away in a great rush and swirl of stone wings and launched into the blighted air.

NIKO COUGHS OUT heated air. His numb hands cup the cigarillo to protect it from the biting wind. The warm smoke hurts his frigid lungs. He'd swear he feels them thawing as he drags in deep. Maybe it's purely psychological. Who gives a shit as long as it keeps him going. Go ahead, tell me how bad smoking is for me.

He thinks about the cabbie ferrying him through the city streets and below the world, her poise amid calamity. The cigarillos were her gift to him. Could she have known I wonder?

An enormous shadow moves upon the ice. Niko sees nothing in the sky and not enough light to cast such a shadow. He watches it moving and realizes the shadow is beneath the ice, a cruising whale-sized figure swimming somehow through the frozen medium. The souls embedded here are stopped midthrash, agonized faces almost without exception angled skyward.

The black shape slides across the pale ice under Niko's ragclad feet. He feels caught in the dark beam of some kind of antispotlight. He fights an urge to run. Where he'd run to is moot. He can barely keep up this dragging pegleg pace as it is. But the icewhale passes underneath him, and where it passes many of the frozen damned are gone and in their place there floats a bloody silhouette marking where they were, contorted human stencils painted red.

Niko turns to watch the silent shadow continue along the ice into the distance. Behind the ochre band of the Lower Plain the black line of the Ledge provides a false horizon.

The icewhale momentarily blots out a dark shape standing upright against the pale fluorescence of the frozen lake. Niko frowns. Something's following him across the ice.

Niko has long since stopped trembling from the cold. He peers ahead and only sees an endless reach of ice mottled with frozen bodies. Maybe he should try to dig himself a hole. Or just curl up on the ice. Just to give himself some warmth and rest. Just for a little while.

But he keeps walking. Jemma's out there somewhere, a glowing feather in a glass jar. So many knights forgot their way and lost their spirit in the lifelong search for their elusive grail.

Against his throat his locket burns.

Stone wings flap out in the alien dark.

Somewhere on a riddled plain a patient hand scrapes free beneath a granite block.

Somewhere on the Upper Plain a metal hammer rings against a chisel on a marble eye and a mad dog anchored to an ancient gate jerks in its manifold sleep.

Somewhere drinking light along its black contours a parked car pings beneath its hood as its huge engine cools.

In deserted tunnels beneath a city of angels a Checker Cab's headlights probe ahead like searchlights unshrouding the ocean floor.

Somewhere out there in the turning world lost people who will meet are strangers yet. Somewhere crowded strangers meet. Somewhere consequential people fall in love. A woman dies and maroons the man who loves her on the crowded globe alone. Somewhere in history strong hands clasp and hold. Somewhere myth demands a terrible release. A penitent soul will not let go. Plucked guitar strings conjure tears. Vapor ghosts from liquid bubbling on a heated spoon. A lyre chord resounds while riots burn a city down. Siren song a singalong for old dogs' howls. In rank apartments needles carve cuneiform on blueveined roadmap flesh, a plunger pushed to summon dreams in sepia. Somewhere cold along the Mission District a cancer riddled ragman stops and grabs his chest with sudden vivid memory, some lost love's perfume. His callused fingers numbed by blues he played for her for thirty years in crappy underpaying bars where groping drinking paying people talked above his naked pain. Somewhere east of downtown there's a blind man and his halfblind dog waiting for a train that never comes. In Hollywood dark deals are clinched inside a restaurant closed for many years that caters to a private clientele. In a bar where gazes never meet a jukebox gulps a coin and blank eyes become ghosted by a generation's past as everyone and no one hears a steel guitar begin to sob. In a drawer in a desk in a secret room lie sixteen yellowed stapled pages and a signature in blood.

Alone in a house on the continent's edge a brokenhearted father sobs and sinks beneath the burden of his grief.

In a silent house in the Hollywood Hills a body on a bed grows cool.

Somewhere on a windswept frozen plain a resolute musician falls.

XV

COME ON IN
MY KITCHEN

NIKO BLINKED AT HIS BROTHER in the late morning sunshine. Van didn't say a thing, not hello, not even surprise, but his expression clearly said Jesus Niko you look like hell. Niko silently opened the door wider and turned his back on his brother and drew his ratty bathrobe tighter as he went back into the apartment.

Van followed him inside and stood dumbfounded and turning about in the still and musty living room. Knotted bedsheets curtained the windows to perpetual twilight. A faded Navajo blanket rumpled at the foot of the threadbare couch. On the other end two stained bedpillows without cases. On the coffee table within easy reach lay empty Nehi bottles, chip bags, In-N-Out sacks, paper plates, tv dinner trays, a pizza box. Cigarette butts and crumpled wrappers everywhere. The coffee table scarred around the edge closest to the couch where butts had been left burning. The possibly tan shag carpet matted and sprinkled with detritus. Cottage cheese ceiling waterstained and earthquake cracked. The silent old tv tuned to General Hospital and bathing the room in some awful light. An unplugged lamp sideways on the stand beside it, next to a kilnstretched Pepsi bottle.

From where he stood Van could see into the kitchen where foodcaked dishes swam in gray water. The toilet droned in the bathroom, needing only a jiggle to shut it up.

Niko flopped onto the couch and began searching for his cigarettes as he stared at the mimetic soap opera.

Van wrinkled his nose and breathed out and said Jesus.

"Wrong apartment. He's a couple doors down. Tell him you're a Jehovah's Witness." He snorted.

"Don't you have a bed?"

"Yeah. It's in the bedroom." Niko found his Kools under the pizza box and tamped the pack. "You want something to eat?"

"This may be the first time I've been glad I ate on the plane."

Niko lit a smoke. "Haw haw, that's a good one bro."

"Where's your girlfriend? What's her name?"

Niko smiled a private sleepy smile. "Rumor has it she's just hunky-dory." He looked down at himself exposed by the bathrobe when he flopped onto the couch but didn't bother adjusting anything.

Van looked at the floor and sighed. He left the room and a moment later came hollow metallic jiggling. In the living room again he said, "Your bathroom is disgusting."

Niko tapped ash into the pizza box. "I piss in it, man, I don't eat off the floor."

Van glanced at a poster of a mouse giving the finger to a diving eagle, THE LAST GREAT ACT OF DEFIANCE.

The sobbing toilet quieted.

Van found the Trimline phone under a stack of unread newspapers. He clicked it several times but got no dial tone. "You disconnected your phone?"

"Ma Bell did it for me."

"Niko." Van stood over Niko now. "Dad's been trying to get hold of you for three weeks."

"You make a better wall than window, Van."

"What?"

Niko made a brushing gesture for Van to get out of the way of the tv. Van stared at him a moment longer and then turned around and banged the tv off. "Look, you want to crawl into a bottle and sit there in your own crap, that's your business. You're thirtysix hundred miles away from us and we all know what a grownup you are now."

"You came all the way to Califor-ny-ay just to tell me I can do what I want with my life? That's a real shot in the arm, bud." He laughed. "Speaking of which." He glanced around the coffee table and then started to get up.

"Niko, Mom's sick."

Without replying Niko went into the kitchen and opened Jemma's Cookie Monster cookie jar.

Van followed him. "Did you hear me? I said Mom's—"

"I heard you." He reached into the cookie jar and pulled out a baggie.

"I didn't come out here because she's got the flu, Niko. Dad thinks it'd be good for her if you—" Van stared as Niko removed his rig from the baggie. Teaspoon and syringe and cottonballs and a tiny cellophane packet of china white. Cut with baby laxative but hey. Beggars can't be choosers. Also a length of surgical tubing but Niko no longer bothered with it.

"What are you doing?"

"Making breakfast." Niko measured a fingernail sized pinch of whitish powder into the spoon and added water from the dripping tap. He grabbed a matchbox from the foodcaked O'Keefe & Merritt stove. "Most important meal of the day you know." He scraped a match alight and held the flame beneath the spoon and watched the powder liquefy and quickly bubble. "All your recommended daily vitamins and minerals."

"What the hell are you doing?" Van's tone was curiously empty.

"Well I'll tell you, brother mine." Niko stirred the spoon with the hypodermic needle and pressed a cottonball into the liquid. He pushed the needle into the cottonball and slowly drew the plunger. "I'm cooking my heroin because snorting it just don't float the boat no more." He held the filled syringe up to the light and turned it to look for cotton filaments. Instead of pulling up the sleeve of his robe he unbelted it and dropped it just to piss Van off even more. Sickly thin and bareass naked in the filthy kitchen he held the syringe away from himself and glanced at the crook of his elbow. Three square meals a day for the last six months had not collapsed his veins and Niko took a certain pride that he still shot in the ditch. Not between his fingers or his toes and not under his tongue or behind his balls or in his neck or stomach like some fuckedup junky. Sure these regular meals had gotten steadily larger but hey, that's what appetites are for. An eighth a day, big woop. A real junky'd call that a fucking tease. And hell, look at this arm. Pinpricks sure, but nothing like some of the road atlases he's seen. His last abscess was a fading purplish memory. Good healthy veins. The better to—

That was when Van hit him. Van was taller than Niko but much lighter and he'd never been much of a fighter. The blow was more haymaker slap than punch but Niko wasn't expecting it and the hypo sailed out of his hand and onto the baggie which promptly turned over and emptied every last expensive necessary grain of china white into the filmy gray dishwater.

Niko gaped. For a second he seriously wondered if he could shoot up the dishwater.

Van looked as surprised as Niko, as if he had just been operated by remote control.

"You asshole." Niko made to go around Van but Van was ahead of him and rounded the counter and saw the syringe on the carpet and stomped it. Then he whirled around with his fists up but Niko only stared in total disbelief at the ruined syringe and the wet stain on the shag carpet like some backwoods king whose tiny kingdom has just vanished out from under him.

"You dick. What the fuck do I do now?"

"I guess you'll have to do without like the rest of us."

Niko lunged. He got Van by the collar and pushed him back into the kitchen and bent him back over the counter and put his face inches from his brother's. "I got a special bulletin for you, Father Vangelis." Flecking his brother's face with spittle. "That wasn't yours. Who told you you could show up here uninvited and fuck with my shit?"

Van tried to push back but Niko pushed him first and then turned away. "Fuck. I got no dough for more smack and my connection might as well be in Antfuckingarctica till tomorrow. Jesus in a fucking sandbox, man." Suddenly he turned toward Van with narrowed eyes. "You came here with money didn't you? Sure you did. Our father who art in Florida wouldn't send his baby boy out west without a little pin money."

"I'm not going to give you money to buy drugs."

Niko clasped his hands and looked piously skyward. "And somewhere an angel gets its wings."

Van watched perplexed as Niko stomped out of the kitchen and came back with a wrinkled Cheech Wizard shirt and a wrinkled pair of pants drawn from a laundry pile.

"Look Niko, whatever we need to do I'm sure we can both—"

Niko tossed a set of keys and Van caught them. "You broke it," said Niko, pulling on the pants he'd grown too thin for. "You can help fix it."

"Where are we going?"

"Trolling." Niko slid his feet into a pair of rubber thongs.

THE INTERIOR OF Niko's white Ford wagon looked a lot like the inside of Niko's apartment. A for sale sign taped to one window, useless because the phone number on it was disconnected now. On the rear windshield some wag had written Test Dirt—Do Not Remove! The engine's idle sounded like an offbalance washing machine on spincycle. Niko slumped in the passenger seat and yawned at the roof. He sniffled and wiped his nose with the back of his hand as Van backed out of the driveway and onto Las Palmas.

Niko gave Van directions to a payphone on Highland and scrounged up change from the seat cushions. He was out of the car before it stopped moving. Van watched him run into the booth and slam the door and drop the change and dial and light up a Kool and try to pace the eighteen inch length of the booth. Niko's face brightened when someone answered. He got out maybe five words and then frowned. He said hello a few times and then batted the receiver into the phone and left it hanging. He got back in the car and slammed the door and sat there scowling at a torn flyer for some band at Gazzarri's.

"Niko—"

"Shut up man, I'm trying to think." His face was covered in sweat.

"I'm not going to help you get any more of that shit."

Niko looked at Van as if he'd told a bad joke. A thin clear trickle of snot ran onto his upper lip.

"I mean it. I won't have anything to do with it."

Niko pursed his lips. Finally he nodded. He sniffed loudly and held out his hand. "Okay. Give me the keys."

"What are you going to do?"

"You're gonna take a cab back to the airport and tell Mom and Dad whatever the hell you want. If I can't get hold of my guy I'm gonna drive to Watts."

Van pulled the keys out of the ignition and held onto them. "Are you crazy?"

"The brothers don't care who they sell to."

"You're not going to Watts and I'm sure as hell not driving you there."

Niko waved at his brother as if batting away flies. He yawned hugely and spat out the window. "Spare me the party line, little buddy. I don't really give half a shit if you approve. I'm facing the day without my usual rosy smile and it's all your fault. So this is your chance to make it right."

"I'm not going to help you buy drugs."

Niko wiped sweat from his forehead. "If I was a kid and you broke my toy you couldn't just say So what, kid, I don't like your toy. Right?"

Van stared at him as traffic went by on Highland. "That's some seriously messed up logic."

Niko shook his head. "No it's not. You break my toy, you owe me a new—"

"It's not a goddamned toy." Van slammed the steering wheel. His eyes were tearing. Frustration, anger, pity, some combination. "Jesus look at you. What the hell have you done to yourself out here? Mom's got cancer, do you understand me? She's going in for radiation treatments and Dad thought it'd be good if you were home. I've been running interference for you for a month. I told him you're a musician, you keep weird hours, maybe you fell on bad times and your phone got cut off, maybe you had to move, it's a tough life, flying by the seat of your pants, blah blah blah. And then I show up and—" He waved at his brother as if he could dispel him like smoke. "What a fool," he said and Niko knew Van meant himself. Somehow that was worse than him calling Niko a fool. Because something in Van's tone said, I should have known better. You're a screwup and I should have known better.

Van clamped his eyes shut and turned away from him. Niko looked at the cigarette burned nearly to the filter in his fingers. He chewed his lower lip and scrunched his face up like a gambler figuring odds. Then he ground out the butt in the overflowing ashtray and set a hand on his brother's shoulder. For the first time since he showed up on his doorstep Niko realized his little brother was still just a kid. He'd just gotten out of, what, his first year at UF? Only two years separated them, but Van was just a kid.

"Van. Van. I'll go with you. Okay man? I'll go home."

Van turned toward him but his guard was still up. "Just like that huh?"

"Almost. You gotta cut me some slack man. It's like six hours to Florida. I'll be a mess."

"Poor baby."

Niko was dying for another cigarette but he wasn't about to relinquish his brother's attention now that he had it. "It's like medicine, Van. If I don't take it I'll get sick. I just want to be sure I'll be okay until we're home, that's all. I need to score. Just a little bit. Just enough to get me through the flight okay. And then we'll be home and it'll be fine. I'll see Mom and you guys will help me through this."

Van looked at Niko's hand still on his shoulder. His mouth scrunched up and he looked worried. It was the expression Niko'd learned to seek every time he wanted to talk Van into something. Letting him borrow a dollar from the uncirculated coin set their grandmother had given them, loaning him money in Monopoly so he wouldn't have to quit, letting him ride his brand new birthday bike. Of course somehow it always worked out that those mint coins never got replaced even with regular old coins, or he came back strong in Monopoly and trounced everybody and wouldn't offer to bail his brother out, or he clipped a curb with the bike and laid it down hard enough to bend a pedal inward till it scraped the metal trouser guard every time Van rode it from then on.

Niko saw that look and saw that Van wanted to believe him so he pushed a little more. "I just need a little. Enough to get me home. I won't buy any more than that, I swear."

Van looked at his lap. "And you'll come back with me?"

"I'll eat the peanuts and stare at the stewardess's butt."

Van shook his head. "Why do I let you do this to me?"

"Cause you're my brother." Niko grinned and sniffled and shook Van's shoulder. "That's what brothers do, man. You know I'd do the same for you."

Van started up the car. "No I don't. Because I'd never ask you to."

THEY DIDN'T GET a hundred yards from the Gulf station five blocks away from Niko's apartment.

At the station Van gave Niko some money to fill up the car and buy more cigarettes and then sat there shaking his head and getting madder in the early summer heat. Niko went in and in a moment the pump activated. Van shoved the nozzle in and squeezed the handle. Niko came out of the station and went to a door and found it locked. He shook his head and walked quickly back into the station and came out and waved a restroom key at Van. Van frowned. Was Niko going to the bathroom to shoot up? How could he? He was clearly out of heroin.

The nozzle cut off and Van reinserted it and squeezed the handle again.

He kept trying to feel sorry for Niko but what he mostly felt was anger, and something that couldn't be called betrayal because it was not entirely unexpected. Niko was the hell bent for leather one, the one without a brake pedal, the one who went too far. He had always stuck up for Van in fights with other kids and had always been fun to tag along with because he was restless and mischievous and always coming up with new diversions. But it seemed you always ended up standing beside him hanging your head and apologizing to someone for breaking their window, talking their son into jumping off a roof and spraining his ankle, getting into the birthday cake before it was served. Something in Niko didn't know how to stop.

When Niko entered high school and Van was still in junior high they began to drift apart. Niko took up guitar and joined a band and discovered girls in earnest. Van stuck with the schoolbooks. He knew Niko was drinking and probably worse and it made Van a little cool toward his brother and a little sad. After Niko left for California seeking fame and fortune as a rock star, like every other American male of his generation who could even get his hand around the neck of a guitar it seemed, not only did Niko have no brake pedal, his wheels came off. In California you could do anything and no one seemed to care.

Van shook his head. Go west, young man. So you can fall off the goddamned map.

Niko came back from the restroom already lighting up a Kool and looking fidgety and happy the same time, a jester desperate to keep the king entertained and avoid losing his head. His wrinkled T-shirt was soaked with sweat. He kept rubbing the back of his head and scratching his arms. His nose would not stop running and he kept sneezing and spitting and swallowing.

The tank filled up and Van topped it off. Niko went to get the change and Van stood watching him in the hot and smoggy California day. He was somewhere he had never been before and about to go commit a felony with someone who might as well be a total stranger to him.

But no. However far gone he might be Niko was his brother, and Van was here for Mom and Dad. Because Mom might not have a lot more chances to see Niko after she went into the hospital. Though maybe the best thing Van could do for her would be to tell her that he couldn't find him. Tell her Niko moved, no forwarding address. What good would the truth do her?

Niko came back holding two sweaty Cokes and a little tube of Bufferin. He passed a bottle to Van and opened the tube and tapped two tablets into his mouth and toasted Van with the Coke bottle and then chugged it and belched loudly. "The pause that refreshes," he said.

Van made a sour face and Niko laughed and drummed the roof and got in the car and rubbed his forehead with his Coke bottle.

Niko leaned to look out the driver's window, grinning that hideous fake grin, eager to get on the road toward his shitty little Shangri-La. "Something wrong, Van-man?"

"Gosh, I don't know." Van got in the station wagon and shut the door. "What could possibly be wrong?" He started the car.

NIKO'S STOMACH HAD started cramping while they were driving to the station. From the cold sweats and the tingling on his ass he'd known that everything he ate last night was about to blow out both ends. Naturally the bathroom door had been locked and Niko had to ask for the key, which meant keeping his cool. But if there was anything he was good at it was keeping his cool. He couldn't do much about the physical symptoms but even when his hands were shaking and his nose was dripping and he was sweating like a thoroughbred he could bygod stand there in front of the Gulf Guy and say May I have the restroom key please? with his asshole clenched so tight you couldn't pound a nail in it.

On the john he leaned his head over the sink and let go. It was as bad as he'd expected. On the way back to the car he could see Van looked steamed. Niko lit up a Kool. Showtime, folks. He kept quiet and let Van gas up the car and then went back to get his little brother's change and also used his little brother's dough to buy his little brother a nice cold Coke and got himself one too along with some Bufferin. He made sure Van saw his hand shake as he handed him his drink and downed the aspirin. He'd left his face wet from the bathroom sink so he'd look even more sweaty than he was. Do the vulnerable frail thing a little bit. Not exactly a stretch right now.

Sure enough when he leaned across the seat to ask Van what was wrong he saw Van's anger turn to pity, saw the pity become guilt for judging his big brother so harshly. This suited Niko because Niko was getting thin. You could set your watch by a junky's dose and he should have fixed hours ago. The way he felt now was nothing compared to what was coming if he didn't score. Right now was more like an itch between the shoulderblades he couldn't quite get to and he needed Van and Van's bread to help him find a backscratcher. There wasn't a virgin's chance in

Hollywood he was going back to Florida and the white picket fence trip that was their parents' house. No way José. That would be like doing bad drugs even if his bloodstream were pure as angel's piss. No, he'd ditch Van at some point after he scored. He'd think of something.

But right now Brother Van was Niko's ticket to ride and he didn't want to piss him off. So he got Van's change and got him a Coke and joked a little too desperately and laughed a little too loudly and got him thinking maybe he'd get Niko on a plane after all. But most of all he got them moving.

The car shuddered idling at the entrance to the service station as they waited for a gap in traffic. The monotonous clack of the left turn signal was driving Niko nuts.

"Hey, let's go to Vegas," Niko said. "It's a lot closer than Florida. Lot more fun too."

"We are not going to Vegas. One shithole a year's my limit, thanks."

"Just joking. Jesus." He smiled. "You think L.A.'s a shithole?"

There was no reason for what happened next. No cause. It was so simple. Van drove out onto the road in no special hurry. No opposing traffic. They turned left into the lane. The closest car a pale blue Dodge van waiting at the light in front of them. Niko saw the van in plenty of time. He even thought Hey if we don't slow down we're going to hit that van. It never occurred to him that Van would do anything but stop.

Van didn't stop. He drove into the van. He wasn't speeding. Wasn't talking. Wasn't looking anywhere but straight ahead. He just plain didn't see it.

When they hit there was a single solid crunch and a mild smack like two bowling balls bumping. Not even very loud. Niko was wearing his seatbelt and he jackknifed forward but got his arms up in time and hit the dashboard with his palms and sprained his left wrist. That was it. Accident over. No shrieking brakes. No blaring horns. The van ahead of them rolled a foot or two and its double back door sprang open and a big cardboard box fell out.

Niko looked at his brother to ask him Didn't you see that van? He was going to make a joke. Van hits van, film at eleven, yuk yuk. But Van was still slumped forward with the side of his head against the steering wheel. He looked at Niko with his tongue lolling and a doofy slackness to his face. Niko laughed. Yeah really cute, this stupid little fenderbender was the death of you, I get it.

Then a red bud bloomed in the white of Van's right eye. It blossomed to the size of a penny. Dark red blood trickled from Van's nose and flowed across his lip and still the bloodrose spread its petals in his eye. The dark blood trickled down Van's jaw and welled and dripped onto the floorboard. The crimson flower filled Van's eye now. Everything so quiet Niko heard the plop on the rubber floormat when the first drop hit.

"Van." Niko's voice small and lost inside the odd quiet of the station wagon. "Hey." He touched his brother's shoulder and his brother's head lolled in an ugly boneless flop that leaned his body back against the door.

Niko jerked back. He looked out the windshield for help, anybody, someone who could do something. The driver of the pale blue van was just now getting out to see who had hit him. He looked annoyed but that was all. The cardboard box that fell out the back of the van had spilled cheap patchwork ragdolls onto the hood of the station wagon that beheld their liberation with vacant stupid grins that would haunt his nights for decades.

Moments that solidify the path of a life. Niko's course was not bound by his brother's death but instead was fixed when he looked upon his brother's horribly unmoving form and thought How the hell am I supposed to score some dope now? Just a fleeting thought but there it was. That alien flower bloomed inside his brother's head like something had invaded him and cored him like an apple, and all Niko could think to do was get away and hide and not talk to the driver of the van or to the police or anybody else, to gain a few more hours of freedom because every cell in his body was yelling that he had to find some god damned way to get a fix.

Niko glanced around the car. Hadn't it been a while since they hit the van? Why wasn't anyone coming to help them? Where was the driver of the van? He should have been back here by now.

Niko stared. The driver was still getting out of his van. One leg in broadcuffed jeans and scuffed workboots extended toward the pavement. An unlit filter cigarette clamped between his lips. The door half open as if he'd started getting out and then realized he'd forgotten something important.

Traffic was stopped all around the street. Drivers expressionless as if awaiting further orders. In the back seat of a white Impala two kids frozen in the midst of whacking each other as if posing for a portrait while their mother, hair wrapped in a floral print scarf and wearing enormous buglike Polaroid sunglasses, stared into the rearview and did not look away.

Nothing moved.

Niko looked at Van and had the insane thought that his brother had somehow done this. Somehow stopped and took all motion with him. Only a moment ago breathing and moving and thinking and now slumped here empty and inert and all the world outside him gone to silent stillness.

Niko found the doorhandle. Opened it. Couldn't get out of the car because his seatbelt was still fastened. Unbuckled it and backed out of the car and did not look away from Van. As if he might suddenly grin at the terrific prank he'd pulled on his big brother the fuckedup junky. Good one huh bro? Because Van couldn't possibly be dead. They'd only been going twenty miles an hour for Christ's sake. Niko'd only sprained his wrist. Life could not possibly be that fragile.

Outside the car time was transfixed as if Niko had stepped into a photograph. Smoke hung suspended like dirty cotton in the midst of belching from a yellow Camaro stopped as it was pulling from the curb. Its jowly driver staring through blackframed glasses at motionless opposing traffic. A frozen guy in a Peruvian vest staring at a billboard advertising Levi's. The ragdolls staring and staring on the crumpled white hood.

I'm hallucinating. You get thin and you get the shakes and you get cramps and chills and sweats and fever, and then you hallucinate. But that shouldn't be happening yet. The accident must have brought it on. What else could it be?

He rubbed his thumbs across his fingers to test their solidity, their reality. Their sibilance distinct in the silent street.

He turned full circle beside the station wagon and still nothing moved. But it seemed he heard something. Some approaching sound.

Niko faced the intersection where a faint deep purr grew to a rhythmic gargle. Then it glided into view, long and dark and predatory, an old black sedan like a luxury car in a gangster movie. The only thing moving anywhere in sight. The big black vintage car turned right and came toward him and eased to a stop in the opposing lane beside the station wagon. The pale and uniformed chauffeur got out but left it running. He touched the glossy bill of his cap impersonally to Niko who could only stare as the driver opened the suicide door of the passenger compartment.

The man who got out was nattily attired like a movie producer trying to dress like an English rockstar. His hair in perfect disarray. He saw Niko standing confused and afraid there and he grinned as if he knew him. As if they were old friends long separated and finally reunited.

Petrified and sweating and dripping snot Niko stood with the station wagon between himself and this man. The station wagon in which his brother lay impossibly dead. The grinning man approached Niko holding a stapled sheaf of papers and a pearlescent fountain pen that gleamed in the Hollywood sun. With one hand he uncapped the pen to expose the gold nib and turned the pen in his fingers and slid the back end into the cap, all in one smooth motion without looking, like some kind of bureaucratic samurai.

Behind the man the chauffeur stared without expression at the driver's window of the station wagon as he tugged a white silk kerchief from the breast pocket of his uniform jacket. Niko paid little attention to the natty man as he came around the car with a hand held out and grinning as if they had just consummated a used-car deal. He could only watch the chauffeur as he produced something from his jacket, something that glittered, and began walking toward Niko's car.

The beaming stranger called Niko by his full and absurd name just as Niko saw that what the chauffeur held as he bent to open the driver's side door of the station wagon was a small glass jar.

XVI

FLOATING BRIDGE

N IKO WAKES UP WANTING A drink. Before he opens
his eyes, before he has time to think I'm alive, he has a
sense of lifting a tumbler of brown liquor to his lips and drinking
it down to feel the good sharp burning tunnel to his stomach and
settle there as before a hearth to spread warmth throughout his
limbs and ward off the—

Chill.

Niko sits up and gasps. He turns his hands in front of him as if
he has never seen them before. He thinks clench and they clench.
His skin burns. At first the pain is good. A reminder he's alive. But
then doubt creeps in. I have seen a world of pain down here and no
one feeling it has been alive.

Well how do you know you're alive, cowboy?

Niko tables the question. Right now there are less philosophical
matters to attend to.

He is in a tiny room of ice. His shadow wavers on the curving orangelighted wall, cast by the small and cheery fire crackling
before him. His black guitar case stands against the white wall
like a cutout silhouette. His socks and hiking shoes are on his feet.
Laces doublebowed.

As if waiting for his attention his feet begin to throb with frostbite. The soles burn as his scabbing cuts begin to thaw.

Niko touches the tender swelling on the back of his head where he got slugged. Did getting cracked upside the skull do something to his memory? How would he know if it did?

Something about the fire bothers him. The fact of it is puzzling enough. And it's burning branches. When did he last see anything that might be used as kindling? The ice room is a little igloo six feet wide and maybe four feet high. There's no hole to vent the smoke and provide fresh oxygen to feed the fire, or for Niko either. And without an airhole he should be choking on woodsmoke that doesn't seem to be there. There should be water everywhere. It should have put the fire out. But the smokeless fire burns and no ice melts.

The fire's heat is far from soothing. Niko has barely escaped freezing to death and the close warmth makes his skin feel sanded with an emery board. His cheek throbs where it's cut and bruised. The eye the Aussie gouged continually waters.

But unquestionably the fire has saved his life. Who down here would build it and return his shoes and disappear? Not one of the damned. They are long past caring even for themselves.

One of the demons then? Why in or underneath the world would they do that? At best the demons seem amused by Niko. Most are perplexed by him and even a bit fearful. But hold on. Dexter/Sinister said there was a pool on whether Niko'd go the distance. One of them had bet in Niko's favor. Who else might have? What might it cost you here to help out the underdog? Who would take that awful chance to win a bet?

For a moment he conceives a secret cabal, an organized resistance to the tyranny in Hell. The Sub-underground. He snorts. Yeah right. His voice is flat in this small space.

Who then?

Niko rubs his forehead. His headache's back.

He remembers the vampiric waif who tried to drain the life from him near the foot of the Battlements. Something had streaked into view and knocked her away. Probably saved his life. Many times he's caught motion from the corner of his eye and turned to look to find it gone. He remembers looking back across the icy reach to see a figure limned against the whiteness of the frozen plain, following him.

The fire's heat should make him sweat but he's too dehydrated. He sits back against a buttress of ice and taps the toes of his hiking boots together three times and says There's no place like home.

He sits up straight. Maybe I wasn't rescued at all. Maybe I'm inside a bubble frozen a thousand miles deep within the ice, sealed up with a fire to eat up all the air.

Suddenly the curving walls are very close. The ragged collar of his filthy shirt is choking. He needs air. Needs out. He turns toward the wall of ice to dig or pound his way out. An unfamiliar weight on the right side of his jacket makes him stop. He reaches into the pocket and his hand encounters the neck of a bottle. He pulls it out and stares at it sparking highlights from the fire. Full and sealed it calls out like a twentydollar whore who knows his name. A fifth of Jack Daniel's.

NIKO'S GUITAR CASE is embedded in the wall. Niko works the case till it pops loose and leaves a guitarshaped hole looking out onto the windless luminous plain. He sticks his head out like a dog at a car window and sucks in breaths of frigid air, deep and cold into his lungs. The cold feels good despite his pain. He opens his eyes and looks around. His little ice cave is a bubble on the reach of ice.

The fire gutters in the draft that follows when he ducks back in. He pulls a brand out of the fire and holds it to the curvaceous opening. Immediately the ice begins to melt. So why hasn't the whole igloo melted down?

He should have learned to stop asking these questions.

Niko collects the runoff in his palm and sniffs and tastes it before allowing himself to drink. Sure he's dehydrated but this ice is a medium in which the bodies of the naked damned are trapped. It is impossible not to picture their encased forms as he slakes his thirst. Every hour it seems he learns something about the places true desperation can take him.

Arrhythmic hissing startles him. At first he thinks a creature is in the igloo with him, some bristling reptilian thing calling out a warning. But the fire's deepened crackle and sudden steam tell him that the igloo's finally melting. Got to move before the fire drowns. He holds up the whiskey bottle and only hesitates a moment before cracking the seal. He pulls three branches from the fire and sloshes whiskey on the end of each.

A small glass tube spills from the liquor bottle and clatters onto the ice. Rolled up inside the glass tube is a piece of paper. A message in a bottle.

The fire steams and crackles with dripping water. The igloo is getting humid. A tiny rain patters him now, and won't being wet be fun when he steps back outside.

Niko scoops up the glass tube. The moment he touches it he wants a drink the way a drowning man wants air. His very tissues cry out for alcohol. Immersed in the smell of whiskey Niko drops the glass tube into his jacket pocket and pokes one of the doused branches into the dying fire. Sputter spark catch. He holds the brand away from himself and sets the whiskey bottle down to thrust the remaining doused branches through the belt of his jeans like toy swords.

He kneels beside the liquor bottle to put the cap back on and hesitates as he looks down at the open neck. Just a little nip, buddy pal. To warm your insides when you're on the ice again. What harm could it possibly cause by now? What, you worried about your health? You've already started smoking again. Guess you know you ain't gonna die from cancer huh? You won't have time for cancer. So come on. Knock one back. Man if anyone in history ever deserved a drink it's you. Jesus H. Himself yanked a cork or two when he knew they were gonna turn him into God's own decoration.

Niko screws the cap back on and wipes his trembling hand against his pants. Attaboy. Now look away from it. Come on. Leave it.

He grabs his guitar case and kicks the hole in the wall a little wider. He bends to crawl outside but halfway out he stops and yells Shit and shoves the hardcase out ahead of him and backs into the slagging igloo and picks up the bottle. Fuel. I'll need fuel. The air is sauna thick as damping fire steams. Niko puts the fifth in a coat pocket. Its weight an anchor as he hurries from his shelter's rain.

Mortality Bridge

* * *

Trudging on the frozen plain and holding high a makeshift torch a few hours later Niko feels the temperature begin to rise. An oddly warm wind gusts. Niko lowers the guttering torch and draws a deep breath. Rot decay corruption. He glances behind him. No one here but us chickens. Somewhere back there his igloo has melted to a puddle and frozen again.

Niko sets the guitar case on the milky ice and pulls his last branch from his belt with stonestiff fingers. He transfers the flame from the dying brand to the new one like a lost Olympian and shields it with his body against the mild breeze until the new branch catches. It brightens right away. Well, how bout that. The torch is passed.

Niko continually trades torch and guitar so that his hands can recover some mobility and feeling. At one point the shadow of his torch wielding hand falls across a face caught screaming in the ice and Niko's shadowfingers form a figure. He says Bunny and makes it hop.

Niko's feeling pretty danged good. He was just breathing in a room full of whiskey vapor and he's buzzed for the first time in a quarter century. Thanks to his old anesthesiologist pal Dr. Daniel his scrapes and cuts and bruises are now dull background throbs. If he makes it off the ice his wounds will probably sing an aria as his body warms again. Meantime thankee Dr Dee.

The abortive toast he'd shared with Phil to commemorate the Deal twentysomething years ago had been Niko's last taste of alcohol. Drinking champagne beside a wreck that held the body of his brother and convinced he was hallucinating. The whole episode brought on by head trauma after the accident, with a dash of withdrawal symptoms thrown in for good measure. The Mouton Cadet had barely cleared his palate before he was on his knees in the middle of that preternaturally quiet Hollywood street and retching while above him Phil-for-short had grinned and grinned. "If you think that's bad, wait'll next time you try shooting up. Welcome to sobriety, Niko-holic."

From that moment on the very smell of alcohol made Niko queasy. Drinking it was out of the question. Any other drug was inconceivable.

But now he wants to suck on that old JD bottle like a baby at its momma's tit. He has it in his power right this very second to fall off the wagon hard enough to get road rash and it sounds like a terrific idea.

I should throw the fucker out on the ice right now. But I might need the alcohol for fuel. Besides it's a test.

A test, buddy pal? Like the smoking test you failed with flying colors in the cab and on the Battlements? You know you're digging yourself a hole that leads straight down to china white.

He holds high the burning torch and continues his determined march across the frozen plain, Prometheus in rags.

Now with the air warming and his last torch burning Niko suddenly remembers the message in the bottle. Shit, how could I have forgotten it? Well you're juggling a lot of balls here buddy. He sets down the guitar case and feels in his pocket for the glass tube. His fingertips brush the box of matches and the cigarillo pack. Traveler's charms. He pulls the glass tube from his pocket and examines it by paltry torchlight. Thick as his pinky and sealed with a cork. Niko yanks the cork out with his teeth. Fuck it tastes like whiskey. His mouth waters as he spits the cork out on the ice. Litterbug.

He taps the note out and unrolls it and unfolds it and stares at it in utter disbelief.

Buddy pal—
   One for the road.

Thick ivory laid cardstock paper with a deckled edge. Thin-stemmed broadcurved letters in the calligraphic style of a broad-nibbed fountain pen. No signature. No need for one because the handwriting is Niko's own.

SHORTLY AFTER THE final torch has guttered out the ice grows slick with standing puddles. Niko has discovered Hell's own springtime thaw, a change of seasons measured by a progression not of days but of miles. In the distance is a line that seems to mark the end of the ice. Beyond it is a redlit gleam that must be water runoff from the melting plain. Beyond that it's hard to see.

Niko's hiking shoes are not exactly built for trekking over plains of melting ice. He's already pratfallen several times and bruised his tailbone.

The whiskey bottle taps his hip in time with his walk. With the branches burned away his rationale for toting booze has gone up in smoke. Why doesn't he heave that bottle as hard as he can just to hear its satisfying smash upon the ice?

The melting plain begins a slight downslope toward the river. A constant runoff flows around his heels. His frostbit feet throb with the water's cold.

The icy reach is dotted now with body parts uncovered by its melting. Upthrust clenching hands and idly kicking legs and staring faces brought toward the light however dim. The closer Niko gets to the river the more there are of the indifferent dead emerging from the ice, till at the slippery bank itself the icebound souls are embedded only from the waist down. Several are free above the knee. Blankly they stare at Niko as he passes among their transfixed number like an orchard keeper. He tries to tell himself he doesn't care. All he wants to do is find a boat, a bridge, a way to reach the inner shore.

If the plain of Hell is infinite and the earthquake-created Ledge is infinite and the Lower Plain and frozen reach are also infinite then perhaps the river carrying the runoff and the thawed out damned is infinite too. Infinitely long but not infinitely wide; the far bank is only a quartermile away. Swimming distance, if Niko were a decent swimmer even unencumbered by the guitar case. If the water were not cold enough to freeze his joints motionless within two or three minutes. If the rapid current were not laden with the detritus of bodies like a logflow.

It looks as if a thick line runs from bank to bank downriver in the distance. A bridge?

As he heads downriver thousands upon thousands of naked freezing bodies tumble in the shallows of the sloping shore, huddle into fetal shapes for warmth, hold one another as the current sends them downstream to bump and smash along the shore, tissue frozen but not numbed and feeling ripsaw cold in every isolated nerve.

Suddenly an enormous black thing breaks surface, streamlined like some creature evolved for life in windtunnels. A gash of sawblade mouth opens as it arcs back into the water, and where it disappeared it leaves a large red stain that spreads and quickly dissipates.

Niko stares at the placid water where the thing knifed out and in without a ripple. Finding a bridge is definitely the thing to do.

A MILE OR so later Niko finds a small patch of ice free of emergent hands or legs or faces or backs. He squats on the frozen riverbank to rest his feet as best he can without actually sitting in the chill runoff.

The frozen dead around him stare. One woman is embedded in the ice up to her thighs. She continually slaps her paleblue face as if to make herself feel something, anything, even pain as substitute for warmth.

Ahead of Niko two embedded men face each other a dozen yards from the water. One buried to midthigh, the other to midshin. One large and fat and covered with thick black hair, the other slim and pale and nearly hairless. Both scream hoarsely at each other. Apparently each thinks the other more fortunate. They aren't close enough to hit each other but that doesn't stop them from trying.

Weary sore and injured Niko decides to stop and rest. He lights a cigarillo to ward off the chill. He closes his eyes and takes a long deep drag. It's the little things, it really is. As he enjoys the one small pleasure he has known down here he becomes aware of a lingering silence. He opens his eyes and takes the cigarillo from his mouth. The two men have broken off their argument to stare at him. Niko exhales gray smoke that roils away, underlit by faintly glowing ice and oddly beautiful.

The cyanotic woman has stopped slapping herself. Her paleblue hands now on her ample hips. Gaze direct and frank. She's quite attractive in a drowned sort of way.

The two staring men begin to scream at Niko, loudly asking what the fuck he's done to warrant clothes and cigarettes and matches. Has he been sent to torment them further, to sit there clothed and warm with packets of fire at his side just to remind them of what comfort their damnation has deprived them?

Throughout their tirade Niko simply sits there smoking. His mind an empty canvas for the moment. When the cigarillo is down to the butt he starts to stub it out upon the ice but changes his mind and picks it up and stands. As the two men gape, as all the transfixed dead around him stare, Niko approaches the pale woman who had looked on him so directly but with no hint of rancor. He holds out the smoking butt of cigarillo and raises his eyebrows.

Her smile is sly as she accepts the butt and keeps her gaze on him and inhales deeply. The cigarillo burns down so low it has to be burning her fingers. Probably she can't feel it or maybe she doesn't care. Her eyes close. Her face all gothic sensuality.

Niko recovers his guitar case and nods at the smoking woman. The more hirsute of the two angry men shouts that if he were free he'd kick Niko's ass for mocking him.

Niko sizes the man up from head to toe. Big and burly and quite hairy, potgut but still muscular. He really does look like a bear. Niko can't place his accent. "If you and your friend would stop arguing long enough you could probably pull each other out of here."

"I wouldn't soil my hands with him," says Bear.

"Fuck you," Thin Man agrees.

Niko shrugs and says Oh well and recommences his long walk. A few minutes later he looks back. The two men are yelling at each other again, arms waving wildly as they fling their accusations. The beautiful drowned woman beyond them to one side. She sees Niko looking and waves slowly like an underwater frond. Niko waves back and turns around and laughs despite himself. Flirting with death.

A MILE LATER Niko sees a man struggle free near the frozen riverbank. Who knows how long the man has waited for the runoff to wear away the ice enough for him to free his frozen legs? Ten years, a hundred, a thousand. However long, Niko witnesses the moment when the man frees his legs at last from out his icy prison. The man stands and lifts clenched fists like a victorious boxer. The man grins as he jumps up and down and then bends to slap his feet and massage some feeling back into his legs. Naked and barefoot on cold running water on a plain of ice and happy as a dung beetle in a manure factory. The man bows theatrically though no one cheers him on.

Niko wonders what the man plans next. Escape? Do they really think of escape here even idly? But escape to where? The sunlit world that judged and found them wanting? To another possibly worse part of Hell? To enlist with Niko's imagined Sub-underground cabal, an Underground Railroad ferrying desiccated souls out of perdition to a place more merciful? Where would that place be?

The man who freed himself is running now. He slips, he falls, he slides. He gets up laughing. He bows low to the jealous crowd. Niko is all set to cheer him on when from the water near the frozen bank there bursts a black eruption, enormous glossy and alive. It arches from the water and hangs suspended there, for a moment a work of art or architecture, and then it yaws and glides onto the ice. Its front end yawns like some fanged funnel and it slides along the ice and leaves a darker trail of wet and scoops the freed man up and rolls back into the water and leaves behind only a broad wet swath upon the ice and the small twin holes where a pair of legs had for how long been encased.

THE BLACK LINE Niko has been heading toward is definitely a bridge. There's something odd about it though he can't quite figure out what just yet. Something about it he doesn't like.

BEFORE TOO LONG the air before the bridge seems to shimmer like a road on a hot day. Niko's socks squish in his shoes as he navigates the hadearctic waste. Across the broken reach he hears the flattened groan of straining ice, a sound a bit like leather stretching. Small flat icebergs dot the river. With the rising temperature the shore of ice has begun to calve in places, causing cracks and upthrusts in and on the plain.

Everywhere the ice has parted Niko sees remnants of embedded frozen bodies ripped apart by glacial motion, torn off at leg or waist or neck and even lengthwise. Redcored bodies float like flies in amber all about him, distorted by pale ice.

When he looks up again the bridge has his complete attention.

What he had taken for wavering air is the writhing of the bridge itself. The bridge is built of bodies. Thousands of them naked and freezing and huddled against the icy current forever breaking against them and crying moans so terrible they sound like pleasure. Some of those who clutch along the outside mass fight off the clammy grip that binds them to the others and they roll into the river to swim furiously toward the frozen bank. But however hard they swim the current brings them thrashing back where they are gripped and reabsorbed into the coruscating mass. It reminds Niko nauseatingly of ants swarming a dead animal. But these aren't ants, they're people. Human beings.

Half a mile later they aren't just people. They're people Niko knows. The bridge is built of the bodies of people he has met throughout his life. Out there on the water they're a living groping bridge and Niko knows them, knows every damned one. Friends lovers partners. Producers critics roadies. Groupies dealers bandmates. Managers clubowners bartenders. Waiters waitresses restaurateurs. Schoolmates teachers playground bullies. Lawyers doctors deejays shrinks. And if Niko is the thing they have in common then Niko is the reason for their present suffering. There are so many.

Niko thinks about looking for another way across but knows there will be none. He considers moving on and trying to swim across but no. If he doesn't freeze and drown he'll end up as an hors d'oeuvre for the black leviathan or the current will sweep him to the clutch and press of those he knew who may not wish him well. And if that doesn't happen, well, Niko has a funny feeling about the water itself. He knows the story of the river Lethe. Or perhaps remembers it.

Damn you Geryon. If only you had flown a little farther. But of course you left me there so I could make this trek. What you said about crossing the ice. "If you survive the walk across it, well then. You will cross that bridge when you come to it." It's all a kind of trial isn't it? Or maybe just an entertainment. But one man's trials are another's entertainment, yes? Were you warning me then? Not against Hell but against myself? That if I fail it will not be due to obstacles but as a consequence of my own insufficiency? Who I am is my undoing. We are what we have done.

Geryon you are arrogant and cruel but there is something about you I cannot help but like. You—showed me something? Took me—somewhere? I can't quite remember. I think within the confines of your unforgiving laws that you were trying to help me.

But there's the ice and there's the water and there's the farther bank. And between the two are piled contorted and screaming all of those I've ever known who died.

Niko looks up at the cavern sky. You bastards. How I despise you.

But in this old drama playing out inexorably as a spring unwinding metaphors are manifest and traditions and rules inviolate as natural law. So Niko picks up his guitar case and heads out to walk across the bodies of those he has known.

From the first rubbery step it is horrible. Their flesh yielding as they writhe beneath him. Some grab his ankle to restrain him. The grip always feeble but just strong enough to make him shake it off and then feel shamed. As he knows it is meant to. But still he casts them off and staggers across their terrible mass with his guitar case held high out of their reach. If he falls they will surely drag him under.

All of them moan his name.

Niko cannot meet their eyes. Cannot give them what they want. Acknowledgement and recognition. But he has no choice. If he looks stonily ahead he can't see where to step and he will surely fall. And to fall here is to stay here. He has to look down and in looking down must meet the desperate jealousy and need in the eyes of those he barely knew, the recognition in the eyes of many he was familiar with but hardly would call friends, the regret in the eyes of those few to whom he has felt close. Some of those he walks across he does not recognize. They're much older than when he knew them, they're naked, they're gruesomely out of context, their acquaintance was too fleeting.

But they're people, Niko! You can't ignore them, you knew them! There to one side is Ray, his bus driver through most of junior high school, batting aside the outstretched arm of a woman who looks just like a grownup version of Anne Ellison, the freckled girl with braces who vied with him for the spelling bee championship throughout all of elementary school and for whom he'd harbored a secret painful crush. Anne reaches out for Niko and Niko makes himself look away from her woman's face which even agonized and crying out his name contains a ghost of the girl she was. He forces himself farther onto the nightmare bridge and steps on the reaching arm of Mrs. Bouduin, his first housekeeper, who died of a heart attack after working for him for a year. Overweight and slow but thorough and always nice and thoughtful she had stolen thousands of dollars' worth of silver and Jemma's jewelry over the course of her employment.

Now among the voices crying out his name is that of Erin Farrell, a whiskeyvoiced singer he had dated once and slept with twice and never called again though he had later worked with her on several gigs. He hears her voice but does not see her as he jerks his leg away from Mrs. Thompson, his firstgrade teacher, plump woman with a broken blood vessel worming one eye that he had stared at whenever she came close. She had seemed the very picture of an upright moral Godfearing woman, what was she doing here? Niko's leg as it jerks from her hand kicks the jaw of Stevie Dane, his old drug buddy and high school bandmate in The Spanish Flies. Stevie Dane who rode a needle right into the ground.

"I'm sorry," Niko calls out to them all. "I'm sorry. I'm so sorry." But his cries are lost within the manythroated imprecation of his name.

Keep moving. You can do that can't you? Can you do that? What are you if you can?

Which of course is why they're doing this to him.

Niko sidesteps Gary Calvin Watson, who could twohand tap Two-Part Invention in D Minor on his Rickenbacker bass. Watson had got sick of the business and bought a ranch in Wyoming and got gored to death by one of his own bulls if you can believe that. Niko stumbles past Watson and brings his foot down on some half-remembered interviewer's shoulder. Rearing from the awful seething now is Bobby Harris, more Jem's friend than his but Niko had always respected and admired him. Bobby died of AIDS ten years ago. He'd been a good man, what was he doing here, Bobby was a good man.

Bobby's knocked down by a woman Niko would have known no matter how much older she became because she has the reddest hair he's ever seen. "Betty," Niko calls. "Cousin Betty." Her name unuttered for how long now. Betty's batted aside and buried in the undertow of crawling damned. He had lost his virginity to Betty Towers, Cousin Betty because they were distantly related and they'd taken secret pleasure in the forbidden nature of that fact. He still wondered about her sometimes. Where she was, how she was, who she was now. And now he knows. She's dead, she's damned, she's doomed to unending persecution here, used as a pawn to be used by him.

Niko screams a wordless howl. This is more than he can bear. More than can be borne. He risks a backward glance and sees he's barely come a hundred yards. The bridge must be a quartermile long.

Harden your heart Niko. They're dead and damned and it doesn't matter any more. But Geryon's words keep cycling in his anguished mind. Your armor is the very weapon they will use against you.

As Niko heaves and tears his way along the population of his life his scream becomes a wordless curse against the forces that have led him here to walk across the living corpses of those he has known. All to save one of their number venerated by his heart. He sobs his rage against whatever mind could send good people into Hell and punish them forever for the arbitrary sins of an eyeblink mortal life, a mind that could use their own humiliation just to show one man what travesty and selfish desperation he'll commit.

Thrust against him now is a baldheaded girl whose name he can't remember. She was young, twelve or thirteen, the Make A Wish Foundation had forwarded to his management a letter she had written. She was dying of leukemia and wanted to hear him play. He'd sat beside her hospital bed surrounded by newscameras and hospital staff, an acoustic guitar on his lap. Chemotherapy had left her bald and she had seemed a homesick fallen angel propped by pillows there. He'd asked her what she wanted to hear and she'd said she didn't really know, whatever he wanted to play was great. Her mother and father were there and she had glanced at the cameras and reporters and at Niko, nervous and starstruck, and Niko had asked everyone but her parents to leave and nearly pushed the media from the room, and then he'd sat and played for her and her alone. As if sound waves from vibrating strings could save her. As if whatever tore its way from Niko's core could enter her and make her anything but worse. Unbelievably she had asked him if he knew "Aint Misbehavin" and he'd laughed and picked his way through it like a beginner, remembering it really but asking her to hum the melody for him anyway so that he could pick it out and gradually perform a duet with the poor sad dying pale bruised and hollow-eyed gaunt girl tubefed and smiling there on the whitesheeted bed. He tried to play upbeat but he was saddened she was going to die, sad and angry that she would never make love, never be a mother, never toast a happy couple, wear a prom corsage, hold hands in a movie theater, pay her own electric bill, fret over what to name her baby. Never grow up.

And here she is still twelve or thirteen, dead these many years and damned for reasons he and probably she doesn't know and doubtless would not understand, a naked thin baldheaded girl who clutches at his feet as if he is some bogus prophet come to trample his deluded flock and give them nothing but his reluctant and unhealing touch.

She calls out Mr. Niko. Mr. Niko.

Her name, what was her name? You don't remember do you asshole? You played her some songs and joked in a hospital room and all it cost you was a day and a plane ticket, and when you left you were sad but still given some cold comfort that at least you were able to fulfill her wish and make her happy for some little while. And then she died and you forgot her.

Whatever flimsy truce of old he forged with his own inner demon shatters at the touch of her small hand upon his ankle. The old ebb tide of self destruction washes through him with an awful and familiar surge. I won't do this. I can't do this. I will not partake in their humiliation. Will not degrade these people for your own amusement. You win. Fuck you, you win. I want no victory if the cost is this. I'm done. I surrender.

Niko stops his forward struggle. Hands claw at him. Cover him. The bald girl reaches up toward his face and his hand intercepts hers. Their fingers touch entwine and clench. She says Mr. Niko. Niko weeps but doesn't know it. He feels a tug on the guitar case long clutched in his hand and lets it go. Feels a tugging on his foundering soul and lets it go as well and is dragged down.

THE COLD TOUCH of the dead swarms all about him. Jem I'm sorry. I tried, I tried my best. It wasn't good enough because I wasn't good enough. Will it hurt when they tear into me. Will I drown freezing in the water below. Will there be a sleep and a forgetting. And after I am husked and my flayed soul is thrown out like a rind into this awful universe of garbage will I see you ever Jem. And will you forgive me if you do. A part of me hopes you don't. I carry that hell with me as I live and breathe.

Niko's body turns and turns. His hair is pulled as he is passed among them. He swims amid the cacophony of his name. Will they crush him, will they tear him apart like mad Bacchantes? Will he drown beneath the press of cold and naked bodies? What are they waiting for?

He opens his eyes and there is only blackness. He stares upward at the cavern ceiling. All beneath him is a jostle.

They're carrying him. He is borne aloft atop a coruscating sea of reaching hands. Passing him overhead like a concert stagediver. Delivering him across the bridge of themselves.

For a panicked moment Niko thinks they mean to bring him to the gaping maw of some mad chewing thing that will devour him and so commit him here forever. But look at their faces. Look in their eyes. Even in the midst of such despair there is a kindled spark of gleeful rebellion, possibly the first joy or defiance they have felt or shown beyond the closure of their mortal lives.

Turning now in their collective grip he faces downward. A man he doesn't recognize, with a split brow and a missing eye, smiles piratic up at Niko as his hands raise up to take their share of Niko's weight. My God, there below him now is Andy Brand, his favorite session drummer, dead in a motorcycle accident how long ago now. Andy holds his hands up with the rest of them and gives Niko a look that is only reassuring and somehow conspiratorial. And now he sees, it can't be, it's Ave, Avery Kramer, his old manager, bald and fat and wearing the shiteating grin Niko always pictures when he thinks of him, the grin that implied he was getting away with something because he usually was. Too far away to hold him up but reaching for him anyway. Avery, Niko shouts. Avery. He forces a hand through the forest of upthrust arms and reaches out to Avery. Their fingers touch and their hands clasp. A brief squeeze and then the current carries him away.

Joy floods Niko's heart. It hurts, it fills him with a trembling exultation. It makes him want to die. He lives within its fleeting heat like a moth dived headlong into consummating flame. Joy.

How his friends have managed this rebellion Niko doesn't know. But manage it they have, for this brief moment in their endless suffering, and they carry Niko across a patchwork history of his peopled life. Can he really have known so many who have died? In fleeting glimpses and brief touches he encounters glad remembrances and sorrows, and passed along and past.

Now he sees the far shore nearing, sees his guitar case handed off across to it like a bucket in a fire brigade. Niko himself is being delivered like a hometown hero.

A figure stands upon the farther shore. Niko strains for a second sight of it as he is jostled and bumped and turned about, and in his narrowed focus misses many calling figures from the stages of his life. His brief joy now stained by sudden doubt. It had looked like. It couldn't have been. They wouldn't.

His buoyed spirits sink now in a morass of premonitory fear. Of course they would. Of course they have. Of course they saved the best for last.

Standing on the far shore just beyond the bridge, past Eddie the ice cream truck man who used to give him credit and Jake the club owner who had paid off Niko's gigs in drugs, there with hands held out to welcome him, with the face so like his own, the face that Niko last saw sightless and unmoving against a steering wheel in a crumpled wreck.

Van.

XVII

IF THE RIVER
WAS WHISKEY

NIKO STILLS HIS HANDS UPON the strings. The only music now the mindless babble of the river Lethe. He looks down at the still guitar and wonders What did I just play?

He feels a forlorn sadness at his own return. As though he has not regained but instead has lost something. But what he's lost he doesn't know. He knows it by its absence. By the shape it leaves behind.

Patient in his armor the Achaian watches. Waiting as he comes back to himself. Niko thinks he likely has not waited long.

Niko lays the Dobro gently in its case. As if tucking in a sleeping child. Softly shuts the lid and shuts the latches slowly as if to keep from waking the encoffined steel.

"You are changed," says the Achaian.

"I am diminished." Niko regards the case upon the sand before him. Then nods and picks it up and turns to face the stoic soldier. "Akileo, I am sorry to see you in this terrible place."

"I am sorrier to be in it. So you remember now."

"I remember. I would thank you but this was no gift."

The barest nod of helmeted head. "Not to be born is best. Failing that, then not to remember. But now you do and you will try to resume your mission, and so I must carry out my own."

Niko wipes a palm against a thigh of his damp jeans. "I guess there's no talking you out of this."

"I have few words. Already we have talked too long."

Niko nods. "I don't want to hurt you."

"Your music is stirring, Orfeo. And I am the worse for its reminder of my living days." A smile ghosts the even line of the Achaian's mouth. "But do not flatter yourself."

"All right." Niko feels adrenalin surge at the certainty of the coming fight and tries to breathe evenly and keep himself relaxed. "Anything else I should know?"

The spear levels at his throat. "Only that you are mortal."

"I know it with every breath. But you?"

The Achaian seems amused. "Nothing painful is inflicted here in vain. Stay your trepidation and tend your own house, winesack."

"Okeydoke," says Niko. And swings the hardcase at the spear. It slaps the bronze head. The Greek has anticipated this and follows the deflection to strike with the spear's unbladed end. Niko is no longer there. He's behind the soldier's right shoulderblade, hardcase dropped and his hands on the soldier's hands, and he mirrors their motion and continues it and exaggerates it to redirect the parabola of the strike until the arc intersects the sand. The soldier's body follows the spear's arc and lands hard on its back. Niko continues the motion as if enacting some wellpracticed choreography. They might be dancing. In fact they are.

Now Niko holds the spear. Someone watching would have seen the soldier seem to hand it to him. Beside them lies the guitar case.

The soldier tries to twist away and Niko steps upon the bronze breastplate. Strong hands grip his calf and Niko pushes down to gain time and brings the spearpoint to the soldier's throat.

The Achaian grows still. Sweat wells Niko's brow and drips to patter bronze.

"So there is more to you than music."

"There's more to anyone than the stories people tell."

"Yes. Yes I know."

Niko takes a deep breath. "So I guess it's not just your heel any more that's, you know—"

The doomed man snorts. "Such a thing if ever true was mortal as was I. No more."

"And Hektor's armor?"

"No longer his nor mine." Bronze plates shift: the Achaian shrugs. "This was forged for me from chamberpots behind the walls of Dis. It keeps me weighted at the bottom of a lake of burning piss." The strong chin juts. "Palaver has never been my talent and I weary of it now. Do what you must do my ancient. Do not falter."

"I'm sorry."

"We are ever victims of our duty and our selves. A favor?"

"If I can."

"Throw my corpse into the Lethe. Do not leave me here. The water is all that can sunder me from the misery of my existence before I am found and reawakened to resume my eternity of pain."

And with that Niko understands the source of his deep sadness at his own resumption. "I will, Akileo."

The Achaian smiles. Not grudgingly but openly and shockingly boyish. "How good it is to know my name is still remembered on the earth." And sits up.

Niko tenses as through the wooden shaft he feels the bronze slice flesh and grate against a vertebra. The soldier lies back down with a liquid gurgling sigh as if relaxing. A soft rhythmic hiss, and the sand around him reddens. Bubbles float in that brief red pool. The rhythm slows. The soldier stares up at Niko the whole time and Niko watches the blue eyes until their light is mere reflection. Then he braces his foot on the fallen soldier's breastplate and withdraws the leafshaped blade. He thinks to do the chivalrous thing and set the spear beside the body and close the cooling fingers round the haft. But no. Not here where the body's death is so shortlived. Instead he takes a dozen running steps and hurls the spear out on the sandy plain. The arc of its flight is lost in the dark but Niko hears the faint chuff when it strikes ground.

He stands a moment looking out at what he cannot see. The river's hiss behind him.

That deep sadness upon returning to himself. Because he'd crawled up from these icy waters with no notion who he was. Nameless in Hell he'd held no memory of despair. No loathed and cherished demon clawed inside him. He was not a man who'd signed away his soul or lost his love and did not remember what all myth and history related he would lose. What he has lost countless times in many forms. For the first and only time in Niko's life and lives he'd been at peace. And the sadness he had felt upon returning to himself was grief at peace's loss when memory infected him again.

He turns toward the frigid peopled Lethe. You're it, aren't you motherfucker? The cowabunga fix. The motherlode whiskey river. I've been looking for you all my life. And there you are, oblivion, there you are. I could take a running jump right now. Couldn't I? Dive on in and do the very opposite of drowning. And never know a moment of remorse. And why not. Why not.

Niko looks away from the river Lethe and turns his back on his forgetting.

On the sand the soldier's body has already begun to twitch. Niko hurries to him and links hands under him and lifts. Jesus christ. The guy may be short but even without that armor he'd weigh at least one eighty.

Niko staggers with the soldier to the riverbank and lobs the body as best he can. He watches the Achaian's limp form splash into the water and flop unwilled as it rolls until it drops beneath the surface, weighted by armor and more than armor and carried by the current as it quickly sinks from sight and memory and all else but the lying mirror that is myth.

Niko collects his meager belongings from the sand. The whiskey bottle still full and sealed. Hadn't it been empty? He looks at the river and then hurls the bottle out over the water. Its splash is lost in the river's rush.

The message on the parchment the Achaian delivered. *Buddy pal: Here's the short version.* Niko reads it now with eyes once more haunted by untold lifetimes' memories behind them. As with the note in the makeshift igloo the handwriting is familiar because the handwriting is his own. He rolls the parchment and flattens it again and slips it into a pocket and then picks up his hardcase. Wet grit clings along one edge. Red discoloration on the fine blond sand.

Looking inland Niko narrows his eyes. It will be different this time you goateyed son of a bitch. It will. The song will not remain the same. Walks on.

XVIII

MIDNIGHT SPECIAL

WASTED, WEARY, NIKO NAVIGATES THE inner shore. His ragged shirt is soaked with sweat, his calves are cramped from walking on the sand. It's hot and muggy as New Orleans in August but the sky is murky and the air is curling dark and the light is ochre red. And that sure as shit ain't the Mississippi behind him.

Niko treads the hardpacked sand, pulled by instinct like some migratory bird that senses its direction but has lost all sense of why it travels or where it will arrive. Perhaps his journey has made him a little crazy. Going crazy seems the only rational response to this ceaseless parade of torment and despair.

He comes upon a narrow stream that runs inland from the river. Rather than ford it Niko follows it. Soon a forest lines the rivulet banks. The smaller trees bear pale yellow fruit the size of softballs. Beneath the trees are knots of obese damned so gravid that they cannot lift themselves enough to pluck the fruit their starfish hands strain toward like massive babies blindly groping toward a toy. They look halfmelted and drowning in themselves, blubber spreading in a doughy mass and features buried under wrinkles like bleached

Shar-pei dogs laboring to breathe, their gender blurred to indistinction and imprisoned in their convoluted flesh.

Four demons lounge around the base of one spreading tree, playing cards and eating fruit. They laugh and shout insults at each other and shuffle and deal. One says I knock and raps the ground in front of him with his sharp knuckles. Without looking he lobs the slim core of a gnawed apple over his winged shoulder. The sessile damned are groping for the scrap before it has stopped moving. The lucky winner is the one who rolls a few inches to one side and feebly grasps the core in his chubby fingers and brings it to his gaping mouth to chew and swallow mindlessly, seeds and stem and all.

In a moment three of the demons groan and complain and pitch their cards to the grinning dealer who then shuffles for another round. One demon gets up grumbling and idly hooks his trident in a branch and jerks it up and down. Heavy ripe fruit thumps down around the rotund dead who strive to gorge themselves upon it. The demons break off their game to watch the obscene feeding. They nudge one another and chortle and point out favorites and place bets.

One of the obese gluttons lets forth an awful highpitched keening and begins to rock like a dinghy on a choppy sea. His enormous belly shudders and convulses and heaves and his jaws work and his eyes are terrified and agonized as they look out from their fleshy pits. From deep within this struggle of bloat comes a mild purring terrible to hear. One demon whoops and shouts and slaps the shoulder of the one beside him as the purring enloudens and becomes a rip on the fat man's belly that spreads across his massive floundering gut as if he's being disemboweled by an invisible assailant. The curved rip widens and reddens like a smile and the smile vomits an engorged stomach and stuffed-sausage intestine and bile. The body wheezes but it cannot scream because its diaphragm is torn in two. The wound's lips flap with a thick fart of venting gas. The corpulent explosion grips great handfuls of its own ruined guts and stuffs them in its mouth and chews and swallows and spews them out again from its exposed digestive system only to grab and swallow them again. Around the gluttonous display recycling itself the other swollen dead grab whatever of the spilled sweetbreads they can hoist into their engorged selves.

The happy demon does a little dance and tells the others to pay up. Niko hurries on into the woods.

Naked bodies shackled hand and foot against the boles of fledgling trees of some lost species never named. Many of the dead seem barely inconvenienced by their long confinement as they talk casually among themselves. Others are stretched taut and lengthened over the course of many years as the trees to which they're bound have grown and slowly pulled apart their chained and moaning decorations in the agonizing grip of the slowest imaginable rack. Manacles on taller trees hold only stumps of tornoff limbs.

Demons with tackhammers and awls patiently transcribe entire narratives onto the trunks of certain trees. The bark shudders at every stroke and Niko sees that these trees have an eerily human shape. As if long ago the seeds of human beings were planted and grew elongate and distorted. Some bear fruit that demons pluck and eat to conjure muffled sobs from deep within the rooted flesh.

Demons with enormous axes chop at other trees that exude blood instead of sap. Scabbed stumps sprout limb saplings born again from parent trunks. From the deeper forest comes a hornet whine of chainsaws, a grating keen of buzzsaws, a chortle of woodchippers, pounding of hammers, intermittent chopping. The vibrant tone of human wood filed down to powder.

Several times Niko glimpses odd apparitions. Waisthigh Bosch-like naked chicken creatures mostly leg and running blindly through the woods. He can't figure out what they are until one such strange and awkward thing slams against a tree and falls back kicking and convulsing to regain its footing. Against his better judgement Niko goes to help the flopping thing only to pull up short in utter horror at the realization that the creature is a human being. A woman rendered unrecognizable as such because her spine has been snapped and bent double and her entire head shoved up her ass. The flailing arms find purchase on the ground and hoist the contorted body upright. The extruding pelvic bones and lower back are cut and bruised and scabbed and swollen where she has sprinted into trees.

The woman scampers off like some kind of maimed blind spider. Niko does not follow.

THE SOUND OF powertools flaying wood grows louder as Niko presses on and soon emerges from the peopled wood and stops before an appalling sight. Ahead on the denuded plain thousands of demons work the living lumber and drive teams of shackled damned to chainhaul soul-encasing logs to a low enormous building, itself made of timber rough and doubtless conscious. The logs go into one end of the building and emerge from the other as eightfoot lengths of finished four by fours. The air smells heavily of sap and blood, sawdust and rotting meat. The building is both slaughterhouse and lumber mill. A slaughtermill.

A wooden platform runs the slaughtermill's length, and beside the platform runs a railroad track emerging from the thinning forest on Niko's right. A signal at the platform's end glows steady green. An odd jewel of color in this monochromatic red.

The railroad signal's green turns flashing red, a color nearly white in the ochre light. Niko feels the rumble grow until its thunder fills the world. A great sculpted black iron locomotive howls braking from the wood of the gluttons with a sound like a nation of fingernails clawed across a vast clean chalkboard plain. The locomotive's front is shaped like a frenzied gargoyle head with a great maw gaping to devour whatever lies before its bound life screaming on the rails. Its behemoth breathing carries across the clearing as it bellows to a stop beside the platform. A load of naked dead disgorges like fleas abandoning a corpse, to be rounded up and herded along by whiphanded demons who direct them to piles of finished beams. The dead are made to pick up two beams each and drag them along a twinrutted trail etched deep into the plain by centuries of just such wooden beams dragged likewise. Niko feels dread certainty about their fate as his gaze follows the rutted path into the distance where inverted phonepole crosses crowd the flat horizon.

The train bleeds forth a ragged thousand of the damned, then winged demons search the cars for those who cower fearful in the dark. What wretched bodies they prise forth are carried struggling high into the weighty air like baggage. The demons chortle and cavort and dogfight one another, playing chicken and making diving airplane noises as they bash the bodies against each other in the raven air. When they tire of this the demons dive toward the gaping head of the locomotive and feed the limp pulped bodies to the waiting train like offerings to some allconsuming god of industry. The venting engine steam turns bloodred like the spout of a mortally harpooned whale.

Soon the train is thrumming again, a neverending growl like some entropic engine of the night unraveling the fabric of nature itself. Niko feels the locomotive's urge to tear along the track and devour all that lies along its fated way. The boiler builds up its head and begins a labored breathing. Slaved wheels spin to grate sparks from the rails beneath. Demons scatter powdered bone onto the rails. The wheels gain traction and grind on. The angry god of locomotive shudders and convulses waking. Boxcars jerk into motion as the gaping metal maw once more eats up the neverending miles.

Niko is up and running before he is aware of what he's doing. Running awkward with the guitar case in hand and free fist pumping. Running toward the leaving train and watching thick red smoke vent from the locomotive straining deeper into Hell. The demons on the nearby platform have their whip hands full with this new trainload of tormentees but Niko clothed and carrying a guitar case and running fullout is bound to attract attention.

And he does. A demon looks up from lashing a sobbing girl's naked bleeding back and sees Niko making for the rear of the train and frowns. He cracks his whip about him to clear a space and gets a running start and spreads his leather wings and takes to the irontainted air.

Niko veers more sharply toward the train. He glances over his shoulder at the demon on the wing. It's going to be close. At the last moment he cuts left to run in the direction the train is going. The train has picked up speed and sobs along faster than Niko can run with the guitar case. Only a few feet now. A freightcar with an open doorway glides into view. Niko throws caution to the winds and his case into the door. The case bangs the edge and spins into the deeper darkness of the car. Niko jumps in after it. His shins bark the boxcar's edge and he pitches forward and his arms and chest slam the filthcaked wooden floor. His hands scrabble and slide and catch. His body cants toward the spinning metal wheels that want to mill him into pulp.

Something thuds onto the boxcar just above him. Niko looks up and sees the demon clinging to the side of the train like a browneyed bat. Its arms are tapering tendrils, leathery whips coiled around freightcar handles and protrusions Niko could never reach.

Niko glances frantically. Metal walls, the freightcar's dark interior, the edge of the opened door.

The demon grins and draws a tendril idly back and flicks it forward. The serrated tip brushes Niko's forearm and the searing pain makes his arm jerk free. He flails, he hits the door edge, he catches it. Bearing Niko's weight the freightcar door is sliding shut. His ribcage scrapes along the bottom edge of the car. The ground rolls by just beneath him like a giant sanding belt. Niko fights to get a leg up without losing his grip.

The demon's tendril wraps above the doorway and the demon swings over Niko's head and into the dark car. He wraps his wings around himself and watches mutely from deep within, shadows shrouding his indifferent face as Niko struggles for his life beneath him. Niko glares pure hate into the demon's face. The son of a bitch just stands there. The train rocks and Niko's legs fly out and his hand slips off the freightcar door. The demon's tendril whistles through the air and wraps his wrist. Niko's hiking shoes scud ground and then the demon leans back and lands him like a large-mouth bass. Niko convulses gasping there beside his scarred guitar case on the filthy freightcar floor. The wind knocked from him by his fall. His wrist seared where the living whip has branded it.

The demon sets serpentine limbs against the clattering door and slides it shut. Now the car is dark and the air is close. The clanking chaos of the train drowns Niko's wheezing struggle to regain his breath. When he can speak again he addresses the darkness. "Why. Did you help me? Who. Are you?"

And the darkness replies in a familiar voice. "What's the matter, buddy pal? Don't you recognize me?"

Niko stares and feels an awful deepdown recognition grow.

Familiar laughter in the closed and rocking space. "After all the years we spent together." Niko's heard thousands of recordings of himself. Enough to recognize his own voice replying from the shadows.

"Here." Snap of leather, and a supple tendril bearing a jaundiced yellow light the color of a failing flashlight moves between the two figures in the boxcar, one supine and the other kneeling, to render in Rembrandt chiaroscuro a funhouse visage floating disembodied in the dark. "Better now?"

Niko takes in deepset eyes reflecting steady cold light, a broad brow, thickbristled eyebrows, mottled brown hide, wide face and prominent jaw, large nose, broad cheekbones and gaunt cheeks. Twisted and contorted, sinister and mutilated, the demon's face still recognizable as his own.

"You're me?"

In the sepia light the full lips curve in a lopsided grin. "Close but no cigar," says Niko's voice from this thing's mouth. "I'm your demon."

HOT WIND FLUTTERS Niko's tattered coat as the boxcar clatters deeper into Hell to carry its divided load along its destined route. The walls and floor are slimed with human filth, the stench is overwhelming. For once he's thankful for the dimness.

Near one wall the demon sits crosslegged like a huge statue of Niko carved into a gargoyle, swaying languidly with the boxcar's rocking, not resting against the wall because of his wings but hunched forward with mottled tendrils hugging pointy knees and waiting silently for Niko to absorb this latest development and looking all the more horrifying in his sure familiarity.

The strange thing is that Niko doesn't need much explanation. The creature before him looks exactly like the demon he has always pictured, the supple critic and whispering adviser who for so long lived within his mind. Urging him Have another drink. Admonishing him Don't let her tell you what to do. The self aggrandizing voice that exhorted him to put his own needs first, then told him what a selfish prick he was. The voice that on a rooftop whispered Jump. Here is the demon he has wrestled all his life. The enemy he has come to protect because he believes that to exorcise it is to tamper with the engine that drives his art. The imagined creature manifest and sitting across from him in a filthy boxcar on a rocking Hellbound train. And the face it wears is Niko's own.

The desecrated face smiles as Niko begins to understand. The ruined head nods. Acknowledging his acceptance. Their tacit communion.

Niko snorts and ducks his head. His demon grins.

Niko looks up at him again and nods back. His demon laughs and nods back. Niko laughs too, finally, with the finality of understanding. What else is there to say? They're twins after all, however out of true the likeness. The moment hangs unspoken in the boxcar air.

Soon they quiet down and listen to the locomotive's soulhulling horn whistling in the dark while it ferries its load of misery and pain farther into the territory of despair. A cargo seeking mercy from creatures without conscience. Finally Niko nods again as if the iron language of the train has spoken to him in a primitive and private tongue and he regards the demon, his demon, sitting patiently before him.

"You're taller than I imagined."

His demon laughs and Niko follows. The train screams boastful oblivion. Many miles away, mulchosaurs glance up from their gut-strewn prey and scream replies to the iron challenge shrieked across the tortured air beneath the world.

From the folds of its wings Niko's demon produces a bottle. Sealed cap, white letters on black label. "I believe you dropped this." He leans forward and holds the bottle out.

Niko takes the whiskey from him. "I believe you're right," he says, and breaks the longshut seal.

A HUNGRY TRAIN howls down the gloom and feeds its pace by eating souls on rails set in the poisoned land like stitches in a rotting wound while Niko takes the offered drink and smoky liquid floods a tunnel decades dry. His demon nods approval as the man drinks from the bottle and the trainhorn blows an aching note as his charge on a Hellfound train falls off the wagon like an ousted angel.

Down the hatch the demon says in Niko's voice.

Lookin at ya Niko toasts. He holds the whiskey in his mouth expecting that his throat will clamp and when it doesn't lets the liquor trickle down his throat and waits. No pounding skull no clenching gut no breaking sweat. A faint but not unpleasant burn of smoky liquid in his mouth.

He swallows. His eyes tear up, his face turns red, he feels he's going to sneeze. But it has always felt like this or worse.

"Like falling off a bike," his demon says.

"Or a wagon." He lifts the bottle one more time but hesitates.

"Go ahead. The second stroke won't make you more unfaithful than the first."

But Niko bangs the bottle on the rocking floor and watches amber liquid sloshing with the freightcar's motion. "So," he tells the bottle. "You're back."

"Sort of."

"Sort of. What's that mean?"

"I'm back but not the way you think."

"No shit, Sherlock. Now if I want to wrestle you I can do it with my hands."

His demon's smile grows fond. "Not what I meant, bud."

"Don't call me that." Niko grabs the bottle up and takes that second swig and does not see his demon's look of undiluted pleasure.

"Let me deal you some cards here, buddy pal. One, a cute little succubus clamped onto your leg like a horny little poodle dog. Two, a toasty fire inside a comfy little igloo. Three, two lovenotes in your own crappy handwriting, Exhibit A sealed in a bottle of Tennessee's finest, Exhibit B delivered via Greek Express."

"You wrote the notes."

"No shit, Sherlock. And built the igloo. And made the fire. And knocked that little sucker off your leg."

"But why."

A helpless shrug. The ravaged face wears something sad and tender now. The demon wraps his wings about him as if cold and now it's his turn to stare bleakly at the whiskey bottle. "Because, you poor fuckedup loser," he tells the bottle, "I love you."

PITCHFORKED DEMONS STOKE the famished engine with a coke of anguished souls. Niko in the stifling boxcar feels the old familiar fuse burn in his belly and he looks away from his own demon swaying with the boxcar's languid motion. He senses the demon's embarrassment and feels embarrassed for him.

"It's an occupational hazard," his demon says. "Sometimes we get a little too fond of the thing we're decimating."

Niko slides his guitar case between himself and his demon.

"See, I'm part of you. Which means I'm also partly you. Mostly you never needed me. Did you know that? Mortals often don't. You undo yourselves just fine without us. But sometimes you flog yourselves right up to the brink and then just stand there wavering. That's where we come in." He mimes a little push with S-shaped tendrils.

Niko undoes the catches and raises the lid and stares into the case like a man at the funeral of an old lover. He takes another swig of booze. Three old friends getting reacquainted on a train. Can I have a hallelujah.

"But it's hard to watch you do it to yourselves and not feel sympathy for you poor bastards. We get to know you so damn well. It's our job. And to understand is to forgive, right? So even while we push you just that final bit it hurts."

Niko exhumes the Dobro from its case and slides the metal tube over his ring finger.

"You think you need us to keep you angry. Keep you producing. You defend us even when you know we're out to get you. You think we're part of you. Somewhere inside. Well, that works both ways buddy pal. Mostly when we feel the urge to help you out we just ignore it and go on and do our job. But sometimes we sink your boat and then throw you a line. We can't help it. I mean there you are floundering around in hot water you usually boiled yourselves, and we ought to be laughing our ass off at how easy you make it for us, and then this little voice inside us says Hey, why don't you give the poor schmuck a break, and next thing you know we've thrown you a line and we're hauling you in." The demon shrugs and looks a little sad. "That little voice is you. Sometimes you're our demons."

Still not saying anything Niko holds his empty hand out and his demon wraps the bottle with a tendril and offers it. As Niko drinks his demon watches like a voyeur at an orgy.

Niko holds the bottle out and meets his demon's eye. His demon takes it back and takes a long hard gurgling pull and then recaps the bottle and sets it sloshing on the clacking floor beside the guitar case. He grins at Niko brighteyed and belches satisfaction. Smells of liquor, lighting matches.

Niko tunes the steel guitar. The watching demon shivers at approaching harmony. Some dread resolution.

Niko shuts his eyes and hears the train. Feels the rocking. Finds a rhythm. Lets it move his fingers on the metal strings. The Dobro cries.

Out there in the peopled abyss demons pause their endless nail-gun crucifixions as a dark refrain comes from the passing boxcar rocking gently as it rolls beyond their stations of the cross. Pinioned souls allowed a brief and unplanned respite moan and twist in parody of sexual release as this sad dopplered lullaby weeps out across the neverending night.

As his fingers play the trainsong Niko realizes that the locomotive horn is blowing rhythmic harmony to take the top part of the melody he improvises in a plaintive slow and unarticulated speech from disenfranchised nations crying out its cureless loss.

He opens his eyes.

The trainhorn stops when tendrils lower from a leathern mouth.

Niko mutes the metal strings and lets the train conduct itself to iron down the flattened plain. The demon grins a feral grin and bangs its bony hip to knock hot spit from the harmonica that gleams between its snakelike tendrils. Not a trainhorn then.

Fascinated Niko hugs the Dobro while his demon blows a high downbending chord that finds the trainbeat in its motion and before he knows it Niko's strumming long and sheeting heartbreak chords above that wailing harp. Chords that hover dip and glide like gulls above a churning ocean. Whiskey humming in his veins. Music's in your blood they say.

The soultrain groans along its iron fate, tie and spike and rail and wheel. Niko in a drunk duet upon a midnight special of his lost soul's forging. Who he is has led to where he goes as surely as the route on which he runs, tie spike rail wheel, tracks as damning as the ones that once had mapped his arm and leading to the same conclusion.

He keeps his eyes closed and plays on and while he plays his demon talks. "Here's the trick, buddy pal, here's the rub. I remove some obstacles and you think that I'm helping you." The slide sobs high up on the Dobro's neck. "That's why I'm just like you. That's why I'm torn." Grounds the crying on the bottom string. "I want you to succeed. See? I want to watch you get away with this." Arpeggios his doubt. "Because when I help it shoves you right into the mouth of it. You make it easy for me. I want to thank you and I want to kick your ass." Lets a held chord bleed while reaching blindly for the bottle. Feels it pressed into his hand. Drinks deep and holds the bottle out and feels it taken. Winces not uncomfortably at the little detonation in his gut. Hello old friend. "But here's the grand prize question. What will you do when you get there?"

Niko mutes the strings and lets the trainsong play unaccompanied. Measure for measure, tie spike rail wheel. "What do you mean?"

"I mean when you get to where you're going and it's time for you to walk the walk how are you going to fuck it up?"

A clatter from ahead goes through them and behind them as the train runs over piles of bones.

"Who says I'm going to fuck it up?"

"You've never done anything but. It's the nature of the soul who lives in you. He ruins his life, he comes down here, he screws the pooch. Over and over, life after life. You know why? Cause he's a fuckup, that's why. It's that simple."

"Fuck you."

"You fucked up club gigs when you were just starting out because you were using. You fucked up every time you tried to sober up or kick."

"That was a long time ago."

"It's fair to say what happened to your baby brother was a fuckup don't you think?"

"Shut up."

"Why? You've heard all this for years. I'm just saying it out loud this time. You fucked up every band you were in so much you had to hire session players on your albums and tours. And how about Jemma, old buddy old pal? El Fuckuppo Grande. What, you think being rich and famous keeps you from being a loser? You've got assloads of cash, you're famous as shit, and you fucked up your whole life. You always have. So why in the world should I doubt you're gonna fuck up again?"

Niko hugs the Dobro with his eyes clenched shut. He thought his demon had defected, jumped ship to help him on his sorry way. Why is he doing this to him now?

But let's be honest, buddy pal. Something inside you wants to hear all this. Something believes every word this son of a bitch says. Always believed it. Isn't that why you shot up, why you drank? To shut him up or build a wall to shut him out. But all it ever really did was shut you in there with him. Like you're in here with him now. Tie spike rail wheel. Soulmates, cellmates, oneman show. He can't help himself, he's what he is. We are who we are. It's that simple.

Niko puts the guitar away and shuts the latches on the case. His demon's brighteyed scrutiny. He sits there still a moment, sad hand on the black case remembering Jemma's hand. He reaches for the bottle and the bottle meets him halfway. He sips and cranes his neck and swallows loudly. Lets the bottle go. It doesn't hit the floor.

Listening to his demon guzzle Niko stands unsteadily. Bends to pick up the case and nearly falls. Stumbles to the door and slides it open and leans the case against the wall and stands with one hand clutching the edge of the door and watches the protean blackness gliding by. That voice inside him whispers Jump. Still inside him whispering even as its embodiment sits drinking across from him on the filthy wooden floor of the clacking train. Like staring at a cancer growth cut from your galbladder yet still feeling its hard protrusion beneath your belly. It doesn't end, it never ends, it never goes away, however much of it may surface in the world.

"I used to drop acid," Niko says to the metastasizing dark. "Long time ago. Not really my drug. There'd always be a moment where things seemed right at the edge of turning bad. You'd look at things, even the air, and it all wanted to erupt and decay and rot. Jemma used to tell me you had to remember that you were the one driving. You had to be able to point at something going rotten and say And now it's not. And it worked. It really did." He laughs and shakes his head. "And now it's not. It's like being a kid and believing you can point at something and make it disappear."

"It's a beautiful story, Niko."

Niko turns and glares. Three sheets to the wind on the floor of Hell. He points his finger at the demon like the barrel of a gun. Delighted and surprised his demon barks a laugh and pats himself with snaking tendrils and then shrugs and shakes his head. "Still here."

Niko nods. "Still here." He picks up the guitar case from where it's propped uncertainly against the swaying wall. "And now I'm not," he says. And jumps.

XIX

ROADHOUSE BLUES

NIKO PASSES ON INTO THE fabled dark. The plain is black and empty now, a starless void through which he staggers like a blind man groping, ignorant of the shape and substance of the world around him and the possibility he creates it with his every step. The scarred guitar case clutched in his uncertain hand the only thing outside himself to hold. The ground beneath his hiking shoes is solid but he cannot see it or even hear a footfall. See him from on high with a dark-adapted eye, a small blot struggling against emptiness.

A struggling blot with its first hangover in twentyfive years. And oh is it a stellar event. Every flutter of his torn and filthy jacket flails his eardrums. His scalp is wet leather tightening as it dries creaking across his skull. His entire body has a migraine. Gravity alters as he walks.

He shuts his eyes, for all the difference it makes here in the heart of the abyss, and pinches hard on the bridge of his nose. Roman candles explode inside his eyelids. He chews skin on the inside of his cheek to make the little pains distract him from the larger ones. His world and mind are narrowed on the object of his quest. Jemma hovers now at the edge of consciousness numinous as angels are said to be and become for him as mythic. Her existence somewhere up ahead the evidence of things unseen. Her captive soul's light seen through eyes of faith. Something to believe in. At last. At last.

He lowers his hand from his nose and opens his eyes and blinks. It seems out on the plain he sees a shape that's blacker than its dark surround. He stares into the unremitting dark and tries to mark what form lies out there brooding.

Niko stops walking.

How did I get here?

He glances behind him. Little difference that he can see. An empty unlit stage awaiting props. Hadn't he been on a train? Playing his guitar and singing? Drinking Jack Daniel's and getting stinking drunk with his demon?

A ravaged leathery version of his own face looms in memory and grins to show yellowed needle teeth. His demon?

Had it been a hallucination? I mean you were pretty drunk there buddy pal.

And where'd that whiskey come from in the first place?

A leathery tendril wrapped around the neck of an offered bottle of Tennessee's finest. Okay, not a hallucination. Your own personal demon. And you got drunk with the damned thing. You played the Dobro while it blew the harmonica for Christ's sake there in a stifling freightcar rattling down the gullet of your very ruin. Oh he remembers that all right. Smoking again. Drinking again. Hanging out with lowlifes. What's next?

But of course we all know what's next. Don't we buddy pal? What looms like the Empire State Building on our personal landscape of addiction.

But how has he gotten here? When had he left the train and how? It's as if he has been walking in his sleep and suddenly awakened, the only evidence of his drunken transit with his demon on the train a few blurry mental photographs and a bruised chest and the mother of all hangovers.

The train. His demon. Drinking. Jamming. An argument. And he'd jumped off the train? Yeah that's right. Took a deep breath that smelled of iron and hot oil and grabbed the guitar case and hesitated at the opened doorway and then jumped. Flying a whole minute it seemed with the wind hot in his face and his jacket fluttering like a broken bird. The train a churning juggernaut beside him. The sudden openthroated howl of horn. He had waited for the fist of ground to punch the life out of him. And then. And then.

And then a sudden scrape of shoes upon the unseen plain. As if he were merely gliding across the causeless dark. He literally hit the ground running and he tripped and tumbled and the guitar case flew off to clatter loudly as he rolled to a stop. And then?

And then nothing. He'd drunkenly examined his cuts and scrapes and bruises and he'd found his guitar case, and with it once more in hand he had started following the railroad tracks.

Niko resumes his long downtending walk and heads toward the distant shape that's darker than the black around it.

I should be dead. Or at least lying beside the railroad tracks with broken legs and shattered ribs. Bleeding internally and trapped inside the coffin of my ruined body waiting for my life and thoughts to wind down to a stop like the last ticks on a forgotten watch. That train had been going sixty, seventy miles an hour. You don't walk away from a jump like that.

Had his demon somehow helped him?

Niko doubts it. It seems more likely that his demon drove him toward it.

Then how had he survived? Just plain old good luck? I don't think so, Cisco. No one's that lucky.

He glances up.

The lidded sky.

AS HE NEARS the waiting soulless shape he feels a thrumming deep within his chest. The purring of a predator asleep and dreaming of the hunt. The shape is tall as a building but asymmetrical and set about with curves as if halfmelted. There is no light to see it by yet see it Niko does. The shape itself emits a kind of black light that registers beneath vision the way some stars are only seen by looking away from them. When Niko looks away from the towering shape it leaves a violet smear and a bitter taste of lead. His fillings ache and his skull resonates with that awful thrum. In wary awe he walks around the radiating shape and as he does he sees that he's approached it from behind. Here is the front.

It's not a building. It's a sculpture. Standing on the empty plain the giant naked figures of a man and woman hugging. Arms sunk into one another's sculpted flesh. Her face turned up toward his turned down. Their faces where they kiss are fused. Features indistinct like artist's dummies. Caught halfmelted into one another as if petrified by nuclear detonation at the moment of their embrace. Pompeiian lovers unearthed from the foot of Vesuvius. Horrible and beautiful they loom above his faithless pilgrim gaze.

He falls to his knees before their silent reproach.

The forlorn silence lying hard about the plain.

The train. He remembers the argument now. "When you get to where you're going and it's time for you to walk the walk how are you going to fuck it up?" The most terrible thing about his demon has never been his goading or persuasion but his unrelenting truth. Here is the thing you cannot run from. That no leap leaves behind. No drug or music silences. The irreducible particle of truth: you fuck up everything. You killed your brother. You killed Jem. Traded her for fame. For money. Sold her for a song.

And the wall around his heart gives way at last. It falls without a last defense and Niko pitches forward and cries out. His heart a redhot coal. It hurts so bad that he must surely die. What have I done. What have I done. She is gone. Jem is gone.

Niko sobs before the silent reproach of entwined lovers. Pounds the barren ground with balled scabbed fists.

Gone. The word an anchor on his penitent soul. Jemma is dead. Really dead.

We are mayflies all. We live we love we die. And you have hastened even that. Her face. Her touch. Her voice. Her life. All gone. Taken from the world too soon because of you. Jemma died, and you put on your hiking shoes and left to rescue her from death itself like some damned christ. Came down here to win her back into the daylit world. Who are you fucking kidding? Who do you think you are? You're not going to weasel out of this one. Someone who could sell his soul out for a song is not going to play his heart out to the buyer and reverse the natural order of the world. She's not some carnival prize, hit the devil and win the girl, oh I messed it up this time, here's another dollar. She is dead. And you are on your knees within the heart of all damnation because you are not enough to win her back. Because you are going to lose. You have already lost. Have always lost. You have fought your way across this afflicted plain armed with nothing more than vanity. The arrogance that you can turn back the tide. That your talent, will, determination, love amount to anything at all against the immutable boundary of death itself.

Jemma is dead. Abandon your hope. Let it go. Let go.

Hope falls from him like a scab.

HALF AN HOUR later Niko lifts his face from the plain and rubs his swollen eyes. A certain calmness wells from deep inside and spreads across him. He shuts his eyes again and rubs his throbbing forehead and then looks around the plain. Just the darkness, just the darker duolith rearing entangled before him. He notes his steady breathing. Sees his hand grab up the guitar case. Sees his body stand. Rides along as it limps to the statue's base. He turns his back on the lovers and slumps against them and blows his nose on his ragged coatsleeve. Counts ten deep even breaths. All right. Okay. Well what now? Turn back?

Niko laughs. And fight your way back as far as you have come with not a thing to show? The old riddle, what's the farthest you can go into the forest?

Halfway.

I'm so tired. God I'd love some coffee. Hell, I'd sell my soul for a cup of—

Tortured stone begins to creak against his back. Niko scrambles to his feet and cranes upward to see the giant forms elongating, stone like taffy stretching. For a dizzy moment Niko feels that he and the plain are sinking and he falls backward and lands on his tailbone. The stretching stone splinters and branches out to angle and stab down like spiderlegs. Niko backpedals and gazes up in awe and fear. The warm ground rumbles and the blighted air aches with moans of stretching stone. A vast shape rises on the barren plain. The fossil skeleton of some unimagined beast long dead now being given up by the very earth that housed it across the countless centuries. For a gibbering insane instant Niko thinks it is a living creature, some mindless voracious thing sent forth to fetch him to his long appointed doom. But as it coheres he sees it is the solid and imposing framework of a building extruding from the ground like something loudly growing from a magic beanstalk. Rising dark before him it joins growing bone to growing bone to form girder and arch and joist and wall, ledge and window and column and door. It settles creaking with its own weight like a wooden ship and for a moment it sits whole and still and blank and hollow before him, a gaunt dark cathedral. Then from out the formless darkness beaded colored lights rain upward in entwining strands that swirl across the building's face. A steady hum grows with the flashing light. Machinery. Electricity.

Now across the stone facade are coruscating lights that flash a spade, a club, a diamond, a heart. Motion on the glass entryway is no longer reflected light but activity within.

Niko turns to look behind him. Black air and empty plain, lidded sky and no horizon. He turns back.

A casino stands complete before him. Light smears the entryway as a door opens and a uniformed valet comes out to take up station in the empty driveway. He adjusts his ridiculous little cap and stands with hands clasped before him, dignified and patient and absurd.

A carhorn blares and startles Niko nearly senseless. He whirls, fists raised, and squints at approaching headlights. A white slab-sided 1968 Cadillac DeVille fourdoor hardtop sedan roars toward him and swerves at the last second and shoots past. Glimpse of fat man grinning lewdly as he gestures with a fat cigar while a jowly woman holding his arm laughs meanly. The Caddie pulls up to the casino and the valet helps the corpulent woman out. The driver joins the woman and blows cigar smoke in the valet's face. The valet drives the car away as the casino door opens for the couple and they enter and do not look back. As the Caddie pulls away the valet's exact twin walks out of the casino and stands at the curb with hands clasped before him, dignified, patient, absurd.

Niko heads toward the island of light here in the middle of nothing. The valet flicks his gaze at Niko's weary impoverished approach and his posture stiffens. He does everything but say Hmmph.

Niko doesn't give a ratsass. All he wants to do now is see this thing through and make the motions and say his lines and let the curtain fall. He makes for the entrance and has every intention of pushing on into the final stage of his little drama without a backward glance, but

filling the view before him

oozing across the entrance glass

like a timelapse film of growing cancer

on distorting panes and metal frames

a black reflection slides

a black reflection of a car

a black reflection of a 1933 Franklin Model 173 seven passenger sedan.

Niko turns in time to see it glide up to the curb like a docking submarine. To hear the purring engine die and see the lights go dark. Niko turns and always turns to see the brakelights die as a leather wingtip shoe lifts off the pedal, always turns to fight the story he enacts, turns to thwart the hammer of tyrannic myth that nails him to his fate, turns to see a driver's door open and close with a solid heavy chunk, to see a black cap with a glossy bill over evershadowed eyes deep in a paperskinned and jaundiced face, turns to see a pale thin hand hold up a sealed glass jar.

XX

HOOCHIE
COOCHIE MAN

DUMBLY NIKO WATCHES THE DRIVER approach. It can't be this easy. Not after all this.

And of course it isn't. Weary and heartsore as Niko is he braces himself for some conflict but the Driver heads toward the casino entrance cradling the mason jar and spares him not the slightest glance. As the Driver passes by him with that tightly lidded jar in bony hand he sees that held within and glowing not at all is not a blacktipped feather but a lump of coal. Not Jemma but some other purloined soul.

Niko stays whatever provocation or obstruction might have welled up from within. However much he loathes and fears the sallow son of a bitch the Driver is still just a delivery boy. Do you want to spend what little you have left in you on the thing that brought Jemma here or on getting Jemma herself?

Follow him then. See where our delivery boy delivers.

The valet nods at the Driver but makes no move to park the Black Taxi as his twin had parked the Cadillac. No one but the

Driver drives the Black Taxi. The Driver ignores the valet and strides past the huge glass doors that open before him and pulls the jar a little closer as he enters the casino.

Niko takes a deep breath and starts after him but then he stops. Looks back at the car. Oh no way. It's too obvious.

Nonetheless he follows his hunch and walks to the Black Taxi and hoods his eyes and peers through the driver's side window. Nope, nothing there. Niko gropes beneath the left front fender. Nope. He tries left back and right back and right front and son of a bitch there it is. A rectangular magnetic keyholder stuck to the underside of the fender. He shakes it and a key rattles.

Niko laughs bitterly and looks up at the godless sky and spreads his arms. Almost a parody of crucifixion. If he'd thought to look for a spare key outside the gate however long ago he might have simply driven here.

He drops the keyholder into the inner breast pocket of his jacket and then turns toward the coruscating light and glitter of the big casino, astonished that his heart is not pounding, that his hand is dry on the hardcase handle, that his breathing's even. Either he's too numb to care any longer or there's nothing left inside him that will risk it.

His way is blocked and he looks up to see the valet frowning down. He steps aside and the valet steps with him. He sighs. The valet nods at the guitar case in Niko's hand. "Back door, chief." He jerks a thumb that way and looks through Niko and loudly chews his spearmint gum.

Niko sizes him up indifferently, then sets down the guitar case and moves to step past him. The expected hand comes up. Niko grabs it and ducks under it and turns clockwise with it and folds it down. The pop of dislocating elbow echoes in the driveway. Still twisting the arm Niko brings the wrist down to the pavement. The valet follows until his shoulder lands on the back of his own hand. His eyes are wide. His mouth works like a gaffed bass. Niko straightens and picks up the guitar case and steps past him. The doors open for him automatically. Ye who enter.

LIGHT AND SOUND envelop him. Polyglot hubbub and cries of pain, flashing neon and shattering glass, ringing bells and howling laughter, strobing lights and screeching brakes, striking klaxons and consumptive coughs, whirling gears and baying hounds, growling buzzers and screaming children, rattling dice and yowling cats, shuffled cards and cocking guns, clicking roulette wheels and churning tank treads, chuckling chips and ticking bombs, keno chimes and funeral bells, clapping hands and cracking whips, payoff gongs and marching jackboots, croupiers calling and rifle bolts clacking, tinny lounge music and air raid sirens, ringing coins and murmured treasons, roaring ovens and crackling ice swirled in glasses of smoky liquor. Smells of beer and cheap perfume and cigarettes and money and hideous endless desperate need.

The casino stretches off as far as he can see. Thick corinthian columns recede to infinity. A nicotine pall hangs on the sickly air. A constant rush of furious and pointless activity swarms like a stomped anthill. The floor is plush carpet, hunter green with a florentine pattern in burgundy and cream. Columns and walls are white marble veined in pale blue. The carpet fiber Niko treads is woven human ganglia, nervous systems of the tortured damned. The pale blue veins in the marble walls and columns are human veins once pumping blood but surging now with burning lye. Stretching off for miles are banks of slot machines run by naked patrons seated on the upturned mouths of slavering creatures slowly gnawing them to bloody gobbets. The damned are fused to their machines, right wrist merging with the arm of the one armed bandit and pulling, ever pulling, no scrap of humanity or personality remaining as their flickering consciousness focuses on the whirling bars, all their remnant being fixed upon the hope of one two three whirling eyes. Every millennium or so the eyes align and sweet relief comes as the monster beneath them ceases chewing for a solid minute. The only pleasure here the absence of pain. The eyes on the whirling bars are blinking and alive.

Tuxedoed demons of many shapes and sizes stride about like hurried maitres d' and snap their fingers or claws or tentacles and fire off orders to misshapen dwarves who push preposterously laden carts past fishnet stockinged women wearing posture collars and tottering on nine inch heels while balancing huge drink trays crammed to overflowing.

Some tables hold demons, others imprison bleary desperate alcoholics chained to hard and angular chairs to order drinks that never come. At one table holding several dozen demons a waitress with eyes so sunken her face looks like a skull takes down orders as fast as she can write. One Coke with a cherry, one Diet Coke no cherry, one Cherry Coke with a cherry, one Diet Cherry Coke no cherry, one Coke with a lemon slice, one Lemon Coke, one Lemon Slice with a slice of lime, one Diet Lemon-Lime Slice with a cherry. And no ice on that Lemon Coke, hon.

Haggard waitresses of all ages and sizes and races queue before a brassrailed bar that stretches to a distant vanishing point and call out orders to gaunt and wide eyed bartenders who move as fast as they can to fill orders that will never stop or even slow.

One walleyed waitress turns away with a laden tray hoisted to her bony shoulder. She gets five yards before a demon sticks out a hoof and trips her. Tray and contents fly and mindless alcoholics strain their chains to suck spilled liquor from the living carpet. The tortured filament nervous system develops a fuzzy buzz. The little demon who tripped the waitress orders her to clean it up and fetch another round. The eternally harangued waitress bends to obey and passes out from the posture collar as a demon at a nearby table licks her nylon covered ass with a slobbering tongue.

Variations on this scene are repeated everywhere Niko looks. The din is deafening. It feels so strange to be indoors and in the light after all this unknown time.

Now a tuxedoed demon all angles and propriety strides toward him, rapier nose cutting the dense air and his expression a per-petual snit. He stops before Niko and eyes him up and down and glares at the guitar case. He shoots his cuffs and actually sniffs. "And where do we think we're going?"

Niko lifts the guitar case slightly. "Gig."

"I suggest we take a less conspicuous route."

"I'm here to play for the boss."

"Aren't we all?"

"You tell me where to find him?"

"If we don't know where to find him we certainly have no business seeing him."

Niko wants to argue but Snit here is right, when you think about it. "Got a point there," he says, and turns away and walks among the tortured throng who cry out not for aid or comfort but simply to give voice to their despair. Past hope past want past care. The farther in he goes the thicker Niko feels. Detached from self and surround. The cacophony become distant sussuration. Eyelids heavy. Feet hovering above the living carpet. Skin thick and itchy. All about a hollow echo like a giant transit terminal at rush hour looked at through a lens of fever dream. Guitar case a dead weight in his nerveless hand a thousand miles away. These sensations naggingly familiar. Maybe just exhaustion. But no. No. Something else. Something elusive. Like the unrecalled name of a former lover. Memory on tip of tongue awaiting utterance to fix it in the world.

Fix.

Niko stops amid the seething ruin of souls. He stares unseeing and listens to that old peaceful whisper suffuse into his mind like friendly fog. Like an old habit, yes?

Niko grips the case's handle harder. His free hand brushes his locket as he moves to scratch and scratch his collarbone.

What you gonna do boy? You gonna shrug off a rush? Gonna jump this train?

Nope dont think so. Nothing to be done for it now. In for the longhaul. Rollercoasters left the starting gate and seatbelts come undone. Clack clack clack. Niko has left the building. Ride it out. Let it ride the highrollers say. Ride the white horse.

He shakes his head and gapes around the casino. Blur he fix recedes on tunnel down carpet footed ground, headed sky. place ace yer bets ets. faraway walls, jackpot bingo snake eyes craps, round and round she goes, just move a foot, just one. i gobble dug dare you.

A battered filthcaked hiking shoe slides forward. Now the other one. Just keep doing that. One foot in front of the other. That's the ticket.

Looking only at the floor he makes his thickened way. Just walk. Don't look up. Don't listen. Just walk. He pictures his slack body on his living room floor in the Hollywood Hills. Empty syringe nearby. Someone faraway slapping his face. Come on bud stay with me hang in there breathe.

How could he have been dosed? Cause that's sure as shit what's happening. He's rushing like a dog with its head out the window of a Ferrari. That old familiar glow heating up his veins. Each thought like a card in an evershuffled deck, lost and unremembered as the next one comes along. He hears down a narrow tube. Sees through the big end of the binoculars. Feels over a bad phone connection. Wants to sleep. Maybe is.

What's worse is the awful happy familiarity of it. As if his body's cells contain a memory of his leaden junky days and now they're pricking up their ears and standing on hind legs to bark and yap for more.

It would be so good to just sit down. To lie back and sink into the carpet. Sink into the floor. Through the floor. The ground. Past mantle. Past magma. Down deep. Down to bask in Hell itself. Down.

NIKO'S HEAD JERKS up. Shit. How long?

Around him the awful traffic flows, the roaring din continues. Always flows, always roars.

Fight it god damn it. After all this battle with the outside world will you finally be laid out by a little pinch of chemicals in your veins? You need to move. You need to keep moving.

Come on Hiking Boy, get them shoes in gear. Walk.

AFTER A TIME he couldn't estimate Niko realizes he is staring down at his unmoving feet. What's the deal? He orders his left foot to move but it stays where it is. He orders his right foot to move and it stays rooted too. Niko frowns. His thoughts are congealed gelatin. A slug exudes a slime trail in his brain. His ears ring.

He glances up. He's looking down a corridor paneled in mahogany. He frowns and glances at the deepgreen carpet. When he looks up again he's standing at the end of the corridor and staring stupidly at the woodpaneled wall with no memory of having walked here. The casino tumult left behind.

Niko turns to look back down the length of the corridor and jumps when he sees someone turning toward him a few feet away. This man jumps too. The man is bearded gaunt and strange eyed. Long hair matted and grayshot. Filthy jacket shredded and frayed.

Jeans blown out at knees and ass. Clothes all mottled with filth and shit and blood dried brown. Pale skin bruised and scabbed and scraped and draping from the skeleton that wears it. The knuckles of both hands swollen and arthritic. His ragged beard is streaked with gray and his face is purely haunted. The expression of a sole survivor of some epic rout. A patch of scar across his forehead. Recently broken nose healed out of true. He looks old and tired and sore abused.

Niko drops his guitar case and the man drops his guitar case. Niko is facing a mahogany wall dominated by a tall mirrored door where a moment ago there was a corridor.

Niko silently regards the silent mirror's gaunt inspection. But for the filthy beard his face is nearly that of his demon self on board the train. Every painful step of his descent etched there. A strange flat light of calm acceptance in the dark unblinking eyes. Long past surprise or horror. Some mad prophet gone into the desert looking for his god and come back having found him terribly.

To the mirror's left a lone round button. ☋ He's in an elevator. Beside him his guitar case. Battered and scarred and stained and filthy, ancient faithful bloodhound still and patient on the floor. All right. Okay.

Niko reaches out a hand. Beyond the mirror's border his and his reflection's fingers meet unseen and push the single button and the button lights. A faint suck of air drawn into an enormous long wet fleshy throat. Niko's stomach floats. He jumps up and his reflection leaves the floor and takes too long to come back down. Apart from the hollow in his stomach and a strange tight feeling in his balls there's no other indication of the car's plummet. He can sense it though. The deepening earth around him.

Cool air softly blows and cheesy Muzak plays from unseen speakers overhead. It takes a while for him to recognize the Muzak as attenuated versions of his own work.

He sighs, he stands, he waits.

Twenty minutes later the elevator still drops. Niko leans back against the wall and wearily slides down until he's sitting beside his guitar as a Muzak version of Roll the Bones from his first album with Perish Blues begins. Christ. He shuts his eyes. He dreams he's sitting on the leather couch of his Hollywood Hills living room. Beside him Van reads the Sunday paper. He's still dead but it's okay. Niko asks Have you finished the sports section? and Van hands it over. Niko says Thank you but somehow it is understood he means I love you and I miss you. Van nods absently and searches for the funnies.

Niko wakes up crying. The elevator still drops. Niko has to piss. An hour later he has no choice and pisses in the corner. The Muzak plays. Niko sits beside his guitar case and caresses the scarred curves. He thinks of taking out the Dobro and strumming some sad old tunes but doesn't. He'll either be playing along with the Muzak or against it. Either way he wants no part of it. And to be honest he's a bit afraid to play right now. Swollen knuckles and unsteady hands. He's coming down from his rush and he's got the shakes. It only took one fix. He's sweating like a lathered horse. The Muzak's driving him insane. The elevator drops.

All that day, assuming it is day, he paces in the elevator and clears his throat and spits and blows his nose. He tries stretching out to ease the fidgets and avoids the wet spot in the corner. He studies his reflection and makes faces and flips himself off. He sings along with the Muzak. His stomach cramps. He dryheaves. He takes a tortured nap and is grateful not to dream. The elevator drops.

Niko wakes with chapped lips and growling stomach. The elevator reeks. He's thirsty and he's hungry. But he no longer wants a fix either, so that's something. Always looking on the bright side, that's me. He wonders if this is the private hell that has awaited him. Trapped forever in an elevator listening to Muzak versions of his own music. At one point he tries to pry open the mirrored door, to no avail. Probably best.

He's counting hairs on the back of his hands when some change in sound and motion makes him look up. He feels heavier as he struggles to his feet and presses his back against the wall. He shuts his eyes and feels for changes in the elevator's motion. A soft chime sounds and he opens his eyes. The down button is no longer lit. His knees buckle with returning weight as the elevator slows and stops. He watches himself watching. No fear and neither arrogance. Not impatient but not calm. He looks like someone begging at the back door. Well, that's what I am. Sing for my supper.

The door glides open and wipes him away. He looks out on an executive office, Danish Modern with high ceilings, lots of right angles. Well-appointed in muted gray and russet with teal accents and brightly lit in afternoon sunlight streaming in from the lightly tinted glass that takes up all the back wall. Basking in the sun outside the window is Los Angeles.

The view is from on high and facing south. Niko sees the tangled bands of Harbor, Golden State, and Santa Monica freeways. Something wrong though. To his left stands the ranked array of downtown skyscrapers through which he was ferried by the Checker Cab, chasing Jem a life ago it seems. Library Tower rises pale green above the other buildings. In the distance straight ahead lies the long geometry of LAX. Beyond it angled coastline. Past that he can even see the outline of Catalina Island. In the middle distance the miniature downtown of Century City, and immediately before him Beverly Hills. But to the right are the Hollywood Hills, the three domes of the Griffith Observatory, the crooked teeth of the Hollywood sign. He shouldn't be able to see all of this at once from the same window. And certainly not from this high up.

No cars on the freeways. No motion on the streets. No toy planes stacked up for LAX approach. No street traffic or police helicopters. Ten million people gone.

Nonetheless as Niko looks out on his adopted city a sudden knife of homesickness slides between his ribs. I want to wake up in our bed with Jem beside me. I want to make her a cup of that nasty lapsang souchong tea she drinks. I want to be stuck in traffic on the 405. I want to hear the breaking waves on Malibu and watch the sun sink toward Japan. The living map of half his life is spread before him, so unexpected and heartbreakingly real that Niko simply stares until nearby motion brings him back.

Behind a curved executive desk is a black leather swivel chair, and Niko has a moment as the chair turns toward him to discern with fevered distinction the desktop cluttered with papers, opened envelopes, Post-Its, a pencil cup holding scissors and a letter opener, stacked in and out trays, an Apple laptop, an intercom phone, a cherrywood display rack holding antique fountain pens, a placard reading THE LUCK STOPS HERE. A moment as the chair turns toward him to note the room is strident with the ticking of an unseen clock. An awful moment before the chair turns around in which he knows who he'll see sitting in it.

Niko stares at retro shades above a perfect grin. "Niko-mancer. What took you so long?"

NIKO PICKS UP his guitar case and leaves the stinking elevator. It closes silently behind him. He firms his grip and heads slowly toward the son of a bitch behind the desk. He wonders how he feels.

"Sit down, sit down." Phil waves at one of the chairs facing his desk and presses a button on his intercom and says, "Salome." A door opens and a sad abomination enters the room. Long and tan and lean and lovely, a naked pair of woman's legs strides across the plush gray carpet with a jingle of bells. The pubis is sparse haired, the wide hips end bluntly at the waistline. A silver edged glass tray rests on top. A woman sawed in half and made into furniture. The tray bears a Waterford ship's decanter filled with gently sloshing brown liquor, a matching oldfashioned glass, a matching ashtray holding a book of matches and a pack of Swisher Sweets, a baggie of white powder, a floral patterned silver teaspoon, and an antique glass hypodermic syringe with fingerloops on the barrel and plunger.

Niko stares as the human serving tray stops beside him. Several toes have silver rings. An anklet of little silver bells jingles and the liquor in the clear decanter sloshes gently with the legs' faint tremble.

"Go on," says Phil. "The whiskey was distilled at Old Oscar Pepper; the china white's uncut. The Swishers, well." He shrugs. "I've got some killer Dunhill Cabinetta Robustos over here, but to each his own. Go on, help yourself."

Niko finds he is not too exhausted or indifferent to hate. He knows Phil expects him to refuse out of pride or defiance or unwillingness to feel obligation. Instead he sets down his guitar case and pulls out a chair and sits down heavily and pours himself a stiff one and then opens the pack of Swishers. Phil watches like a man watching a woman undress for him as Niko knocks back the whiskey and lights a cigarillo and reads the matchbook cover as he smokes. Enjoy Travel Luxury on the Pennsylvania Railroad.

"People who collect those, you know what they're called?"

"Yeah, I know." The happy burning in his gut. That's the best god damned rotgut he's ever tasted and he's tasted a lot. The cigarillo, well. It still feels good. He puts the pack in his jacket pocket and is startled to feel something already there. Oh right, the magnetic keyholder.

Phil just can't take his eyes off him. "I gotta tell you, Niko-pedia, you just keep on surprising me."

Niko blows smoke Phil's way. "Makes two of us."

Phil glances at the baggie on the tray. An eyebrow raises above the rim of his shades.

Niko shakes his head. "I know when to stop."

"Do you."

Niko says nothing. He polishes off the doubleshot of whiskey and finishes his smoke. The unseen clock counts down the time. The whiskey goes to work and by the time he finishes the cigarillo he's buzzing like a bumbly bee and who the hell cares. Maybe that's the way it ought to be right here and now.

When the cigarillo is down to its final inch he stubs it out in the ashtray and looks at Phil.

The human serving tray turns and jingles from the room.

Phil watches Niko watch the legs stride off. "Perfect isn't she? You can set your drink on her and fuck her at the same time." He slaps the desk again and laughs. Sees Niko isn't going to play along and nods. "You want to get down to business I suppose."

"My business is with your boss. You're a glorified mailman."

"Well that's a little problematic, Niko-lonic."

"I don't care. You know how this all goes down."

"Oh I do indeed. It's an old song and we've all heard it a hundred times before. And after all this time and all these tries you never learn."

Niko stands to leave and Phil stands too. The air turns ugly. Niko senses that the walls and the desk and the view are all props for his benefit. That just beyond them decimating chaos lies waiting to tear through. But the game they're playing has been played enough to have become a ritual and the players myths. He is certain Phil will abide. Perhaps is even constrained to somehow.

"I'm not here to argue with you. I'm here to play for your boss."

Phil's grin is perfectly insincere. "Then let's take you to him." He steps away from his desk but then remembers something and presses the intercom. "Mr. Alighieri, push my appointments back—" he looks Niko up and down and then glances at his huge Rolex "—an hour. Got that?"

Terrible raw screams come tinny and distorted from the intercom. Phil grins at Niko as he comes around the desk. "We've got him translating Dan Brown into terza rima." He gestures at the elevator standing open for them. Niko hesitates and Phil touches his elbow. "You've got to trust me, Niko-mander. You got nowhere else to go."

Niko glances sidelong at Phil's inscrutable shades. He doesn't trust the son of a bitch as far as he could throw a fit. But Phil's right. He has nowhere else to go. He has almost literally hit bottom. In his experience what you likely find there is a shovel.

He pulls his arm from Phil's grasp and picks up his guitar and steps into the elevator. Maybe this has all been willed. Maybe as the prisoner of myth there is only one outcome and my choices matter not one bit. But I'm damned if I'll be led.

THE URINE STINK is gone. The button no longer has a down arrow but a large **B**. Phil presses it and the mirrored door closes and the car starts down. Niko and his nemesis in this small plunging room.

"Mind if I ask you something?"

Niko shrugs.

"Why do you do this to yourself? I mean it's clear to me that even you don't believe in this anymore. You're just going through the motions."

Niko stares at empty space beside his bedraggled reflection. What is there to say. What difference could it make.

Phil shrugs and looks up at the ceiling and nods. "Just curious."

The elevator slows and stops and opens onto a bright white corridor. Phil gestures after-you and Niko steps into a long white hallway set with black doors.

Phil searches his coat pockets as he walks ahead of Niko. "It's funny. These deals, these contracts. They're all sucker bets, you know that?" They stop before a featureless black door and Phil pulls out a ring of long oldfashioned iron keys. "The people who sign have the talent not to need them." Phil selects a key and inserts it into the door. "I mean, you think we give you that?" He smirks and glances at Niko. "A guy either hears the music or he doesn't. All we do—" he twists the key "—is open doors." He pushes the door and it seems to disappear as it opens in on blackness. "And you all sell out so cheap." He turns toward the room. "Hey Lou. Brought you a visitor."

Niko hears scrambling and heavy puffing and a certain rustle he has come to recognize as leather wings.

"Go ahead," says Phil. "He'll love seeing you. No one ever comes here."

"After you."

Phil grins. "You gotta have more faith, Niko-statin." He steps into the room and darkness swallows him. After a moment Niko leans his guitar case against the white wall and walks in after him. His shadow falls into the trapezoid of doorway light. All he sees is white floor unidentifiably stained and the ghost outline of Phil nearby.

Rustling wings again. Something large moves in the darkened room and by the time he registers its motion it has rushed into his little island of light and he is all enfolded by its wings. He staggers back and raises his hands to strike the reeking thing that whimpers as it holds him slobbering. It's huge and muscular and dark with skin the texture of a shark. Still holding him it slides down his body's length to kneel before him sobbing loudly. Great convulsions heave its muscled back. It cries his name in a voice that stirs dim recognition buried deep within his cells like the encoded cancer trigger that is humanity's heritage. A primordial self has argued with this voice. Nations have fallen beneath its easy guile. The strong and crumpled figure hugs Niko round the knees like a mournful child and a horntip rasps his jeans as the sorry creature turns its face up to him. Even in the scant light Niko sees the goldleaf shine of its goat eyes, the glint of tear tracks on the jetblack leather face.

Niko reaches out, he cannot stop himself, he reaches out and pats the Devil on the head.

The dark beside him laughs. "Now isn't that sweet?"

Niko cannot look away from the idiot madman grinning up at him with a cannibal's drooling mouth of sharpened teeth. "What have you done to him?"

"Me? Not a thing, Niko-lepsy. Poor bastard's crazy as a shit-house rat."

The Devil cries and cries at Niko's feet.

"It was the job. The old bat just wasn't cut out for it in the long run. It all got to him."

Niko looks toward where Phil's voice emerges from the darkness.

"Nobody did this but him. Scout's honor." He shakes his head at the pathetique before him. "He was the fairhaired boy before he got handed this gig. Never got over getting the boot. Used to pine all the time. That Milton, he had him pegged. All heart, no brain, attention span of a gnat. Took everything personal."

Niko wants to push away from the ruined glory of the abject figure before him yet he also wants to give it what mortal comfort he can provide. As the fallen god that Geryon showed him chained to the mountain had radiated patience, so this creature radiates sorrow. Infinite grief from eternal sundering, sad and passionate as a graveyard statue. And truly deeply mad.

"You want to know why your old story always played the way it did?" the disembodied voice continues. "There's your answer. Mr. Passion. Mr. Impulse Buy. Every time, you come down here and you want to make a deal. You grind away at the poor sap until he gives in and lets you play. You're so blindly hopeful and he's such a sucker for anything that lets him feel something. It's pitiful to watch. And of course your music nails him every time, because the spongehearted son of a bitch would cry if a butterfly kicked him in the head. So he hands you back that whore you just can't live without and you and Resurrection Barbie skip on out of here, Jack and Jill go up the hill like their asses are on fire. But whatever mask your punkass soul is wearing there's always a catch and it's always the same. Don't look back. Just like Lot's wife in my favorite bedtime story. Three simple words, no big deal. And even though you've committed more violations than a priest at a whorehouse to come down here, and welshed on an agreement and then even dickered a new deal, even after you get what you want but don't deserve and head on out of here, you still go right ahead and fuck the dog. Don't you, Niko-lama? You just have to look back and screw it up. You want to know why, Niko-wafer? Because you're a loser. A fuckup wetbrain hophead loser."

Niko crouching looks into mad goldleaf eyes. The Devil smiles, the Devil drools, the Devil croons his name. Niko's very soul shudders. "Well. Thanks for the newsflash." He touches the Devil's cheek and the Devil nuzzles his palm. Tears spring to Niko's eyes. Why this should be tragic he doesn't know but it is. It is. He feels he's present at the fall and plunder of some great and frightening empire. Niko firmly pats the great dark burly shoulder. The gesture of a man bidding farewell to a horse about to be put down. Gently he unfolds the shuddering wings from around his legs and unclenches the enormous hands. Stands and pulls the Devil upright. Nods up at that hopeful insane face and then turns toward the door.

"Where do you think you're going?" asks the darkness.

"To get my guitar."

"No can do, Niko-naut."

Niko stops with his back to Phil as a black flower blooms in his chest. "Crazy or not," he tells the bright white hall, "my deal is with him."

"Your deal is with whoever's in charge."

Niko looks at his shoes. They've sure covered some ground haven't they. "I thought you were just a messenger."

"We all have our public face. Don't we, Niko-modius?"

Niko turns back toward the room. The Devil huddles just beyond the doorway light. Phil's form is convoluted dark before him. "So the inmates have taken over the asylum."

"The inmates are the asylum, Niko-varitch. Always were. Let's just say there's been a corporate restructuring at the executive level since your last little venture down this way. Carpe nocturnum, and all like that."

"And you won't let me play for him. Is that it? It's all been just some big joke."

"Oh no no no. I wouldn't let you come this far for nothing. Who am I to mess with a tried and true old story? Everything's the same.

The masks may change but not the play. You'll still have your little audition. And if your music does its thing well hey. We'll hand the man his Kewpie doll. It could happen."

Mephistopheles steps into the light and smiles. "But you won't be playing to win him over. This time out you play for me."

XXI

NOTES ON HER SLEEPING

THIS TIME THE ELEVATOR'S SINGLE button bears an **L** and when it opens Niko looks out on the sterile and depopulated lobby of an office building. Phil walks briskly through the lobby without waiting for Niko, and when Niko emerges from the building blinking in the bright Los Angeles afternoon Phil is standing on the sidewalk with his hands in his pockets and looking bored. Hot dry clear late summer day. Niko begins to sweat under the first sunlight he has felt in a long long time. The air smells like nothing at all, and that is pure perfume. Niko puts his hands up to it. Wants to linger here and gape at the unbelievable fact of Los Angeles around him, a city become near mythical as the reality of Hell usurped it.

Then he sees what waits for them at the curb. "No way. Fuck you."

Phil smirks and pulls out a pack of nicotine gum. "Now now Nikotchka. I went to a lot of trouble to get just the right venue for your little show." He unwraps a stick of gum and throws the wadded wrapper to the sidewalk. "We gotta get there somehow,

Nico-rette." He folds the gum in half and puts it in his mouth and offers the pack to Niko.

Who ignores it. "If your elevator can open out on this it can open on wherever we need to go." He means to sound angry but he hears the note of desperation in his tone.

"All part of the act, Niko-matic. If you can't stand the heat." He shrugs and smacks his gum.

Niko scowls and knows he has no choice. He's come here making demands. If he wants Phil to abide by them, he'll have to accommodate Phil's whims in return. They both know he's standing on shaky ground.

Niko turns toward the curb and hoods his eyes against the glare. For a moment the only three sounds are the intermittent wind, the wet smack and pop of Phil's gum, and the subtle purr of a rare and immaculately maintained twelve-cylinder engine as the Black Taxi idles by the curb with the Driver holding open the suicide door.

THE BLACK TAXI cruises empty Sunset Boulevard in the middle of the sunny afternoon. From the spacious passenger compartment Niko looks in wonder at lighted traffic signals, storefront neon, motionless streets. Somehow Los Angeles has evacuated ten million people but left everything running as if they will return at any moment. An urban Marie Celeste. Not a car in sight. Litter-free streets. Clear air. Unnerving quiet. The only sound the deep gargle of the Franklin's engine.

Niko looks away from the window. Beside him Phil texts on his iPhone and ignores their surround. Between them lies the guitar case. There's plenty of room for it on the facing seat but Niko prefers it close at hand and between himself and Phil.

Straightbacked and unwavering the Driver steers them east through Hollywood not half a mile from where the Checker Cab pursued this very car through Friday evening traffic a thousand years ago when mortals ruled the earth. They pass the Hollywood Palladium. Amazing how fast you travel in an empty city.

Niko leans back on the leather seat. Smells of leather, lemon oil. Birdseye maple sidepanels polished to a liquid gloss. The ride quiet yet surprisingly rough. Well, fortyfive hundred pounds of car on an old leafspring suspension on illkept L.A. roads. But apart from jostling the car itself is unaffected by the world. The ridged rubber siderunners bear no hint of wear or even shoeprint. No trace of blemish mars the paint. The spotless chrome displays no pitting. The windshield glass so clear it's hard to see the frame holds glass at all. Bugless prow of huge front grille. Clear and spotless rings of whitewall tires. Beehive hinges on the suicide doors. Deep maroon upholstery pristine. Thick layered glossy paint like liquid holding shape through some miracle of surface tension. The Franklin's utter black is even more amazing in the sunlit day. They travel like a carshaped hole along the boulevard.

Niko bolts upright.

The smooth white balls of Phil's blank eyes peer over the top of his shades. "Forget something, Niko-lirium?"

Niko sits back and looks out the window. "No. Nothing. This is all just too strange, that's all." In truth he hasn't forgotten something, he's remembered something. In his coat pocket is a little box and in the little box is the spare key to this very car.

Niko tries to quell his sudden urgency. What're you gonna do, cowboy, wait'll they stop to take a leak and boost the car and drive it home? Sure your house is less than five miles from here, but look around you. This might be L.A. but it sure as hell ain't your L.A.

Nonetheless the knowledge of the spare key on his person reassures. An ace up his sleeve.

At Western they turn left and head north toward the Hollywood hills. Western hooks right to become Los Feliz Boulevard and they speed along the undulating road. Before Hillhurst Niko sees a sign and realizes where they're headed.

Phil sees the sign as well and frowns. "Aw, Niko-lizer. It was supposed to be a surprise."

The sign whips past.

← GRIFFITH OBSERVATORY
← GREEK THEATRE

Niko leans back in the seat again and shuts his eyes. "It still is. Heck, I haven't been to the observatory in years."

A long quiet pause. The Black Taxi hangs a left and begins to climb the hill in earnest. Then a hand claps Niko's thigh and a sharp barking laugh opens his eyes. "Niko-median. You had me going for a second there."

Niko turns away again. "You've had me going a lot longer than that," he tells the window.

IT ISN'T THAT the show will start soon. It's that it never stopped. Phil was right. All that changes are the masks we wear. I was born for this moment. Have been borne toward this moment many times before. Chained to the turning of the wheel. And what brings me round to this point every time, what makes the wheel turn in the first place, is my belief that I can free myself from its vicious circle.

Then why bother? What's different this time around?

In the cradle of his nemesis he rocks toward his culmination as the Franklin climbs and climbs the winding way.

Jemma. Jemma's different this time round. She doesn't belong here chained to someone else's story. She deserves better. She always did. And if I can only get her out of this it doesn't matter what becomes of me. I will have broken the circle. Sometimes victory and success are not the same.

Can you do this?

They break from the treelined residential section. Niko looks at his guitar case. In the light of day it's really beat to shit. He sets his hand upon it as if feeling for a pulse.

Phil looks up from his cellphone. "Flop sweat, Niko-star?"

Niko looks at him and marvels that he doesn't feel a thing. Out there on that empty plain he really did surrender something. "Weapons check."

THE BLACK TAXI pulls up smoothly to the curb beside the unattended box office near the entrance to the Greek Theatre. The Driver gets out and holds open Phil's door. Niko grabs his guitar and gets out of the big black car. He stares pointedly across the roof at the Driver but the Driver looks into some middle distance that renders Niko invisible.

The Driver shuts the door and takes up station beside the Franklin.

Niko faces the theatre entrance. The hot and steady wind feels cleansing on his face. Phil comes up beside him, hands in pockets and smacking gum. "Nice venue."

Niko shrugs. "Never played it."

"You kidding? You've played the Greek for ages."

"Cute." Niko heads toward a turnstile.

Phil stops him with a hand on his arm. "Make you a deal."

Niko does not look back. Through the gate he sees the scalloped rows of open air seats. "Blow off the gig," Phil says. "Get in the car and go straight to your front door. The real one in the real L.A. No strings, no catch. You go home no worse off than when you started, you don't come back, and we call it even and the original Deal still holds. No harm no foul. What do you say?"

Niko imagines it. Going back home to his life and picking up the pieces and plunging back in to the remainder of his mortal days. With Jemma left down here. He shrugs off Phil's hand and walks toward the turnstile.

"Okay. Final offer."

This time Niko doesn't even slow.

"Blow off the show and go back home and I tear up your contract. Null and void. We don't owe you and you don't owe us. Even steven, just like we never met. How about it?"

At the turnstile Niko stops. "And Jemma?"

Phil looks around as if asking Do you believe this guy. "Niko, buddy, be reasonable. While you're at it why don't you ask me to go back in time and make sure Eve is herpephobic? We can't walk away with nothing. Just like you don't go back to nothing. She's dead and that's forever, like the songs all say. Let it go."

Now Niko turns around and looks at Phil and Phil's expression falls as Niko slowly, coldly smiles.

NIKO ENTERS THE South Terrace near the stage. The bowl of empty seats curves up before him. The proscenium has been built to suggest a classic Greek design. Niko has been here many times, or at least been to its doppelganger on the populated earth, but only to attend shows, never to play one.

A large band on the stage stands mute with silent instruments. As Niko climbs onto the stage they do not look at him but stare blankly outward. Niko recognizes most of them. Some he's met before, others he knows from grainy pictures on old album art. A bony man wearing halfrim glasses and a shapeless fedora sits before a battered upright piano. A man with a pale and angular face shadowed by his broadrimmed black hat wears a serape over one shoulder and his guitar on the other. A ruddyfaced man with a hangdog look holds a harmonica limply in his gnarled hands. A heavyset man stands like a zombie with his alto sax before him. Motionless behind their mic stands are a very dark woman with a rotting orchid above her ear and a small pale woman with long kinked hair. There are many others, fallen stars and great unknowns now summoned forth from their torments to hear one of their own howl out his pain and so compound their own.

One tall thin man wears a large and unkempt afro, a bright drum-major jacket, purple elephant bellbottoms. Thick and sensuous lips, large and liquid eyes. Niko met him just the once, a drunken allday jam that took his music places it had never gone and ended with an introduction to his great white hobby horse, but he has always looked back on him as a friend. It breaks his heart to see him here. The man just stares through Niko like the others, leaden and abandoned and emptied and wanting. The light of mischief in his eyes extinguished. At his hip a Fender Strat slung lefthanded but not restrung.

Feeling like an uninvited guest Niko passes before the blank yet watchful faces and thinks he feels their silent reproach. Perhaps it is only expectation.

At center stage is a wooden stool, a mic stand and effects pedals and the bare end of a jack leading to a rack. Monitors around the stage emit a faint electric hum. Niko glances at the empty benches as he walks toward the stool. Sitting tenth row center Phil waves obligingly and grins. How many times before how many thousands have I walked onstage guitar in hand? Yet I have never felt the weight of eyes upon me as I do now. Am I afraid? Of course.

He sets the guitar case beside the mic stand and kneels beside it and looks up at listless faces staring outward like Easter Island statues. Singers and musicians all. Mostly living hard and dying old when they were young. One day I'll count myself among their anguished number, take my place among them as some other poor damned soul steps up to his last stage.

The silver locket hot against his throat. He opens it and the ring spills out and rolls on the stage. He picks it up and kisses it and slips it on his little finger. Unlatches the hardcase with nerveless hands.

"Haven't got all day," reverberates from the stands.

Niko opens the case and reaches for the Dobro resting in its plush coffin. His hand stops. He stares. His breath catches. His stomach turns to ice. Oh. Oh no. Of all the things that could undo him. Oh no.

Niko pulls the guitar from the case and limp strings loop like entrails as the neck falls away in his hands, broken where it joins the body.

When could this have happened? He played before the bonfire at the demon Onyx's request. Serenaded Franz to his sick fate at the head of the convoluted line. Played on the rattling boxcar with his demon's howled accompaniment. And after that, and after that?

After that he threw the case out of the train and jumped off after it. And never opened it. Never checked it.

He rocks back on his heels and looks up at the clear blue sky and shuts his eyes.

Behind him Phil's laughter echoes in the empty amphitheater.

Well that's it then isn't it? Show's canceled folks. No refund, do not pass go. You lose you lose you lose.

A shadow falls across him. He opens his eyes to see a slight and darkskinned man with closecropped hair and yellowed eyes. One of them drooping. A battered pawnshop acoustic guitar on a frayed strap like an albatross around his neck. The man looks down at Niko with a face that reveals nothing and then raises up his arms to show his fingers have been fused into a single mottled mass of useless flesh.

The rage that smolders deep behind those Louisiana bluesman eyes. Eyes that have regarded him from blurry photographs on fraying covers of crackling recordings that had tried to capture a way of playing that had made men glare into their beermugs with a killing hardness, raw notes that had widened women's pupils and made them walk pulled by their hipbones. A music that could turn a jukejoint to an orgy and a brawl. A blues nailed to the earth with iron brought back from the crossroads by a hard and young man taken down again in 1929. Young and hard and taken down and standing now above him rudely carved from ebony and rooted to the stage and rendered mute by his ruined hands.

He lifts his mangled hands and shrugs from his guitar and offers it to Niko.

Who at first can only stare.

The face impassive as the dark head nods.

Niko accepts the gift in startled wonder and puts the strap across his shoulder.

"Nigger," comes Phil's reverberating voice, "you are gonna hurt for that."

Robert Johnson slowly turns toward the seats and gives a little shrug. Then backs away to take his place among his mute and watchful band of fellow sufferers.

Stunned to silence Niko stares and hopes his gratitude shows in his eyes.

And then looks down at the guitar. All the finish worn away. Wood gouged as if illiterates have tried to carve their names. He strums a G. It's badly out of tune. The tone is awful. Bottom strings rattle on worndown frets. In short the guitar of a blues player.

Niko opens the storage compartment of his hardcase and removes the metal slide. He slips it on his finger and pulls out a broad tortoiseshell patterned pick. He perches on the simple stool. No pickups no mics no rack no effects. Bare bones. He mutes the strings, his fingers ready. All that's left now. Heel hooked on a rung his foot counts off, five six seven eight.

He plays.

SHE SAT IN on a few numbers at their regular gig one night. She was a friend of Joel, their bass player. He had never heard a voice like that. Graveled, sexual, muscular, feminine, and assured. Halfbagged he flirted with her through his guitar.

And that is minor chords low down on the neck, brown tones rasping as the metal slide wavers on the frets.

Wearing a stained apron and a pensive look she watched him take his first taste of the first meal she ever made him, a secret family recipe she claimed. He had no idea what was in it but couldn't get enough. She said I told you I could cook and he said I didn't think you were talking about food.

And that is a bright harmonic arpeggio.

The sound engineer held a hand on his headphones and looked from her face behind the Neumann boom mic to Niko watching beside him at the board. "God damn, she's like a beautiful Joplin." Niko only watched her through the window and felt a white alarming joy inside his heart.

And that is melody quickening, minor and graceful, an eidolon haunting taut wire.

Her deep breath and creaking grip on the brass headboard, looking up at him in defiance almost before she shut her eyes and turned her head and pulled him closer.

And now the ghost of sex walks syncopated on the bottom strings.

Her voice a chocolate covered cherry. And melody coheres as tempo picks up. Her walk all lazy parabolas like a gently rocking boat. And that is his desire scratching chords. Her face pale and thin above her waterbeaded body wrapped in a white thick towel after he hung up the phone and told her Dr. Abkagian wants you to come in right now. And that is high notes crying as they bend. Her small hand holding his inside the scented CAT scan tube. Upon their bed as they lay cooling. On a roughweather airplane trip as they touched down. Within a lost unlighted cavern. A final clenching time before her final breath.

And that is deep and gaping sorrow at the loss of her.

Niko plays and what he plays is simply Jem. Simple music for a simple grief. Notes no talent could call forth without a lifetime's pain behind them. Like Jem the melody's direct and pretty with a dark edge lurking, and like her always on the brink of bursting into something more. And like Jem the music slows and darkens to a fading ember that flickers and then dies.

And that is what was lost.

The last notes fade across the empty amphitheater. The guitar in his hands. Wood body on his thigh. Warm wind across the hills. No insect sounds, no calling birds in this Los Angeles.

Niko's fingers move again upon the strings. Playing of their own accord a coda for a life not his. A sad small wave before the ship sets sail. Look down on him from high up in the stands. A lone man with an old guitar perched on a chair. Shut our eyes and listen. What we hear is just a good man feeling bad.

Niko rocking back and forth, the guitar silent in his hands. And then he stops. He has no idea how long it's been since he stopped playing. Isn't even sure he played at all.

The musicians still behind him. Poor ruined people brought to silence here. Phil still there beyond the stage, sitting bolt upright with his arms folded and his sunglasses like holes in his skull.

Niko removes the guitar and walks to the front of the stage and stares at Phil.

Phil's expression is impossible to read as he reaches down beside himself and pulls his pale leathercased iPhone from out of nowhere and types on it and then removes a white business card and a limited edition Michel Perchin Fabergé Gold Ribbed Columbian Emerald lever action fountain pen. He uncaps the pen and stabs it into his arm and works the little pump, then pulls it out and licks the nib and scribbles something on the card. He caps the pen and returns it to the case and turns the iPhone off and puts it away and beckons curtly to Niko.

Niko has no idea what to expect as he sits on the edge of the stage and slides off and walks up the steps toward Phil. He holds the guitar out of the way as he sidles along the tenth row.

Phil continues staring toward the stage. Twin sunlight stars glint from his shades. He holds the business card up like a distracted bidder at an auction. There is only the faintest tremble.

Niko takes the card. One side is blank, the other has several indecipherable words scrawled in deep purple.

"Take it to the cashier," says Phil.

Niko stares at Phil and Phil continues to refuse to meet his gaze. Niko thinks he sees a glint of sunlight on Phil's cheek below his sunglasses.

Phil turns away from Niko. "Come on, come on. You think you're the only thing I have to deal with?"

Niko puts the card in a pocket.

Phil rubs beneath his sunglasses. "I'll give you five minutes. Starting the second you leave the casino." He produces his iPhone and begins tapping it. "After that I unload on you. The works. Both barrels. Got it?"

"Where do I find the cashier?"

"At the casino you moron. Don't worry, you'll have a ride."

On the stage the brilliant souls worn to the quick have turned like sunflowers toward the two men in the stands. Robert Johnson motionless as furniture and looking naked with his guitar gone.

"You still here?" Phil tells the air before him. "Go on, get out of here. I'm sick of looking at you."

Niko turns and walks away among the empty seats. On a sudden impulse pulls the locket from around his neck and flings it away. He clambers back onto the stage and passes among the silent damned until he stands before the young man with the cruelly mangled hands. He holds out the guitar but the man makes no move to accept it. Niko is about to put it on him when the man inclines his head at something and Niko turns to see his broken steel guitar beside the empty stool. Niko nods. A final gesture then. He goes to the front of the stage and holds the wooden guitar by the neck and raises it high and comes up on the balls of his feet and drops and brings the guitar down like a man at a midway trying to ring the bell with the big hammer. The guitar smashes all to hell with beautiful chaotic dissonance. Niko drops it beside the corpse of the Dobro and glances back to see the man's reaction but there's no longer anybody there. The stage is empty.

Again he looks out at the stands where Phil pretends to work his phone. He feels no sense of triumph or relief. Nothing is yet returned to him and he is not returned.

Niko turns to leave the stage but stops when Phil calls his old name. He waits to hear the coming admonition.

"You think you've won something here. But you always win this part." Phil is looking at him now across the safety of some distance. "It's what comes after this. That's the part you always fuck up. It's all just a dance we do here. The costumes change, the story doesn't. The old rules still apply. The second you step out that door you're Lot's wife. One look back, one backward glance out of the corner of your eye, and that's it. Game over. Got it?" Laughter sounds like grating metal. "Pretty simple, huh? Don't look back."

Don't look back.

XXII

RAMBLING ON MY MIND

THE WIZENED DEMON BEHIND THE counter gapes at the scribbled card. "You gotta be kidding me." His voice is keening and unpleasant. His "k's" cause a repulsive shudder down Niko's spine and conjure teeth sliding on aluminum. Behind the wideset bars the wrinkled demon squints beneath his darkgreen banker's visor and shakes his head. He taps the shoulder of the demon beside him who is sorting teeth exchanged for playing chips. "Hey Clarence."

"Thirty, thirtyone, thirty—shit." Clarence looks over. "This better be good."

The visored demon waves the card. "You ever see one of these?"

"What, a piece of paper?" He shakes his floppy eared head in disgust and rakes the bloodrooted teeth into a pile again. "One, two, three—"

"Not a piece of paper. A Property Requisition Slip."

"A who?"

"Property Requisition Slip."

"Who's he when he's at home?"

Niko presses his lips and grips the edge of the counter.

"They're for retrieving guest arrivals set aside for processing."

"Since when do guests get anything retrieved?"

"That's my point." Visor flutters the card. "They don't. Not that I ever heard anyway. But here's a form."

"Let me see that." Clarence takes the card from Visor and examines it. He frowns and clucks and tuts and shakes his wattled head. He looks up to see Niko standing on their side of the counter and his frown deepens. "That side, meat pie." He points a gnawed claw at the other side of the bars.

Niko grabs the demon's turtlehide neck and bends close to one scabby flaccid ear and ignores the awful odor steaming from the hairy waxy pit of it. "You've got the form. It's signed. Now get my item or the guy who signed it will be signing you with a rusty churchkey."

Clarence wrests himself away. "All right, okay, criminy." He hands the card back to Visor. "Here. He brought it to you."

Visor blinks owlishly. He looks as if he's going to protest but then looks at Niko and changes his fledgling mind. He furrows his mottled brow and huffs away.

Niko leans against the counter's edge and hopes it doesn't show that he feels he's about to pass out. He has truly shot his wad. He watches in blackrimmed detachment as Clarence goes back to sorting moist teeth gobbets.

"Thirtyone, thirtytwo." Clarence beams and scoops the bloody teeth into a drawstring bag and tosses the bag onto a heap of similar bags and then licks the edge of his palm clean. The green felt blotter on the counter before him dark with fluids. Clarence lowers his hand and looks at Niko. "What's a churchkey?"

Niko ignores him and the demon shrugs and returns to his work. Niko shuts his eyes and draws a deep and ragged breath.

THE JOURNEY BACK to the casino had been strange but uneventful. The Black Taxi had ferried Niko out of the silent hills and onto the southbound Golden State freeway where it sped along the empty lanes toward a downtown abandoned as if a swift and purely fatal plague had swept across the world. The city so familiar and so alien.

At the East L.A. Interchange they got on the eastbound 10 and headed inland toward San Bernardino. Niko stared at the back of the Driver's head and wondered what kind of ride he was being taken on. But Phil had spoken the agreement and it was binding and irrevocable.

At one point he had bolted upright. The guitar. Where was the guitar?

Then he remembered and settled back down on the spacious seat, heart hammering. He'd carried the Dobro so long that its absence was more conspicuous than its presence. Poor guitar. Niko felt as if he'd mistreated a faithful pet.

When he glanced out the window again not five minutes later the Black Taxi was exiting the 10 and curving round the fishhook ramp onto the northbound 15 toward Las Vegas. They could not have come this far this fast. That exit was forty or fifty miles from L.A. But to the left was the sprawling consumer mecca of the Ontario Mills Mall. They were headed toward Vegas all right.

A few minutes later daylight began to ebb. Niko looked left but saw no sign of sun. It had been bright afternoon at the Greek ten minutes ago. When he looked forward again the Black Taxi was coming down out of a long mountain pass and an island of multi-colored light lay scattered on a dark and empty plain ahead. The air turned hot and dry and redolent with rotting meat and shit and an iron tinge of blood. Niko rolled the window up. He was back all right.

As the casino hove into view once more Niko thought of Van, whose dismissal of Las Vegas had been the last words he ever spoke. Is that where you come from, Niko asked the lighted structure as the big sedan pulled up against the curb. Did they pull you from my head? Was this whole mess tailormade for me? In his mind Phil shrugged and said What difference does it make?

The suicide door opened and Niko stared a moment before getting out. He patted himself down and glanced around the huge interior of the Franklin one more time. The Driver staring like a mannequin with the opened door between them. Niko searched for some smartassed or provocative comment but finally he just turned and walked toward the casino and pulled Phil's scribbled card from his ragged coat pocket as the doors opened for him and he was swallowed again by light and sound and pain.

NOW THE DEMON Clarence hums as he sorts bloody gobbets. Somehow the demon's throat produces two separate notes at once. The top note slurs and wavers over the lower octave and in the dissonance of their modulated harmonic a third note is produced, birdlike and warbling, something like a cricket and something like a didgeridoo and beautiful.

Niko fidgets. From some vague where Jemma is being brought to him and soon he will take her back into his arms. Together they will flee this vale of tears and hold each other in the daylit world. He drums his fingers and rocks from foot to foot and paces the tiny space behind the counter. The demon Clarence hums his ethereal polyphony as his ivory claws sort teeth scored with plier marks and in the sight before him Niko sees embodied all the sad and absurd horror and awful epic beauty he has seen and felt and heard and even made since he went down beneath the earth.

Now the demon with the visor gimps back toward him, and held in Visor's claw is a mason jar with a blacktipped feather softly glowing inside.

"What the fuck is this?"

Visor draws up short. "It's the item on your Property Requisition Slip. I doublechecked, there's no mistake."

Niko advances on the demon. "Is this some kind of joke?"

Visor is claws and angles and spikes and teeth but he shrinks before Niko's advance and holds out the slip of paper like a shield. "Read it. Read it. Here."

The humming has broken off and Clarence watches now.

"Jemma." Niko's shouting now, not at the demon but generally to wherever Phil must still be laughing to himself. "Give me Jemma you fucking shit."

"Sir. Sir. Sir." Visor holds up the jar. "This is her, really." Niko realizes the demons are afraid of him because of that slip of paper. Because of Phil's handwriting on it. "There's a Property Identification

Number listed here and I matched it to the storage coordinate on the temporary storage shelves for Property Assessment and it's impossible to confuse it with any others because they never get removed. This is very irregular, and—"

He stops at Niko's inarticulate shout. Niko stands there red-faced and panting like some confused and angry bear. His fists clench until his hands are completely white. He looks at the ceiling. You just won't give me a fucking break will you? I mean I didn't expect Jemma with pompoms and a whistle but goddamn.

The demons glance at one another as Niko forces himself to calm down. Clarence makes a small questioning gesture and Visor shrugs back. Finally Niko holds a hand out and Visor hands the jar to him like a runner in a nitroglycerin relay.

Niko's Grail is just a glass jar with a metal lid. The feather within just looks like a feather, white with black edges along the top third and flecked with black specks. Its faint glow gives off no heat. Jemma. You couldn't even read by its light. The glass is cool in his rough palms.

Visor and Clarence trade glances again as the meat pie holds the jar up like a priest blessing the Host. They watch him slowly lower it and run a hand over it and smell it and then press it against his cheek and squeeze his eyes shut. Visor twirls a hookclawed index finger by his temple. Clarence gets a knowing look and nods. Finally the meat pie opens his eyes and lowers the jar. He nods and then mutters something and then turns away. Visor clears his throat. "Uh excuse me but umm."

The meat pie turns back cradling the jar. Visor hesitantly holds out the Property Requisition Slip and a pin. "Could you just sign this? Sir?"

The meat pie takes the paper and the pin and cocks his head at it. He shuts his eyes and begins to tremble. The demons glance at one another and Clarence casually reaches for a marble paperweight to whang the meat pie on the skull if he gets violent. But the meat pie laughs. It's a weird laugh because it seems almost as if he's crying. "I thought," the meat pie says but can't get out what it is he thought. He sets the jar on the counter and sets an elbow on the jar as if he's afraid the jar will disappear if he loses contact with it.

"I thought. I thought you." And he pricks a finger with the pin and squeezes. "I thought you recognized me. I thought you wanted my autograph." He scrawls something that might be his initials across the back of the Property Requisition Slip.

Visor snatches it away and waves the signature dry. "It's just a release sir."

The meat pie nods and wipes his eyes. "Okay. A release. So I'm released now."

"You may leave with your property, yes sir."

The meat pie does exactly that.

Visor and Clarence watch him thread his way through the mutilated assemblage. "And don't let the knob hit you on the ass on the way out," says Clarence. Then one of the hunchbacks dumps another cartful of teeth in his bin and he has to sort doubletime because he's gotten so far behind.

Before he leaves the casino Niko makes a final stop.

The Sports Book is pandemonium. Cavernous and crammed with demons and canopied by sickly green cigar smoke and cacophonous as demons cheer and jeer team contests played out in the air above their heads. Irate fans shit into their palms and hurl it toward the losing teams. Where it hits it hisses and steams and melts to bone.

A wake of silence spreads from Niko's entrance like a gunslinger movie cliché. Demons nudge each other and point toward the mortal man with the glowing mason jar heading toward the huge row of betting windows along one wall. As Niko moves among them they draw back to form an aisle. As if he is on his way to receive a medal from some alien ambassador. The vast room enstilled.

Niko approaches a barred window and the demon behind it looks up from biting someone else's fingernails and squawks and sits upright and waves his rubbery hands. "Oh no no not this window no no no—"

Niko sets the jar on the counter and pulls out his wallet and removes all his cash. Amazingly still there. Then again what would anyone have done with it? He says Popoudopolos to win and does not look back at the murmur behind him.

The demon glances warily at a wager board. "Eight fifty to one."

Niko pushes the money through the space beneath the grille. The demon flaps his hands and slaps himself hard and glances over his shoulder at his supervisor, who lifts one flaccid breast and squeezes it like a winesack to spray a puslike milk into his own mouth and all over his own face. He licks his lipless dripping mouth with a thick reptilian tongue and grins at Niko and nods at his underling who scoops the cash and calls out Popoudopolos to win.

The murmuring grows louder. The cashier pushes a ticket across the counter and Niko puts it in a coat pocket.

"How you gonna collect if you win?" the supervisor calls.

Niko stares at the obese obscenity fingering itself before him. "It's more fun if everyone knows you owe me." He picks up the mason jar and shoulders through the silent restless hordes soon to pursue him.

EXIT. THE INSTANT he crosses that threshold they'll do everything in their considerable power to waylay stop or ruin him. To make him look back. All the hosts of Hell will nip at Niko's heels. You think the dogs and walls and gates and spears are there to guard the way in? Getting here's the easy part.

Reflections in the glass before him wink and slide and wobble and distort. Thresholds, portals, demarcations. Ye who exit here.

He feels the stares on his back and takes one last look behind him. For an instant just beneath articulation Niko glimpses formless chaos churning there. A fearsome primal mindless maw feeding on decay and terror and the slow uncoiling of the cosmos itself. A universe of evershifting laws and fanged indifference that would smear him across its fabric like a bloated mosquito were it not amused by him. As any hero out of myth was easily defeated who did not amuse or charm the gods. In that instant beneath thought or language Niko glimpses the world caught offguard, the face behind the mask, the true shape of things.

But Niko turns. And as he turns that horrible glimpse reverts to the casino and its enslaved patrons, not staring at him as he had presumed but going about their neverending business, eternal commerce of punishment and penitence.

Again he heads toward the exit and again he stops.

Beyond the carnival-lighted glass the Black Taxi is still parked against the curb. The Driver is nowhere in sight. And a plastic case in Niko's pocket holds the key.

XXIII

TERRAPLANE BLUES

NIKO LEAVES THE CASINO WITHOUT ceremony and pulls the keyholder from his pocket as he heads directly for the Black Taxi. He opens the keyholder with one hand and shakes the key out of the box. At the driver's door he extends the key like a man making an offering to a blind man's cup. His arm feels guided as the key finds the slot without jostle or fumble as if it had eyes. Niko turns the key and pulls the handle and opens the suicide door. Son of a bitch. His heart is yammering. He ducks into the car and through the flatpaned windshield sees stalking toward him the uniformed valet whose elbow he dislocated. Quickly but carefully Niko sets the mason jar on the leather bench seat. He starts to get out but stops suddenly. Don't turn around. Don't look back.

Quickly he turns and backs out of the car, straightening as the valet, swelling like a posing bodybuilder, extends an arm to shove him over. "Away from the car, chie—" Niko grabs the hand and turns it funny and a giant knucklepop cracks across the casino entryway and once again the valet's elbow dislocates. Niko follows through and slams the blanching valet on the ground facefirst and yanks him onto his back and stomps his throat. The valet curls into a ball and tries to choke but can't because no air can escape his crushed esophagus. Niko doubts he'll choke to death because he's probably already dead. If he ever was alive.

He steps around the writhing valet and slides behind the wheel of the Black Taxi. The mason jar tips toward him as he sits and Niko wedges it against his hip. He takes a deep breath and shuts the solid heavy door and elbows down the lock. Wary as he is of this car Niko feels protected now. Encased. But let's not be lulled. Driving this car is sleeping with the enemy. Perhaps it senses who is driving it. Will it try to throw me?

Well you're in the gate and you've got about ten seconds to take stock of this bronc before the buzzer sounds. You better cowboy up.

Smells of leather, lemon oil, age. A locking glove compartment. Birdseye maple instrument panels. Large round dials. A roman numeralled clock the size of his palm. XII. Midnight or noon? The speedometer goes to 120. The odometer reads 186282. The tripmeter shows a row of zeroes. Gas gauge full. No radio. Huge steering wheel. Small brake pedal, the size of the clutch. An absurd amount of legroom. The gearshift long and spindly. The passenger compartment stretches behind him like the rear of a limo. The hood sticks out a good eight feet. Its glossy black the ink of water at the bottom of the Marianas Trench. This thing is a fucking boat. Everywhere around him is metal. The car must weigh five thousand pounds. Casino lights flash and flow along the polished chassis. Something odd about that, what is it? And remembers. Above the ground the Franklin had reflected no light at all. Had been a shadow without a casting object. But here the black chassis is polished to a high gloss like a lacquered bento box.

No seatbelt. Guess that was part of the luxury package. The clutch feels like a weighted legpress. Terrific.

He looks up to adjust the rearview mirror—and jerks his head aside and bats the mirror askew.

Does a mirror count as looking back?

Table that one for now. At least there are no side mirrors to compound the issue.

Niko racks the shift lever and slides the key into the ignition. Once more his hand feels guided to the spot. Okay Houston all systems go.

Before he turns the key he looks through the slanted windshield at casino lights reflecting along the Franklin's nightshade hood. The lights now melt toward the ground like heated wax, coalescing light cascading down the hood like thinning watercolors washing down to dim and fade and die. As it has risen like a beanstalk from this unhallowable ground so now the big casino collapses groaning back into the plain. Niko keep his gaze fixed straight ahead as the dimming structure growls and creaks and sputters and diminishes. Soon the plain is dark again. As if the casino were never there at all.

Unnerving silence follows the casino's demise. Without the light to lend it shape the body of the Franklin is invisible now. In this lull that Niko senses will be very brief he grows aware of the key in the ignition, warm in his fingers like a living thing. He switches it on and nothing happens.

Where the casino was there now begins a growing rumble.

Niko glances around the instrument panel. Remember it's an old car. There. Starter button. He presses it and the engine turns over but doesn't catch. Now the heavy air is imminent with something straining to be born. Now he feels the rumble through the car. He pumps the gas and tries again. Again the engine doesn't start. Briefly he considers getting out to push start the car. Yeah right.

The rumble strengthens. It sounds as if it's somehow widening. Niko dares not look to see what's going on but it sounds as if the ground itself is opening up. Don't look don't look don't look.

A knob beside the steering column catches Niko's eye. Choke. Don't mind if I do. He pulls it and hits the starter button and is rewarded with a deep leonine purr barely audible beneath the minor earthquake rumble all around him.

Something shouts behind him and he glances at the rearview but thank god he's knocked it slantwise. Something heavy lands on the rear of the car and Niko fumbles finding first gear and slips the clutch. The Black Taxi bucks and stalls. A leathery slap on the rear window now as Niko knocks the lever into neutral and jabs the starter button again. The engine purr resumes. The rear of the roof dents with a dull gong as Niko lets out the clutch. Still the Franklin doesn't move.

Handbrake. Niko squeezes the brake lever and slams it down. The big car starts to roll. He doesn't even feel or hear the gear engaging when he eases off the clutch. It's so dark that only the motion of the speedometer needle reveals the car is moving. Behind him an awful bellow like a foghorn grips his heart. Niko gropes for the headlight knob and pulls it. Meager patches of dull red ochre plain flow toward him as the '33 Franklin begins the drive reluctantly across the Lower Plain of Hell.

IT'S A WRESTLING match from the word go. With the casino vanished Niko has no reference point. No sun no moon no stars to steer by. No compass, no compass points. He is not north or south or east or west of anything.

He searches for second gear and finds it and forces the gearshift in. Goddamn it's finicky. Half an inch to either side and it won't go. He lets up on the stiff clutch and surges forward.

I need to turn right. I need to be at least ninety degrees from the direction the car was pointing when I boosted it.

Then it hits him. Holy Jesus Pez dispenser, I stole it. I boosted the Black Taxi. Oh that sallow son of a bitch will be so god damned mad. Oh yes. Niko laughs out loud and drums the steering wheel. I would pay to see his bony face when he comes back and finds it missing. But I won't see it because I will be gone baby gone. Many miles away like the song says. Hell on wheels.

He glances at the silent glowing mason jar. Yes yes yes. I'm gonna do this thing. He pats the jar. We are going to do this thing Jem. We will bring you back into the living world and reunite you with your castoff flesh, and breathing in that living air we'll live our span of years as man and wife. And whatever fate awaits my mortal soul I will have nonetheless escaped at last the nightmare of my history, the prison of myth. And you will have escaped, period.

Her castoff flesh. What has become of it? Was she found? I've been gone so long. What if she is buried? Did Hank come in from Oregon and find his daughter on the bed in their deserted house? Oh no please no. But we will cross that bridge when we come to it Jem my Jem, and if there is no bridge then we will build one.

So exalting Niko turns the car. If he turns more than ninety degrees eventually he should converge with the railroad tracks. Assuming they are still there. Assuming the landscape is not malleable as a fevered dream. But what else to do but go on assumptions? Don't we forge ahead on faith?

Feeling that he drives more than just this car he speeds along his earthbound way.

And feels the Franklin fighting him. He should be shifting into third but both hands are on the wheel to keep the huge car from going abeam. The massive aircooled engine whines and reluctantly he lets up on the gas.

Something clatters across the roof. Wotthefuck. Niko looks up as something big clambers toward the front of the car. He brakes and tries to weave. The engine shudders and he slaps it out of third and hunts around for second with his left arm straining on the right side of the wobbling wheel. The car wriggles pathetically toward the right.

"Okay you piece of shit." He abandons the hunt for second gear and mashes the brake and yanks the wheel twohanded. The big car leans hugely left like a lopsided boat and overhead that foghorn bellow sounds again. A heavy weight lifts from the car and the headlights sweep across something huge and pale brown with too many limbs tumbling on the ground with birdbones snapping and their blunt ends shredding thin membranous wings. Niko notes the direction of the creature's roll because it's where the car was headed before the power slide began.

The mason jar rolls off the seat and hits the gearshift lever and bounces out of sight. The Franklin comes to rest facing the way it came. Niko clenches his eyes. Feral cat of engine purr. Niko looks at his lap. His hands tremble on the wheel. Go. Don't wait till you stop shaking. Go.

Staring firmly at the floorboard Niko forces down the clutch and mauls the gearshift and the Franklin grumbles into motion. Tough shit, car.

If anything was chasing you you're driving toward it now.

Niko forces the wheel to the left. A compass would be a godsend now. Yeah right. And where's the north it ought to point to?

Niko straightens out the wheel and takes a deep breath and looks up from the floorboard. Nothing vanishes. Reality does not shred. The enormous front grille of the Franklin eats up red ochre hellfloor rushing in beyond the headlamps' reach.

Beneath the passenger seat a pale light glows. Niko taps the brake and the mason jar rolls out onto the floorboard. He reaches for it and the steering wheel yanks from his grip. Niko bolts up and shoves the jar against his crotch and wrests control of the car. "Bad bad bad," he tells the car.

He struggles into third gear and puts the hammer down and rocks forward as if to urge the Franklin faster. Headed where? Anywhere but here.

CRACKED VOLCANIC GROUND rushes from the dark before the lengthy hood as the Franklin glides along the dark flat plain. How fast can he go? The speedometer goes to one twenty. He's doing maybe eighty right now. But he is in a place where how fast you go and how far you travel may be very different things.

Something dashes in front of the car and Niko glimpses large eyes long limbs red skin. He jerks left but the big car resists and the rightfront fender clips the running creature and chunky red sprays half the windshield. The car is so damned heavy Niko barely feels the impact. He hunts down the wiper switch and the overhead wipers draw cartoon smiles in the ichor on the angled glass.

The front right headlamp now shines down and to the right. Its light ruddy with splashed gore. And yet the wayward beam drifts slowly left and up to rejoin its companion as the curved fender unbuckles itself and smooths until it is symmetrical again. A faint and distant groan of metal somehow healing. Gradually the ruddy light whitens. Niko starts to turn the wipers off but the switch moves just before he touches it. The windshield is spotless once again. Niko's nervousness at piloting the Black Taxi returns. He sits within the gullet of a beast.

Out of habit he checks the rearview. It's all akilter and he remembers slapping it so. That mirror sure does worry him. Does it count as looking back to look into it? Is the issue the actual act of turning to see what's behind him, or is it the mere fact of what lies behind him being visible in any way? Perseus guided himself with a reflective bronze shield until he could cut off Medusa's head. What was absent from her reflection that petrified in direct apprehension? And does it apply here?

The only way to find out is to straighten out the mirror and take a good long gander. A session player friend of his called this the highnote test. To learn the highest note you can play on your guitar you play the E string at the last fret and tighten the string until it breaks, and it's the note just under that. The rearview mirror is the Cadillac of highnote tests. If a single accidental glance were to undo him after all he's gone through he might as well floor it and head straight for the nearest immovable object. To avoid the possibility he snaps the rearview off the windshield and tosses it into the back.

Niko rolls the window down and hot stale air invades the car that speeds along the vacant plain. The only sound the fluttering of alien wind.

NIKO JERKS HIS head up and yanks the wheel. He looks around but sees nothing. Purring car and whistling wind. Some loud bang awoke him though. He hit something or something hit him. Exhausted and drained and lulled by the thrum of engine and the hum of tires on the flat cracked plain he fell asleep at the wheel. Just for a few seconds probably but that's all it takes. That's all it took for you and Van to slam that car. Two seconds of wandering attention and a whole bunch of lives changed forever.

All right. Enough already. Keep your eyes on the road and your hands upon the wheel.

Soon the railroad tracks are back. Rusted iron on ruined ground. Driving beside them Niko wonders how long he rode the train during his drunken encounter with his demon. A few hours at most. That train had sure been fast though. A couple hours could easily cover a hundred, a hundred fifty miles. Maybe more.

He frowns and raises his reclaimed love's lantern soul to the instrument panel. The gas gauge still shows full and he's doing ninetyfive. The tripmeter and odometer numbers roll in a slotmachine blur. His clock runneth backward.

Crucifaxes dot the landscape now. Tortured souls nailed upside down on X shaped crosses interspersed along the plain like gruesome railroad crossing signs. Niko swerves around the crucifaxes and tries to parallel the railroad tracks because they are an arrow pointing the way back. The crucifaxes brighten before him and their shadows shift and lengthen on the ground. An awful howl sounds just as Niko realizes that a train is churning down the track and slowly drawing even with him. Soon he sees it eating up the night incarnate. Thick red spewing from its demon head like the final snorts of a gored bull. Iron jaws wide to scoop whatever lies along its path. The awful screech of train horn sounds again, the grinding of a million porcelain teeth.

Clinging to the side of the train are demons. Wings tucked tight against the strong headwind or unfurled and flapping behind them like leather flags. They shake their fists at Niko speeding beside them.

Niko glances forward just in time to dodge a looming crucifax. His headlamps catch the resigned look of the inverted soul tormented there. The car that hurtles toward it merely another in an infinite series of punishments to be endured. He feels the Franklin wants to plow into the upright wood, fusing meat and bone and metal, and he muscles the car around the spraddled man. The gruesome X blurs by and gone.

The forest of crucifaxes thickens, a pinioned nation growing before him.

Something hits the side of the car and Niko swerves. On the train the demons hoot and highfive one another and then make room in a boxcar doorway for another demon who holds a naked Asian woman in his great hands.

Niko dodges another crucifax. The landscape itself is forcing him closer to the train. Up ahead the only place the car will fit is on the right of way.

On the train the demon twists the woman's head off like an apple stem and dangles it by its long black hair and reaches back and winds up like a pitcher on the mound. A muscled leg comes up headhigh and then stomps down as the great scaled arm lashes forward. The gaping head shoots toward the Franklin like a comet trailing hair. Niko brakes and the train pulls away and the head streaks past the hood. The demons boo. If they want to stop him they can probably do it any time they want. Smash him from above or open up the ground before him. Peel off the roof and pulp him like an overripe tomato. But that's not the deal. The deal is that Niko's free to try to get out with the bottled soul of his lady love in tow so long as he does not look back. And they are free to do everything in their formidable power to make him look back. What could be simpler?

And, of course, Niko is perfectly free to fuck up on his own.

Less than twenty yards now separate him from the train. Crucifaxes whip by like demented roadsigns on his left.

A demon separates itself from the freight of demons screaming out their joyous wrath. Its wings flat along its muscular back as tigerlike it gathers itself and springs, body seeming to elongate as it arcs from the train with tendrils reaching overhead and wings unfolding like parasols to rake back and guide.

Once again Niko slows the car, this time to no effect. This missile is volitional and banks toward him. The Franklin's chassis rocks when the demon hits the side. Dodging crucifaxes as if playing a deranged video game Niko glances at a monstrous face that leers in the passenger window. The demon clings to the doorhandle and crouches on the rubber runner. A moment later Niko realizes that the demon is circling the tip of one tendril in a gesture for him to roll down his window.

Niko scowls. Fuck that. Dodge crucifaxes, don't hit the train, shake the demon off the car.

Another glance at the demon's face and he revises his game plan. Holy shit. Without another thought or word he leans across the seat and pulls up the doorlock.

The demon shakes his great leathern head. His expression says You moron. He points at the rear doorlock and Niko understands that the demon can't open the front door without knocking himself off the runner and the back door is locked.

Niko jerks the wheel to avoid squeegeeing the demon across a crucifax. Then the car breaks into a clearing in the cruciforest and Niko nearly stands in his seat as he blindly reaches back and tugs up the lock. Foul hot air invades the car as the suicide door opens and the demon tumbles into the back. "Nice driving, buddy pal," his own voice says behind him as its owner slams the door. "Now let's get the Dodge out of Hell."

XXIV

TAKE ME TO
THE RIVER

I t's a Franklin actually."
"Say what?"
"The car. It's a Franklin."
"Whatever. Hey look out. Ooh that was close. Cut right cut right cutright."
"I don't have room."
"You have room."
"I don't."
"Trust me."
"Yeah right." Niko cuts right. There's room, barely.

His demon bends a tendril to wave bye bye at the crucified woman they have nearly sideswiped. "Nice car."

"Thanks. I stole it myself." Niko's palms are slick on the wheel. A stunt driving ace he is not. He's gotten ahead of the train, but the thickening profusion of the crucified is giving him nowhere to drive.

Suddenly ahead there looms a chasm. Redlit from below, miles wide and untold miles deep. The only bridge across it is the slender rampart of the tracks themselves atop a frail and narrow truss bridge that looks like a thread strung between the tops of two skyscrapers.

Niko feels as if he's been dashed with icewater. "No way. No fucking way."

"We've got to," his demon urges from the back. "It's the only way across, and if the train gets there ahead of us it'll stop on the tracks. We've got to outrun it."

"Goddamn."

Thunder rumbles and the ground trembles. The tremors' ripples shudder through the long and slender railway bridge.

Niko's demon sticks his head up front. "I strongly advise you not to use such language once you're on the bridge."

"I really don't want to do this."

"Okay." The demon withdraws into the passenger compartment. "Pull over and stick your thumb out. Maybe they'll give you a lift."

Niko dodges a crucifax. "There's no way I can drive on that."

"The car can do it."

"I know the car can do it. I don't think I can."

"Sure you can." The demon glances back. "The train's two hundred yards back and gaining but you'll have plenty of lead if you don't slow down. Hey did you know your rearview mirror's back here?"

"Yeah." Niko eases the car toward the tracks. The crack in the plain looms like the end of the world. "Where'd this thing come from?"

"Same thing that caused the Ledge."

"I think I'd remember going over this."

"We were getting bagged on the boxcar when we went across. Good thing you decided to jump later, huh?"

Now they're right beside the rails and near the point where the choice is hop on top or sail into the great divide. Niko takes a deep breath and says Hold on and yanks the wheel and steers the car onto the rails.

"Go. Go. Seriously go."

"It won't go any faster."

"Then we're SOL buddy pal."

"How far now?"

"Hundred fortytwo yards. The rate they're gaining, a minute before they hit us."

"I can't fucking believe I'm doing this."

"Drive."

The unbordered tracks look like a slash across a landscape painting of a Martian canyon. Close-set crossties shoot from the vanishing point and disappear beneath the car.

"Where's Jem? Where's the jar?"

"I've got it. You just keep us on the rails."

"How can you be so calm?"

"Cause I'm the one with the wings."

Humming tires run atop the narrow rails before the gaping train behind them bearing down. Niko struggles not to blink. He's so terrified he wants to cry. His mouth is dry, he fights an urge to sneeze. He wants to scream but all he does is clench his teeth. His palms are sweaty on the wheel. He dares not look away from two slim lines on which the big car rides above the deep crevasse without an inch of play on either side. Maybe that's best. They're balanced like a clown bike on a tightrope and if he looked down and saw nothing but miles of empty space above a redlit and unfathomable bottom he would surely lose whatever fraying thread of nerve he still possesses.

"How far?"

"Forty yards now."

"We gonna make it?"

Another pause. "No."

Niko narrows his eyes. "If I'd stopped every time I thought that." An awful pressure builds between his shoulderblades as the voracious iron engine burns down the heated night toward them. Worse than looking back to see the locomotive gullet straining to engulf them is not being able to look back at all. Now his demon is his eyes and ears.

The very iron trembles with the resonance of hurtling weight behind them. This bridge should not support its own weight, much less a locomotive, but it does. The rolling thunder gains and Niko swears he smells its heated iron breath. His demon yells Faster but the pedal's on the floorboard.

"Maybe if we lost three hundred pounds of deadweight," Niko says.

His demon whoops and snaps a tentacle with inspiration and before Niko knows it the backright suicide door has been flung open and the demon has leapt from the car. The door rakes back in the airstream and suddenly the car wants to veer right. Niko's neck aches from the effort not to turn his head. Then his demon forces shut the door and leaps from the siderunner. He glides alongside for a moment and then spreads great batlike wings and snaprolls out over the uncontainable immensity of the canyon. Relieved of weight the Franklin gains some distance on the hungry metal hurtling behind it.

The cliff edge of the fissure's other side is bottomlit hot lava red. Half a mile maybe. Niko's face hurts and he's paralyzed with muscle tension.

The car's own shadow now precedes it, shortening and growing more opaque as fierce behind the car the massive train crowds up until its headlamp glowers down upon the roof. A sudden primal scream of trainhorn nearly causes him to veer off of the rails. Five hundred yards. Come on come on. Thick hot oil smell. Screaming demons over thundering metal and rumbling rail. Iron lip of loco-motive kisses polished bumper chrome. The car is pushed along the tracks now by the unrelenting train. Niko knocks the gearshift into neutral and clamps both hands on the wheel to keep the tires on the rails. The Lower Plain's resumption is a thousand feet away now. Distant crucifaxes stubble the flat ground.

Something lands on the back of the car and Niko stops himself from looking back so fast he pulls a muscle in his neck. His hands twitch on the wheel. He yells God damn it. Distant thunder dimly rumbles. Niko's breath catches. O what have I done.

The rails shudder beneath him and he remembers tremors rip-pling down the gossamer length of railway bridge. He imagines an iron tidal wave rolling his way like a moving hump in a flicked gar-den hose. Roused from monstrous sleep the bridge beneath him groans. Bucking in the metal surge the light behind him wavers. Niko screams but cannot hear his voice in all the clang and thunder. Iron screams on iron and the car is lit by flashing sparks behind it as a thousand tons of locomotive angles off the slender bridge of rails. The train horn howls its outrage at the death that is the price for breaking free from its conscripted fate, tie spike rail wheel, howls out as the massive locomotive plummets from the trestle bridge to arc over the precipice.

The Black Taxi's rear tires thump off the rails and the car begins to slew and then the edge is past and the interrupted plain resumes. Behind him now two hundred thousand iron pounds of locomotive missile slams the anvil of the sheer cliff face. The Franklin bucks on crossties. Unbelted Niko is airborne and anchored only by his grip upon the wheel. Then he lands back on the seat and stomps the gas and the car gains traction and rooster tails a gout of red plain floor as it speeds away from empty rails and a murdered locomotive.

No sooner is he off the rails than Niko's dodging crucifaxes. He nudges the wheel and the car slips between two inverted souls staked to their fate. No way he can keep this up. But wait. With the train gone now he doesn't have to drive fullout. Duh.

As he slows the car he catches motion in the passenger window and sees a whippet thin and windraked demon opening the door.

A crucifax looms dead ahead. Its inverted tenant gaping like a deer at the oncoming lights. Niko speeds up and jerks left. A thud and a crack and the demon is gone. Clotheslined by the crucifax crosspiece.

Niko slows and threads his close way through the cruciforest till he breaks into a clearing. Ahead lie piled lumber and massed demons and the herded damned of the slaughtermill. The 4:07's gonna be a little late today boys.

Niko gives the station of the cross a wide berth as he drives along his ruthless way.

A steady forty mph is both the slowest and the fastest Niko dares go right now. He's shaking and his breath is ragged, senses overloaded. He wants to drive walleyed into what unmarked path lies leading where. Wants to let go the wheel and let the car itself take him where it may. Wants to get out of the car and get on hands and knees and shake until the shaking stops. Instead he holds the car at forty.

Now his route has led him to the forest. Trees swell toward him and flash by, souls entombed in living wood and someday to be wedded to the fleshly dead by iron spikes airgunned into the conscious pulp of their incessant being.

The roof above him buckles. Niko readies for another salvo but it's not another assault. It's his demon, who has glided overhead like a carrion bird to watch the car escape the train and then returned. Once again he lets his demon in and once again his demon fills the spacious rear compartment. A swath of blood that might not be his gleams his enormous chest.

"Nice flight?"

"Lost my baggage." His demon looks backward at pursuing shapes not apprehended by the mind of man. "Go for the woods. They can't fly there, they'll get tangled up like kites."

The wood is sparse compared to the forest of the crucified. The ground is rough and the Franklin's passengers are bounced around as Niko threads among the rotund gluttons imprisoned in themselves exactly as he left them. Jouncing headlights glance upon the pale bruised creatures with their spines snapped backward and heads shoved up their rectums to look so like the plucked and headless corpses of turkeys. The suicides run horrible and blind like panicked fawns. They trip over branches and gluttons and stumble across roots and slam into trees.

From behind approaches arrhythmic pounding. Niko's about to ask his demon what's going on when suddenly around them gallop emaciated horsemen on elongate mounts like anorexic jockeys on enlarged greyhounds. They part around the Franklin to the left and to the right so spindly on their matchstick legs they cannot possibly support their famished weight. Yet they dart like nimble antelopes and flash so quickly in and out the headlamps cone that some dozen of them have sped by before it can be seen that horse and rider are not separate entities at all but joined and of a single will. Running easily beside the car are centaurs. Not the burly robust creatures of Greek myth but gaunt and predatory frames supporting taut thin flesh the gray of crematorium ash stretched near to piercing by protruding bones. If there are eyes within those hatchet heads they are so deepset or black that they appear as twin holes only, painted patches like dark spots on the wings of dusty moths. Their hooves kick up no leaf or twig or clod. Three dozen of them run before the Franklin's prow like shepherd dolphins before a schooner's bow, their hoofbeats' number not accounting for the distance they advance. In their aspect more like insects than like creatures with a meated heart. They part to flow around the bleeding trees and sessile gluttons and argus demons they encounter, each obstacle revealed to Niko moments before he might plow into it. He dodges and swerves, and he curses the centaurs because of course it is their aim to lull him into fallen logs and stone outcrops.

A headless snake jabs past Niko's shoulder as his demon points. "There's a trail there."

Niko heads for it. "Does it lead out of here?"

"Yeah but we're not out of the woods yet."

Niko drives along the rough and winding path. "Why'd you jump?"

"To make the car lighter, stupid."

"I mean from the train."

Silence from the back. Then, "I don't know. It seemed like a good idea at the time? I might ask you the same question you know."

The car spits from the forest like offending gristle out across the open hardpan, the horsemen left behind. Across the fearsome night they drive. Niko and his demon and a faintly glowing jar. See them from a sky that never saw a dawn: carshaped blackness inching over ancient plain, paltry white light leading and dim red light behind, some luminescent bottomfeeder hugging the flat plain floor to follow currents or magnetic lines because its route is charted in the very helix of its twining DNA. And so prowls on. Mercifully oblivious to the indifferent vastness of the deep it crosses. More must yet unwind from out the Stygian dark. This the route the car must forge.

Within minutes they are come to the shore of frigid Lethe, the river of forgetfulness. Scant light gleams from its obsidian liquid.

"How are we supposed to get across?" Niko says to the back seat.

"We'll burn that bridge when we come to it."

Niko glares at the dark instrument panel. Once again he fights the urge to look back at the smug inhuman bastard he chauffeurs.

"If you know something tell me. There are gonna be enough surprises without you adding to them."

"I don't know something." The whiskey voice grows closer as the demon hunches forward. "I'm making this up as I go. Same as you." Niko's nostrils flare at the rot of his demon's breath. His skin has the sour smell of a threeday bender. Mercifully the demon leans back. "When I want to go across a river I fly."

They drive until the river flows before them.

Niko's demon says Go right and Niko turns right. On his left the river flows. How much of my mortal life did I waste returning to that memory-cleansing water? I might still be bathing there had not the grave Achaian delivered my guitar, and the voice of it returned me to my self. Akileo, Akileo. Somewhere on this hardpacked shore I bested you. A feat no Homer will relate. Possibly your disgraceful armor weighs you still beneath those very waters. For your sake I hope it does.

Though the sand is hard and flat the car is still a little squirrely. It wants to get away from him again.

"We're not headed out anymore," says Niko.

"Why thank you Daniel Boone. No we're not. If out is north we're headed east."

"What are we looking for?"

"A bridge would be nice."

"I don't see one."

"There isn't one."

"Then we're looking for the narrowest spot we can find."

"You can never find the narrowest spot on an infinite river," says his demon.

"The narrowest spot in the next five miles then."

"Whyyy?" Like an obstinate six year old.

"Because we're going to cross it your way."

"How's that?"

"We're gonna fly."

It's more like ten miles but finally Niko finds a promising spot. Here some obstruction, probably logjammed bodies, has caused the mounding-up of runoff sand over uncounted centuries until a respectable dune has formed. It projects perhaps a hundred yards into the river and rises maybe thirty feet. From the end of the dune to the frozen far side of the river is about fifty yards. Using the slightly up-angled dune as a ramp, assuming the sandbar is hard and firm all the way, driving at a top speed of around ninety miles an hour ought to land the Franklin just about smack in the middle of the river.

Which is why Niko's demon is on the roof as Niko backs up the car without looking. The mason jar is clamped between Niko's thighs and his head is half out the window like a happy dog to hear his demon's shouted directions.

"Right. Go right. More. Good, now straighten out. Ah nuts. Hold on, will you?"

Niko stops. The car rises as his demon jumps off the roof. "Let me do the talking."

"Someone's coming?" Niko doesn't want to idle here. He must keep moving.

"One of my compadres." He puts on a big ole shiteating grin and through clenched teeth says Look the other way, then nods amiably to whatever's coming toward them.

Niko looks the other way. In his peripheral vision an obese demon waddles to the car. One side of her face looks halfmelted, one eye two inches lower than the other. The bottom of her face thick with caked-on food. A standard issue trident in one clawed hand. She glances at the car and Niko promptly looks away. Niko hears her say Howdy.

"How do."

"What brings you guys to our neck of the woods? You're a little off the beaten path."

"Well. We're delivering a cake. A big gooey chocolate cake with creamy rich frosting thick as dogshit."

"A cake." Her voice is suddenly pure sex.

"Bout yea big. In fact—" His demon's voice lowers seductively and Niko can't make out the rest. As she listens lustfully the obese demon's gaze slides hopefully toward the Black Taxi where she sees Niko trying to look innocuous. "Say," she says.

Niko hears a soft grunt and a strangled squawk and a meaty thump. By the time he looks his demon stands above the corpulent demon writhing with the blunt end of her own trident piercing her head. Her lower eye halfpushed from the socket by the length of iron rammed behind it. Niko's demon has his foot on the trident to hold the bucking bloated figure down.

"Well, I see you did the talking."

"My favorite form of communication. Wait here. I gotta take out the trash." The vanquished demon's mouth works spastically.

"We don't have time for this."

"Fnuh fnuh fnuh," says the fat demon.

Without looking Niko's demon bends to the ground and loops a tendril to scoop a healthy load of sand into the fat demon's mouth. "Look, do you know what'll happen if they catch me?" He snorts and deposits another load into the sputtering mouth below him. "They'll take me apart and put the pieces in boiling oil and cook them for a hundred years in a pot full of piranhas while they decide how they really want to punish me. They have rules about you but it's open season on me, buddy pal. They can do whatever they want to catch me, and when they catch me they can do whatever they want to me. Forever and ever like the lovesongs say. So I'm unloading Shamu here before she decides to collect on the book the casino has surely put on me by now, or before she calls her wicked stepsisters in to share the loot. Okay?" He lifts the trident onto one powerful shoulder. The fat demon dangles like some bloated thing bagged out of season. "Bathtime, skinny." He glances at Niko. "The less they bother me the easier it'll be for you." He turns away like some sick parody of a little lost devil running away from home. "We're in this together sweetheart," he calls over his shoulder.

"What else is new," Niko mutters.

"Fnuh fnuh fnuh," the fat demon says.

"You ready up there?" Niko calls.

"I still think you're crazy as hell," from the roof of the car. "But insanity's helpful in someone I'm supposed to torment."

"That's not your job anymore."

"I can moonlight. Let's go."

Niko reaches around the ungainly seatcushion his demon tore from the back seat and set across his lap in lieu of an airbag, and he puts the car in gear. Awkwardly he shifts as the Franklin lumbers up to speed. The breeze that blows into the opened front windows contains a chill from off the frozen plain across the river.

Above Niko his demon's tendrils, wrapped through driver's and passenger's sides of the window, reposition for a better grip.

They race toward the dune projecting out into the river Lethe. All their calculations say the car can't make it by itself. And his demon can't possibly ferry the fortyfive hundred pound sedan a hundred fifty feet across the river. But perhaps the mongrel airfoil of his demon's outspread wings can give them enough glide ratio to make the farther shore.

Niko keeps them straight and here comes the edge of the dune and son of a bitch it's hard not to hit the brake. The ground drops below the windshield and Niko winces and his foot stays on the gas as the ground drops away and the engine roars and the whitewalls spin on nothing. Above him his demon spreads his wings and holds them as taut and wide and flat as his considerable muscles will allow.

The car soars off the dune. Black rock of sky beyond the hood. The mason jar wedged by the seatcushion between his clamping thighs. The car tips forward and the windshield fills with the frozen line of the far bank dotted with embedded figures. Solvent water rushes upward. Water that once delivered Niko from his haunted heart. The icy bank is twenty yards away now. Ten. Will we reach it?

The schooner hood dips down.

No.

Niko just has time to bring the cushion up between himself and the steering wheel before the car slams water like Icarus on wheels. The mason jar flies free and hits somewhere forward. Without a seatbelt Niko shoots into the seatcushion and it smashes against the steering wheel and he cracks a floating rib. With the wind knocked from him Niko sees black water engulf the hood. Hiss of heated metal hitting water. The Franklin rights itself and Niko is pushed back into the seat. Water splashes his shoulder neck and ear, and where it touches him his skin goes numb. The cushion hits him in the face and he bats it aside.

The spinning whitewalls spray a rooster tail behind the car. The icy shore is only yards away. Blue and naked in the cold the embedded damned stare as the heavy sedan rages forward. The Franklin hates him but the Franklin doesn't want to drown. If it settles to the bottom of the frigid water like some pissant Titanic will it too forget? Niko thinks it will. Niko thinks the Franklin's fighting for its shady life.

Above him his demon shouts Come on, come on. Why doesn't he fly away?

Niko looks around for the mason jar but only sees its glow. He still can't breathe.

A strange and rhythmic thunder comes from overhead as Niko's demon beats his wings with all his might to help the car glide forward. They're barely moving now and Niko doesn't think they're going to make it. The invisible fist lets go his gut and Niko draws a great pneumonic breath.

Something bumps the car's right side. One of the naked dead, paperwhite and dripping, grabs the door with bloodless hands and clambers on. She is beautiful and dead as a lawn statue and moves like an automaton. Niko leans across the seat to pry her fingers loose and wonders even as he does why he is bothering since he's about to join her in her bath of long forgetfulness. Her fingers lifeless cold. Beneath her nails the skin is nearly lavender. Listlessly she watches Niko try to force her fingers from the door.

The car surges forward and tilts starboard. Niko knocks the Franklin out of gear as he falls sideways. His forehead touches the aquamarine of the woman's cheek. The surge continues and something slides hissing across the rear of the car. One of the river leviathans. The wake of its passing propels the Franklin forward and the front bumper scrapes the shore.

Niko slides back behind the wheel to put the car in gear. He glances at the clambering woman who looks up as if sighting a diving hawk. Something yanks her from the car and she splashes back into the river never to remember her escape attempt. Niko's demon jumps down in her place, standing on the runningboard and hugging the side of the car and grinning evil glee. "All ashore that's going ashore."

The front wheels touch the sloping icy shore and the Black Taxi slows. Niko revs the engine and the back tires spin and water gargles as the rooster tail resumes. The car glides forward until the rear tires touch the shore and spin on the ice. Niko's demon is leaning away to open the rear door when the tires grab and the Black Taxi bucks and surges from the water. The demon looks surprised as the car shoots out from under him and he falls backward. He lashes out a tendril but he misses and he drops from sight. Niko hears a heavy splash as his demon falls into the memory scouring waters of the river Lethe.

XXV

WALL OF DENIAL

The Black Taxi skims across the ice. Niko holds it to the highest speed that he can go and still maintain some measure of control. Mottled patches blur before the headlamps' revelation, bodies of the frozen dead beneath the ice.

The Franklin really wants to get loose. The tires slide on watery patches and bump emergent corpses. One such has already sent the car into a slide in which the back and front ends threatened to trade places for at least a mile while Niko held the wheel cut to the right and rode it out until he felt the tires bite beneath him and he straightened out. He must maintain his focus every moment. Must bear down on the frozen sea that's ever forming from the dark ahead. The moment his attention wavers the Black Taxi will get away from him. It's sweaty work. The big sedan is squirrely on the ice. Like piloting a grand piano in a downhill soapbox derby. Niko isn't driving so much as aiming. He wishes the Checker cabbie were behind the wheel. This would be a walk in the park to her. Oh well. He wishes her well wherever she is.

At least he's found the heater controls and floor vents. The trip across the icy reach is markedly warmer this time out. Small comfort. Things are going downhill fast. In the first place there's his passenger. Wet and chilled to the supernatural bone his demon huddles in his leather wings shivering on the restored back seat hard enough to shake the car. His great teeth clack like porcelain castanets. Though Niko cannot look at him he knows his demon's face is oddly childlike and earnest as it regards anew the world outside the window.

In the second place—oh but that doesn't bear thinking about, no oh no.

You play the hand you're dealt, buddy pal, whispers the voice that apparently has not left him despite its incarnation in the seat behind him. Drive.

In the second place, beside Niko on the front seat is the mason jar with its feather floating, and jagged along the surface of the jar like a photograph of distant lightning is a hairline crack.

Niko drives and the night goes on forever and Niko drives.

WHEN NIKO HEARD his demon splash into the river he got out of the dripping wet sedan, the engine still running and steam glowing in the headlights as it rose from the Franklin's dark contours. Niko looked up at the solid roof of night and realized he couldn't run back to the water to help his demon or even look to see where his demon was. From behind him came splashing. "Hey," he called to a Polynesian man embedded in ice up to his waist. "Can you see what happened to the demon who fell in?"

The man nodded agreeably and said something Niko couldn't understand. Near the rear of the Black Taxi a chubby man with a patchy beard was embedded up to his thighs and bent over as far as he could to warm his hands in the car's softly puttering exhaust. "Yo," he called to Niko. "He's right there. You blind?"

"I have a curse. I can't look back."

"Ooh, some curse."

"Is my, has the demon gone under?"

"You kiddin? He's standing right there like he lost a fuckin contact lens. The water's yay high." The man put a hand near his hairy genitals. "Hey. You're that guitar guy aren't you? Nike, some shit like that. My fuckin kids used to get stoned and listen to you.

— 322 —

Bouncin around the house with their fuckin hair and pretendin to play the guitar. Dope dealin little bastards. Fuck, I sent one of em down here." The man straightened from the exhaust pipe. Melted ice puddled beneath the car. "So you're here too huh? Like I'm surprised. Weren't you a junky or something?"

"Or something. Listen—"

"So I guess you're just mister big fuckin rock star huh? Clothes and a fuckin gangster car for the big celebrity. Whose big ol devil dick did you suck, Mister Dope Fiend?"

Niko started looking around for another source of help. "It's not like that. I'm sorry but I'm in a hurry—"

"Oh he's in a hurry. He's got a fuckin schedule. No shit, I'm glad you're even talking to a nobody like me. Before you go I wonder if I could get your fuckin autogra—"

"Could you yell for him to come here?"

Patchy Beard crossed his arms. "Fuuuuck you." He nearly sang it.

Niko glanced at the Black Taxi. The well of its reflection on the melted ice. "Call him over and I'll pull you out."

"You're fuckin A, Jackson." The man made longhorns with his fingers and whistled piercingly and then cupped his hands and shouted. "Yo Batman. Hey ugly. Cmere." He put his hands on his hips. "He's coming. Hey how the Yankees doing? Been in the series lately?"

"They lost."

"Damn Yankees."

Niko heard his demon splashing toward the shore. "What did you say to me?" his own approaching voice said.

Patchy Beard stopped with his yap half open as he recognized the demon's voice and then the demon's face. "Well put my dick in a blender. He's fuckin ugly as you."

Niko sidestepped and backed up until he stood before his demon and he craned his neck to look the waterlogged creature in the eye. His demon's face was changed. The expression lacked the gleeful hostility and brooding menace hewn into cheek and brow and lip. More, his demon looked lost. Still frightening. Still powerful. But lost. "Do you remember who you are?" said Niko.

His demon's look was unlike any Niko ever saw him wear. The pure befuddlement belied its very design. The demon slowly shook his head and Niko felt a little tug of pity. He sighed and walked past his demon's burly shoulder, treading carefully on the ice, to open the passenger door. "Climb in," he told the demon who did not know he was Niko's demon.

"Whyyyy?" He sounded like a child.

"Because I can tell you who and what you are and why you can't remember." Niko smiled as he gestured for the demon to get in. "Trust me."

Now Niko listens to his passenger shiver and shift on the seat behind him. My demon. "Your name," he tells the thrumming night unspooling there before him, "is Nikodemus."

"Nikodemus."

"Does that ring any bells?"

"No."

"Okay." Niko bites his lower lip and takes a deep breath and glances at the mason jar beside him. He doesn't need to see the hairline crack, he feels it in his fissured heart. Is the feather's glow a little dimmer? It seems to be. He gently lifts the jar and holds it out behind him without looking, left hand steady on the wheel. "Here. Careful with it." He hopes he sounds less nervous than he feels.

Tendrils wrap the jar and take it from him. "What is it?"

"It's somebody's soul."

Greenish shadows shift. "It's broken."

"It broke when we jumped the Lethe a few minutes ago and you fell in."

"The Lethe."

"It's a river. The water causes amnesia."

"I fell in?"

Niko nods. "It's why you're soaking wet."

"I don't remember falling in."

"That's because you fell in."

"I'm cold."

Niko adjusts the heater. "Better?"

A long pause. "You're mortal?"

"Very."

"I'm helping you?"

"You've been assigned to me. We're like partners in a race. There's a bet on whether we can get the jar to the gate. A lot of people are trying to stop us."

A tendril taps the jar's screwon cap. "Why don't I just fly this to the gate?"

He is startled by the suggestion. But no. "There are conditions. I'm not allowed to look back, but you can. They can't try to stop me but they're allowed to try to stop you. You'd catch hell if you tried to make it out with that." He glances toward the rearview to gauge Nikodemus' reaction and once again is glad and frustrated at the mirror's absence.

The demon actually scratches his head with a tendril as he concentrates. "Okay. Anything else?"

"If anything happens to the jar we're screwed."

Green light shifts. "But something's already happened to the jar."

"I think it's still okay. Just don't let it break." The Franklin slurs on a wet patch and Niko nudges the wheel in the direction of the mild skid. The tires regain traction and the Franklin straightens out. "Any other questions?"

"What's your name?"

Niko senses Nikodemus is distressed by the absence of what he feels should be there. Niko remembers the sensation well. He grips the steering wheel tighter. "Niko."

"Niko."

"Sound familiar?"

"No. It sounds like my name though. Are we friends?"

Niko frowns. "Well. We've known each other a long time. You kind of work for me."

"Oh. Okay."

Niko drives another mile with his mouth pressed tight. The darkness weighs around them with oceanic pressure. We do not drive across so much as tunnel through.

Finally he bangs the steering wheel. "Look," he tells the hollow dark, "you don't really work for me. We're not partners. I made that up. I'm sorry."

"Oh. What are we then?"

"You were assigned to me, but not for some bet. It was your job to lead me into temptation. To give me a nudge when I was wavering."

"But now I'm helping you."

"Apparently."

"How come?"

"I don't really know. I think you feel sorry for me."

"Sorry for a mortal?"

"I don't really know. I'm not sure you do either."

"You could just be telling me all this too."

"I could. But I could have not told you you're my demon at all and you wouldn't know any better."

"How'd we end up in this, this situation?"

Niko barks a laugh and feels a sudden craving for a cigarette. He drives, and as he drives he talks to the advancing night that never tires of its own disgorgement. And for once he tells the dark the truth. And for once the darkness listens.

"So that's the deal." Niko's throat is raspy and he wants a drink. Water, but he'd chug a double whiskey without a thought. He's exhausted and his side is throbbing where his rib is fractured and the pain is probably all that's keeping him awake by now. They've left behind the plain of ice and drive again upon the barren floor of Hell. Somewhere in the gloom a mountain rises, somewhere on its face a fallen god is chained. Far ahead a thin black thread has formed the flat horizon of the Ledge. Niko watches as it slowly thickens and he clears his throat. The heater's off now. The windows are open and a hot and septic wind plays through the spacious car.

"And this is all true," says Nikodemus.

Niko's very aware his demon literally holds Jemma's life in his—well, his tendrils. "Every damned word."

"And if I go back they'll obliterate me."

"After they hurt you a lot for a long time, yeah. That's what you said."

Shadows shift as the jar is held up and turned about. "Will my memory come back?"

"Mine did. Eventually. I don't think it's gone, I think you just can't get to it." Now he sees the faint outlines of the ascending hills of the mounded dead fallen from the Ramp. The Meat Pie Mountains.

"Okay," his demon finally says.

Niko frowns at the prow of the car plowing the dark. "Okay what?"

"Okay, I guess Nikodemus is an all right name."

Tears sting Niko's eyes. "Okay," he says. As much to himself as to his darker version.

"So what do we do now?"

"Is anyone behind us?"

"Not a soul."

"Okay then." Niko takes a deep breath and yawns deeply and arches on the seat and stretches to his fingertips. He shakes his head and rubs his heavy eyelids. "Now we teach you how to drive a stick shift."

HE WAS ROWING on Lake Arrowhead. The water red and the sky dark. From the bow Jemma grinned at him and said Pass me a bun, hon. Niko shipped oars and picked up the paper sack from the seat beside him. When he opened it something green and glowing flew out and disappeared into the sky. He smelled Jem's perfume. He looked at Jem to ask her if she'd seen what just happened but Jem had turned into a husk. Her body collapsed as he watched. He knew he had to get her back to shore and get the green thing back into the sack but when he picked up oars again he saw there was no shore. Only bloodred water far as he could see. He called her name. Not to the empty Jemma suit that rippled like paper in the breeze but to the vacant air. He began to row without direction. Calling and calling her name.

"Hey. Wake up."

"Mnmn."

"Niko. Come on, get up."

Niko opens bleary eyes to find himself on the back seat curled around the mason jar as if he's cold and it gives forth some form of heat. He sits up and his injuries are tallied and handed to him in one lump sum. An invisible knife is wedged between his ribs. His shoulders throb and his feet ache and his neck is stiff. "Whadissit. Jus laid down."

"You've been asleep for two and a half hours."

This wakes him up a bit. "Are we there yet?"

"Not quite. But we have company."

"Um gotta pee."

"Can't help you there, buddy pal."

"Who, who's behin us?" Niko feels as if he's trying to think thoughts his brain is too small to contain.

"I don't know. Headlights."

Niko blinks. "A car."

"Niko, you have to wake up. I'll never get this thing up the Ramp. It's all I can do to drive it straight with nothing around us."

"Nnkay." Feeling drugged unsteady he carefully sets the jar on the front seat beside Nikodemus and climbs over the seatback like an old man. Nikodemus' bulk takes up most of the space in the front of the sedan. Riding shotgun for a moment Niko collects his wits and stares at the obsidian Nothing filling the windshield. "Where the hell are we?"

"Coming up on the Ramp."

"I don't see anything."

"That's the Ledge. It's so big you can't see it all. Here." He turns right and the Franklin angles more obliquely toward the infinitely wide upthrust fault. Now Niko sees the distant knife edge of the Ramp itself against the vast undifferentiated black of the Ledge's face, angling down until it merges with the Lower Plain. The Meat Pie Mountains begin as small hills at the foot of the Ramp, undulating ever taller off into the starless distance. Beyond that a dull glint from the sluggish surface of the sea of blood.

Nikodemus steers them straight toward the Ledge again and once again the view is vacant black. It looks simultaneously as if the car is floating motionless in an empty universe and as if it's constantly about to hit a wall.

"Go straight again. That's making me sick."

"Screws up your perspective doesn't it?" Nikodemus turns the wheel. "I see what you mean about the car. It doesn't like being driven."

"Mmm. I wasn't kidding about needing to pee."

Nikodemus grins and holds out the mason jar.

"Aren't you a fucking riot."

"You could try peeing out the window."

"Look, I've learned I'm capable of a lot of uncivilized things. But I've got to draw the line somewhere."

"Do you want me to stop?"

Niko clamps his knees together. "How far back are they?"

Nikodemus' head swivels far enough to break a human neck. "Eleven and a half miles."

"I don't think I can hold it till the next gas station. Better stop."

Immediately Nikodemus whips a tendril around the shift lever and puts the car in neutral and hits the brakes. They're still creeping along when Niko jumps out and tears open his fly.

And stands there waiting and feeling foolish.

"I thought you had to pee."

"Quit staring."

The demon looks puzzled. "Whyyyy?"

"Stop looking at me dammit."

Shaking his gargoyle head Nikodemus lets the clutch out with the Franklin in gear and the big car bucks like a bronco and stalls. Nikodemus lets it roll a few feet. Brakelights make the patch of plain look like the surface of Mars. Nikodemus starts the car but forgets to take it out of gear and the Franklin lurches and stalls again.

"Oh heck" from inside and then the engine starts.

Niko finds himself staring at a pristine vintage car idling on the floor of Hell while he holds his penis in his hand and tries to pee. Yessir, I'm on me a heroic epic type journey.

Something monstrous shrieks nearby. Niko jumps back and pees on his own shoe before he realizes it's Nikodemus leaning on the Black Taxi's horn. Niko shouts God damn it and his knees buckle as the ground quakes and a roaring spreads across the sunless sky.

As quickly as it came the tectonic spasm passes. Niko runs for the car.

"Now you've done it," says Nikodemus.

"Slide."

"I was just getting good at this." But Nikodemus slides and watches Niko put the car in gear and get them moving again.

Niko drives in silence for a moment. They're closing in on the bottom of the Ramp and Niko heads a bit away from the Ledge. Soon the Franklin speeds past more dead than Niko thought had ever lived upon the earth. The untold millions of bodies of the Meat Pie Mountains heaped upon each other like an obscene snowdrift against the obsidian of the Ledge.

"I see you've started remembering things."

"I have?"

"You've called me buddy pal at least three times."

"Buddy pal. What's that?"

"Pet name."

Now the Franklin is pelted on the right side. Niko and Nikodemus hastily roll up the windows. Entire disenfranchised populations wander torn and broken sobbing here, robbed of self and hope and dignity. Tearing at themselves or at each other as they wail and as they curse their births and lives and deaths. They see the headlights speeding by and hurl insults and stones and handfuls of verminous shit and bile. How many of their number were delivered to their mournful estate by the very carriage that now speeds by?

In the distance to the left are buildings and the ruins of buildings. Dim light renders them soft and indistinct as underwater relics.

"What are those?" says Niko.

"I seem to recall Gorgons."

"What, do they live there?"

"They turn people's bodies into stone and the bodies are cut into bricks and the bricks are fitted to make the buildings."

"Cute." Niko gazes across the unlit distance at the houses of pain reared and tumbled there. Here they think in geologic scales. Punishments meted out across whole epochs.

And then there's no more time for rumination because they're heading straight toward the Ramp.

NIKO CAN ONLY gape at the scene before him. A ceaseless torrent of the damned disgorges from the foot of the Ramp, flooding ever forth like a living river of insatiable army ants destroying everything in its relentless path. From the Ramp's terminus the dead eventually scatter all about the Lower Plain as they head on to the endless variations of their future punishment. The base of the Ramp where they are thickest is a pullulating sea of wretches.

Behind this carnography of wounded flesh the Ramp itself angles upward, and even though the angle of its rise is slight it covers such a distance along the Ledge's face that it rises and recedes until it disappears into the measureless dark. A road wide as a fourlane highway carved from out the naked rock by hands wielding crude implements, a work begun back when this cliff was made two thousand years ago, and every inch of it seething with naked festering bleeding scabrous broken rended suffering sobbing maimed humanity herded pushing stumbling running trudging crawling fighting falling crushed and crushing in an endless current streaming down its length to join the wounded nation at its base.

Niko blinks and shakes his head as if to ward off bees. The writhing masses here before his inundated eyes. Suddenly nauseated he is filled with revulsion and blind mortal panic and something like religious terror in the face of his own insignificance, in the face of every body's insignificance. Teeming billions suffer here while hidden hands direct the reins of infinite space and eternal time. How can a mortal mind contain a single brush stroke of this horrible vast canvas? What overwhelms me now is but a fragment of the whole. But could I absorb the naked entirety of this place I would be struck gibbering mad. Had I seen this going in would I have gone? Did Geryon spare me this on purpose when he flew me to the Lower Plain? This is what I've set myself against. I must be out of my fucking mind.

The broken mirror of his demon's face gazes earnestly at the human tide before them. "That's an awful lot of people."

Niko glances at him but Nikodemus seems sincere.

"Then again, it's a lot of awful people."

Niko slows the car. "Lock the doors."

"Whyyyy?"

"Lock the damn doors."

"Okay okay. You don't have to yell." Nikodemus locks the doors and gazes out the window as Niko stops the Black Taxi. "I don't think this will do much good if all these people get hold of us." He glances behind them. "The headlights are getting closer."

"I need a minute." Niko rubs his eyes and face and temples with shaky hands while the engine thrum fills the car.

Sixty seconds later Nikodemus says Okay.

"Okay what?"

"Okay it's been a minute."

Niko sighs. "I think I liked you better when you were mean."

"I was mean?"

"If we left the car and I held onto Jem could you fly us to the top?"

"To the Upper Plain? I don't know." Nikodemus peers upward through the windshield. It's like trying to see the Man in the Moon while standing on the lunar surface. The wall is so big and so close it can't be seen as an object.

"Haven't you flown it before?"

"I don't remember. I guess I must have."

Niko frowns at the steering wheel. "I can't do this. I can't drive up that."

"You drove across the Rift."

"One epic deed a day's my limit."

"We can take turns."

"Are you crazy? They'll tear us apart. If we can even get through them."

"They're afraid of demons aren't they?"

"So."

"Well." Nikodemus shows his needle teeth.

"What, you're going to scare off a hundred million people? Even you aren't that ugly."

The feral grin deflates and Niko realizes he has hurt his demon's feelings.

"Why don't we at least try flying?" Niko says. "If you get tired we could glide back down."

"You said the demons chasing us are allowed to stop me and distract you. I think both of those will be a lot easier for them if I'm holding onto you in the air. And if you drop the jar the whole thing's over anyhow."

"Oh." Niko tries to imagine Nikodemus engaging in some kind of aerobatic dogfight while burdened with Niko. Guess not. He narrows his eyes at the epic ebb and flow of ruined souls before them. He breathes deeply. "All right. We drive." He's scared off his ass. Resignedly he puts the Black Taxi in gear. "This is going to take days."

Nikodemus leans back as best he can in what for him are the cramped confines of the passenger side. "Bitch bitch bitch," the demon says.

At a guess it took four days. Lacking day or night it was hard to tell and the car clock made it worse by running backward. Mostly Niko drove while Nikodemus crouched on the hood like some nightmarish ornament, a cargoyle shouting and lashing his tentacles to clear the way. The docile dead obliged like sheep. Rarely getting past first gear Niko would drive until he was falling asleep at the wheel and then Nikodemus would take over while Niko tried to sleep in the back seat curled around the haircracked mason jar and getting so used to the soul unmooring shriek of the Black Taxi's horn that sometimes he would pop awake because it stopped. His dreams were filled with faceless cordwood bodies he drove over as they reached out cold dead unavailing hands.

The car stopped often. When the surging dead would not or could not yield. When it became impossible to tell whether the car was heading up the Ramp or toward its edge. When Niko had to deal with unavoidable human functions. For the latter Niko was at first afraid to leave the car, certain that the jealous dead would set upon him. His fears proved groundless and he did his business unmolested in their midst. Having come so far the dead were numbed past caring by their torment, crazed by the irrevocable certainty of eternal perdition, hopelessly resigned so deep into these regions of despair that they were become more cattle than human beings. Hell itself had worn them to the nub. Ceaselessly the mutilated and afflicted dead jostled and swarmed and pushed with no more will than snowflakes in an avalanche. They never looked back and neither did he. Not once did he see any of them try to buck the tide. Even those forced over the edge by the swell and press of their fellow sufferers fell with a complete indifference awful to behold.

Sometimes a member of this destitute parade would grab onto a doorhandle and sometimes even get the door open. Nikodemus kept forgetting to lock the door going on and returning from cargoyle duty. Twice one of them actually made it into the car. Once a teenaged boy with buboes that opened to show little teeth, once a tiny Inuit woman who sat quiet and still upon the seat. Niko was so surprised by her sudden appearance and then so fascinated by her calm centeredness that he had gaped at her and done nothing. In the midst of all this horror she had seemed a saint. Niko was content to let her ride along with them, though where she thought she was going was anybody's guess, but Nikodemus yanked her from the car.

Continually the car ran over fallen trampled souls too injured to regain their feet. Their regeneration set back even further now by two tons of bulldozing vintage sedan. Niko tried to tell himself it wasn't the same as hitting them in the mortal world. They could not die and they would heal. But their pain was still pain, and the first forty or fifty made him feel awful. Soon they were just speedbumps.

Several times Nikodemus left the car and flew away to return hours later bearing water in a smooth scraped swollen bladder that had to have been a human stomach. Desperate and dehydrated Niko drank the cloudy water anyway, his body grateful even as his mind resisted.

Nikodemus also brought handfuls of raw food. Niko tried not to think about what he might be eating as he chewed and swallowed without looking. The alternative was starvation, and he had learned as many had before him that when faced with real and lasting hunger and no certain end to it in sight a man will eat anything put before him that might give nourishment without killing him and not complain. Niko ate and drank and did not complain.

During all this upward crawl the Black Taxi never ran out of gas. The aircooled engine never overheated or stalled or stopped or even missed or knocked. Odometer and tripmeter turned and turned and turned.

Whatever had been following them was lost now among the crush and press of millions of dead in the miles between. Or perhaps their pursuer had left them to their epic and mundane labor.

There was only one place they could emerge after all. Easy enough to have cohorts waiting at the head of the Ramp.

At first Niko could not help staring through the windshield at the continuous exodus parting before the Franklin's prow. As if entranced by some overstocked aquarium of grotesqueries. Vacant faces and empty eyes, tribes of Adam, tribes of Shem. A diaspora of the penitent damned everfleeing the holocaustic closure of their mortal lives. At first he sought among their drowned expressions faces he had known upon the living earth but glimpses of their anguished faces were too fleeting for his memory to fit a name. They trudged and stumbled past the Franklin as it made its salmon trek upstream and the only impression made by those endless permutations of recombinant DNA was a palimpsest of handprints on the windows of the car.

Nikodemus did not talk much when he was in the car but instead watched the passing faces, brooding and introspective.

Niko wondered about atmospheric pressure. The Ramp rose higher from the Lower Plain than Everest rose above sea level but the temperature remained hot and dry and the air pressure did not decrease. How could that be? If the millibars were normal on the Lower Plain they should be breathing near-vacuum by now. And if they were normal on the Upper Plain, the Lower Plain should have been dense enough to crush bone.

To pass the time he concocted science fictional solutions involving massive airpumps and recirculating vents carved through the Ledge by some long-vanished race to equalize the pressure. And then he looked around at the endless stream of immortal souls made flesh to be forever punished, at the interior of the car that never ran out of gas and that he knew to be somehow alive, at the perfectly inhuman version of himself hunched and pensive on the hood with wings tucked tight and tendrils wrapped around mahogany knees drawn to massive chest, at the cracked jar that contained the glowing essence of Jemma's soul. And he laughed at himself until he cried and then wiped his eyes and wondered if he truly had gone well beyond the pale.

Blind black wall to the left of them, blind abyss to the right, the staggering dead between. They rode a tightrope between solid nothing and empty perdition and they played out this numbing odyssey so long that it became hard to remember a time they had done anything else, which was almost literally true for Nikodemus whose smoothed mind had done little else, when the end hove into view.

THE STEERING WHEEL saws and Niko's arms jerk back and forth as the Black Taxi jounces over yet another fallen soul. Nikodemus asleep in back, sorting through the desecrated attic of his memory. The demon has stopped his icebreaker shifts because a fine red mist of blood is falling steadily on all and sundry now, windborne from the bloodfall somewhere up above. The dead flow past and passed. Niko plods forward and lays on the horn and drives over the fallen and occasionally turns on the topmounted wipers and thinks about how horrible it is that you really can get used to anything. How repetition drains an act of meaning. Of consequence. I wash a load of dishes and it's boring. I wash a thousand loads and it's something my hands do while my mind wanders and I no longer see the dishes. I kill one man and never forget his face. I line men up and shoot them by threes and fours all day long for years and only want a beer at the end of the day. Drive across a thousand suffering souls in Hell and just want airshocks and allwheel drive.

All those demons at their labor. Tormenting the damned for as long as there've been people. Their numbing work unending. Bored senseless and craving variety. Torture their only entertainment. Some are numbed to drones by their inflictions, some become creative just to ease the monotony of another working day. Most of it a gray undifferentiation of repetitious sadism. And Niko understands that in his journey up the Ramp he's found within himself some hint of what the demons feel. Truly there are things about yourself it's best to never know.

Niko is so deep within this rumination that the Battlements have been in view awhile before he notices them. What makes him finally straighten on the seat and draw a quick breath is a familiar sight from what seems long ago. A tiny distant flare of orange rising briefly out to limn the feudal Battlement walls as yet another burning soul is hurled to streak out shedding sparks and screaming high across the Upper Plain.

XXVI

STONES IN
MY PASSWAY

WELL WELL WELL. LOOK WHAT the cat dragged
in." Pignose grins through the windshield.

"What's the matter, fellas? Cat got your tongue?" Batface leers
through the passenger window.

"Let's let the cat out of the bag." Ramhorn's face appears upside
down from where he lies prone on the buckled roof.

The Black Taxi is parked below the Battlement walls just past the
head of the Ramp and near the shore of the Rio Rojo gouting blood
out over the Ledge. The corralled dead so thickly streaming past
them on the way to their prolonged descent it seems as if the car is
moving forward but it is not. It is stopped, and Niko and Nikodemus
look out at the stone gargoyles who have flown from their Battlement
perches to land on it. The fenders press against the tires. The car so
weighted down it cannot move. Any of the gargoyles could peel back
the roof like the lid on a can of Vienna sausages. This respite merely
toying before the kill.

Nikodemus looks more thoughtful than alarmed or even worried. His tendrils wrap each other like caduceus snakes entwining and disentangling. Nikodemus' version of wringing his hands.

The tendrils part and Nikodemus looks out the windshield at Pignose waggling his fingers with his thumbs in his ears to the large knuckles and sticking out a gray stone tongue at least a foot long. "They're forbidden to do anything to you," says Nikodemus. "It's me they want." And with surprising grace and speed he jumps into the back seat and wraps a tendril round the doorhandle. Realizing what his demon is about to do Niko starts to turn back to grab him but then stops and balls his fists and yells in frustration because he can't look back. Nikodemus yanks the handle and pushes open what truly is for him the suicide door.

BATFACE IS CAUGHT by surprise when Nikodemus surges from the car and knocks him off the runningboard. Pignose and Ramhorn gape stupidly as Nikodemus bats aside the damned like bowling pins and spreads his wings like a dark thing flowering. Half a dozen running steps and then he's kicking air and canting forward with legs spraddled like a swimming frog's. His leather wings beat furiously as he arcs above the ever congregating dead.

The Black Taxi groans and nearly bounces when the two remaining gargoyles push off from it. A loud bang sounds behind the car. Niko thinks it's a shotgun blast, someone behind them firing at the flying gargoyles like a demented skeetshooter, until he understands that the Black Taxi has blown a tire. Batface regains his stone feet and glares at Niko and raises a warning claw at him before turning away and launching into the air to join his confederates in pursuit of Nikodemus. Niko stares a moment as the sea of the dead closes around the car again.

Then he becomes all frantic motion. Put the car in gear and lean on the horn and lurch away. The naked dead before the car jump back but can't go far before they run into the wall of their own kind. Niko drives about ten clear feet and then plows into them. The first two fly backward like circus acrobats. The next slams the hood and clings there after the bumper breaks her shins.

She claws the black metal and pulls herself along the hood toward Niko. He swerves and she rolls to one side and away. Tires bump across her soft body.

Jouncing on the yielding logs of bodies the car can't pick up speed. At fifteen miles an hour there's time for many of them to get out of the way but not all. But it's run them down or join their ruined ranks. He keeps his foot on the gas and grips the wheel and clenches his jaw and plows through them.

Soon the car breaks free of the clustered damned and emerges onto open plain with both frogeyed headlamps askew. One beam projects directly down in front of the car and the other angles up to light a shaft of air. The left front fender is bent down into the tire which sends up smoke and a stench of burning rubber. The right rear tire is blown and the car feels sluggish and handles even more reluctantly than before. All four whitewalls redstained rings now like the smoldering irises of demons. The hood and grille and front bumper are covered with blood that cooks on the hot black metal with a slaughterhouse reek. Fine red droplets constellate the windshield. Niko leaves them be. Turning on the wipers will only smear the windshield and leave him blind.

The dead still flock toward the arch that opens onto the head of the Ramp but here they are spaced apart enough that Niko can avoid most of them.

Now the Black Taxi limps across the dimlit plain at twenty miles an hour, right rear tire flat and cockeyed headlamps a lighthouse beacon blazing Here I Am. The only light the distant glow of the enormous nazi bonfire. The flaming bodies that streaked out from the Battlement walls to light the plain are absent now that all the gargoyles are off pursuing Nikodemus.

Niko hopes his demon will evade them. Since Nikodemus emerged from the Lethe with his memories shed like the water that ran off him, the demon has been an oddly endearing soul. Not innocent but naive perhaps. And still he risks himself for Niko's sake. Risks not his life which he does not possess but risks oblivion itself. For him. For Niko. Damned Niko. Reneging Niko. Who has put himself ahead of all the world and sought to contravene the fate his own hands sealed in blooded letters of his name.

Why is Nikodemus doing this? Niko has no answer. Nikodemus has no answer either. But whatever luck exists in such a forlorn place as this, Niko wishes all of it upon his demon in his desperate flight.

And speaking of desperate flights. Have to stop and change that tire. Won't that be fun.

Now the Franklin moves among blackened lumps of thrown burned bodies heaped about this section of the plain. The remnant cinders lying in their nerve-seared pain who wait for muscle and tendon and skin to regenerate enough for them to resume their pointless ways. Niko avoids them as best he can, but they are many and the headlamps are cockeyed and the plain is dim. The intermittent crunching underneath the tires is unnerving.

Those able to hobble, crawl, or drag themselves move among their roasted kindred. The mindless insane headed toward what punishment will greet them next. See here this one poor soul. Man or woman Niko cannot tell for all the burned flesh cracked and glistening like a boar gone upright off the spit. Standing rooted like a tree struck bare by lightning. The seared bark of its flesh gleaming with pus as it turns to watch the car roll by.

Niko frowns. The charred soul is clearly visible in the dimness. Lit by headlamps that have realigned themselves. Niko peers out over the steering wheel. The downbent fender has resumed its former curve, the smell of burning rubber gone. Niko waggles the wheel and the big car responds. He gives it some gas and shifts into third. Forty, fifty miles an hour now. Dodging bodies lying burnt. The tire is no longer flat. In the few minutes of Niko's rumination and worry for Nikodemus the Black Taxi has healed itself.

A coppery hot slaughterhouse reek emerges through the floor vents.

It's the blood. The Franklin used their blood to heal itself. As if the car contains within itself some complete memory of its ideal form, as a starfish holds its blueprint or a lizard its own tail. And fed vampiric on human blood is fueled to shape back to itself. Restored as fully as the dark idea it is.

Jesus christ. Niko's dread at being contained within this awful conveyance is reborn. I am swallowed. Alive within the guts of some remorseless predator marauding an alien ocean and not the pilot of this thing at all.

He dampers his horror to swerve around a large black mound that is in fact a pile of reconstituting mulchosaur shit. How could he have forgotten?

And because that is the way things go in this demented world, as if on cue he hears from out beyond the headlamps' reach an awful rhythmic clacking like a nail caught in a tire. Sure as Hell is all around him there it is, twentyfive feet long and angling toward him on its many legs, its crescent head held low before it to ingest whatever lies along its hungry way.

Niko floors it and cuts right and the creature moves to intercept. Niko cuts left. Five thousand pounds of famished running digestive tract respond.

Shadows shift inside the Franklin as the mason jar rolls. Niko herds the jar against him without taking his gaze from the sidewinding creature growing in front of him. He can't turn around to outrun it. He'll have to drive right up on the son of a bitch and hope he can swerve past it.

"If you fuck me up I'll let it eat you," Niko tells the car. "And I swear to god I'll get away, and I'll laugh while I watch it tear you into scrap."

Distant thunder shudders as the raven sky convulses and the ground shakes with his utterance of the word that is down here profane.

Niko's pretty sure the mulchosaur can't match the 298cc V-12's top speed. He's about to find out, though, because there the son of a bitch is, head raising off the plain and crescent shape all sawteeth mouth and wider than the hurtling car. Niko holds the Frankin straight and feels it trying to get loose from under him. He shouts No and wrests the wheel back to avoid a head-on with a mulchosaur. The eating machine before him jags to follow. Niko yanks the wheel left and now the Franklin responds like a bored-out Corvette. The back end skids and tires fight to maintain traction. The mulchosaur scoops dirt where the Franklin would have been before the final swerve.

The Franklin fishtails and the right rear fender smacks the creature's opened jaw. It's like hitting a wall. The heavy car rebounds and Niko grabs the mason jar and jerks like a doll. He protects the jar but hits the dashboard with his shoulder and then feels another booming impact followed by a chorus of highpitched keens over rhythmic clacks. An entire pack of the creatures is after him.

Niko has managed to keep his foot on the gas and the Black Taxi is still moving at a good clip when it plows into something huge but yielding. Niko's shoulder hits the dash again. For a few seconds he beholds nothing but raw white pain and he cries out and makes himself sit up and then he sees that most of the windshield and the driver's window have turned nearly opaque brown. A nauseating stench from the floor vent fills the car. The stuff on the windshield looks like mud. Niko finds the wiper knob and pulls it and the wipers smear the chunky brown pudding to a paler ale that thickens dark and lumpy at the end of the wiper's arc. The front left side of the car is covered with a muddy brown batter writhing with thick stringy worms and chunked with stuff that might be bone. The smell is sickening.

It's digested mulch. The Black Taxi has plowed through a bank of excreted remains human and otherwise. Mulchosaur shit. The car is covered with it. Gobbets of it fly off into the slipstream. A worm-riddled clot slithers along the driver's window by his head. It looks like one of those chocolate turtle candies. Niko's stomach lurches. Saliva floods his mouth. He tries not to look but how can he not? He grits his teeth and pushes the vent knob. The hood is caked with cooking shit. Close behind him he is sure an always starving pack of two-ton food processors clacks and keens and cranes enormous crescentshaped mouths toward him.

Drive.

The heaps of blackened dead are thinning now. Even the most Olympian gargoyle throw can carry only so far. Up ahead and to the right is the giant rock near the stone altar that serves as the source for the lake of blood. Niko swings wide of it and the landscape shifts like a bad acid trip to bring into view the vast and convoluted line of bureaucrats waiting decades for their absurd fate. Niko wonders where Franz is out there.

Fleeting glimpses of punishments and atrocities all about him on the plain. Blurred sufferings and flashes of torment. Myriad sadisms enacted without origin, outcome, explanation. I have walked through this.

Niko drives among the toppled statues of forgotten icons carved in living stone dissolved by acid guano. Demon workcrews cover giant transfixed shapes like army ants to chisel and carve and hammer while manlike batshapes flock the pestilent air. Niko slows to thread through the massive ossuary. Headlamps pick out pale quarried flesh lying cracked and broken and bleeding from a thousand lightning fissures. Icon faces worn to anonymity across geologic time. Beneath the tires a steady crunch of marble gravel, broken chunks of broken souls. The ruddy light that dyes the bone of their hard flesh is generated by the massive bonfire fueled by burning hides of skinless nazis staked and branded on the gritty ground. Here I played dark melodies for genocides and their tormentors, here spoke with a titan. Here a demon lost her soul on my account. The whole despairing landscape is a kind of journal, ink of blood on every page narrating woe and loss, despair and pain. Drive.

IN THE STAGNANT air above him claw rakes wing and barbed tails twine and grapple as his newly christened demon fights alone unseen and desperate, moved by what strange urge his mortal counterpart may never know. The air about the dark combatants beats and shudders and corrosive blood rains down upon the damned. Far below the living airwar two small white lights glide steadily across the grim and sunless plain.

HERE THE DECAPITATED stagger clutching their own heads. Blind they trip and fall and drop their burdens and their groping hands recover the wrong ones and collaborate to reconnect their proper selves. Here are screaming children pierced by rods to march in perfect lines. Demons flaying women to the bone and past. Now the lengthy wooden platform hung with populations of the skewered hugging their greased poles. Bowels lanced by splintered wood. The Franklin's headlights pass them soundless by like some portentious comet. Crows the size of men pluck out men's eyes with sharp hooked beaks and toss blackfeathered heads to gulp them down like olives. Eyes that see throughout their own digestion. The lips of flatterers sewn to the rectums of diarrhetic misers.

The Franklin shudders from some impact on the plain behind and once more Niko stops himself from turning to look back. A creeping feeling grows between his shoulderblades and as it strengthens he decides to trust his intuition and yanks the steering wheel left right left.

A giant granite block slams the ground he might have occupied had he not dodged. From high above come indecipherable curses.

God damn it. They're not allowed to stop me. Are they? No. The deal was clear. They're just trying to get me to look back.

Wait a second. The granite blocks?

Sure enough the plain is dotted now with slabs of granite dropped upon the running damned and left to weather away in a place that has no weather. Now the plain looks like an unkempt graveyard for some vanished race of giants. Sam Gamundi lies beneath one of these nameless markers. Digging and digging as he always will, world without end amen.

On impulse Niko honks the horn. The sound that emerges is the bellow of some ancient sea creature decrying its own extinction, an awful nightmare alarm calling to the very soul to strip itself from mortal flesh and prepare to be delivered from its bound estate. Niko shudders in his very core.

Did you hear it out there Sam? Did you know that it was me? That I'm returning with Jem's soul in hand? I think you did. And I think that you will bless and curse me at the same time. As always.

Now a thin white line out on the dimlit distance like a scar. Can it really be the marble wall? Demarcating here and there? Niko blinks and rubs his eyes but can't be sure. The white line blurs and fades and as it does a sound grows round the Franklin, rustling at first like swishing taffeta but quickly growing louder and more sibilant.

What had he encountered before running into Sam? So much has happened. So much is jumbled.

Strong gales buffet the heavy car. Streaking sand illuminated by the headlamps looks like rain. But this rain would not drench, this rain would flense—

Twisters. He remembers now. Enormous dustspouts scouring a baked plain intaglioed with the polished bones of the patient dead.

A stuttering rumble shudders the dirted air and a terrible coil dances past the car and lowers an undulant finger toward him like a mindless searching god. Flayed bodies flail within the spinning redlit gray, sailors drowning in a maelstrom. Constantly they bash each other and stain patches of the living wind a brief dull red.

The back end of the Franklin saws. Niko lets up on the gas and turns the wheel in the direction of the threatened spin. If the tornado touches him it could lift this car and sling it tumbling and set it smashed and crumpled on the plain with Niko pulped inside it and the glass shards of the mason jar catching the last fading glints from the feather's dying glow.

The tires sing across a sea of polished bone as Niko swerves around the roaring serpentine. The tornado lurches and then lifts. Niko evades it and heads toward the false horizon of that thin white line. A wrenching groan behind him like some alien god sobbing in its tortured sleep. The air itself is humming now. It glows and sparks with static from the rubbing sand.

The funnel stabs toward the ground in front of him and darkens as it feeds on sand and rock and living bone, a deadly churning arabesque. Niko veers again. The whirlwind spits out some projectile that javelins toward the car. Just before it hits he sees it is the half flensed body of a man. Niko screams and swerves and ducks. The body slams the passenger side of the windshield and glass and blood and shit explode into the car. The glass is not tempered and Niko's hands and forehead are cut by tiny shit-infected shards.

Niko sits back up. The pulped body is wrapped around the pillar post it has buckled.

The twister now meanders toward the car. The mason jar has got loose again and thumps across the floorboard. The ghastly body screams a sickening gargle and sprays teeth and bloody gobbets from its ruined mouth. Niko waggles the wheel and the body flops but does not fall of off the car. The mason jar thumps again.

With his side of the windshield starred he's driving blind. The freight train rumble of the closing whirlwind loud and growing louder. The smashed body flails its macabre puppet arms as it tries to crawl

into the car with Niko. Niko grabs the warm red mush of nearly jellied head by its matted clotted hair and tries to force the body off the
hood. It feels like tepid oatmeal. The damned soul's scream sprays
warm blood mist across his arm. A gore drenched hand grabs Niko's
wrist and pulls the broken body farther into the car. For one long second mortal and tormented gazes meet. In the raw steak of the dead
soul's face one eye is crimson and the other burst. Niko glimpses
awful fire in that remaining ember eye. The depth of this soul's pain
a counterpart to the abyss upon which it must look forever.

Niko pushes the man's arm and slams the brakes. His bruised
chest hits the steering wheel and his busted rib screams bloody
murder as it grates. The clinging soul's scalp peels away in Niko's
fist with a horrible soft purr and the body plows a furrow of caked
brown shit as it slides along the dented hood scrabbling and clawing
and slipping off to leave behind a red swath of itself. The car bucks
over the fallen body.

Niko hits the gas and nothing happens. He didn't let the clutch
in when he slammed the brakes and the Franklin stalled. Now the
car is barely moving.

The twister's roar is deafening now and the bloodsoaked car
interior is coating with fine sand. The abraded chassis hisses. Niko
tries to start the car and the car lurches. Stinging sand sticks to his
bleeding arms. Niko stomps the clutch and turns the key again and
the engine catches and then something hits the front of the car hard
enough to knock it aside two feet.

Niko stops the car and finds reverse and drives backward. All
he can see is spiderwebbed glass in front of him. He hunches in the
seat and brings up his left foot and kicks out the broken windshield.
A sliver gashes his ankle. He sits back up and there it is, a wall of
spinning air before him. He grips the wheel more tightly and he
presses harder on the gas. He screams Go at the car. His ribcage
throbs. Go, go.

The gearbox whines.

Niko's eyes sting with grit.

Assbackward deeper into Hell and blind to boot. If anything
besides the tornado is chasing him, gargoyles or mulchosaurs or
demons or sherman tanks or marching bands with bagpipes for all

he knows, he's about to join their party bigtime. But it seems he's outrunning the whirlwind even going backward.

The twister lights with static lightning. Angry god deprived of sacrifice. Across the surface of the plain its cursive body writes an endless nightmare rhapsody in some alien script.

The funnel lifts.

Niko stands on brake and clutch. The heavy car skids backward to a halt and Niko pops it into first and puts the hammer down. Shadows shift as the mason jar rolls and hits again. The slowly rising whirlwind finger stops and poises and strikes. Niko works through gears and forces the car straight and drives directly under the living funnel as it augers onto the plain intent to write his epitaph. Niko drives. He drives and the funnel touches down where he just was. The heavy car is caught within the grip of vortex winds and Niko shuts his eyes as stinging sand assails his skin. The rear end of the car tries to get away from him. He lets off on the gas and feels the car gain traction. For a moment Niko thinks he's got control and then the Franklin spins. Niko turns the wheel in the direction of the spin. He averts his mortal gaze and feels himself turn round and round. The tires' scream is faint against the cyclone's freight train thunder circling and circling.

And comes to rest.

The rolling mason jar taps Niko's shoe. He picks it up. A cold blade stabs his heart when Niko sees a tiny triangle of glass has been knocked out. But within the feather glows. And a faint smell of Jem's perfume. The smell that filled him with when he hugged her long and hard after months away on tour. It smells like Jemma. It smells like love.

Carefully he sets the jar upon his lap and starts to look out the kickedout windshield. And stops. Which way is forward? Which way backward? The Franklin spun so many times there's no way he can know for sure. He can hear the twister roaring down the plain—behind him? Yes behind and to the right. Then ahead and to the left is where he wants to look. Right?

Probably. But what if it's not? The twister's had time to move.

Niko sits unmoving in an agony of doubt. God damn it. You can't just sit here. You've got to look up sooner or later. Got to pick a direction. Got to have a moment's faith.

He takes a deep breath and holds it. Jem. The solid certainty of broken mason jar held his bleeding hands. All right. Okay.

He looks up and sees a redlit white wall separating ground and sky. All breath escapes him.

The engine that had been so well tuned idles roughly now.

The tornado closing from behind him.

The heatless jar in his cut hands.

Go.

XXVII

EVERY GOODBYE
AIN'T GONE

AND NOW THE MAD AND headlong race across the final
stretch of plain. Niko pushes the Black Taxi to the limit
with the pedal to the metal and hands clenched on the wheel and
the broken mason jar wedged firmly at his crotch.

The engine keens. A rapid chuffing sounds beneath the tires
like a speedboat rushing through a modest chop. Constant around
him are bangs and thumps as metal unbuckles. The dented hood
slowly smooths and the right side roof raises as the crumpled pillar
post straightens. The Franklin looks as if it is inflating as it eerily
heals itself. A crystalline lattice spreads across the empty windshield frame like a web weaved by an unseen spider, bowing in the
steady wind and making it difficult to see what lies before him.

Niko rolls the window down and hangs his head out. Something
smacks his forehead and he flinches back and wipes away a whitish
paste and dark brown bits. A kamikaze cockroach. The chuffing
from the tires is the Franklin running over hordes of roaches
carpeting the plain.

Unable to look out the window Niko rocks from side to side to triangulate a view through the thickening lattice of reforming windshield. Occasional dead shine ghostly in the headlamps' glare as Niko heads obliquely toward the growing line of marble wall that stretches probably forever away in either direction. Up ahead in the far distance he sees a darker patch within the wall. The gate?

Niko has become afraid to hope for anything but now he cannot help the hot anticipation that uncoils in his chest. The end in sight. The end in sight. He reminds himself that he has made it past the end before, in submerged memory, in different guise, and still looked back. And still lost everything.

I will break this. Whatever else it costs me I will break this chain.

Before him grows a steady creaking as the windshield glass reforms. It's nearly impossible to see out now. Niko blindly heads toward the wall. When he nears it he cuts right and drives alongside it. He ought to come upon the gate soon.

He cannot shake the sense of unseen legions nipping at his heels. Surely they will not just let him waltz on out of here. Surely they've got something special planned.

Well let's hurry up and find out what it is.

THE WINDSHIELD IS a solid pane of glass again, lined with a network of filament cracks that slowly thin until they disappear and leave clear spotless glass when they are gone. If the mason jar would only do that.

Suddenly the gate whips by. Niko yells and stands on the brake and then fumbles into reverse and backs up until he's sitting in the idling car beside the massive gate. Staring out the window wondering what to do next. Beside him looms the massive iron grillwork of the gate. Just beyond that crouches the giant insane dog growling growling growling.

He forgot about the goddamned dog. This time it has no need to strain its anchorchain leash as it faces him with slobbering feral grins. The dog is posted less to keep people from going in than to prevent their leaving. If Niko tries to get past it, it will have no problem at all tearing him into bitesized chunks. No jumbo milkbone gonna save your ass this time buddy pal.

MORTALITY BRIDGE

While the dog quivers like a drumhead just beyond the gate Niko surveys the wall. Featureless white marble smooth as glass rising at least thirty feet. No way in hell he can scale it. He fights to quell a white blind wave of desperate panic that will own him if he lets it break. Like trying to figure out a chess problem while a bomb ticks down to zero underneath your chair. Come on. It's just a dog for christ sake. A hydra headed dog the size of a small elephant but still. Just a stupid fucking animal. Come on smart boy. Can't you outthink a watchdog on a leash. That old bumper sticker, My Karma Ran Over Your Dogma. Yeah well my karma's pretty much become—

Niko draws a deep breath as a desperate idea is born. No oh no.

But he goes into action before he allows himself to think about it. For thought would surely paralyze him now. He sees his hand reach toward the shift lever. Don't do this, old son. Miles away his foot lets in the clutch. You won't survive this. His remotely operated hand fumbles until it finds reverse. Jemma won't survive this. He lets out the clutch. God damn it you stupid grandstanding asshole you won't make it. As the car backs up he turns it to the right until the gate glides into view again in front of him. You think there's an airbag in this thing? You don't even have a seatbelt, you moron, you're gonna kill yourself. He straightens out. The grated gate and eager monstrous dog beyond it shrink as he backs up. The view through the nearly regrown glass is slightly fractured, but the dog remains kaleidoscopic even when the glass is whole again.

Something heavy lands on the back of the Black Taxi. Niko flinches. Guess you were being followed. Oh well.

He stops about a thousand yards from the gate. That should be plenty.

Now winged figures land along the top of the marble wall above the gate to perch like heckling ravens on a power line. They dangle hooves or claws or feet and grin and nudge each other and wager and cackle as they hold up tridents and rocks and bricks.

Niko regards their ballpark camaraderie and on sudden impulse hits the horn. The soul-cleaving shriek cuts the chronic night and batwings spread and flap. One demon jerks hard enough to fall off the wall and land on his head. The others laugh and several jump up to piss on him. The fallen demon grins and opens his mouth and drinks and bows like a courtier. His wings flourish like a sable cape and then he leaps up to his former perch.

Niko lets up on the horn. The sudden reigning silence nearly as painful. He watches the wall a moment longer. Gathering for the pounce. He revs the engine. Ready or not boys.

Why are you doing this?

He puts the Franklin into gear one final time.

What choice do you have?

He looks toward motion to his left. Something big stands on the runner and its leathery brown face fills up the window. Niko calmly elbows down the lock and looks away. Screw it. You want a ride, I'll give you a ride.

The suicide door explodes open, wrenched off its beehive hinges. Niko's foot slips off the clutch and the Black Taxi lurches and stalls. Motherfucker! Niko turns to confront whatever has confounded him, not really giving a shit that it just tore the door off a car. It grips him with powerful tendrils and hauls him before its battered and demonic likeness. Niko has a moment to take in darkly bleeding clawmarks raked across the craggy face, an ear shredded to flapping ribbons, a pulped eye lying wet on the swollen cheek, and gleaming bone beneath the ripped scalp before he's pulled from the car and thrown to the harsh warm ground beside the wrenched off door.

Niko lies there with the wind knocked from him and watches Nikodemus get behind the wheel. He whispers No.

Nikodemus starts the car.

Niko struggles to his feet. "No," he says. "It's not your fight."

Nikodemus looks at him and even though his demon's face is a bleeding bludgeoned ruin its expression is one of pity.

Niko trudges stiffly toward the car as if poisoned by curare. It doesn't matter. I will not let my demon do this. This is my job.

But he is stopped by Nikodemus touching his chest. It's not a whipthin tendril the demon presses against him but the hard curve of a glass mason jar.

Nikodemus fixes Niko with his remaining eye.

Finally Niko looks down at the jar. The gesture also an accepting nod. Gently Niko takes the jar and the tendril withdraws.

The demons waiting on the wall. The jar he cradles close. Smell of perfume rising from the broken glass. Is it fainter than before? His eyes burn and his lips press tight.

Nikodemus gives a little nod and hoarsely whispers Thanks. Because we all want absolution, all want to atone. And then he puts the car in gear and Niko steps back and watches Nikodemus smoothly drive away.

Niko doesn't know he's crying until a tear lands on the cracked glass in his hands. Son of a bitch sure learned how to drive a stick.

A THOUSAND YARDS:

Niko watches from this safe distance as the headlamps light the gate like prison searchlights. In the glare the six mad fires of the waiting dog's reflecting eyes. The engine roar diminishing. Receding taillights blurred by tears. After all he's done to get this far he stands alone now on the outskirts of Hell with the cracked jar held fast in his arms and watches his demon and his friend accelerate across the thousand yards toward the iron gate.

On the wall they scurry to their feet and hooves and claws. Shouting reaches him across the distance. Tridents rocks and bricks are poised.

The Black Taxi impossibly sleek and smooth and doomed streaks toward the waiting metal.

Just before the crash the demons throw. Missiles smash on grille hood windshield roof.

The mindless dog's anticipated leap uncoils.

The nightblack car holds steady. Silently hits the iron gate at eightyfive.

The front end accordions. The taillights lift.

The gate buckles then bursts outward.

The front end hits the leaping dog. Meat and metal merge.

The engine plunges past the firewall.

The fused mass of enormous car and monstrous dog slams down beneath the portal.

Blood and burning oil gout the air.

The collision's thunder reaches him.

Niko runs.

* * *

DESPERATE AS HE is to reach the gate he cannot run the whole distance. Niko is too injured and too tired and too goddamned old to sprint a thousand yards. Within a few hundred yards the run becomes a trot, the trot a jog, the jog a power walk. It takes a sundered lifetime to get to the wreck. He's wheezing and holding his ribcage by the time the portal looms above him once again. All around him on the wall stand demons and gargoyles and abominations. The hot air heavy with their rustlings but they say nothing nor do they shout or move. Unmolested Niko walks beneath their alien scrutiny. They stand in mute witness at the passing of something. Midwives to the death and birth of myth and humbled in their pensive silence.

Niko approaches the steaming ticking wreck. Dread and caution. The terrible marriage before him barely recognizable as creature or car. Blood and oil and shit and gas and fur and metal everywhere, bucketfuls hurled against the portal's white marble hugely stained about the smoking wreck. The Franklin half its former length. Bent around itself and warped around the bleeding meat and protruding bone of guardian dog. The blighted air thick with smells of burnt rubber and cooked flesh. A clotted headlamp shines straight up. Cooling metal pings. A palmwide studded collar wraps a redringed whitewall canted outward and still slowly turning like an abandoned playground toy.

Tensed as if expecting a blow Niko rounds the wreck. Looking for any sign of Nikodemus. Afraid that he will find it. He stares at a gap in the metal so crumpled and compressed he doesn't recognize it at first. And then the shapes around the gap make sense. There's what used to be the roof. There's a slanted length of bench seat mashed against the bent steering wheel. Niko's looking through the space where the driver's door used to be. Between the seatback and the steering wheel a bloodsoaked shape that must be Nikodemus. But it can't be Nikodemus. There's barely three inches between seat and wheel. But it is.

Niko looks beyond the wreck. Beyond the gate. Past the threshold. Outside. Half a dozen steps and you're out of here. One two three four five six and free and then you win. Come on. Come on. Let's go. There's nothing you can do for him. Leave him here or what he did for you will be for nothing.

Shattered glass crunches as he takes a step. He glances at the wreck. The bloody shape within.

A shadow stretches on the ground. Thin. Elongate. Human. Someone standing close behind him. All Hell holds its foundry breath.

"He's not alive," Niko tells the empty waiting air before him. "He never was." He looks up but sees only the marble top of the arched portal and the bent overhang of ruined gate. "He wasn't mortal so he can't die. Right?" Cold marble flattens his voice. Speaking to the shape behind him. He can't look back to see it but he can guess who it is. "You've come to take him. Haven't you?"

The shadow's hand comes up to touch the bill of its shadow cap.

Crunching glass resumes as Niko returns to the wreck. It takes all his will to bend and gently set down the mason jar he holds like some rediscovered fragment of Atlantis. I can't let them take him, Niko tells the jar.

When he moves toward the car the waiting shadow falls across the jar. The feather's green glow dims. The shadow's arm comes away from the jar and its shadow hand now holds the shadow of a jar. A jar in which there is no shadow of a feather. A new jar then. Empty and awaiting capture of the firefly soul of Nikodemus.

Mortal threats occur to Niko but what threat can he make, what power does he have? He must have faith in the bond of uttered vows. Abide. Abide.

He turns away from the jar. Through the flattened and serrated wedge where the windshield smashed and the roof caved in Nikodemus sits crushed between steering wheel and seat, his huge body crammed into an impossibly small space. Niko pushes on the seat but it won't budge. He reaches through the collapsed doorway and grips Nikodemus but his hands slip on the blood. He leans in as far as he can and tries again and gets a grip but still can't move his demon's bulk. Three hundred pounds of Nikodemus are wedged in tight.

Niko's pressed against the wreck with both arms shoved inside it when something jumps below his feet. He lets go and looks down.

It's the dog? The car? Crackles and pings surround him. Metal slowly smoothing. Drip of fluids recirculating. Dog and car are resurrecting, each feeding on the lifeblood of the other.

The waiting shadow falls across him now.

Niko tries again to pry his demon from the wreck but it's no use. He slaps the lifeless bloody face and screams his demon's newly given name but still the hulk of him lies boneless pinned and unresponsive.

Sudden light shines from beyond the gateway. It brightens and shifts along the wall and as it does a familiar knocking gargle grows. Niko feels a pang of fearful joy as the source of that noise glides into view and stops with a highpitched squeal of wornout brakes. The door yipes open and the driver gets out and looks across the yellow roof at Niko standing in the wreckage and she lowers the cigarillo from her mouth to blow pale smoke into the air beyond the wall. "Holy shit," the cabbie says.

XXVIII

I'm Tore Down

HE CABBIE GAPES AT WRECKAGE and the mob behind it. When she looks at Niko her eyes hold no hint of recognition. Well who knows how long it's been since she saw him last? He knows what he looks like now. Thin, bearded, scraggly, filthy, beat to shit.

Niko waves. The cabbie flinches. Niko sees her realize who he is, and with that startled recognition her gaze shifts to what he can only imagine must be gathered behind him. Now the cabbie's astonishment is colored with something like admiration. She waves her cigarillo, mutely asking You caused this? Niko shrugs.

With remarkable aplomb the cabbie steps around the Checker Cab and opens the rear door. Her gaze shifts between Niko and the unnerving quiet crowd he feels behind him as she keeps one hand on the handle and beckons slightly with the other.

Niko feels as trapped as Nikodemus. He's never been happier to see someone in his life. Every cell in his body urges him to pick up Jem and run to the cab and dive into the back seat and haulass out of here and not look back. But he balls his fists and stands where he is. "Someone's trapped in there," he tells the cabbie. "I have to get him out."

The cabbie looks puzzled but she nods and selects a key from her crowded keyring and opens the trunk. Niko feels a terrible cold spot between his shoulderblades while she rummages. She lowers the trunk and puts her cigarillo back to her lips and heads toward Niko bearing a crowbar and dragging her wheeled hydraulic jack like a little dog on a leash. She raises an eyebrow at the glowing mason jar on the ground and guides the jack around it and stops in front of Niko.

"Hiya."

Niko wants to laugh but if he starts he might not ever stop. Instead he simply stares. She looks exactly the same. Same clothes. Same loosely knotted tie. She left him at this very gate how long ago now? Nikodemus led him to suspect his fugue on the banks of the Lethe had lasted months at least and maybe longer.

The cabbie leans to one side and looks past him and takes a deep drag from her cigarillo. Looking into the face of her nemesis, Niko realizes. Her opposite number. She juts her chin in a look of acknowledgement but not respect and leans a little farther to blow smoke past Niko and toward her opponent. Niko could kiss her. He wants to ask her how she knew to be here now but a black fog spreads across his vision and things go far away.

"STEADY." HER HAND on his arm. "Here." Glass crunches as she walks him backward to the wreck, grimacing when some wet organ squishes beneath her battered leather tennis shoe. She peers at Nikodemus through the crumpled doorway gap. "Um."

"He's alive."

She nods doubtfully and goes to work with the crowbar. Banging prying straining. Niko wants to help her but he feels encased in something. The cabbie tries to fit the jack sideways into the compressed doorway but can't hold it in place and work the lever at the same time. Pure shame releases Niko from his immobility and he hurries to the cabbie. They trade a glance and she nods. Hers is the first human face he has seen in a long long time with any kind of life or light in it.

Niko holds the jack steady while the cabbie works the lever. The lifting arm touches the doorframe and metal begins to creak.

The car flinches and the cabbie draws back with her eyes wide and the jackhandle coming up to strike. But there's nothing to hit really and she glances again at Niko and goes back to work. "We need a jaws of life," she says.

"I'm surprised you don't have one in that trunk."

The opening groans wider and soon Niko reaches inside the Black Taxi and grabs Nikodemus' inert body while the cabbie sits on the crumpled hood with both legs through the windshield frame and both feet pushing on the demon's burly bleeding shoulder. They get him loose enough that the cabbie can come around behind Niko and pull on Nikodemus' naked legs while Niko leans into the desecrated car and guides the body under the wedging jack. On the deformed dashboard past the bent steering wheel he glimpses the tripmeter he reset at zero when he left the casino. The numbers now read 31415. Above it the odometer shows a row of zeroes.

Something tickles Niko's arm and he jerks away. Beside Nikodemus on what's left of the passenger side in the middle of a pile of shattered glass and stringy entrails a severed doghead the size of a beachball lies crushed. What fur is not peeled back to show bare skull is matted with blood. Inches from Niko rotted yellow teeth the size of fingers clack. A single brown and insane eye glares pure malice at him.

"On three," the cabbie calls behind him.

Niko scrunches away from the doghead and braces both hands on Nikodemus' shoulders. With the demon's legs hoisted underneath her arms the cabbie calls out One two three and Niko pushes and the cabbie pulls and Nikodemus comes free and spills stillborn from the car.

The disembodied dog's jaws snap frantically and Niko jerks away and bangs his head against the buckled roof hard enough to scatter pinprick lights. He blinks and shakes his head and carefully backs out of the murdered Franklin. Niko and the cabbie grab a tendril apiece. The whiplike tentacles are smooth and muscled as any strong arm and not reptilian at all.

Niko and the cabbie drag his demon through the wreckage, mopping a swath through blood gas bile glass ichor oil meat and metal. Niko's bruised shoulder feels as if it's glowing.

"Jeez, what is this guy, a statue?"

Niko stops beside the mason jar. "I need that."

The cabbie wipes sweat from her brow as Niko carefully lifts the jar until he holds it against his hurting ribcage. The smell of perfume definitely fainter now. He nods at the cabbie and they start pulling again. One more step remains to take him past the threshold and at long last out of here. Niko is about to take it when he hears a voice.

"Leaving without saying goodbye, Niko-tizer?"

Niko stops. He expected something like this. "I've already said everything I have to say to you," he tells the air before him.

"Not to me, Nikster. To her."

And Niko hears the only thing that could stop him as no wall or beast or power has stopped him all this awful time.

"Niko," says Jemma.

NIKO DROPS THE mason jar.

It lands on Nikodemus' belly. He lowers Nikodemus and straightens feeling cold. As if a rifle's pointed at his back.

"Niko. Where are you going?"

Niko shuts his eyes. She sounds so afraid.

"What's wrong?" the cabbie asks.

"Niko please."

Niko stands stock still with eyes clamped shut. "You don't hear that, do you?"

"Don't hear what?" says Jemma.

"Hear what?" says the cabbie.

Niko opens his eyes. The yellow Checker Cab roughly idling ten feet away. The rear door open. Yellow dome light inviting as a fire on a cold night.

"Niko, I don't understand. Why are you leaving me here?"

"You okay?" the cabbie says.

I could just go. Pick up the jar and drag Nikodemus and be out of here. Nothing to it. He looks at the jar trembling on Nikodemus' belly.

"Niko?" Doubt cloud's Jemma's voice.

"I need a second," Niko tells the cabbie.

"He needs a second, folks," says Phil behind him, laughing now. "Maybe it's just occurred to this fuckup junky that he's about to trade his little sweetie pie for a jelly jar and a feather dipped in glowing paint. Which this numbnuts got from us. That's how dumb this asshole is. He'll waltz out of here with that thing like it's a midway prize he just paid fifty bucks to win while we all laugh our ass off here. Wind him up and watch him go, every friggin time. It's better than tee vee."

Niko stares at the jar. The hoops they've made him jump through. It would be so like them.

But how to know? Could he learn anything by opening it? Or will her spirit rush from its container? It's another highnote test. How can he learn if this is Jemma without destroying what is Jemma?

"Look at him, darlin. Your little white knight's about to leave you to the wolves and sail on out of here. He'll probably even tell himself it's all his fault. Later on, of course, when there's nothing anyone can do about it. You know why?"

"Niko please," calls Jem. "I'm sca—"

"Cause he's a martyr, pusspie. That's why. He's happier suffering on his cross than getting his sorry ass off of it. He always was. Why else would he fuck this up every time it all goes down." Phil laughs. "He knows it's you he's leaving. The poor dumb bastard can't suffer if he gets the girl. How he gon play de blues good iffin he don feel bad? You done been sacrifice fo art, babygirl. Aint that right, Niko-lostomy? You'd sell your mother for a song if it was sad enough. Wouldn't you?"

"Jem," says Niko.

"Niko don't listen to him. I know you love me." He can hear her crying now. "Just get me out of here. Take me home."

Home. That's good. Niko looks at the cabbie. "Do me a favor?"

"Sure."

"Anything," says Jemma.

"Look behind me and tell me what you see."

"Niko—"

"I see the gate. I see the wreck."

"Niko, what are you—"

"Some guy in sunglasses and a sportcoat who looks like he wants to sell us something."

"Niko who is this woman, why won't you talk to—"

"I see our old pal in the chauffeur outfit trying to stare a hole in me."

"Don't leave me here Niko you can't—"

"There's a couple dozen scary monsters who look like they belong with your buddy here."

"You can't just walk away from me—"

"They've got their backs to us and they're guarding the gate against a lot of naked people who look like they want out real bad." She spreads her hands.

"No one else?"

The cabbie shakes her head.

"You don't need me anymore, is that it, Niko? You used me like you used everyone you ever met, used me up and threw me in the trash, and now you're going to leave without looking back. Is that right?"

Niko nods at the cabbie. His face stone.

"Is it worth it, Niko? Worth being a selfish son of a bitch who lets his dead brother take the fall because he doesn't have enough spine to face up to what he did? Who steals money from his friends to buy drugs and steals their talent to make albums? Who eats up the best years of someone's life because he can't stand to be alone? Who lets her love him and then sells her down the river to save himself. I'm here forever Niko. For ever. I loved you and you pawned me like a watch."

"Anything else?" His voice sounds odd, his voice sounds old.

"Tell me to my face," says Jemma. "Be a man and look me in the eye and tell me you're letting me go."

"No," the cabbie says. "Jeez, isn't that enough?"

"Come on, Niko. If you're going to dump me like an ashtray and go on with your charmed little life at least have the balls to do it to my face. Instead of slinking off like some kind of thief. Like you always do."

Niko nods and says Okay. The way the cabbie's watching him he wonders if she isn't hearing everything after all.

"Give me a goodbye, Niko. Is that too much to ask? I wasted my life on you."

The cabbie carefully picks up the mason jar and holds it out to Niko. He takes it from her and nods thank you. This time out he held no hand on his ascent. The letting go is different now.

"What'll it cost you to be a man for once and face me, Niko? You'll be fine, you always land on your—"

"Ready?" the cabbie says.

"Yeah." Niko nods. "Thanks."

She shrugs and picks up Nikodemus' tendril. "No problem."

"Niko look at me. I didn't do anything. I wasn't part of this. You can't just walk away from me. You killed me. You sent me here. Look at me. Niko look at me you selfish son of a bitch."

Niko hoists up Nikodemus' tendril. "Nice try, Phil. You had me for a minute there."

"Be seeing you, Nik-orpheus."

"Niko—"

Niko and his guide and his demon and his love cross over.

XXIX

HELLHOUND ON
MY TRAIL

OLD SPRINGS CREAK AS NIKO and the cabbie deposit
Nikodemus on the dark green bench seat. They're not
sure what to do with his wings. One is torn near the thick muscle
padding where wing joins back. It does not bleed. One long thin
birdlike wingspar bone is broken.

Niko and the cabbie settle for turning Nikodemus on his side
to face the seatback so his tattered wings can overhang onto the
floorboards. Blood is everywhere on the cab and on their palms
and clothes. The cabbie has a smear of it along one cheek where she
wiped unthinkingly.

Niko's eyes tear when he regards the trailing pulp of Nikodemus'
jellied eye. The demon is still unconscious. No pulse, no respiration.
Was there ever?

Is it wrong to bring him along? Maybe. But it's more wrong to
leave him behind.

don't leave me here niko you can't

Niko pats his demon's chest and wings twitch with a sound of
rustling taffeta.

Before he backs out Niko looks at floorboard litter stirred by Nikodemus' restless wings. All exactly as remembered and welcome as a lifeboat to a struggling swimmer in a freezing sea.

He is suddenly impatient to get moving again and backs out of the cab. Ahead of him the cabbie stands holding the passenger door open.

Niko glimpses something blurring toward the cab in time to push the cabbie out of the way. She lands on her ass just as a hurled mallet slams the windshield and tempered glass explodes across the front seat and dashboard. A bellow cuts the tarnished air. The enraged Thor who threw this hammer rushes from the darkness toward them.

"Encule de ta mere, je vous tuerai!"

Auguste the sculptor runs fullout with arms outstretched and fingers curled. Beard a trailing banner and bright eyes crazed.

Niko is in no shape to fight anyone but he sets Jemma on the front seat and steps around the open door and braces himself to meet Auguste's mad rush. Past the bellowing Frenchman the toppled ladder lies beside carved marble cracked and alabaster arms and heads amputated from the wall by the Black Taxi's collision with the gate.

"Philistin! Assassin! J'arracherai votre coeur et violerai le trou! Mangeur de merde!" Auguste looms like a bear with arms spread wide and spittle flecking his beard. Niko drops into a squat and Auguste is suddenly overhanging him. Niko calmly stands and raises his arms and winces at the sharp pain of his broken rib as Auguste arcs high and loudly thuds onto the hood of the Checker Cab. For a moment the Frenchman lies there blankly staring up, and then he's off and after Niko once again. Niko lifts his leg to kick Auguste in the kneecap but his leg just won't cooperate and the Frenchman bowls him over. Niko slams the ground with Auguste on top. The hands that have spent lifetimes wresting life from inert rock now clamp his throat and bear down. Niko bucks like a fish on a deck. Maddened eyes glare inches from his own. Coarse gray beard tickles his purpling face. Tongue bloats in mouth. Buck again. Throw him off. No good. Grunt with effort. Nothing comes out. Scream. Throat pinched shut. Vision red edged. Heartbeat rhythm bludgeons skull. Face swells. Bursting. Auguste's incoherent screams. Spittle patters face. Tight against him. Find his thumbs. Pull back. Relieve pressure. Not enough to get air through, strong hes strong. vision disperses. last sight flat mad light of his eyes. sorry auguste. sorry. think id have done the same

A distant thump. Auguste scowls. Blinks rapidly and tosses his head. Another thud. The pressure lets up on Niko's throat. Auguste's eyes cloud and he pitches forward against Niko. Who worms from under the unconscious lump and draws a great long wheezing gasp. His hands go to his throat as if to open it wider. Air just won't come fast enough. Breathing through a clotted straw. The dark veil slowly lifts and the cabbie's standing there. Her mouth says Are you all right? All he hears is steady ringing. Helps him to his feet. He tries to tell her I'm okay but nothing will come out. Nods instead and thinly coughs. Hockey puck in windpipe. Every time he coughs a sharpened wire stabs his broken rib. Niko motions I'm okay, let's go, get in the cab. She agrees and then he sees she holds a tire iron in one hand. Ah. Thank you. Again.

The cabbie swipes broken windshield glass off of the seat and helps Niko get in the cab. He huddles round the mason jar and stares at chunks of glass that rim the windshield. Bet it doesn't grow back on this car.

The cabbie shuts the door and seals him from a universe of wretched suffering and pain. Give it a parting glance? Can I do that now? Give it the finger? Give some goodbye anyhow. Isn't that what the forgery of Jemma said?

The cabbie brushes glass away and dusts her bloodstained palms and gets behind the wheel. She shakes her head at the jagged windshield frame. "Man."

Auguste's mallet lies between them on the seat. The cabbie picks it up and tosses it out over the hood. "Poor Auguste. Wish I hadn't had to do that."

She shuts her door and buckles up. "Seatbelt."

Without looking Niko points to where the battered gate lies broken open. He hoods his eyes like a ship's lookout and points at himself and then points again at the gate and draws a question mark in the air.

The cabbie purses her lips. "Orpheus held Eurydice's hand all the way to the entrance of Tænarus cave. He never looked back the whole time. Until he stepped into the sunlight and turned to tell her how happy he was they'd made it. But she was still in the shadows and he lost her."

Niko draws a ragged breath and looks heavenward. Brings the jar up and turns it in his hand and forces himself steady. It isn't over. Won't be over till they're back up on the world. Okay. All right. He nods and shrugs.

"We'll get there," the cabbie says. "They won't go past the gate. The hard part's over." She slaps his leg and smiles. "Besides, I never dropped a fare off anywhere but where he said he was going." Then she glances at the wall and her expression changes.

Niko tugs her sleeve but she shakes her head. "Nothing. Never-mind. Let's ramble."

They inch forward.

"Wave bye bye." The cabbie's cheer sounds forced but Niko does it anyhow albeit listlessly. Goodbye. Goodbye.

The cabbie edges forward around the unconscious body of Auguste. "Désolé, Auguste," she calls. "Pardonnes-moi."

When she's past the laidout Frenchman she tells Niko to shut his eyes and she turns the cab in a wide circle. Headlights sweep the screaming figures frozen in the stone and shifting shadows lend them motion they will never know. Then the headlights reveal nothing but the cracked bland floor of the empty plain until the cab is heading away from the gate and all that lies behind it. Niko uncovers his eyes. A deeper well-like darkness far ahead must be the tunnel entrance.

Hot air buffets them through the glassless windshield. "This is gonna be a pain," the cabbie says. "I better not go too fast. One good bug and pow."

Niko ducks his head and lifts the jar to his face and breathes in deep. Faint sachet fading. The glow seems dimmer too. We have to hurry. He wants to tell the cabbie but his throat clamps shut whenever he tries to speak. He starts to check on Nikodemus and stops quickly. Looking Nikodemus' way is looking back. God damn.

Niko shuts his eyes. The hot wind against his skin. The gate and all the fractured plain behind him dwindling. The endless demolition of the hopeless damned receding. Goodbye, goodbye. I am escaped yet not delivered.

Niko taps the cabbie's shoulder. "How. you. know. be. there?"

"How'd I know to be there?"

Niko nods.

"Well." She fidgets on the seat. "I dropped you off and drove away and I got maybe as far as we are now and I heard this huge crash. I thought Wow, it didn't take him very long to get in trouble, and I turned around and headed back to see what happened and there you were."

Niko stares. "How. long?"

"How long what? How long did it take me to get there?"

Niko shakes his head. "How long. from let me off. to pick me up?"

The cabbie looks him up and down. Trying to reconcile his gaunt and weathered ruin with what she tells him next. "I couldn't have been gone three minutes," she says.

RIDING ON THE rails again. In the distance a pale green glow.

Unlike Niko the cabbie can check her rearview mirror and she does, continually. But every time Niko croakingly asks her what she sees she only shakes her head. In the back seat Nikodemus stirs. The cabbie lights a cigarillo. "So who's your friend?"

Niko watches the brown tube of tobacco like a predator. "My demon." He taps his forehead.

She takes a drag and nods. "Ah," she says in smoke as if that explains everything. Maybe for her it does. She catches Niko's longing expression. "What happened to the pack I just gave you?"

"Fell in a river. Long time ago."

"Oh." She pats her pockets and fishes out a fresh pack of Swisher Sweets and hands it to him and he taps one out and sniffs. Oh yeah.

The cabbie indicates the jar in his lap. "That what you came for?" The lighter knob pops and Niko lights up. The happy scratching in his injured throat, the little death inside his lungs. He holds up the jar and turns his head to blow out smoke that dispels in the hot breeze blowing steadily against them. "That's her."

She nods. "So. Where to, mister?" She says it lightly like a joke but Niko thinks a moment. Fueled by nicotine his mind feels widened. He feels he's thinking clearly for the first time in a long time. What was it the cabbie had said? *I never dropped a fare off anywhere but where he said he was going.*

Three minutes. *I've been gone three minutes.*

And the final act unspools before him like a scroll.

The mason jar. In the absence of Jem herself returned to him Niko had naively thought that Jemma's soul would somehow turn back into Jemma when they crossed over. The spell would lift and she would change like some enchanted frog into a sleeping princess. Yet they had crossed over and her bottled soul remained a glowing feather. Not that this light, this essence, isn't Jemma. A lifetime's length it rides within the flesh, a passenger bound until the vessel makes some farther shore.

But if what the cabbie says is true the rightful container of Jemma's soul lies in her bed not one hour dead. Not found, not taken in an ambulance, not cut up and examined, not made over and exsanguinated and filled with alien fluids, not eulogized and wept over and bid goodbye and sealed inside a coffin and ensconced within the quiet earth and left to dwindle to the elements during all the long and struggling time of Niko's absence from the roofless earth.

Not an hour dead. And Niko holds her outcast soul upon his lap. But she diminishes. She slips out through the cracks. *I cannot let her gutter while I hold her in my hands. What will I do?*

What he will do—oh. Oh.

Faust in all his hubris never contemplated such alchemy as Niko now considers.

"Home," he tells the cabbie. "Take me home."

THE FAINT GREEN glow around the speeding cab is phosphorescent mold jellying the tunnel walls. To either side the afflicted stumble, pale-eyed Morlocks absent of past or future. Unwitting guardians of this borderland adorned in ragged relics of a dim-remembered world long left behind. Greateyed Jeremy out there somewhere, side pierced like some mutant christ. Niko hopes the simple monster will recover from his wound. Compared to creatures he encountered later Jeremy was a muppet.

He remembers something with a start. "Hey. Do you still have those candybars?" He's already reaching for the glovebox when the cabbie says sure. His mouth floods as he opens the glovebox and pulls out a shapeless foilwrapped Chunky bar. His hands shake as he hurriedly unwraps the halfmelted candybar and shoves it into his mouth. The sweet explosion almost unbearable.

The cabbie nudges him and points out the swath in the slimy wall where the Checker Cab jumped track and blew a tire and scraped along the side. Niko nods. Written passage.

The moonish creatures press against the gelid wall and let the cab pass unmolested, their blinding encounter with the yellow car a blob of painful recent memory in their meager minds.

Niko shuts his eyes and feels the damp air on his face. It reeks of rot but he no longer notices.

The glowing length of tunnel is behind them now. Bare brown brick conjured from the dark ahead. The iron rails on which they ride are no longer rusted and the crossties are no longer rotten wood. Tie spike rail wheel.

"Your bud back there," the cabbie says. "What are you gonna do with him when you get back?"

Niko coughs to clear his injured throat. "I haven't thought that far."

"I think he might be in for some trouble when we leave the tunnel."

"We'll make him keep his head down."

"Not what I meant." The cabbie glances in the rearview. At what, at what.

"Then what?" Niko feels thick and stupid and filthy and weary and sore.

"Well. He isn't mortal is he? Like you are?"

Niko notices she doesn't say Like us. "No."

"Well I think he might be once we're back."

Niko blinks. "Might be mortal?"

She nods. "I don't know. I mean it's just a theory, right? But these guys." She hooks a thumb at the back seat. "They don't get out much. I think somehow the game is rigged against them.

Otherwise they'd be taking vacations in Disneyland and screaming in the Haunted Mansion. Don't you think?"

"But." Niko scrunches up his face. He's thinking about his good old buddy Phil with his trendy shades and his Rolex Oyster Perpetual Daytona Cosmograph and his hair in perfect disarray and his iPhone cased in human leather that appears from nowhere. Mortal when they're in our world? How many times has Niko wanted to kill the supercilious son of a bitch? "Well so what if he is?"

The cabbie eyes him. "He's bad hurt. Injuries like that probably would have killed a mortal man."

"Yeah but he's not a—oh."

She stubs out her cigarillo. "Oh. If we take him to the surface it might kill him when we cross over. If he stays down here he'll definitely heal."

"If whoever's following us doesn't catch us first."

She looks at him sharply.

Niko points out the window. "You can see their light on the walls. Behind our headlights. It's him, isn't it?"

She scowls at the rearview. "It's a pair of headlights."

"It's him." That goddamn cold spot creeping back between his shoulderblades. "He waited for the car to heal itself and then he came after us." Niko looks out the window at light from the headlamps shining far behind them. "How far back is he?"

"Hard to say." She chews her lower lip.

Niko senses more bad news. "What now?"

"Black Taxi driver's kind of an independent contractor. He follows company rules but he doesn't really work for the company." She glances again at the rearview. "His rules let him go past the gate. And he's not mortal on the world. Otherwise what use would he be?"

"So he'll try to distract us all the way back up."

"At the very least."

"Well, we'll just try to outdrive him until we're out. What else can we do?"

"I don't think it'll stop there." She indicates the jar.

"But they gave Jemma back. It ends when we're back, when we're out of here."

"They really like technicalities. Loopholes. She's not back until her soul's back where it belongs. He'll try to get her before that."

"What, does he work on commission? He already did his job."

"You stole his car and wrecked it."

Niko stops. The rushing dark ahead looks exactly the way he feels inside. "So now it's personal."

"I'd be pretty pissed off if I was him. I'm sure he'll win employee of the month if he brings your lady back too. But I doubt there's anything he can do if you can put her back where she belongs."

"And Nikodemus?"

"That's his name?" She seems amused. "I think someone will have to come up after him. He doesn't belong where we're going."

The tunnel walls are growing smooth and pale gray. In the distance floats a faint green dot. The first of the rail signals.

Niko puts his hands over his scabbed and bearded face. "So I've at least got to get Nikodemus somewhere safe or drop him off before we come out in case he goes all mortal on us and his injuries kill him. I've got to get Jemma back into…Jemma, before the Driver catches up to us."

"That pretty much covers it."

Niko lowers his hands. "The jar's broken. I think she's… leaking out."

The cabbie shakes her head.

"Do you know anything about that?" Niko holds up the jar. "About putting these back where they belong?"

The headshake continues. "I drive a cab. I take people where they're going. I don't know how to do that."

Niko and the cabbie both jump when Niko's own voice comes from the back seat.

"I do," says Nikodemus.

XXX

CAN'T FIND MY
WAY HOME

T HE TUNNEL IS MODERN AGAIN, three steel rails, prestressed concrete walls, equidistant lights. The distant cries of Red Line cars call out across an unknown distance, ghosts of dinosaurs haunting the chthonic world.

"Two hundred yards," calls Nikodemus. Hunched in the back of the Checker Cab he stares out the rear window at the Black Taxi eating up rails and steadily gaining on them. The demon's shredded wings flutter in the constant rush of wind into the car.

Niko and the cabbie told Nikodemus what they fear may happen to him when they cross over but the demon insisted on coming with them all the way. "In for a penny, in for a pounding." His tone had brooked no argument.

The cabbie squints intently at the lights unspooling from the dark.

"Hundred fifty yards," calls Nikodemus.

Up ahead the tunnel splits. The cabbie's going to try to cut over to the righthand tunnel at the last possible moment. "One twenty." If she cuts over too soon the Black Taxi will easily follow her. "One hundred." Too late and they'll miss the tunnel and the Black Taxi will be right on them.

Niko sees the switchoff now a thousand yards ahead. A faint curve of wall, another set of rectangular lights branching out to the right.

The tunnel walls grow bright around them. "Train," yells Nikodemus. "Train behind us. Two hundred yards and gaining fast."

"Where the hell did that come from?" says Niko.

"It's running down the—no wait, the black car's going faster."

"Shit." The wind blows harder as the Checker Cab speeds up. "I keep thinking it's you talking back there," the cabbie tells Niko. "He sounds just like you."

The cab fills with an eerie lamentation. The siren song of the pursuing Blue Line train reverberating down the rails and through the passenger compartment.

"Don't look back," chants Niko. "Don't look back. Don't—"

A blast of the trainhorn fills the tunnel.

Nikodemus yells from the back seat but Niko barely hears him. The branchoff is dead ahead. His peripheral vision picks up bright lights from the passenger side mirror. The trainhorn's about to powder his skull.

The Checker Cab veers off the tracks too soon. Niko slams against the restraint as the car bounces over crossties. He tucks the jar against his stomach and hears the cabbie yelling and Nikodemus yelling and ricocheting all over the back of the cab and the trainhorn's liquefying his brains and he can feel the awful closing pressure of the Black Taxi practically being pushed into them by the speeding Blue Line train and the tunnel switchoff gapes before them now too late to turn into it but the cabbie yanks the wheel regardless and Niko's thrown against her and Nikodemus is hurled against the side as the Checker Cab bounces off the crossties and rumbles onto the adjoining track and as it leaves the first track bygod something smacks the rear bumper and the back end slides and the left rear scrapes yellow paint onto the tunnel wall and then they're jouncing along the crossties of the adjoining track and the cabbie jerks the wheel right-left and the cab leaps onto the new set of rails.

The bumping stops. The vibration stops. The worldfilling apocalypse of trainhorn diminishes down the tunnel they have left behind.

And the Black Taxi?

Once again the cabbie checks the rearview. This time she grins. "Nothin to it," she says. Already fishing the cigarillo pack from her shirt pocket.

Niko doesn't realize he's pulled something in his back until the muscles unclench painfully and all at once. The relief throughout the cab is palpable.

Niko quickly checks the mason jar. The same, the same. The glow barely perceptible, the perfume a faint memory on a garment.

The cabbie taps his leg and points and Niko squints into the wind against his face. Length of tunnel stretching out ahead of them and now a bright amber light set in its middle. Jesus christ another train. There's nowhere to go this time. No convenient switchoff or nick-of-time escape hatch. They're about to meet their fate headon without a prayer.

But the cabbie seems amused and waves her cigarillo at the hovering amber light. "It's okay. It's a streetlight."

Niko gapes while she slouches on the bench seat and loosens her thin tie another inch and drives on the rails with one-handed confidence.

Nikodemus pokes his huge and one-eyed head between them to stare with eager trepidation through the open windshield.

The cabbie grins. "Sometimes," she says, "the light at the end of the tunnel really isn't an oncoming train."

AT 8:23 P.M. on no special Friday night in late summer a battered Checker Cab ferrying its battleweary passengers emerged into the open air and crowded light of the Blue Line platform at Flower and Seventh Streets beside the purple lighted Staples Center in downtown Los Angeles, California, home to ten million working sweating fucking eating driving laughing sleeping struggling human beings in homes slapped onto hillsides or gridded into the Valley or cobbled together from duct taped cardboard boxes, and not a soul among them saw the tired yellow metal creature lumber from its subterranean lair, saw it swerve and bump off rails and onto smooth paved road, watched it glide to a stop, observed the brakelights flash, heard the gargle of its idle as the passenger door opened, witnessed the terribly thin man sore abused and homeless looking in his filthy ragged clothes who cautiously backed out of the phlegmatic beast like some old arthritic. Watched him straighten slowly, one hand going to his back as if it pained him while the other held some kind of moonshine jar that could hardly be seen to be glowing in the everpresent city light.

No one to see him stand there facing westward for a while. Toward the land's end and the everdrowning sun beyond. No one apart from those who traveled with him saw him draw a ragged breath and clench his fists and nod and slowly turn
turn and look back
look back at the way he came
and saw him break the cycle of tyrannic myth.

Whatever else might happen Niko had escaped the bonds of his conscripted fate. The future that befell him was to be his own.

On that unusually deserted street he stood a moment as if something belonging to him had fallen out the window of the cab and he was trying to remember what it was, let alone glimpse it back there on the road. No beggar, no broker, no hardhanded worker saw him raise the fractured jar, for all the world a pauper king proposing a toast, or saw his free hand rise above it with one long middle finger pointing toward the bottomlit and heavy sky.

THE UNIVERSE ACKNOWLEDGES neither gesture and after a moment Niko lowers the jar and turns back to the chugging cab. "Thanks for stopping. I guess—"

In the back seat Nikodemus' mouth is open and his one good eye stares fixedly beyond the metal roof, beyond the roofless night.

The cabbie sees this and hurries from the cab and opens the back door to lean over Nikodemus. She pries open a dark leather lid to check his lone pupil, uselessly because his eye is such dark brown.

Niko wants to check for pulse but ends up feeling stupid with one limp tendril in his hand. Instead he sets his ear against the

— 378 —

demon's chest just as the cabbie brings her cheek near Nikodemus' mouth, and Niko and the cabbie bump heads.

The cabbie says Owee.

"I think his heart stopped," Niko says.

She points her cigarillo at the Blue Line tunnel mouth. "Probably when we drove out." She backs out of the cab and straightens. "You know CPR?"

"Yeah."

"You work on him. I'll be right back."

Niko sets the mason jar on the curb and climbs on top of Nikodemus and tilts back the huge and battered head to clear the airway. "You gonna call nine one one?"

"Not yet." She goes to the front of the cab and pulls the hood latch.

Niko grimaces as he swabs the demon's airpassage with a finger and then pinches the nostrils shut. He takes a deep breath and only hesitates a second before he puts his lips to his demon's lips. The jellyfish of Nikodemus' ruined eye is warm and wet against his cheek. Niko blows. It's like trying to inflate a hotwater bottle. He blows harder and Nikodemus' burly chest rises. Niko lifts his mouth and the chest deflates and foul breath washes over him. Well his own breath can't be much better. He bends again to fill his demon's lungs. Two breaths and thirty chest compressions. Assuming the same rules apply to refugee demons in cardiac arrest in the back of taxicabs.

The cabbie goes to the back and opens the trunk.

Niko checks again for pulse and respiration. Nothing. He scoots back and sets one palm atop the other on the demon's sternum and leans down into it. I swear someday I'll laugh at this. One and two and three and four. Nikodemus' body moves but Niko can't be sure it isn't just a reaction to the compression.

The cabbie pulls a set of heavyduty starter cables from the trunk.

Twentyeight twentynine thirty. Niko pushes stiffened fingers against the turtleskin neck. Nope. He bends to the slack face again and exhales hard. It's like playing a tuba. Nikodemus' unwilled lungs push corpse breath into the reclaiming world. The graveyard sigh fills Niko's nostrils. O I cannot take this, it's too much like it was with Van. I am haunted, I am haunted. He slaps a blood-dried cheek. "Come on, buddy pal. Come on, goddammit. Come back." Niko moves to compress his demon's chest again. One and two and three and four.

The cabbie ducks her head in. "Nothing?"

Niko shakes his head. He's covered in sweat.

"Okay. Help me drag him out."

Niko doesn't waste time asking what she has in mind but instead backs out and helps the cabbie pull the heavy body from the cab. At the gate when they had dragged the demon through the wreckage to the waiting cab he'd wondered if Nikodemus was dead. Now there is no doubt. What the difference is he couldn't say. But he feels it and he knows the cabbie feels it too. A certain bonelessness. A stillness different from sleep or mere unconsciousness. Dead weight.

"What are we gonna do?" says Niko.

The cabbie goes to the front of the cab and picks up a set of starter cables. "We're gonna jumpstart him."

"Are you out of your fucking—no, wait, never mind. Good idea." Niko steps away and the cabbie clamps the black cable to Nikodemus' left chest and then touches the red cable to his right chest. Bluewhite flash, electric sputter, flying sparks, smell of ozone and burned flesh. The galvanized body spasms. A tendril writhes like a detached lizard tail and quickly grows still. A puff of smoke rises from Nikodemus' chest.

"Christ." Niko glances at the sky expecting rolling thunder and quaking ground. He leans forward and feels for pulse and respiration and shakes his head.

A gray Mercedes with darktinted windows eases into the nearby intersection and stops with an abrupt bark. Powerlocks clack down and the sedan speeds away.

Again the cabbie touches Nikodemus with the red cable. Sputter spark smoke. Nikodemus jackknifes as if gutpunched and goes rigid and then goes slowly limp again as if deflating. The smell of seared flesh would be nauseating had Niko not become accustomed to such things. Niko sets an ear against the broad sternum. Still nothing.

The cabbie frowns and holds her car keys out to Niko. "Rev the engine when I tell you to."

Niko limps to the cab and practically falls behind the wheel. The cabbie ducks beneath the hood and moves the red clamp from the positive terminal to the starter coil and then says Okay and backs quickly away.

The engine starts and idles knocking. Flash sputter spark and twenty thousand volts rush lightspeed into Nikodemus.

The cabbie yells Yes and Niko hears a long asthmatic wheeze of firstdrawn mortal breath and then a bellow that can best be called demonic. Then a thud of thrashing tendril denting quarterpanel.

Niko scurries from the cab to see the demon very much alive and on his feet and squared off with his snaking tendrils raised against the cabbie who holds up the starter cable clamps like a horror movie hero brandishing a crucifix against a vampire.

They both turn at Niko's voice. "Welcome to Los Angeles," he tells his demon.

THE CABBIE DRIVES down Wilshire Boulevard. Swerving through traffic caught by surprise at the signals' sudden change. "Sorry to take surface streets," she shouts into the wind buffeting through the mostly empty windshield frame. "The Hollywood Freeway's still a nightmare."

"A nightmare." Niko laughs. He hears the edge of hysteria in it but he can't help himself. A nightmare.

People stare at the cab as it hurries along. Beat to hell, no windshield, a demon filling up the back seat and gawking like the tourist he is. How could they not? But this is Los Angeles and most of them assume there's a movie or a television shoot nearby, or that someone's having a theme party or premiere. Or even if they don't think there's a movie or a party or a premiere, well, this is Los Angeles.

As they drive past MacArthur Park Niko can't get over how clean everything looks. And the people! They aren't covered with blood or shit or scabs or parasites. They aren't buried in stone or broken in half or impaled on pikes. Those kids at the corner there. Six teenaged boys with beanie caps pulled low over shaven heads and loose shirts over baggy pants. Hands stroking belly tattoos. On constant lookout like meerkats. Not screaming, not mutilated, not blank and hopeless but whole and alive. They have no idea how beautiful fleeting rare and frail they are. No one out there has any idea. Not the woman packing up her hotdog stand or the kids dueling with their plastic laser swords or the gaunt man rattling his paper cup of paltry change or the Rasta selling homemade incense on a blanket or the man behind the counter at the doughnut shop filling a pink box with a dozen mixed or the swollenfeeted woman pushing her shoppingcart full of rags. Lucky blessed mortal oblivious and so very much alive. Unique unknowing souls one day to be contained perhaps within rude mason jars delivered to their tailored doom and every one of them worthy of the costliest rescue.

It is an effort of will to look back at his demon. Looking back at anything will take some getting used to. Nikodemus wears a thick gauze patch taped over one eye from a firstaid kit the cabbie brought forth from the Checker Cab's trunk.

"How you doing?"

Nikodemus shrugs and gestures with a tendril out the window.

The cabbie maneuvers the Checker Cab like a porpoise through signals and intersections and traffic. "Thought I'd take Wilshire to Fairfax and take that till it hits Hollywood. That's about the least crowded we'll find on a Friday night without going way out of our way."

Niko merely nods. He would ride shotgun with her on any route she took on earth or otherwise and never question her. The city he knows seems more surreal to him than its unattended doppelganger had. These old familiar streets so new and strange. Perhaps they are not what's changed.

Hard west on Wilshire now. Vermont, Western, Crenshaw. Abstract neon of Koreatown. On the hillside the Griffith Observatory poised between seas of ordered light. The Greek Theatre hidden in the hills nearby. I played there for Jem and yet I've never played there at all. The tall block letters of the Hollywood sign dark beyond.

Through Midwilshire now. Tar Pits, County Art Museum, Petersen Automotive Museum. At Fairfax the Checker Cab turns right and heads north. Traffic thickens as they near CBS Studios and Farmers Market and The Grove. Stopped behind a car at the light at Fairfax and Third Niko glances back to see Nikodemus staring up in mortal terror at a Gray Line Tours bus turning left from Third onto Fairfax.

It's okay, he tells his demon.

Nikodemus nods doubtfully without taking his piratic gaze from passing forms of tourists backlit behind tinted windows as they point down at the smashed and battered cab.

"What you lookin at?" the cabbie calls.

Niko sees a camera pointed at Nikodemus. "Wave," he tells his demon. "Wave."

Nikodemus waves. One for the books.

Nikodemus what do I do with you? I have violated something in bringing you here and I have no doubt the universe will seek to rectify it.

At Santa Monica a homeless man standing gaunt in the street like a bedraggled prophet points at the cab and shouts Motherfucker owe me money. Then the light turns green and they continue unabated across Sunset to Hollywood where they turn right and then left onto the canyon road to begin their snaking climb.

ALL THE OLD familiar places. The gaudy lighted mailbox at 2101. The wrought iron bats of the horror movie director at 2118. The left turn that always seems about to end but in fact turns sharper. Coming home.

Niko doesn't know what to do with his hands. Even after everything his heartbeat quickens and his mouth grows dry and his eyes blink rapidly as they take in what will be catalogued later. My friends beside me. This ruined amazing car. Did ever an explorer come back home from unmapped oceans bearing such cargo as mine? Ferried across the sunless world.

Behind him and below him city light sways and sways.

The last stretch of uphill road. The final curve. The length of white stone wall. The graze mark where somebody sideswiped it some years back. My demon with me still. The flaring driveway. Security light and camera. Jemma snug against my lap and leaking out into the mortal world.

The black grilled gate.
The broken chain of myth.
The Black Taxi waiting in the driveway.

XXXI

WHEN LOVE
COMES TO TOWN

WHAT DO YOU WANT ME to do?"

Idling in the middle of the road the battered yellow Checker Cab faces the sleek Black Taxi. Gunslingers on the main street of Dodge. The space between them electric.

"I don't know." Niko looks past the hood of the cab across the showdown distance. Past the Black Taxi, past the gate, at the mansion at the end of the statuaried drive. You're still there. Unbelievably still there. Through the door and up the stairs and in the room and on the bed where mere hours ago I held you while you drew your dying breath. Hours and ages later I am back with you in hand.

"All right, screw him. We switch to Plan B."

"I didn't know we had one," says the cabbie.

"We didn't."

QUIET NIGHT. No traffic on the high hill road. The Checker Cab's doors creak open and the dome light shines. The cabbie gets out already patting herself for a cigarillo and Niko gets out holding the jar like a Fabergé egg while Nikodemus struggles out. Relieved of his weight the chassis lifts. All stand waiting.

The driver's door opens on the Black Taxi and the Driver steps out. He bids them all good evening with a touch of bony hand to glossy bill of cap and turns the hollow of his gaze toward the lambent jar in Niko's hand.

The cabbie lights another cigarillo. "Hiya, Sparky. TGIF, huh?"

The Driver only looks at the jar. Experimentally Niko slowly lifts it. The Driver's head tilts up. Niko lowers the jar and moves it out to the side. The Driver's head tilts down and swivels slightly.

"Hey, how's my ride?" calls Niko. "Sure is fun to drive, isn't she? Handles like a dream." He smiles. "Man, I fired her up and that bitch just opened up for me and purred."

The eyeless gaze no longer on the jar.

"You know for a while I wasn't even sure who was driving who. It's a shame I had to smash her all to hell—"

A sound escapes the Driver that could not issue from a human throat. Keening and choppy and thin. Chihuahuas bark from the plastic surgeon's estate next door. In the hills coyotes yip. The Driver shucks all pretense of patience and stalks toward Niko with cold murder on his jaundiced face.

Niko says Go.

Nikodemus sprints to the wall and jumps high and hoists himself over. His shredded wings flutter as he drops to the other side.

Niko hands the jar off to the cabbie and hurries limping toward the Driver. He veers around the Driver and makes straight for the Black Taxi where he jerks open the heavy suicide door and jumps inside and slams the door. He yanks the key from the ignition as the door is snatched open behind him.

While the Driver goes for Niko the cabbie calmly goes to the gate and hands the jar through to Nikodemus, and the demon dashes with it up the lighted drive.

Niko scrambles across the seat and gets the door open just as something grabs his ankle. He kicks out blindly and does not connect but frees his leg and tumbles headfirst from the car. He manages a halfassed shoulder roll on the driveway. Sharp pain in his side like a woodrasp drawn across his broken rib. He stands and then falls back against the open door which hits the Driver hot behind him.

Nikodemus opens the front door of Niko's house and runs inside.

Slouched against the closed car door Niko glances at the cabbie and she calmly nods. Behind him the window rolls down and sudden fire rips across his back. The world whites out. Niko gasps and the gasp locks up. Don't you dare fall. He jerks forward and sees the ignition key in his hand. A hot iron pierces his back when he flings the key away. The key arcs into the darkness and lands in someone's yard downhill.

Now you can fall.

Niko falls. The opening car door nudges him. He digs in his heels. Aware of the open window just above his head. His ass grows warm. What's that about? Oh. Blood flowing down his back. Well this sure can't last. Come on bud. Get up stand up, like Bob Marley said.

Niko manages to stand. He pushes from the Franklin and turns around just as the door bursts open and the Driver bursts out. Niko backpedals but the Driver stops in front of him and puts a friendly arm around his shoulder and draws him close as a lover and Niko is so startled by this that he lets him. Lets him draw his gaze up slowly into the churning horror of those evershadowed eyes. He half expects a smell of fetid breath but there is no breath at all. He hears the cabbie shouting out, his name perhaps, but his true name is seldom spoken anymore upon the mythless earth. And Niko does not turn he does not hear he does not fight but only looks into that borderless and leeching face and feels a softening inside, of life of will of want, and he senses the Driver's hand upon his chest, then senses it within his chest and rummaging there for some forgotten thing made consequential only by its perceived absence, by its need to be reclaimed and redeemed, and Niko is about to tell the Driver that what the sure and probing fingers seek is no longer there. Was bartered for a song and sold too cheaply many years ago.

Just about to gently say these things he stops. His breath taken from him as the alien fingers brush the very thing inside him he has never truly believed existed. Never despite evidence and experience felt was really there to sell or trade.

The Driver seizes Niko's soul and pulls. Not hard. Not hard. Instead he coaxes teasing Niko's soul from its asylum like a loose thread in a pattern. His nimble fingers are not cold at all.

Yes thinks Niko as he looks into that jaundiced faceless face. O yes I will go with you. Take me with you, strip me from the prison of my flesh. Take me fuck me o it feels so good to die like this I love you.

He feels his soul enjoined more fully than it ever was with Jemma in their most heated passion or quiet certain love. Stripped down to his foundation he shares—with the Driver! with the Driver!—a naked true communion not known since unborn he shared his mother's body.

The river Lethe was mere forgetting. This is vast enjoining. Who knew oblivion was so intimate? Slide the needle in and push the plunger home. You're gone, youre gone, you are g
  one.

Piercing sirens and howling dogs and rhythmic patting wake him. Someone says Come on come on. He wonders what all the fuss is all about and realizes that the patting is the cabbie slapping him.

He sits up gasping hugely. Ambered overcast, Hollywood night. The cabbie kneeling over him, holding his arm.

The siren is his house alarm.

Where'd the Driver go?

Niko touches his chest. Gone?

But no. He feels his self still there. Now that he knows its shape within him it seems obvious. How could he not have known it's been there all this time?

Sudden tears. The soul I sense inside me now. As if pregnant with my self. And shamed. I wanted to go with him. I loved him. O christ that is his power. That you go with him gladly. A poisoned aphrodisiac. This is what Jemma felt there at the end. This is what she felt. I am cuckolded by death itself and in his embrace would have done the same and happily. I am sick and so ashamed.

He shakes his head to clear his mind and looks up at the cabbie looking down. "What happened?" Nearly shouting in the din.

"He jumped out of the car and ran into you. He hugged you and then your house started yelling bloody murder, so he dropped you and ran through the gate in a big hurry. That part was pretty impressive." Looking not at all impressed she drags on her cigarillo. "I thought you were a goner."

"I think I was. How long ago?"

"Thirty seconds?"

"I have to turn the alarm off or this place'll be crawling with rentacops."

"I need to compress your back. You're bleeding pretty bad."

"Gotta help Nikodemus."

But she's already going around to the back of the cab and opening the trunk. "Can't help anyone if you bleed to death." She shuts the trunk. "Right?"

"Yes mother."

The cabbie removes Niko's shredded jacket and pulls up his flayed shirt. She draws a hissing breath and winces when she sees his back. Quickly and efficiently she puts on a thick compress and wraps his waist with surgical tape.

"I can't believe you have a compress that size." Niko tries to smile bravely and not think about how his back must look.

"Maxi-pad. I can't believe you're not screaming your head off." She smooths the bloody end of the surgical tape across his belly.

"Can't feel a thing."

She looks doubtful but helps Niko to his feet. He hisses like a brand in water. Now the cut hurts, now he feels his broken rib.

The cabbie brushes hair from her forehead and leaves behind a dark red streak of Niko's blood. "Well I guess you'll play the guitar again."

Niko looks up from his field dressing. "Really? I don't think so." And as he says it knows it's true.

"We better get in there," says the cabbie.

"Yeah."

The gate code is the date that he and Jemma floated on Lake Arrowhead and felt themselves begin again. Niko punches in this anniversary and the gate begins to rattle open. "This still isn't your fight," he tells the cabbie.

Her only reply is a get-serious expression and a gesture for him get moving, for which he gives a grateful smile. He owes her so very much.

Niko passes on into his statuaried driveway. Behind him the cabbie takes a last long pull at her cigarillo and flicks it away.

THE FRONT DOOR stands open. Niko and the cabbie look through the doorway at the veined marble floor, cherry knickknack shelves with dried flowers, Lalique crystal, an oval mirror. Niko is struck with sudden fear that he'll see his own body on the couch, an empty hypodermic beside it. All of this the raving of a mind that's shutting down. *I am returned to haunt myself.*

He gives the cabbie what he hopes is an encouraging look and limps into the ululating house. The black leather couch unoccupied. The empty hypodermic rests where it was tossed on the glasstopped table. Sweeping curve of carpeted staircase. No one else in sight.

Niko limps to the security alarm panel and enters the code. Sudden silence jars the house. Faint tick of the moonfaced clock.

Niko jumps when the telephone rings.

"Security company?" the cabbie ventures.

Ah. He hobbles to the phone and picks it up and says Hello.

"Regent Security, sir. We show an activation at your residence."

"Yes. I'm sorry. My uh friend came into the house ahead of me and uh I was unloading the car. I forgot, sorry. It's off now but thanks for—"

"Who am I speaking with please?"

"I'm the homeowner. Niko, Nikkoleides Popoudopolos."

If the man from Regency recognizes Niko's name it doesn't register in his tone. "The alarm has been active for several minutes, sir. I've dispatched a unit to your home."

Niko strangles the phone. Somehow he feels it's all that's holding him upright. "Oh that isn't necessary. We're fine."

"Fine, sir. If I could just get your password."

"Password." Niko feels thick and stupid. "It's eight oh one—"

"Not your alarm code, sir. Your secret password."

Niko looks helplessly at the cabbie. This is just too fucking absurd. Here in his house in the Hollywood Hills there's a dead body, a demon, a messenger of death, a mythic ferry operator, and a leaking mason jar containing his girlfriend's soul, and he has no idea how to stop a bored security dispatcher on a telephone from sending armed rentacops to his door.

"I can't recall the unit without your password, sir," the dispatcher says into the silence.

"I'm sorry, I've just never had to use it, hold on a second."

Something thuds upstairs.

"Sir?"

Niko feels an absurd urge to command the dispatcher by one of the old Keys. Leave me alone, this has been willed where what is willed must be. But that won't play here.

"Sir, I'm afraid I have to—"

"Lyre. It's lyre, L Y R E."

A pause. Niko hears taps on a keyboard. "That's correct, sir. Sorry to trouble you."

"No um trouble. You're just doing your job."

"You have a nice night now, sir," says the dispatcher.

"Too late." Niko drops the phone to the marble floor.

"You all right?" the cabbie asks.

"Fuck no." He nods at the stairs. "Let's go."

The cabbie helps him climb the stairs. Every step a gardenclaw embedded in his ribs and lower back and pulling. By the top of the sweeping curve his compress feels hot against his back and he suspects his wound is bleeding freely again. They pull up short at the top of the stairs and Niko grabs a newel to keep from falling down.

"Darn," the cabbie says.

Down the hall stands Nikodemus, back to them and tattered wings outspread and trembling taut to fill the corridor. Niko starts to call out to him but suddenly the wings retract and Niko sees his demon holding the fractured mason jar and glaring sliteyed at the Driver who stands calm and confident between Nikodemus and the door to Jemma's sickroom. Wearing his perpetual halfsmirk and waiting for the demon to make his move. With Jemma seeping out into the mortal night and Jemma's body soon to pass all hope of resurrection time is on the Driver's side.

The cabbie touches Niko's arm. "Even if he gets by him he won't have time to put her back."

Niko tries to make what the cabbie says mean something but he's having trouble making words connect. He feels he's looking out through eyes not quite his own. But he understands that once again the game has changed and that their hastily concocted plan must be abandoned.

Just to drive home his point the Driver lights a cigarette and blows smoke in Nikodemus' face. The demon whipcracks the air in frustration.

The sound goads Niko to action. "Give me a minute. Stall the Driver any way you can and then send Nikodemus my way when you hear me honk out front."

She nods. Niko glances once more at the silent power struggle in the hallway and then struggles back down the staircase. He clumps through the living room and master dining room and into the big kitchen hung with copper pots. On the tiled wall a green-painted pegboard hung with several sets of keys. He snatches up the black keychain embossed with the winged B and hurries back as best he can through the living room. His lower back throbs in time with his heartbeat. Pain lances his ribs and flares his twisted ankle with every step. I am held together now with paperclips and duct tape. I believe my clock is winding down.

He clutches the keys and heads for the door. How strange to be back among his comforts and accumulations. He hadn't expected to see them again when he left. An hour I've been gone. All this traveling encompassed by a single sweep of any clock. This time he feels no pang of loss at leaving them behind forever once again, and when he leaves he doesn't look back.

THE BENTLEY CHIRPS and flashes and unlocks itself. The burgundy GT Speed looks almost black in this light. Niko nearly falls into the seat. It hurts but the pain is somewhere far away, a noise in another room. He touches his back and his palm comes away red. Well beyond panic at the sight of his own blood he merely shakes his head and wipes his palm on his filthy pants leg. *The dealership's gonna love me.*

He starts the car and half expects it won't turn over, thinking it must have been months since he drove it, but it starts right up and Niko realizes it has in fact, only been a few days since he took the Bentley out.

Niko drives out of the garage. Rounding the fountain in front of the house he sees the cabbie trotting down the driveway toward the front gate. *What gives?*

She glances back at the sound of his car and waves and then gestures for him to stay put. He stops before the front door. When he honks the horn he half expects to hear the bellow of some prehistoric beast. But no. It's just a carhorn and the Bentley's just a car.

What seems like a long time is less than ten seconds before Nikodemus rushes from the house in a blur of wings and tendrils and sees Niko in the Bentley and runs toward him with one tendril wrapped around the mason jar and the other reaching for the door. The demon lifts the latch but nothing happens. The automatic locks engaged when Niko put the car in gear. Past Nikodemus the Black Taxi Driver appears in the doorway of the house. Niko blindly stabs the control panel and his window whines down. Nikodemus is about the tear the door off when Niko stabs another button and the doors unlock. Nikodemus piles in and Niko peels out.

Nikodemus holds the mason jar in one coiled tendril. "I tried."

"I know you did." Niko speeds down the drive past soulless blind statues and surges to a halt before the gate. They wait an eternity for the automatic gate to clatter open. Niko glances at the jar. *Does it give forth light or mere reflection now?*

Beyond the gate the Black Taxi still faces the pummeled Checker Cab, but the black sedan's bonnet hood is folded up. There's no sign of the cabbie. In the rearview Niko sees the Driver strolling down the driveway toward them.

When the gate is open wide enough Niko glides forward twenty feet and punches an overhead button and the gate begins to slowly rattle shut as Niko stops beside the Franklin. The black car's hood folds down and the cabbie looks at Niko with a big old shiteating grin. Her hands are smudged with grease and a smear of it warpaints her forehead beside the streak of Niko's blood. The cabbie glances up the driveway at the Driver coming toward them. "Goodbye, good luck, get going."

"One question."

"Better be quick."

"Black Cab test question."

Her eyebrows raise. "Shoot."

"Shortest distance from point A—" Niko indicates their surroundings "—to point B."

And points up.

Her mouth opens in surprised delight. "Dang I like you. You got brass." And quickly she gives Niko the directions he needs.

He can only shake his head when he hears where he is bound. Doesn't that just goddamn figure? He glances in the rearview and sees the Driver at the gate now. "Thanks," he tells the cabbie. "I'll marry you next time around, I swear."

"You already did. Now get out of here." She squeezes his arm and nods farewell to Nikodemus and slaps the rear of the Bentley as if spurring on a horse as Niko speeds away. She watches the car speed round the corner and listens to the throaty engine dwindle down the hill. Good car, the Bentley. Rich man's car.

She closes her grease-stained fingers over an object in her hand and smiles. Then she straightens her thin tie and turns toward the gate to face the enemy she has faced so many times so many places, the enemy she so truly deeply loves. "I think you dropped this, Sparky," the cabbie says, and holds out the magneto wire she tore loose from the Black Taxi.

XXXII

RUNNING ON FAITH

So. Friday night, Hollywood Freeway north-bound. Traffic not too bad if you don't mind whipping in and out of the breakdown lane at ninety to pass the slowpokes and piss off just about everybody.

Niko doesn't mind. Whatever the cabbie did to the Black Taxi will only be a stalling measure at best. We're talking about a car that repaired itself after an eighty mile an hour collision with an iron gate and a dog the size of a one ton clubcab pickup. So put some miles on, buddy pal.

Speaking of buddy pals. Niko looks at Nikodemus filling up the front seat like a grownup in a schoolboy's desk. The torn and battered eyepatched demon watches cars they pass, watches the city with the open curiosity of a child. He shifts constantly on the seat. Nowhere is comfortable because of his wings. Opposing traffic a motionless head-light river. Must be an accident somewhere past Hollywood. Oh wait a minute. Niko remembers the overturned fueltruck by the Virgil exit. I drove by the cause of this traffic jam an hour ago. My god.

Nikodemus rubs a tendril against the thick pad taped over his ruined eye.

Nikodemus I owe you so much. You haven't even asked where we are going. My dark and ruinous twin you have a faith I never had. Our destinies are linked and always have been. Knowing this should make it easier to tell you what I must. But it doesn't. It doesn't. I still believe in my own volition.

He snakes through traffic as he speaks his demon's given name. "So Nikodemus."

The white patch turns toward him. "That's not really my name, is it?"

Niko shakes his head.

"I didn't think so. It doesn't feel right." The head turns away again. They've reached the downside of the Cahuenga Pass connecting Hollywood and the San Fernando Valley. Ahead to the right the multicolored neon and lighted tubes and spires and pyrotechnic flashes from Universal City Walk hold the demon's attention. Its black tower cleaves the misted night.

"I don't know your real name. I gave you that one after you fell in the Lethe. I had to call you something."

"I'm not mad. It's kind of funny. Nikodemus."

Niko feels like a total shit. He has to tell Nikodemus what he's up to. The demon has the right to know. Especially now that he is mortal.

Ahead the right three lanes split off to form the westbound Ventura Freeway. Niko whips across traffic and into the far right lane. Streetlights all around them dim. How odd.

Then Nikodemus is shaking his shoulder with one tendril and steering the car into the breakdown lane near Laurel Canyon with the other. "Hey. Wake up. Come on, wake up."

Niko grabs the wheel. "I fell asleep?"

They ease into the breakdown lane and stop. Staccato rush of passing cars. Nikodemus studies him. "You're very pale."

The surrounding traffic lights have grown abstract. Niko can't make sense of them. He's cold. Ask Nikodemus to turn the heater on? Can't concentrate. Nikodemus talking. "What's that?" Niko shouts as if his demon is far away.

"I said I think you've lost a lot of blood."

"Oh." Niko considers this. Yes that seems right. He's lost a lot of blood. He shakes his head in great big arcs. "Can't do that.

Wayyy too soon. Got a little ways to go. Then I can bleed to my heart's content."

"How far?"

"Hmm?"

"How far away is where we're going?"

"Maybe thirty miles."

"All right." The car chimes as Nikodemus gets out. Niko's head lolls as he watches the enormous alien figure walk around the car and open his door. The surf of speeding cars grows louder. A horn blows and tires screech. Boy gonna cause him a accident.

Nikodemus leans into the car. "Come on."

"Wherem I goin?"

"Passenger side. I'm driving."

"Smy car."

"All right, I'm driving your car."

"Oh. Okay." Niko sleepily acquiesces and clambers painfully to the passenger seat instead of getting out and going around. Ooh look at all the blood. A cable in his back pulls taut. Niko lifts the mason jar from the floorboards and breathes deeply. Faintest trace of her perfume and not a ray of light. Hang in there baby Niko tells the jar and cuddles it.

"Where is the clutch pedal?" Nikodemus says. "How do I work this lever?"

"Issa automatic. Put it in D an you don't gotta shift."

Nikodemus looks impressed. He fiddles with the electronic controls until the seat is as far back as it will go. He adjusts the rearview mirror and puts the Bentley in drive and abruptly steers onto the freeway. A horn blares and a Honda screeches around them, missing their rear bumper and then the car in the next lane over by less than a foot.

They're doing ninety by the time they pass Coldwater Canyon.

"Umunna go seepy now."

"Where are we going?"

"Malibu Canyon."

"What's there?"

Niko blinks blearily at his companion. "Heaven."

* * *

NIKO GETS A second wind as they climb out of the Valley just past Woodland Hills. He wakes up with a gasp and glances around, disoriented. They're really whipping along the freeway. The speedometer hovers just above one hundred. Shouldn't we slow down to avoid attention? Ah fuck it. What are they gonna do, shoot me?

The fuel gauge is below empty and the idiot light is on.

Niko turns to look behind them and feels that awful pulling in his back. Like a guitar string tightened to snapping. Great, I'm a highnote test.

A pair of bugeyed headlights races in the breakdown lane a couple miles back and slowly gaining.

"He's back there," says Nikodemus.

"I'm cold."

Nikodemus frowns. "The heater's all the way up."

"You want me to drive?"

"I don't think that's a very good idea."

"Okay. We're a mess, huh?"

"We're a mess."

They pass the sign for Parkway Calabasas. Calabasas means pumpkins Niko thinks. Someone named a place pumpkins. "You don't think we're gonna make it, do you?" he says to the road ahead.

His demon drives in silence for a mile. "It would help if I knew what we were doing."

"Okay. In a couple miles take the Las Virgenes exit. Go left and head out Malibu Canyon toward the ocean. Just before Pepperdine there's a tunnel. If we can get to it before the Black Taxi gets to us I think we have a shot."

"Whyyy?"

"Well. As below so above."

"I don't understand."

"As the Red Line tunnel is an entrance to your old stomping grounds, so the Malibu Canyon tunnel is an entrance—" And Niko gestures at a point beyond the roof.

Silence for a while.

"Are you sure?"

Niko looks at Nikodemus. Worry does not sit well on the demon's face. "Yeah. I'm sure. You still don't think we're gonna make it, do you?"

"We might. We could. If the Driver doesn't run us off the road. If your car doesn't run out of gas. If you don't run out of blood before we get there. If your woman's soul is still in the jar."

"Okay, so other than that." Niko leans his head against the window. The glass cool against his forehead. "Thanks for driving. You didn't have to come you know."

"Yes I did."

"Yeah. I guess you did." Niko shuts his eyes. His hands and feet feel miles away. He shivers with some inner cold. All he wants to do is sleep. O Faustus now hast thou but one bare hour to live. I am in the last hour of my life. All I do now a compendium of final things. I have kissed Jemma one last time. I have left my home a final time. The last time I will see my city. Music has left me now. On the road ahead my last words wait for me. Last breath. Final heartbeat. Sight. As always they have lain out there. As for all who ever lived. My enemy and friend beside me drives me toward that meeting I've evaded but anticipated all my life. The unsailed sea that shapes the continent of life itself by giving it a shore. Now my untried soul will brave that deep. As Jemma here beside me has though I have hauled her partway from that drowning.

He turns the redsmeared broken jar in his bloodstained hands. Just glass. Just a feather. Jemma will I see you again? We are spirits I have learned. Something in us immortal and irreducibly ourselves. But paired and forever bound? I don't know. I fear perhaps we intersect we waltz and we move on. The music stops and we are all alone. Well if that is so I can accept it. When I set out to get you back it was because you had been taken from me. But on the way my reasons changed. It was because you had been taken at all. Taking you was wrong. Not unfair, not tragic, but wrong. A violation. You didn't deserve to die. You don't deserve to be there. And I don't care what happens to me so long as I can make that right. My winning or losing no longer matters. I don't deserve you back. I signed my soul away and can't stand on some right to overturn that. Phil was right: a binding contract freely entered into. But you did not. They can have me. But not until we have you safely from them. That's what's different this time. That is what we have a chance of winning here. For even just the fact of change can be a victory.

But now that we have broken free the story's outcome is unknown. What will happen to you when we cross that boundary again? To think that you might simply be returned to where I brought you from.

All I can do is what I do now. The rest is in the hands of the gods. Who are not known for their evenhandedness. Not to mortal men and especially not to those who set themselves against them. Even Orpheus before me did not get so far. Yet he was not blessed with such companions as I've had. Perhaps that was his failure, that he took it on himself. That in truth he went down for himself and not for her.

So hold on Jem. Hold on. Soon we will be home.

THE CAR TURNS off the freeway and Niko opens heavy lids. "Where are we?"

"Las Virgenes exit."

"Go left."

They turn left and pass above the Ventura Freeway. Up ahead a McDonald's and a liquor store and a gas station. "We need gas," says Niko.

"Look behind us."

Niko looks just as the black length of the Franklin turns left off the exit ramp. Shit. Nikodemus puts the hammer down and an invisible hand shoves Niko into the seat. Mournfully he watches the gas station whip by.

The Bentley flashes by an L.A. County Sheriff car parked on a side road before a condo cluster. The patrol car kicks up dust and speeds onto the road where it is nearly broadsided by the Black Taxi before the big black car yaws into the lefthand lane and whips around the black-and-white.

"Cop," says Niko.

Nikodemus merely looks at him.

"Yeah right, never mind." They lean hard into a curve. "This road is sort of glued onto a mountain range. It's pretty curvy so be careful."

"I like this car. It's much easier to drive than that one."

"I'll will it to you."

Colored light plays about them. The sheriff's lightbar. Its strobing backlights the Black Taxi racing between the Bentley and the patrol car and definitely gaining.

Nikodemus sticks the Bentley round a tight right curve. The tires wail as they slide out toward the precipice in a mild fourwheel drift into the path of oncoming headlights. Nikodemus backs off on the gas and cuts in and a black Ford pickup streaks by honking and goes on to barely miss the Black Taxi and the pursuing patrol car.

Whatever else Nikodemus might be he is certainly not the Checker Cab driver. The demon's driving experience consists of three or four days driving a supernatural vehicle up a ramp full of dead people and mowing them down like grass.

Niko tries to think. Okay. So. Malibu Canyon Road runs along the hillside above the sheer dropoff of the gorge that houses Malibu Canyon Creek. Near the crest of Malibu Canyon Road there's Mulholland Drive but few other side roads. Mostly undeveloped state-owned parkland till you get to Hughes Research Labs and Pepperdine University near Pacific Coast Highway at the Malibu shoreline where the Santa Monica Mountains drown in the Pacific. Friday traffic on the canyon road. No wonder that sheriff had been parked there. He's gonna wish he'd baited his line for smaller fish.

Niko massages his forehead. His fingertips are cold. Okay. Stop worrying about the sheriff. He can't stop us and if he radios for help they'll just be waiting somewhere near PCH on the other side of the hill. Where the hell else are we gonna go?

The biggest worry is the tunnel itself. They're not driving some tanklike Checker Cab with special buttons that enable it to do supernatural things. No sir. They're driving a Bentley. A quarter million dollars' worth of fine machine but a machine nonetheless. Its most supernatural controls are a GPS and personal environment controls and memory settings on the seats. When they reach the tunnel it may be just a tunnel. Not a Portal, not a Doorway to some other where. And what then? What if they drive into it and come out still on Malibu Canyon Road and heading downhill toward the highway and a row of Stop Sticks and a line of sheriff's cars?

But officer I can explain. This here's my demon, see, and this jar contains my girlfriend's soul, I was being chased by Death himself, you won't believe the night I've had, can't you just let me off with a warning?

If we come out that tunnel and we're still on Malibu Canyon then the only way to cross that boundary will be the way most people do. By dying. But if we, if we die close enough to the portal the cabbie swore would be there, maybe then the Black Taxi Driver won't have time to strip us from ourselves and trap us like fireflies in a jar and head back to his master with us in hand. Maybe.

We'll jump that bridge when we come to it.

A SHORT BLOOP of sheriff siren brings Niko back enough to make him realize that he's been a little gone. Now he feels a tingling warmth like when you're so cold it burns. The Black Taxi's less than fifty feet behind them now and the sheriff's car is on its ass.

The Bentley's engine lurches and sputters and catches and dies. Nikodemus stomps the gas and turns the key and whips the dashboard with a tendril and swears in a guttural reptilian tongue.

"We're out of gas," says Niko.

"What do we do?"

"Keep driving. It's mostly downhill now."

And it is. The serpentine road hugs the hillside downtending and tight turning. Niko tells Nikodemus to put the car in neutral and go easy on the brake. They're still going so fast they barely have control as they slur around the curves and nearly trade paint with oncoming traffic. In the gliding quiet Niko hears the leonine purr of the Black Taxi's motor and the bored out grumble of the sheriff's car. The sheriff hasn't bothered with the siren again.

"It's harder to steer now," Nikodemus says.

"Power steering went out when the engine died. So'd the power brakes. You'll have to press harder to slow down."

"How much farther now?"

"I'm not sure. Not far. It's the only tunnel on this road."

They lean into a turn.

"What do we do when we get there?"

"Depends on what we find."

They lean the other way.

"What if it's just a tunnel?"

Niko studies his demon. His whitepatched eye and broken wings. The pursuing headlight glare bright against the back of his roughcarved head. "Then I think you know."

Nikodemus is silent.

"You don't have to—"

"What else can I do?" Nikodemus yanks the wheel. "I'm more married to you than she is."

"I'm sorry."

"Don't be." And astonishingly the demon grins. "It's been fun."

"Nikodemus—"

The demon steers them through a narrow S and makes a deep gargling sound that ends in a sharp click.

"What's that?" asks Niko.

"My name. My true name. I remembered it awhile back. I wanted you to know."

Niko chokes back sudden tears. All he can do is nod.

The canyon road is thick with mist from the encroaching marine layer piled up against the hills. The mist is silvered with the rising moon. Powerless the silent Bentley twists and turns among the earthbound clouds. Pursued by laws of man and nature both. Niko checks to be sure Nikodemus isn't wearing his seatbelt. Not that it would have fit him anyhow but just in case. Feeling oddly calm and languid and logical he unfastens his own seatbelt and then leans forward and switches off the passenger airbag.

On a downhill straightaway Niko lowers his window. The road ahead is free of traffic and they dip below the mist and up again into it. The car fills with an ancient odor.

"What's that smell?" says Nikodemus.

"The ocean. It's just over this pass."

"I'd like to have seen that."

In this time of final things. Here in the mountains I feel the sea. The two have traded places many times I know. Nikodemus will never see the ocean or the sun.

On impulse Niko reaches for the radio button and as he reaches somewhere in a place without location on an infinite and sunless

— 403 —

plain a glass tube slips over the ringfinger of a dark brown callused hand and as he pushes the radio button the glass tube slides along tight metal strings and as he scans across the static hiss of exploding galaxies a beatup shitbox of a pawnshop guitar begins to cry a world of pain back at a world of pain and in so doing somehow makes that pain abate. As the antique and ageless car behind them catches up and pushes them and tries to herd them from the mountainside with its own bumper the Bentley's radio catches a weak ghost signal, a music relayed on the mist, a few bent notes on a bottleneck slide. Niko hears them crying on the radio as the rear end of the Bentley gets loose. It seems a mournful voice calls Niko's name as he looks ahead and sees the tunnel mouth two turns away. Hard right and hard left. They head uphill and the Bentley begins to slow. The surging Franklin plows into them and tries to push them off the road.

Now the siren wails again or is that a bending heartbreak chord.

Nikodemus steers them skidding round the righthand curve and they head downhill once again and pick up speed. The Black Taxi falls behind but Niko knows it's just a brief respite. The hills and mist around them strobe red from the sheriff's whirling lightbar. The music Niko thinks he hears picks up a heartbeat shuffle. This last turn is going to be tight. No oncoming traffic. Tires chortle as the demon steers the Bentley toward the wall of mountain and then cuts into the oncoming lane to gain the inside line as he enters the sharp left turn.

The sheriff's car falls back. Maybe they want to kill themselves but the sheriff doesn't.

As they pick up speed toward the tunnel mouth the Black Taxi makes one last try and rushes into their rear bumper. Somehow Niko feels the Franklin's rage. The Driver's cool and certain fury. The Bentley's back end gets loose and scrapes the mountainside. Sparks fly and rubble peppers road. Nikodemus holds the car around the hairpin turn and then he straightens out and they are in the tunnel.

Nothing happens. It's just a tunnel. Two lanes and overarching concrete.

Oh well. Niko glances at the speedometer. Fiftyfive. That should do the trick.

The tunnel isn't very long, a couple hundred yards at most, and quickly they emerge. The road veers sharply right and Niko leans forward to grab the steering wheel but Nikodemus bats his hands aside. For a moment Niko thinks the demon means to outdrive their pursuers and survive. Then Nikodemus yanks the wheel himself, and as the Bentley veers left off the road and up the dirt embankment toward the insufficient guardrail looming in the headlights showing only emptiness beyond, Niko understands that Nikodemus steered them off the road because if he himself had done it everything would be for nothing. Because suicide is a mortal sin.

The car tears through the white guardrail. The airbag explodes from the steering wheel and drives Nikodemus back into the seat. Nikodemus flails and the thick white bag goes limp. The car arcs out into the canyon night. In the sudden quiet Niko hears the ocean's crash. The music on the radio is out of reach now.

Moonlit mist fills the windshield.

Niko cradles the mason jar. Clarity spreads through him. His stomach seems to rise. He floats above the seat. He smells the ocean. Hears the creek below.

The front tilts down. The windshield fills with mountainside and scrub. Here it is. Here it is.

Something dry and snakelike grips his arm. Nikodemus. Niko holds his hand out and the tendril wraps his palm and Niko grips it tight.

See you there says Nikodemus.

Last things. Jemma I am so afraid and I am not afraid at all. Then will I headlong run into the earth.

The Bentley dies against the gully floor.

SHERIFF ANDREW SAUNDERS' report described the suspect vehicle as a late model Bentley sports car, deep maroon. The suspect vehicle violated posted speed limits and disregarded posted traffic signals as it exited the Ventura Freeway on the westbound Las Virgenes ramp. The vehicle was weaving and erratically driven. Suspecting intoxication Sheriff Saunders gave pursuit. The driver of the suspect vehicle was described as a large male, black or hispanic, the passenger a white male. The driver disregarded Sheriff Saunders' instructions to pull over at the next turnout, and Saunders subsequently radioed for backup. Pursuit speeds exceeded seventy miles per hour along Malibu Canyon Road, a posted thirty-five mile per hour zone. The suspect vehicle entered the tunnel at an approximate speed of fiftyfive miles per hour, then exited the tunnel and inexplicably veered from the road. The vehicle traveled up the embankment and broke through the guardrail. At no time did the brakelights flash. Sheriff Saunders immediately pulled over and exited his patrol vehicle to render assistance but the suspect vehicle was at the bottom of the gorge on the far side of Malibu Canyon Creek. Visibility was limited due to an encroaching marine layer and the site was inaccessible until a rescue crew with winches arrived on the scene an hour later to find the vehicle smashed to half its former size. The occupants did not survive. Their remains were transported to the Los Angeles County Department of Coroner for autopsy and identification.

The report made no mention of any other vehicle involved in the pursuit.

XXXIII

BRING IT ON HOME

NIKO CUTS THE ENGINE AND the boat floats on the quiet lake. The air is rarefied high up on Lake Arrowhead. Patchy early morning mist still haunts the water.

She sits across from him, a frayed and faded blanket with a thunderbird design across her knees.

Indistinct the shoreline turns and turns around them. Smell of gas from the outboard.

She has a certain smile. As if she's given him a present and she waits for him to open it.

Niko doesn't move because this moment is a fragile bubble and he doesn't want to break it. Pearlescent mist beads Jemma's hair.

"Hi," she says.

Niko looks around. The boat. The lake. The shore. "We're here? We made it?"

A hundred tiny diamonds fall as Jemma shakes her head. "Not yet."

"Oh. Okay."

They drift and they drift. Happy lap of water on the hull. He wants so much to touch her.

They watch their separate shores slide by. He sees her artist's eye appraise his face, sees the love that guided the hand that set his face to canvas.

Something's missing. And at that thought it's where it ought to be, his old Martin in its case between them there and holding in it unborn tunes.

Niko wants to close his eyes and drift with their own drifting but he is afraid that when he opens them all this will be gone. This is the core of things then. This was always home. We have always shared this little boat, we are what anchors this place.

"You're all right then," says Niko.

"You're in here with me."

"Am I dead?"

Her smile deepens. "You have to wake up."

Out on the mirrored plain a fish breaks the mist and writhes suspended in their alien world before it splashes back into its own.

"I need you to forgive me, Jem."

And he sees the ache in her face. The simple ache when hearts misunderstand. "Oh honey. There's nothing to forgive."

And here at last is absolution.

His face goes tight and he begins to softly cry. Where is the quiet of inner peace?

He puts a hand to his chest and says Ow.

Jemma nods. "If it was easy everybody'd do it."

Niko laughs and she laughs back. Their little boat rocks on the deep.

"Your trip's not over yet you know."

"No?" A shadow dread falls over him.

"Soon."

"How do I end it, Jem? I just want it to be over. I just want you to be okay."

"Then wake up."

"Can I kiss you?"

Jemma laughs, not meanly but surprised, and says Oh Niko. And they bump against the farther shore.

Mortality Bridge

* * *

GRIT AND PEBBLES press his cheek. Niko opens his eyes. He blinks. He gropes. Hard and flat and sandy.

Suddenly sits up and gasps. Not in pain but in expectation of pain. He pats his chest, his head. No blood, no broken bones. Not even a bruise. He remembers his forehead slamming the windshield as the carfront crumpled toward him. The awful roar and tearing loose inside him as the dashboard crushed his chest.

Niko rubs his forehead. Not even a bump. His hand finds his back. The Maxi-pad is gone and there is no sign of the slashes.

Slowly Niko stands and explores himself in puzzlement and disbelief, his own hands assessing like a lover's hands.

Jemma.

Chilled in desert heat he stops. He looks around himself and feels the heart he felt stop beating leap with sudden fear.

The mason jar is gone. How could it not be here, considering what it held? Could Jemma not have made the crossing? Leached into the world, and everything for nothing?

He clenches his fists and glares at the sky. The sun bright, the cloudless sky blue enough to break his heart.

He looks away. He has awakened by the side of a paved road that cuts straight and long across a bright and featureless plain that looks like lower desert.

There is no wreckage. No sign of Nikodemus. No creek no gorge no mountain road. No mountain.

In the distance straight ahead something else lies by the road. Niko hoods his eyes and peers. No. It's much too large to be a jar.

He turns to see what lies behind him and he staggers backward as if struck. Behind him is nothing. Utter Nothing.

Niko spins back around and clamps his hands against his head and shuts his eyes. After ten deep measured breaths he opens them again. Okay. All right.

He begins to walk toward the only feature on this sundrenched plain. The Nothingness keeps pace behind him. His progress destroys what he leaves behind. There is no going back.

* * *

HALF AN HOUR later Niko hears tremendous roaring in the sky. He looks up to see a vintage Old American 260 steam locomotive plunge chuffing from a Magritte cloud and hurtle overhead, pulling half a dozen passenger cars. It looks like the tourist train Niko and Van rode around Stone Mountain Georgia when he was seven years old. Confederate flags and rubber tomahawks. A hokey staged train robbery that had terrified the two boys nonetheless.

The blast of horn cuts off abruptly as the locomotive rushes into sudden Nothing, followed by the passenger cars and the caboose. Then the train is gone and leaves behind an echo of its whistle on the plain, a line of black smoke, a faint smell of hot iron and grease, the fleeting image of a darkhaired boy in the caboose. Waving something that might have been a tomahawk.

Again the plain is silent still. Niko waits a while but nothing else happens so he resumes his walk.

Eventually the thing in the distance begins to look like someone in a hammock. Though what the hammock is lashed to is still too far away to tell. Behind it a small square structure.

He stops again at a familiar sound. He's still trying to place it when a mile away across the plain a boy in cutoffs and a broadstriped shirt comes pedaling a red and white Spyder bike with a banana seat and a high sissy bar. Apehanger handlebars, no gears, pedal brake. The boy leans forward into the wind his moving makes. A white bathtowel safety-pinned around his neck flaps behind him.

Niko stares. The boy bikes by and waves and grins as only boys in summer can.

Niko finds his voice and calls out Van? Van?

The pedals turn to make a rhythmic sound that he remembers well because it's he who banged the bike into a curb and bent the pedal down into the trouserguard.

The darkhaired boy does not slow down as he speeds by. The sound cuts off as the bike rides off the edge of existence. Coming out of memory and passing into memory. Niko's gaze turns to follow it but he closes his eyes because the alien Nothing interferes with something in his brain.

Now the distant barking of a dog. Soon a Rottweiler runs toward him across the plain, trailing gleaming drool and flapping a long pink tongue.

"Rufus?" The name escapes his lips as the memory blossoms. "Hey Rufus boy." Niko squats and calls to the dog and claps his hands. Remembering how Rufus would put his paws on your shoulders and press you down until he stood on top of you licking your face. The day one of his elementary school teachers drove by and saw this and became hysterical and pulled over and got out of her car screaming Get off him, get off him, thinking Niko was being attacked. Dad had thought it was the funniest damned thing.

Rufus had been hit by a car while mating in the middle of the street with a collie from the neighborhood. Dad and Niko had bundled his broken gasping body in a blanket they would later throw away, and driven him to the vet to be put to sleep.

Rufus runs past Niko happy as a dog can be. His bark cuts off as he follows the boy and the bicycle into Nothing, leaving behind only a faint and fading echo in the air to indicate he was ever there at all. Niko's heart breaks just a little more.

Gone.

THE PERSON IN the hammock is reading a book. Whether the person is a man or a woman is still too far to tell.

AHEAD OF NIKO now a cheery carhorn toots. He leaps out of the way as a white Ford Fairlane races by. Greenlettered Florida plates, a man and a woman in the front seat, two boys in the back. The man dark and bearded and smoking. Niko knows they're Lucky Strikes. The woman thin and pretty in a bright floral print sundress. The car gives a saucy wiggle and the woman raises a hand to wave as the car sounds off its cheerful toot

and gone.

Alone again upon the desert floor. Dad had bought that Fairlane new on credit. He had finally gotten promoted to supervisor at the bottling plant and he surprised his family with the car by just driving up in it one day and taking them for a ride all over St. Petersburg. Mom asking Can we afford this? Niko and Van used to pretend to drive it in the carport and Dad would get pissed when he started it up and the wipers came on and the turn signals blinked and the radio screamed static.

So that's the way it's going to be.

Niko squints and shifts the mason jar to his other hand to hood his eyes and peer at the reclining figure reading in the hammock in the distance. He resumes his walk. He doesn't get four paces before he stops.

He just shifted the—

He raises it and sunlight glints from glass contours. It slickens with his sudden sweat as he turns it in his trembling hands. There is no hairline crack. No missing triangle of glass. The lid is tight, the glass clean, the blacktipped feather floats. He knows if he could set it in the shade the jar would glow cool green.

Niko presses the jar against his face. He breathes in deeply but smells nothing. It's sealed tight. Its beehive energy against his cheek. He shuts his eyes.

THE STRAT HAD cut a groove across his thigh and the headphones round his neck were choking him. Graying dawn outside the little bedroom studio. The track still didn't feel right and he knew he was going to try again rather than sleep and lose the impetus that drove him here.

At his knee the tube Marshall hummed like a contented cat.

Niko set down the Strat and rewound the Akai and cracked his knuckles and then picked up the guitar once more to try and figure out the thing it wanted from him, the feeling within that wanted out.

But before he plunged back into that uncharted wood he glanced up. Across from him she curled asleep and covered by a faded threadbare blanket with a thunderbird design. And she was not beautiful asleep. Her expression slack and not angelic. The very ordinariness of it so beautiful he felt a yearning to be something more than he was or could be. And as good a player as he was, he knew as he turned on the reel to reel and hugged the Fender once again that nothing he composed would ever be as beautiful as her ordinary sleep.

Watching her he played the music of her sleeping. And by surrendering made something beautiful.

Niko lowers the jar and opens his eyes. He sniffs and looks around. "Okay," he tells the desolate plain. "All right." He lowers the jar to the road to wipe his palms against his jeans then wipes his cheeks. Get it together bud.

When he feels as ready as he's ever going to be he bends to pick up the mason jar that has been returned to him. Beside it now is a milky plastic bubble. A container from a bubblegum machine. He holds it up against the sun and joggles it and sees that it contains a little rubber monster. Niko remembers pestering his grandmother on a visit to the A&P, Can I have a quarter for the machine, just a quarter, I'll get a monster. She'd rolled her eyes and acted exasperated but Niko knew she was delighted to give him a quarter. And out of the milky bubble had come this little rubber monster with googly eyes and a silly grin and long ropy quivering tentacles. Niko remembers it clearly. Remembers imagining the voice he thought the monster would have if it could speak.

He glances from the little rubber monster in its milky plastic bubble to the feather floating in its mason jar and back again. And feels a sudden stab of hope.

Hello Nikodemus, Niko whispers.

Talismans in hand. The road ahead his unmapped future. Unraveling history and rewriting myth with every step. We are ready for the coda now.

There is no hammock.

When Niko is ten yards away the reclining stranger dogears a page in the book and stands. The hammock stands with him quivers a moment as if shrugging itself and then unfolds. Tattered feathers ruffle in the light hot breeze.

"Howdy," says the angel. The accent broad, the vowels flattened. Niko guesses East Texas. The angel is tall and lean with long straight thin blond hair and a long and fine planed face. The voice is pleasant, a whiskey-rough tenor. His eyes are Parrish blue. He seems to be male though he is more pretty than handsome. Though he is beautiful his wings are frayed and patchy, mottled and kind of beatup looking. They vibrate behind him like tense muscles.

The structure behind the angel is a rundown greasy spoon truckstop currently untenanted but with badly lettered neon sign. PETE'S.

"Afternoon," says Niko.

Niko and the angel regard one another as the wind scatters memories across the landscape of his life.

"Good book?" Niko nods at the paperback in the angel's alabaster hand. Long and slim like the rest of him, that hand would be at home on a Rodin sculpture, a concert pianist, an angel.

The angel looks at the book as if just remembering it. His sudden blush is startling. "Louis L'Amour. Got a weakness for em."

Niko nods. "Well I don't want to keep you from your reading." He makes as if to continue walking but the angel blocks his path.

"Ah ah. Fraid not, old son. Not while I'm standin here."

Niko looks thoughtful. He ought to be sweating in the sun but he isn't. "That's the way it is?"

Worn feathers rustle: the angel shrugs. "Folks familiar with the Good Book tend to be a mite less surprised than them that aint."

"I've read it." Niko smiles. "Except the begats. I'll say hi to Jacob for you when I get where I'm going."

Parrish blue meets placid brown and the angel smiles back. "Tough hombre, old Jake. Good reverse sitout on him. Lot biggern you too."

Niko shrugs. All these gestures movements of a dance.

The angel's having himself a good old time. "Well sir, we can flap our jaws all day long but I just dont see the point, do you?"

"I suppose not."

The angel nods. "Guess that aint corn mash youre totin in that jelly jar."

Niko turns the mason jar in his hands. "Guess not," he says, liking the angel very much.

The angel looks wistful. "Aint had me no mash in—well that dont matter neither does it?" He brushes his pale ivory palms.

"Youll be wantin to put that and your personals down somewheres out the way. Things are liable to get kinda—" he cracks bony knuckles and leers like a hyena "—broke."

"Okay." Niko bends to set down the jar and the gum machine bubble.

"Off the road, son. We get all kinda traffic here."

Niko looks around the desolate plain. Looks back to the waiting angel. "Where exactly is here, if you don't mind my asking."

Another rustling shrug. "Depends. Word like here dont really figure. Not the way you mean. Could be somewhere not a place at all but a bunch a stuff stands for something else." His sidelong grin is sly. "Could be all this is happenin in your head in a hunk a metal at the bottom of a ditch while your poor old bodys callin closing time."

"Could be," Niko says, "I'm nodding off in my living room with an empty needle on the floor beside me and none of this is real at all. Never has been."

"Ive studied that notion too." Now the angel's grin shows yellowed smoker's teeth. "But you get a piece a me, son, you aint gonna wonder whats real and what aint. These battered wings still kick up dust." The mass of feathers rushes from behind the angel to clap in front. A dust devil whirls before him and evaporates.

Niko gently sets the jar and the gum machine bubble a safe distance from the road and from the angel. He gives both a final lingering touch and asks them for whatever blessing they can give and then reluctantly he turns away. He cracks his knuckles and touches his toes and works his head from side to side to loosen up his neck. As he stretches he figures that even in his prime, uninjured and in tiptop shape, he'd have his work cut out for him with this good old boy watching him with patent amusement.

"You bout ready there champ?" the angel calls.

Niko nods. Determined and bemused at how he's come to be once more in this position. He heads toward the angel and tries to ignore the jackhammering of his heart. He surprises himself by saying, "Can I ask you something?"

The angel straightens from his fighting stance. "You sure dont look like the kind that stalls. But fire away, son."

"This may be more a favor than a question."

"Cant make you no promises, but lets hear er."

Niko takes a deep and only slightly shaky breath. "In my wallet there's a driver's license. Taped to the back of it is an obolus. An old Greek coin."

The angel's brow furrows. "You wanna aim for the bullseye there, amigo?"

Niko glances back at the distant jar gleaming in the pleasant afternoon sun. "It's for you. I mean if you. If I don't." He looks back again at the angel, surprised how hard this is to say. "It's a tradition," he tries again, "that you pay the ferryman when you. When."

The angel stands up straight and brightens as he understands what Niko's asking. "Oh hey, dont you worry bout a thing there. Thats all took care of. You did your job just fine and dandy. Tell the truth I won a good bet offa you."

Niko purses his lips. Again he looks at the jar and the milky bubble beside it. "They're okay?"

The angel grins. "Heck yeah, theyre fine. The both of em."

And at last the burden shifts.

But leaves confusion in its place. "Then—I don't understand. What are we about to fight for?"

Once again the angel blushes. "Now I truly do apologize. I thought you knew." And he flows back into fighting stance with wings held high behind him. All tension and poise and tautened spring and alabaster of him. "This time out youre fightin for yourself."

Niko sounds the depth of his being for an emotional response to this and receives no echo. God he's tired. "And when I win?"

"If you win," the angel corrects, "then you just keep on walkin, bud. Grab that little bubble and that lightnin bug jar and head on down that road and over the mountains. Its a fair hike and youre apt to meet up with a lotta your past along the way. But I reckon youll know when you get there. Just keep on walkin and dont stop. And dont look back no matter what."

Niko's laugh is like a sigh. "Is that all."

"Thats it, hoss. But I dont know why I'm tellin you, cause I'm about to give you so many lefts youll pray for a right. Now are we gonna get down to it or are you gonna talk me to death?"

Niko brings his arms to guard position and shifts most of his weight to his back leg. He feels coiled springs in his limbs, feels strength and old resolve awakening. "Let's dance," he tells the angel.

"Bout time." The angel spits into his palms and rubs them. "Till one cant stand or one says give." He straightens and then bows formally and properly.

Niko bows back and does not take his eyes off his opponent. It has been a life of worthy adversaries.

"Round one," the angel says laconically. And saunters out with lazy danger in his every move as Niko, as always and as ever, comes out swinging.

Myths are things that never happened
but always are.
　　　　　—SALLUST, C. 86-35/34 B.C.

ACKNOWLEDGEMENTS

I AM DEEPLY GRATEFUL TO THE following: Scott Kelley for his many suggestions for the downtown chase sequence, for nifty Aikido moves, and for showing me the entrance to Hell. Jessie Horsting for valuable information on automobiles and addiction, and for pointing me toward solutions on confrontations with the devil. Ken Mitchroney, my buddy pal, for always riding shotgun. Richard Curtis, agent of change, who believed right from the start. The Petersen Automotive Museum (www. petersen.org), for supplying the glorious 1933 Franklin Model 173 seven-passenger sedan.

I hope that readers familiar with Dante's *Inferno* (especially the John Ciardi translation), the myth of Orpheus, and similar descent-motif stories—along with the legend of Faust, the blues legend of Robert Johnson and the Crossroads, and many related deal-with-the-devil myths, folk tales, songs, and movies—will indulge my mashup of elements I perceive as mutual and archetypal. Wherever possible I have tried to acknowledge these sources in the text itself, albeit obliquely. "Where I steal," said Michelangelo, "there I leave my knife."

As this story is a combination of many myths and legends, so Hell itself is here a kind of remix that borrows, blends, and disregards (which in some ways is more difficult) elements of Dantean,

Grecian, Roman, Miltonian, and Medieval Catholic hadeography (to use Niko's word) as I felt appropriate to create my own private Hell.

Though I have taken pains to be geographically accurate, when the story required it I did not hesitate to alter or invent physical details and locations of landmarks, freeways, buildings, etc. It's risky to be very detailed when describing Los Angeles, a city that will not hesitate to tear down a cultural icon to put up an apartment complex (as sadly happened with the Belmont Tunnel entrance to the old subway line). Some landmarks became dated during the protracted writing of this novel—and in some cases well before—but I elected to retain them either because they resonated with the novel's themes or simply because I liked them better than their usurpers.

Those who are curious can follow the aboveground chase scenes in realtime using satellite imagery with a custom Google Earth route map available at www.mortalitybridge.com. I'm sure it's only a matter of time before Google can supply us with maps of the remainder of Niko's journey as well.

—Steven R. Boyett

Author's Note

This book was engendered in part by the poet Nancy Lambert,
who many years ago gave me the idea for a story
updating the mythical ferryman Charon
as a cab driver in Manhattan.

Nancy, I like to think you traded jokes
and smokes and breathtaking lines
with the driver of your own taxi
when it came for you.

       —SRB